W. James Beseman
9-16-99
(213)

NIGHT RUN

NIGHT RUN

BY ROBERT DENNY

DONALD I. FINE, INC.
NEW YORK

Library of Congress Cataloging-in-Publication Data

Denny, Robert.
Night run : a novel in honor of the famed night witches of World War II /
Robert Denny.
p.   cm.
ISBN 1-55611-336-6
1. World War, 1939–1945—Soviet Union—Fiction.   I. Title.
PS3554.E575N54   1992
813'.54—dc20   92-53080
CIP

Manufactured in the United States of America

10   9   8   7   6   5   4   3   2   1

Designed by Irving Perkins Associates

To the brave women

FOREWORD

IF YOU ASK people to name women warriors throughout history, most will mention Joan of Arc and, perhaps, the Amazons of Greek legend. Joan, of course, was more inspirational leader than military strategist; the Amazons of Greek legend, according to Herodotus, were fierce warriors who took men as slaves—and might, therefore, be called the ultimate feminists.

But there have been other women warriors as well. If they have been little noted, perhaps it's because most historians have been men. Yet history remembers red-haired Boudicca, queen of the Iceni tribe, who successfully led a revolt against the Romans in Britain in the first century.

And there was a second army of Amazons in West Africa in the nineteenth century that comprised one-fourth of the adult female population of Dahomey.

A flurry of interest arose among American audiences during Desert Storm when news videotapes of U.S. women military pilots appeared on our TV screens. Though technically non-combatants, they flew in harm's way and one, Major Marie Rossi of the U.S. Army, was killed in a helicopter accident.

Desert Storm led reporters to unearth the nearly-forgotten history of America's one thousand WASPS (Women's Airforce Service Pilots), who flew forty-three types of military aircraft—our speediest fighters and our biggest bombers—from factories to advance bases in the United States and Canada during World War II.

But, till very recently, hardly anyone in the West knew that Russia had women combat fliers during its Imperial period and three air regiments of women combat pilots during World War II.

These women, most of them girls in their late teens and early twenties, performed incredible feats of bravery and made an important contribution to the defeat of Germany on the Eastern front.

Night Run deals with the most romantic of the three regiments: the women who piloted and navigated old biplanes that had been built as trainers but were used to glide silently over the German lines at low altitude at night to bomb troop emplacements, ammunition dumps, command posts, and transportation centers.

Unconsciously poetic, the Germans called the young women the "night-witches."

This novel also tells how a young American B-17 bomber pilot bails out of his crippled plane, lands behind Russian lines, and, unable to be repatriated immediately, winds up flying for the Soviet Air Force. Some of our pilots did, in fact, bail out over Russian lines and spend time with their Soviet counterparts. And several regiments of foreign volunteers flew for the Soviet Air Force during the war.

So it is plausible to imagine that a Romeo and Juliet romance might have—and perhaps did—emerge from a chance meeting of these combatants from different lands and cultures during World War II.

It is also true that the Germans had a "smart" bomb that sank a battleship in 1943 and that the Luftwaffe developed a plan to refuel a Viking flying boat in the North Atlantic from a submarine and bomb New York City. Like several other plans to strike directly at America, it was abandoned for one reason or another. Here, I have used the license of fiction to depict what might have happened if the plan had been carried out.

As this recital demonstrates, it's hard to imagine almost anything about history's biggest and bloodiest war that didn't happen or wasn't attempted. And some of its best stories are still known to only a few. My first novel, *Aces*, dealt with the surprise appearance of the Messerschmitt 262, the world's first operational jet fighter, in the skies over Europe in late 1944. If Adolf Hitler hadn't stupidly forbidden his fighter aces to use the new superplane to stop our daylight bombing offensive, it could have changed the course of the war.

Except for historical figures such as Eisenhower, Churchill, Montgomery, Stalin, Zhukov, Konev, Hitler, Göring, Arnold, Eaker, Spaatz, German test pilot Hanna Reitsch, and the Luftwaffe aces Galland and Steinhoff, the characters depicted in *Night Run* are fictional. With few exceptions, I have hewed closely to the documented history of the era and the historical personages spoke and acted much in the manner in which I have made them speak and act.

I wish to acknowledge the help and advice of Roma Simons, who is compiling a history of the night-witches for the U.S. Air Force; Major Rita Gomez, who is intimately knowledgeable about the use of women in aviation roles and combat; Boris Bohun-Chudyniv, Soviet expert at the Library of Congress, who provided valuable advice on Russian language and culture; Russell Strong, author of *First Over Germany*, and historian of the 306th Bomb Group, Eighth Air Force, in which I served; Von Hardesty, aeronautics curator at the National Air and Space Museum who is the author of *Red Phoenix*, a history of the Soviet Air Force; Brig. Gen. Leon Goodson, USAF, Ret., an expert on fighter tactics; and World War II historians Dr. Earl Ziemke and Charles von Luttichau.

Several scenes in *Night Run* were inspired by *In the Sky Above the Front*, a collection of briefing reports edited by K.J. Cottam, 1984; and a non-fiction work *Night Witches*, by Bruce Myles, 1981. Useful sources for data on the Western war were *Flying Forts* by Martin Caidin, 1968; the *Mighty Eighth War Manual*, 1984, by the late Roger Freeman; and the excellent biographies of Eisenhower by Stephen Ambrose.

Over the years, deserved tributes have been paid to the men who flew in World War II. I will be pleased if this novel does the same for the valorous women who also flew and, as we have found, often fought in battle.

Half of this is true;
Half of this is probably not true . . .
Don't hold it against us if we add something or
  miss something.
We're telling you the way we heard it . . .

> —From *Manas,* thousand-year-old epic
> poem of Soviet Central Asia.

. . . what Russian does not love to drive fast? Which
of us does not at times yearn to give his horses
their head, and to let them go, and to cry, 'To the
devil with the world!' . . . At such moments a great
force seems to uplift one as on wings; and one
flies, and everything else flies . . . and a
pedestrian, with a cry of astonishment, halts to
watch the vehicle as it flies, flies, flies on its
way until it becomes lost on the ultimate horizon
—a speck amid a cloud of dust!

> —*Dead Souls,* NIKOLAI GOGOL

PROLOGUE: THE GENERAL

THE GENERAL SUPPRESSED a smile as the young pilot wearing a lieutenant's bar and wings swaggered toward him, halted, popped to what he thought was attention, and saluted. *He's a boy,* the old man thought, *a fresh-faced innocent boy, not more than twenty or so.*

"Permission to speak to the general," the pilot said formally.

"What can I do for you, Lieutenant?" the general asked.

"Sir, I know that Indians don't just walk up and talk to chiefs," the boy said, "but I heard you were here and that you were—well, that you weren't the kind who would mind. I saw your interview on CNN on the Russian business and I've read a lot about you and well . . ." His voice tailed off.

The general looked the young man over appraisingly. Slim, wiry, erect, middle-sized, with bright, alert eyes. The cocky look that marks the hunter. An American fighter pilot right out of Central Casting.

"What've you been flying, son?" the general asked.

"The A-10, sir. The Warthog. In the desert."

"How did you do out there?"

"Got eight tanks, sir. Six with the cannon, two with Mavericks. Also four personnel carriers. And a Mig."

The general's bushy eyebrows rose. "A Mig? In that old clunker of yours?"

The boy nodded and grinned. "Yes sir. It was early on, before we wiped them out or their air force bugged out to Iran. I was low-level, of course, after a tank, and the damnfool Mig pilot tried to mush in behind my tail to get a shot at me. I was flying an old clunker, as you say, but I could turn a whole lot tighter than he could. So I turned into him with my cannon—you know the A-10 cannon—and blew him into confetti. Sir."

The general smiled. "Tell me if I'm right. When you got out of flight school and they assigned you to A-10s, you were disappointed. No young hotshot wants to fly an armor-plated tank-buster that flies on the deck at four hundred knots, right? You wanted to bore holes in the skies in F-15s and F-16s."

The young man looked abashed. "Yes sir, exactly. But . . ."

"But," the general said deliberately, "when you climbed aboard and sat on top of that two-ton, twenty-foot-long, seven-barreled cannon and felt it go off beneath you the first time, you changed your mind, didn't you?"

The lieutenant actually blushed. "Yes sir, there's such a feeling of— I guess you'd call it aggression, power—when you fire that big thing—" He laughed in embarrassment. "I won't tell you what my girl friend said about my sitting on that cannon."

"I can imagine," the general said wryly. "There're some analogy there to what the P-47 pilots felt shooting up trains and barges during World War Two and what the Germans felt in the armored Focke-Wulfs—they even tried out a 75-mm. cannon in that airplane . . ."

The general paused, looking into the past. "It's certainly how the Russian pilots felt flying their Shturmovik tank-busters. They carried a 37-mm. cannon—a little bigger bore than yours, but no depleted uranium ammunition. And nothing like your rate of fire."

"I guess you know all there is to know about that airplane, General. It must have been quite a kick."

"Quite a kick," the old man said. "What's your name, son?"

"Epstein, sir. Sid Epstein."

"Well, good luck to you, Lieutenant Epstein. And, if the need arises again, good hunting."

"Thank you, General. It's been an honor to meet you, talk to you

like this." The boy saluted smartly, did an almost military about-face
—the Air Force was never really good at that—and sauntered away.

The general watched him. As the young officer's gait became a
swagger, the old man smiled sardonically and a thread of envy ran
through him. The boy was on top of the world and only dimly realized it. Flyboys don't grow old as fast as other men do. Their work
keeps them clear-eyed and alert. They don't sit at desks and vegetate,
frowning over sales figures. And when they're young, they expect to
be young and healthy forever.

At his age, Epstein didn't know anything about prostate problems
or failing eyesight or atrial fibrillation or an arthritic spine or—the
old man despised the thought—sexual dysfunction. When Epstein
rolled out of bed in the morning he didn't have to worry about standing up too soon and fainting because his clogged arteries hadn't had
time to get blood to his brain. He could spring out of a chair without
something giving way. And when it was time for it to be up, he
didn't have to think about it: *it* was up.

The general shrugged. But there was a certain satisfaction in being
old enough to look forward and back at the same time. It was wonderful to be young, but it was sad to be unappreciative of the good
things you had that age takes away.

As for himself, he had had the prostate resectioned, digoxen kept
the heartbeat under control, and the knee had been repaired. Bifocals
took care of the eyesight problem. And now, wonder of wonders, it
seemed that the other problem could be fixed, too.

An angel of mercy wearing captain's bars had shown him how. She
was waiting for him now at the door of his quarters.

Kathy was smart and trim in her uniform with the nurse's cadu-
ceus on her lapel. And she was tall, as tall as he was, with clear blue
eyes and dark hair. A musette bag was slung over her shoulder. They
went inside his spartan suite without a word. She put her bag down
and kissed him lightly.

The setting sun's rays slanted through the window and he adjusted
the venetian blinds. "Time for a drink," he said. "The usual?"

"Sounds great," she said. He mixed two bourbons-and-water,
handed her her glass, and they settled into his two armchairs.

"I want to ask you something," the general said, looking into his
glass. "When you were here the last time I was so"—he chuckled in
embarrassment—"the only word that fits is *overwhelmed*—that I
didn't get some things sorted out. I'm curious, Kathy. I'm on temporary recall duty and I wouldn't have any influence in your branch of
the service, anyway. I couldn't do your career any good."

He shook his head abruptly. "You're not that type anyway. So what . . . ?"

She flashed a broad, white smile. "What's a nice girl like me doing coming on to an older man, is that it?"

"A much, much older man," he said. "The standard disclaimer is that I'm old enough to be your father but I'm even older than that."

She nodded and smiled. "And over all these years you've been around enough women—oh, I know about you—to know that sometimes it's best to take the good things you're offered without asking a lot of questions."

"I know, but . . ." he began.

She held up a slim hand. "Okay. I'll sort it out for you and maybe for myself at the same time. Well, first, I suppose it's true, to some degree, that women are drawn to famous men, powerful men."

He snorted. "If I'm famous or powerful it's a well-kept secret."

"Oh come on, General," she said. "You've been on TV and in the newspapers and in books. Sure, that kind of notoriety can fade pretty fast but you command a lot of respect in the military fraternity." She grinned. "And in the sorority. You've done a lot for women in the service. I mean *for*, not *to*."

Her face grew serious. "And there's something that has nothing to do with that. You've lived a long time and you've been through some really extraordinary experiences. You've seen so much, gathered up so much, I guess the word is *lore*, that you're really quite a challenge to be with."

He smiled. "I'm beginning to like what you say. Carry on."

"Well, next, you're a remarkable physical specimen. Oh, I've looked at your chart; I know about your medical history. But you're hard and muscular; you really have an extraordinary body for someone your age. Any age. Very much like that boxer on TV the other night . . ."

"The middleweight."

"I guess. So that's an attraction in itself. And the medical aspect interests me, too. That's my business, you know. Between traumas and medications you've lost a certain sexual capability. But now," she said, grinning impishly, "medical science, in the form of your volunteer nurse, is able to take care of that, too. And do something lovely for herself at the same time."

She reached in her bag and pulled out a vial and tiny syringe. "One pinprick with a tiny needle that injects a very small amount of papaverin and you grow hard and stay that way for two hours. Do you have any idea how many men—I should say, how *few* men—can stay hard for two hours? Continuously?"

"I hadn't thought about it," he said. "Actually, that's a lie. Every man thinks about it. Men gabble about that kind of thing in barracks and locker rooms. Mostly they lie."

She smiled. "Well, that brings up, excuse the expression, another reason why I'm hanging out with you. This may sound a little selfish and maybe even ignoble, but why hold back, right? Given the circumstances, I'm really pretty much in complete control of what happens, aren't I? It's pretty rare for a woman to be in complete control of what happens between herself and a man, and I'm enjoying it. I hope that doesn't offend you."

"Under the circumstances, no."

She rose, slipped off her earrings, put them in an unused ash tray, and began unbuttoning her jacket. "Well, General, if that's enough explanation on my part, why don't we, um, *retire*, as the Victorians used to say? I'm beginning to feel rather flushed, to put it politely. Why are you looking at me like that? Am I a wee bit too liberated for you?"

"I'm not sure," the general said, "but that's not it. Just for a minute there, the way you looked up, those blue eyes and dark hair, you reminded me of someone else. From a long time ago. Someone"—he was amazed that, after all these years, he still had to swallow hard when he thought about it—"someone very nice."

Galina, his mind said.

CHAPTER ONE

THE INNOCENTS

GINNY GIGGLED AS Mike blundered off the beam and lost control of the aircraft on his instrument approach. She laughed aloud when, cursing and sweating, he became disoriented, missed the runway, and, when the altimeter dropped to zero, crashed.

"Okay, Hotshot," she said into her mike. "You're dead. You can come out now." She pulled off her earphones, put them on the table of her operator's station, and, leaning back in her chair, watched the squat Link Trainer flight simulator as it sat, stubby wings leaning sideways, on its pedestal in front of her. A moment later, the hatch opened and Aviation Cadet Michael Gavin, glowering, stepped out.

"Not too sharp on instruments, are we, Hotshot?" she asked, grinning.

"I oughta paddle your butt for calling that letdown the way you did, Ginny," he said. "Maybe I'll do just that tonight."

The smile faded from her face and she looked about the cavernous hanger swiftly to see if any other Link Trainer operator might have heard him.

"You'll do no such thing, Mikeyboy," she said tartly. "Talk like that

7

and you won't get within a country mile of me, tonight or any time. Just do it again and you'll see.''

"Why do I need all this Link Trainer crap anyway?" Mike demanded. It was a foolish question and he knew it, but he felt obliged to make some kind of response.

"Because, Sillyboy, the Air Corps may just ask you to go up when the sun isn't shinin', right? So you have to learn this instrument stuff —and I wish you wouldn't use that word 'crap.' You know I don't like it.

"Look," she said, sighing. "This is really my fault and I gotta admit it. We've been talkin' and horsin' around on the intercom these last few weeks when I should have been makin' you work." She shook her head. "Geez, you can't even orient yourself on a beam, read the dit-dah-dits, much less make an instrument landing."

She brushed her streaked blonde hair from her eyes and pursed her lips in self-disapproval. "I'm bein' paid to teach you this stuff, Mike, and I haven't been doin' it. I'm some great professional Link operator. Okay, tomorrow, we go to work. No more playin' around, okay?"

His face relaxed. "Okay, boss, tomorrow we start working. Just so it's party-time tonight."

She looked around quickly again. "Geez, Mike, keep your voice down, willya? This place echoes and there're people around. I don't want to be known as the base party-girl, which I probably am already. Just sign up with little Ginny and have a roarin' good time. Things are bad enough as it is."

"Honest to God, Mike," she said, rolling on her side and wiping the perspiration from her face and torso with a towel. "Sometimes you scare me, the way you slam into me like that. It's excitin' and I'm not sayin' I don't like it, I do, but it's as if you're mad, really mad. And when I look up at you, your eyes seem so angry."

She sat up, took a sip of her drink beside the bed and, turning, looked at him appraisingly. "You're always mad, or half-mad, anyway. What is it that makes you this way, honey?"

He shook his head glumly and stared up at the spot on the ceiling. He had been looking up at it for the past six weeks, an average of three nights a week, when he could get off the base to spend the night, or part of it, in Ginny's shabby apartment nearby.

"I don't know," he said. "It's just . . . ah, piss-ant." He fell silent.

"Great answer, piss-ant. What's that supposed to mean, anyhow?"

He shrugged. "It's just, you know, an Army expression. Like snafu, bollix, blow it out your barracks bag, something you say when—well, when you're pissed off."

"Which you generally are," she said. "Just sitting with you sometimes, I've watched your face change. Maybe you've been talkin' and laughin' and it's relaxed and then you seem to think about somethin', you never tell me what, and you get all stony-faced and mad-lookin'." She rubbed his head. "What goes on in there?"

"Oh," he said, pulling a wry face, "it's a habit, I guess. I guess you'd call them daydreams. Maybe somebody passes by and looks at me funny and I start to imagine that we have words and it turns into a fight. Or Captain Redman chews me out—which he's been doing a lot of lately—and later I go through the whole thing again in my mind where I flare up and answer back and he has the MPs pick me up and, oh, piss-ant. Angry daydreams, I guess you call them."

"Well, there's gotta be a reason," Ginny said, lying down and turning to cradle him in her arms. "I'd like to know what it is. Fact is, I know so little about you. You know all there is to know about me. Good ol' Ginny, one step removed from West Virginia white trash. Ginny Waller from the holler, now Number One Link Trainer operator here in Augusta, Georgia." She deliberately pronounced it "Jow-juh."

"But you," she said, stroking his close-cropped hair. "I've looked at your 201 file, of course. I know you're from Baltimore, Ball-tee-more, Mary-land. You're oh, five-eleven—same size as I am in heels, about a hundred and seventy pounds of, oh my, hard muscle—sandy hair, sort of gray-green eyes, nineteen years old. God, and I'm an old twenty-three. Your father died—I was sorry to see that—but your mother's alive. An only child, you are.

"You have a really sweet nature sometimes," she said, cuddling him, and you're a"—she lowered her voice to a growl—"a won-der-ful lover. Just dee-vine. But I don't know beans about what goes on in your coconut head except that it makes you angry and impatient. So tell me."

"Nothing to tell," he said tersely.

"Just answer some questions then, okay? I mentioned your father back then and you looked even madder than usual. You didn't get along so good?"

Mike snorted. "He was a big-shot lawyer with a Baltimore law firm, wanted me to crack the books, get good grades, be one, too. He'd talk about his big law cases when he'd come home at night—if he got home at all some nights. I'd listen, I didn't have much choice, and sometimes he'd give me one of those long briefs to read, *boring* stuff—really, excuse the expression—dog shit. I told him as much one night and he went bananas. He was always on my back about my grades in school, anyhow. I was more interested in football and the more he got on me, the less I tried in school. He was always finding fault, criticizing."

"What would he say that was so bad?"

"Oh, I'd hear him telling my mother—nice and loud so I'd hear— 'there's a gas pump somewhere just waiting for that boy.' A gas pump! He'd say it over and over."

"So what happened?"

"Well, to force him to admit I wasn't a moron, I did a lot of reading. It got to be a habit. When I wasn't playing football or baseball I was at the library reading. I got so I enjoyed it. Mostly I read the classics. I really snowed my English teacher; that was one class where I shined" —he laughed—"in spite of myself.

"Over the last six-seven years I've read Homer and Plato and Descartes and Spinoza. Couldn't understand Kant. Also Steinbeck and Hemingway and Shakespeare, especially the tragedies. Read some of the Russians too—my paternal grandfather was Russian; so I read Tolstoy, Dostoevsky, Pushkin, great stuff when you get into it. All about wars, nations, people, love, all those things. I'd drop some quotations at the dinner table to show him I wasn't as big an idiot as he thought. It was pretty obvious kid-stuff, showing off like that, but I'd do it anyway. He still thought I was a lightweight."

"Is reading what got you interested in flying?"

"To some extent. Saint-Exupéry wrote beautiful stuff. But I always wanted to fly. When I was a little kid I took in all the old flying movies, *Wings, Dawn Patrol.* I saved up lunch money and bought a couple of rides from the old barnstormers who used to come around in their biplanes. Beautiful things—Wacos mainly. I loved the smell of the oil, the sound of the wires and struts, like musical instruments, and the feel of the wind, the way it whips at you in an open cockpit.

"I even had dreams about flying—you know, rising in the air, moving your arms and flying in the air over people and houses. I dreamed that kind of dream over and over. Finally I went and looked it up."

"What did you find out?"

"Well, there's a book by this psychiatrist named Jung. Ever hear of him?"

Ginny sighed. "No. God, you're makin' me feel so ignorant."

"I don't mean to," he said gently. "Hey, Ginny, you're a lot smarter than I am in many ways. Wiser, understanding what makes people tick, how to get along. Even if you haven't done as much reading, you're a hell of a lot smarter in lots of ways than I am."

She smiled appreciatively. "Well, thank you, honey, it's sweet of you to say that. So what did this guy say about your dreams about flying?"

His face became glum. "What he said was that people who have those dreams haven't lived up to their expectations. The dreams are an unconscious substitute for feelings of failure."

"That's pretty deep stuff, Mike."

"Oh well, we don't have to get that deep, Ginnybabe. We can just stay on the surface for a while. Like this. You have the smoothest, nicest skin, with just a few very nice freckles," he said, beginning to stroke her with the tips of his fingers. "There's one here—and down here."

"Hold on just a dang minute," she demanded, seizing his hand. "You didn't get along with your father; what about your mother?"

"Laura," he sighed. "I always kind of resented the fact that she always stood back, never said anything *against* me in those blowups with my father, never defended me either. Just sort of passive.

"But there were some nice times, too. My mother's a piano teacher. She taught me some chords, only thing I had the patience to learn. And, sometimes, before Dad came home from the office and she didn't have a student coming in, she'd play songs for me and I'd sing. Mostly pop songs but sometimes classical songs by Rimsky-Korsakov and Rachmaninoff—mainly, I guess, because of the Russian background." He raised his eyebrows. "Never thought of it but maybe that was her way of trying to get me closer to my father."

"I didn't know you could sing, Mikey. Are you any good?"

"Not great. Pleasant, people've said. No big deal."

"So what finally happened with your father?"

His face darkened. "I enlisted just after Pearl Harbor, passed the non-college exam and got in the cadets. A month later, he had a heart attack at his office and died."

She nodded. "So you never got to prove anything, that you weren't a lightweight, I mean. I'm sorry. But I think you've gotta forget that, or accept it or whatever, so it doesn't screw up everything you do. Make you fight every order somebody gives you. You keep on goin' the way you've been goin', gettin' into trouble, you're gonna get yourself washed out of flight school and wind up . . ."

"I know. Shoveling shit in Biloxi, Mississippi."

"That isn't the way I was goin' to put it, but yes, that's what'll happen if you don't shape up."

"I'm shaping up right now, Ginny. Can't you tell?"

"Oh my yes, I can tell. I didn't think you'd be ready again so soon."

"I'm always ready."

"You sure are."

Later, fanning herself, she asked: "What about your Russian grandfather, Mike? How'd he get over here?"

"Jumped ship, literally. He was a sailor. He didn't like the Czar and his Cossacks, but he didn't like the way the revolution turned out either. The parade turned up an alley, he said. One dictatorship turned into another. They needed a revolution, they didn't need another dictatorship. So he escaped."

"What was his name?"

"Gregor Petrovich Gavronov."

"Wow, some name. That's how you got the name Gavin?"

"Right. He had enough sense to change the name to Gavin so my father wouldn't have a handicap, growing up. He wasn't going to get into any big-time law firm with an old-country name like Gavronov."

"What would your name be if you were back in Russia?"

"Well, Mike would be Mikhail."

"Mikhail. That's nice. You're a lovely boy, Mikhail. I'm going to miss you like crazy when you go on to advanced. That's only a couple weeks from now, isn't it?"

"I'll miss you too, Ginny."

"Thanks, but you really won't. You'll get caught up with your new airplane, your flying. You'll find a new girl. And, I guess, tell the truth, I'll find a new man.

"God," she said, shaking her head, "by the time this war is over, I'll be the biggest whore in the whole Southeast Command."

Mike took her in his arms and held her close. "No, you won't, Ginny. You're a sweet, caring woman and, some day, you'll marry a very lucky man. I'd never have made it this far if it hadn't been for you. You're a fine person and I'll never forget you. Never."

Tears filled her eyes. "That's very sweet of you, Mike, Mikhail. Very sweet. And tomorrow I'll start doing somethin' even more useful. Get you back in that Link Trainer and teach you how to navigate on instruments. You aren't goin' to graduate with the class of '42 if you don't learn. And this is your midway point, Honeybabe, the end of basic."

"We'll start tomorrow, Ginnybabe. But this is still tonight."
"I keep forgettin' you're only nineteen."

When he got to the flight line in his flying gear next morning, Mike
vowed he'd stay out of trouble. He kept the pledge for the first thirty
minutes. It wasn't *all* his fault, he told himself later. It was at least
partly Buddy's.

Aviation Cadet Harrison Bryce was a tall, slim youth from Greenville, South Carolina. He had an infectious grin and a breezy personality and was generally known as Buddy. Like Mike, he was acquir-
ing a reputation as a troublemaker. And, like Mike, he commanded a
grudging respect from his superiors for his quick reflexes and apti-
tude for flying. It was natural, perhaps, that the two would find each
other.

They were in the same basic flight training class. The airplanes they
flew were parked side by side. In Air Corps terminology, the airplane
was a BT-13 (Basic Trainer No. 13). To the cadets, the airplane was
known as the Vultee Vibrator.

There was a reason for the nickname. The BT-13 was a noisy, rattling, and sometimes treacherous bucket of bolts. Mike loved it, hated
it, and sometimes feared it. The Vibrator was a stubby single-engine
airplane with an air-cooled 450-horsepower radial engine in front.
The landing gear was fixed. A two-position lever in the cockpit
changed low to high pitch and vice versa.

As putting a car's transmission into low gear provides better trac-
tion for starting out, the low-pitch setting turned the propeller blade
on its hub to take a bigger bite of the air for takeoff and landing. It
also made an ungodly roaring noise.

The airplane had flaps that were raised or lowered by means of a
large spring-loaded hand crank on the left side of the cockpit. When
Mike least expected it, the crank would unwind backward and hit
him on the top of the wrist.

That not only hurt, it smashed the face of his regulation Army
wristwatch. Mike screamed in anger the last time it had happened.
He had had to buy three replacement wristwatches at five dollars
apiece by that time. An aviation cadet made a fairly fat seventy-five
dollars a month, but it didn't take long for a string of five-buck state-
ments of charges to eat into it.

So, as other students had learned, he began wearing the face of the
watch on the inside of his wrist.

The BT-13 sometimes scared Mike, as it did all students, because it sometimes refused to come out of a spin. And, once in a while, for no good reason the mechanics could identify, the engine would catch fire and force an emergency landing.

"Yankee know-how," Buddy explained. "God knows who designed this Rube Goldberg thing (he said "thang") or why the Air Corps bought it. It rattles like a Ford fender. But I do love that big engine. And the ol' clunker can do some pretty good tricks."

Later, they blamed the trouble on Captain Redman, their burly chief flight instructor whom they called Captain Red-Ass. That morning, he lined up the cadets and told them in precise terms what they were and were not to do in the trainers.

Redman was an ex-fighter pilot. His A-2 jacket was fashionably scratched and distressed, his officer's cap was crushed as if it had been worn in the shower, and he sported a pencil-line mustache like John Boles in the movies. He was also a sarcastic SOB.

"Lemme make something real clear," Redman said in a stentorian voice. "You cadets"—he managed to infuse the word "cadets" with contempt—"you cadets are to do exactly what you're ordered to do; nothing more. You will go aloft for thirty minutes and practice stalls and spins; give yourself plenty of room. Get so you can *fly* this airplane [he always said aer-o-plane]; don't let it fly you. You will also practice some slow rolls and snap rolls.

"When you're finished, you will practice takeoffs and landings, touch and goes, for twenty minutes. Stay in train and don't crowd each other. Tomorrow you will mush in over a rope—it will be strung up between two poles like goal posts—and you'll practice short-field landings, like you were landing on the deck of a Navy carrier. Later in the week, we'll do some cross-country flying and check out your navigation."

Redman puffed himself up and held up a warning finger. "What you will *not* do is horse around up there, waste the Army's gas and time and maybe lose an airplane. We've got lots of useless bodies like you around but we can't afford to lose an airplane. So there will be *no* dog-fighting. None. Anybody who does it will get his ass kicked up around his neck. Understand? All right; go to your planes. Go."

He dismissed them with a contemptuous wave. Obviously, Mike and Buddy agreed later, it was really Captain Red-Ass's fault. If he hadn't mentioned dogfighting it probably wouldn't have occurred to them.

"Tell you what," Mike said. "Let's find a piece of sky of our own over the northwest there, the river, and have a dogfight. See who comes out on top. Red-Ass can't be everywhere. He'll never see us."

Mike was off the ground first. He shoved the Vibrator's throttle forward, waited till the bucket of bolts began to bounce and get light-footed, and eased the stick back. The dew in the grass of the nearby field sparkled like a tapestry of diamonds as he cleared the runway.

It was a clear, brilliantly sunny morning. Thin cirrus clouds streaked the bright blue canopy high above as if traced across it by giant fingers.

As he soared up into the sky, he thought: *What a kick! What a helluva kick!* What he meant, and knew he meant, was: *What a thrill! What a beautiful, lovely experience!*

Mike circled over the Savannah River and waited. Five minutes went by and no other airplane appeared. He was about to bank away and start practicing spins and rolls when, at last, he spotted a BT beginning to climb toward him.

"Tally-ho!" Mike yelled, the way the RAF pilots did in the latest Battle of Britain movie. He turned his BT on its back, pulled the stick into his stomach, and let the nose drop toward the struggling airplane below. "Bam, bam, bam!" he yelled as he fixed the BT in his imaginary gunsight.

Mike used his excess speed to pull up into a half-loop and roll-out as the second BT began turning to intercept him. Turning so tightly the G force squashed him down into the cockpit, he dived on the other plane's tail. As the other pilot turned, banked, dived, and climbed, Mike stuck to him like glue.

Growing in confidence, Mike moved in closer until his propeller seemed only feet away from the BT's tail. After another five minutes of aerobatics, the enemy airplane leveled out as if in surrender. Grinning, Mike pulled alongside to wave at Buddy.

But the red face glaring at him from the second BT was Captain Redman's. Savagely, Redman made a cutthroat gesture and pointed downward. Mike let his head drop on his chest. *Ahhh, piss-ant*, he said to himself. Obediently, he banked away, cut his throttle and, losing altitude, moved into the airfield's traffic pattern.

Ten minutes later, sweating and flushed, Mike stood at rigid attention while Redman, sitting behind his office desk, chewed him out.

"Give me one reason—just one good reason—why I shouldn't wash you out for insubordination and ship your ass to Biloxi!" Redman thundered.

"No excuse, sir," Mike said, giving one of the three responses a cadet was allowed to make. The other two were yes, sir and no, sir.

"No excuse, sir," the burly captain said sarcastically. "There's only one reason why I'm not washing you out right now, Mister. When a cadet under my command fucks up, it reflects on *me*, and I don't like that. And the Training Command is on our ass to move cadet pilots into advanced." He pointed a thick finger at the cadet. "So you get one last chance even though you don't deserve it. *One*. Fuck up again and you know what you'll be doing in Biloxi."

"Shoveling shit, sir."

"Exactly. You're dismissed." He waved his hand as if fanning away an annoying insect.

Buddy was waiting for him outside, his thin face furrowed. "What happened?"

"One more chance," Mike said, pulling out a handkerchief and wiping his face. "How come you didn't meet me over the river like we agreed?"

"The engine caught fire at five hundred feet," Buddy said. "It was a fire-drill. I had to bank around, call an emergency, and dump it on the ground. I'm really sorry."

"Not your fault, Buddy. Forget it."

Redman's revenge—or so Mike characterized it—came a week later when assignments to advanced flying schools were listed on the bulletin board. He and Buddy had been posted to twin-engine training.

The two promptly went to the sergeant and requested an audience with Captain Red-Ass. The sergeant smirked, announced them on the intercom, and pointed toward the captain's door.

"Sir," Mike said, speaking for himself and Buddy, "we requested single-engine school. We believe we will make outstanding fighter pilots and preferences are usually honored. But our names are posted for twin-engine school. We request our preferences be honored. Sir."

Redman looked at them as if they were bums asking for a handout. Then he leaned backward in his chair and said coldly: "It may not have crossed your minds, misters, but this war is not being waged for your entertainment. It just so happens that there is a demand for multi-engine pilots at this time. I'm sure you'd like to be hot-shot aces and bore holes in the sky and all that, but that ain't the way the ball bounces this time. It's twin-engine school or Biloxi. What's your choice?"

"Twin-engine school," the boys muttered.

"An excellent choice," Redman said. "Now get out."

The day of their departure for advanced training in Albany, Georgia, Mike met Ginny outside the hangar. "Oh God, I hate to see you leave," she said, her voice breaking and tears filling her eyes. "I'm goin' to miss you so bad." She moved into his arms and laid her cheek against his.

"I'll miss you, too, Ginny," he said, somewhat surprised at meaning it.

"It really isn't fair," she complained. "You cadets come and go and we girls stay behind and, and *grieve*, really *grieve*. We'd be better off comin' and fightin' alongside you."

Mike hugged her and smiled. "That's not what women do, Ginny," he said gently.

Five thousand miles to the east, on a grass field a few miles north of the shattered city of Stalingrad, Galina Tarasova sat in the cockpit of her ancient PO-2 biplane, so small and frail it could fairly be called a *kukuruznik*, and waited for the takeoff signal.

The little bomber's hundred-horsepower engine popped like a steaming teakettle. The sound was drowned out every few seconds by the rumble of heavy gunfire. Behind Galina in the rear cockpit was her navigator/gunner, Nadia Rudnova.

The weight of Galina's responsibility made her small gloved hand tremble as it rested on the throttle. It was her first night mission.

The sun had been down for hours but the velvety darkness was dispelled periodically by orange flashes from the explosions around the city. A pall of black smoke and, with it, bits of tarry debris floated from the southwest to remind the aircrews of the agony that Stalingrad's inhabitants were suffering.

The tarry smell was offensive to Galina not only because of its dreadful source but because it polluted the aromatic breath of Mother Russia—the bracing turpentine scent of the nearby pine forests and the sweet smell of the aspens.

Galina and Nadia were members of the 588th Air Regiment, one of two all-women air combat regiments of the *Voyenno-vozdushnyye sily*, the Soviet Air Force, also known as the VVS. The two regiments flew bombers; a third regiment was equipped with Yak fighters that were flown by men and women pilots.

The 588th flew tiny, thirteen-year-old biplane trainers; each carried four 50-pound bombs on racks beneath the wings. When the moment came, Galina knew, she would release the bombs by pulling a wire in her cockpit. Nadia, who had already flown ten combat missions with another pilot, now dead, would give her navigational directions by intercom from the rear cockpit. If they were attacked by a German night fighter, Nadia would try to fight him off with the 7.62-mm. machine gun mounted on a ring across her cockpit. Both knew that stealth was a better defense.

A green flare blossomed at the edge of the field. It was time. Galina pushed the throttle forward and the PO-2 began waddling over the grass. When it began skipping she pulled the stick back slightly and the biplane took flight. A few seconds later a second PO-2 took off and, a few seconds after that, a third.

Galina made a slow climbing turn to the right and leveled off at three thousand feet. "Remember the plan," Nadia whispered. "Keep turning right till we're south of the city. Then we'll attack to the north. That'll avoid some of the ground fire."

"Understood," Galina answered.

The target was the local headquarters of a German division that had been marked on a map of the city by intelligence. The day's ground battle around the tractor plant had been brutal, with heavy casualties on both sides. There had also been many aerial battles, with Soviet Yak fighters trying to pick off Stuka dive-bombers and Messerschmitt 109s attacking the Yaks. Conversely, ME-109s and Focke-Wulfs tried to shoot down the Soviets' low-flying Shturmovik tank-killers while the Yaks went after the German fighters.

Now the night sky was empty except for the "night-witches," as the Germans called the Soviet women pilots, and the occasional, deadly German night fighter. Below, the Volga shone like polished silver, though the beauty of the winding river was marred every few seconds by drifting clouds of black smoke.

Galina knew that the work of the night-witches was hardly decisive in the struggle for the city. But she also knew that it kept the exhausted German troops from getting uninterrupted sleep and, occasionally, did real damage by hitting a command post, ammunition dump, or troop concentration.

"Take a heading of ten degrees and check your stopwatch," Nadia said. "The target should be in front of us in one minute." Galina swung the PO-2 on the prescribed heading and punched the button on the stopwatch. At the same time, she cut her engine and began gliding silently toward the target. The wires and struts keened in the night air.

When the sweephand touched zero, Galina tossed a parachute flare over the side. Abruptly, the ground turned white. The landscape was a surrealist's nightmare of gutted buildings, piles of stone and brick rubble, and heaps of unburied bodies, only some of them wearing uniforms.

"Dead ahead!" Nadia cried. Below, German soldiers, some—she could see clearly—with officers' badges on their tunics, scurried like rats around the headquarters building. Sandbags had been packed against the brick walls.

A searchlight snapped on and anti-aircraft tracers began streaking up from the ground in globules of light. When they reached her altitude they exploded like huge orange dandelions.

Galina flew through the explosions, nose down, and jerked the wire release. The bombs fell directly on the target. She saw several bodies rise in the air like rag dolls and she shoved the throttle to full power, banked sharply away and, diving, turned back toward the Soviet lines.

One explosion rocked the airplane and she heard bits of shrapnel tear through the fabric of the fuselage. Then she was free of the inferno. Behind her she heard more explosions as the following PO-2s dropped their loads. An instant later there was a very loud boom and a bright flash of red; someone, she thought excitedly, had accidentally hit a cache of stored ammunition.

Moments later, hooded smudge pots guided her into the landing area and she was on the ground, bumping across the grass toward her parking spot beneath the camouflage nets.

When she climbed out of the cockpit, Nadia hugged her. "Good first mission!" she said. "You're a fine pilot."

"Thanks," Galina said. She realized that she was very tired. Some of the fatigue came from the tension of the first mission, she knew; some came from the shortage of food. Even a slim five-foot-four girl of nineteen needed more nourishment than one meal a day of black bread and soup.

There was, however, the occasional chocolate bar—though it was a cause of some resentment—from the men at the nearby Yak fighter base who seemed to have a plentiful supply.

When the other two biplanes had landed, Major Larissa Kravchenko, the regimental commander, spoke to the six women before they went to their bunker to sleep.

"It was a good mission," she said. "All three crews performed well. Evidence is that we hit the command post and Irina here"—the girl's eyes glowed with pleasure—"apparently hit an ammunition dump. I will submit a good report on tonight's work."

The major looked at them seriously. "We play a small part in a very big war, perhaps, but the day will come when they realize the women can do as much as the men. Now go to bed."

She pulled each of them to her ample bosom and administered a motherly hug before bidding them goodnight.

Before falling asleep, Galina mentally reviewed the events of the past two months. She had done well in training and, tonight, on her first mission. Though brief, it had been frightening, but it had been exhilarating, too. She vowed to excel and make it crystal-clear to her superiors that, one day, she should be transferred to fighters.

She was still embarrassed at the dressing-down she had received two weeks earlier from Major Marina Raskova, the famous woman flier who had organized the women's regiments at Comrade Stalin's order. Galina had protested her assignment to the slow PO-2 bomber, pointing out that she had become an instructor at her sports flying club in Moscow, was considered a superior pilot, and was well-qualified to fly a Yak fighter.

Her protest had made the legendary Raskova angry. "Do you think this is a game, Lieutenant?" she demanded. "Our soldiers are dying by the thousands, the millions, sacrificing their bodies and their lives to stop these Hitlerites. We'll be lucky to get through this winter. And here you come whining about the kind of airplane you're assigned to fly. Be glad you can make a contribution, Galina, any kind at all. Now get out."

Galina saluted and did an about-face. But tears began running down her face before she could reach the door.

"Wait!" the older woman commanded. Raskova strode to her, turned her around, pulled a handkerchief from her tunic pocket, and wiped Galina's eyes. "Remember that you were picked from among many, Galina. Many others failed to qualify. Be proud of that. Now go."

Galina felt better afterward, but she still had mixed feelings of pride and a lingering yearning to fly a fast airplane. The new Yaks, she had heard, were the fastest combat airplanes yet. Imagine flying the very fastest airplane! Would they really allow a woman to do *that?*

To sit in the experimental Messerschmitt 163 Komet when the rocket engine was ignited, Flugkapitan Hanna Reitsch said to herself, was to be suspended in the mouth of Hell. The sheets of flame and the savage bellow of the engine were terrifying to even the hardiest of test pilots.

And the Komet—some called the stubby, tailless craft the "power egg"—was not an animal that barks but cannot bite. Already, fellow test pilot Heini Dittmar was laid up in hospital with a spine injury from an earlier test flight.

Hanna had received the respect due her bravery only after her achievements made it impossible for the Luftwaffe aces and generals to ignore her. Reichsmarshall Hermann Göring had laughed when he had met her.

"Five feet and one-half inch!" he had roared. "And this mouse of a creature is the pilot who showed us how gliders should be flown, who test-flew our first helicopter, who tested the device to cut balloon cables in mid-air, who now flies our first rocketship! The body of a mouse and the heart of a lion!"

After she had performed an extremely dangerous test—landing in a net of ropes on a platform simulating the deck of a warship—they had made her an honorary Flugkapitan. The Führer himself had presented her with the Iron Cross. She wore it today over her coveralls.

Now she took a deep breath, said a silent prayer, and activated the engine. From one fuel tank flowed concentrated hydrogen peroxide. From another came a mixture of hydrazine-hydrate in methanol. When the two met, spontaneous combustion occurred and vapor shot out of twelve jets with a backthrust of forty-five hundred horsepower.

The tiny aircraft shot from the ground, slamming Hanna into the back of her seat in a series of powerful blows. She jettisoned the wheels at two hundred feet; the airspeed was already two hundred and fifty miles an hour.

In a few seconds, she was flying at a breathtaking five hundred miles an hour. Pointing the tiny nose upward at seventy degrees, she was at thirty thousand feet in a minute and a half. She leveled off as the speed rose to six hundred and banked sharply. The tiny craft was surprisingly agile and easy to fly, once aloft.

"Wonderful!" she exulted. No one, surely, had ever flown so fast. This would be the decisive weapon to stop the Allied bombers—an airplane so fast that the gunners in the bombers would never see it. Beside the Komet, the Allied fighters would be creeping snails.

And the rocket plane's twin 30-mm. cannons would smash the barbarians who dared to drop bombs on the towns and cities of her beloved Germany!

But there was, inevitably, one major problem and she and the engineers had found no easy solution to it. The Komet had only five to six minutes of flying time before the fuel ran out.

And here it was. The engine flamed out. The breathtakingly fast Komet became a falling stone. She pointed the nose down and banked toward the field. Now, with the stubby wings and no tail, she had to keep the speed high. The approach had to be made accurately.

There would be no pull-up and go-round, no second chance to make a safe landing. This was not an aircraft for mediocre pilots.

Hanna streaked along the downwind side of the field, checked her speed and altimeter, and curved carefully onto the approach. Too high! She sideslipped and the craft shuddered. Careful, don't stall! She straightened out and squared up with the runway. She pulled the nose up very slowly, very gently, and touched the ground with the Komet's landing skid at one hundred and fifty miles an hour.

The skid screeched and she fought to keep the plane straight before it slid to a halt. Hanna expelled a deep breath and waved as the others came running to her. She smiled. Many, she knew, believed that Germany had gone to war prematurely, that the nation lacked the resources to fight a two-front war.

But German science and the bravery of German airmen—and air*women*—would save Germany. Wasn't today's flight a promise of that? She was very proud to be a part of it.

CHAPTER TWO

A GOOD WAR

Bored and weary, Mike and Buddy stood at the supply counter in the quartermaster warehouse at Turner Field, their advanced training base near Albany, Georgia, as a chubby clerk read off a list in a monotone and dumped each item in front of them.

"Bag, assembly, B-4 . . . Bag, flyer's, A-3 . . . Cap, summer, B-1 . . . Cap, winter, B-2 . . . Sunglasses, flying . . . Gloves, winter, A-10 . . . Goggle assembly, B-7 . . ."

"Why issue goggles when we're going to be inside the cabins of the airplanes?" Mike asked.

"You never know," the clerk said without looking up. "Helmet, summer, A-9," he continued. "Helmet, winter, B-6 . . . Jacket, A-2 . . . Jacket, winter, B-3 . . . Mask, oxygen, A-10 . . ."

"Why do we need both summer and winter stuff when we're only goin' to be here ten weeks?" Buddy asked.

"You never know," the clerk droned. He peered at the list and reached in another box. "Parachute, 24-inch seat type . . . Shoes, winter, A-6 . . . Life vest, B-4 . . . Cylinder, CO_2 . . ."

"What are we supposed to do with CO_2 cylinders?" Mike asked.

As the clerk opened his mouth, Mike and Buddy spoke along with him: "You never know."

Being "processed" on and off Air Corps bases was a deadening experience. Earlier, they had had the routine medical examination, lining up naked to have their eyes and ears checked, mouths peered into, groins prodded for possible hernias, and penises squeezed (the traditional "short-arm" inspection) to reveal any venereal discharges.

Afterward, they dressed, slouched to another building, and waited to be interrogated by a human relations officer. Thin, bald, and bespectacled, the lieutenant was the perfect prototype of a non-flying paddle-foot.

"Have you made a Class N allotment for payment of National Life Insurance premiums?" the man asked.

Mike and Buddy answered no and the officer handed each a pen to sign applications for ten-thousand-dollar policies that authorized withdrawal of six dollars a month from each cadet's pay and named his mother as beneficiary.

"Have you made a will?" the officer asked. The two boys looked at each other in surprise at the odd question—a *will?*—and answered no. The man handed each a form to fill out and return.

"Have you written home this past week?"

The boys mumbled incoherently and the officer pointed to a long table in the corner where other cadets were scribbling and said: "Do it now. There's pencil and paper over there. Put the envelopes on my desk on the way out."

The mess hall was a huge and noisy replica of the mess halls at their primary and basic flight training bases. And the food was the same mountain of monotony they'd encountered before: filet-of-gray-meat with gravy, mashed potatoes, peas and carrots, a piece of sticky cake, milk, juice, and coffee.

Ground school began at 8:00 A.M. the following morning after the most terrible of all excuses for a breakfast: chipped beef on toast, universally known as shit-on-a-shingle. Disdaining it, the boys ate an apple, had a bowl of corn flakes with milk and sugar, drank coffee, and then bought doughnuts at the PX.

In the classroom they encountered meteorology, engineering, dead-reckoning navigation, Morse code, aircraft recognition, and Army rules and regulations. When the cadets spoke in class, Mike was struck by the realization that nearly all of them were from southern states.

After lunch—hot dogs and sauerkraut (dogs in the hay), bread, milk, and a banana—they were sent to a hangar for more Link Trainer instruction.

It was two days before they got to the flight line. The instructor, they noted thankfully, was a pleasant, soft-spoken officer named Lieutenant Hurd. Buddy was overjoyed to find that he was from South Carolina.

"Wonderful," Mike said dourly. "You can translate for me. That cracker we had back in primary kept telling me to keep the no-uz stray-ut. It took me a week to understand what he meant."

"You just don't tawk Ewe-nighted Stets," Buddy grinned, thickening his accent.

The airplane was an AT-10, a low-wing Beechcraft monoplane with two 280-horsepower radial Lycoming engines and two side-by-side seats in the cabin. The AT-10 was made of wood so, though the Army tried to call it the Wichita, the cadets dubbed it the "bamboo bomber."

The boys found it harder to fly and, particularly, to land than they had expected. Mike was surprised and embarrassed when, touching the runway for his first landing, the AT-10 bounced high in the air. Pushing the wheel yoke forward and bringing it back, Mike tried to ease the wheels onto the ground. Instead, it bounced again and the airplane bounded down the runway like a kangaroo as Mike, cursing, tried to get it under control. "The damned thing's got a built-in bounce!" Mike yelled, waving his arms, when he and Buddy got a chance to compare notes.

"Don' I know," Buddy said dolefully.

Over the ensuing weeks, the boys were drilled in dead-reckoning and radio navigation, made point-to-point night flights—Mike found that he hated night flying—practiced single-engine emergency procedures, took cross-country trips, learned to fly on autopilot, and studied engineering in ground school.

They were kept so busy they found no opportunity to get into trouble until a cross-country flight was scheduled along a triangular course from Albany to Waycross to Macon and back to Albany. They were pleased at being able to team up on the exercise and take turns flying. No deviations from the set course were allowed.

On the way to Waycross, they saw the beginning of the Okefenokee Swamp on their right. The huge swamp was mysterious and ominous-looking and made its own weather. Fog and low clouds hung over the area in seeming defiance of the sunny landscape and skies to the north. Even the trees and brush poking out of the brackish waters were stunted and twisted.

Unquestionably, the Okefenokee contained many different kinds of living things, some of them slimy, dangerous, and evil. It was repellent, repulsive, and irresistible. And they had been obeying orders for much too long.

"We've *gotta* go over there," Mike said fervently.

"You're right," Buddy said. "Nobody'll know. Do it."

Mike banked to the right, cut the throttles to lose altitude, and glided silently toward the twisted treetops.

"There!" Buddy shouted. An emerald-green pool lay just beyond a patch of heavy undergrowth and ferns. In the middle basked an enormous alligator. Mike dived toward the pool, the airplane's wheels barely skimming the surface, and blasted the throttles.

The alligator reared, thrashed about, and slithered into deeper water. "What a kick!" Mike yelled, rocking the plane's wings.

"Whoop-to-do!" Buddy shouted.

They buzzed about over the swamp, cutting through low clouds and murk, managing to scare a wild pig and stampede two deer. Banking vertically, they saw what looked like a family of cottonmouth snakes sidle toward the water.

"Man, that's no place to go down!" Buddy shouted. It was then that the flock of large birds exploded from a nearby patch of tall grass. One flew directly into the port engine and a second hit the windscreen. The port engine barked and quit and the nose began turning toward the left.

Long cracks appeared in the windscreen; streaks of blood and clusters of feathers made it almost impossible to see.

"Gotta land!" Mike yelled.

"Turn northeast!" Buddy shouted. "Beyond the swamp; there's a grass field over there. Better put 'er down."

"Oh piss-ant," Mike groaned. He banked about and pulled the throttles back as Buddy lowered the wheels. The landing was a good one but the wheels struck a rut when they were slowing to a stop and the aircraft pitched forward, tail-high, caving in the nose, breaking both propellers and several engine cylinders.

"It's Biloxi for sure this time," Mike said somberly when they had clambered out and surveyed the damage.

"Shee-it," Buddy replied. After standing about irresolutely for five minutes, he shagged to a nearby farmhouse, called the local police, and asked them to phone the operations office at Albany.

An hour later an olive-green Army staff car arrived. Out of it came Lieutenant Hurd, shaking his head, a round-faced engineering officer who looked like he had swallowed a lemon, and a gray-haired major. The boys quailed at the sight of the major's oak leaves; attracting the attention of brass *that* high up was bad news.

The major was surprisingly low-key. "Are you men all right?" he asked. When they nodded speechlessly, he asked: "What happened here?" The boys hemmed and coughed and gestured silently to each other to act as spokesman.

The major leaned toward Mike and, pointing at him, asked: "What happened, son?"

Mike told him about the birds and the forced landing.

The major looked about. "I can see what the birds did but I don't see any birds or bird's nests around here. Not even any tall trees. Were you boys on course?"

"Pretty much, sir," Buddy said.

"Pretty much," the major repeated thoughtfully. He stepped forward, peered closely at the wheels, and plucked a few pieces of swamp grass from the undercarriage. Walking around to the tail, he found a tendril from a vine wrapped around the stabilizer.

"We had an AT-10 crash in the swamp over there a couple months ago," the major said, examining the vine. "Cadets were fooling around. The crash killed the pilot. The co-pilot won't ever walk right again. That's besides the cost of the government equipment. Do you know what an airplane like this costs?"

When one boy shrugged and the other shook his head, the major said: "Ten thousand dollars. Think about that. Ten *thousand* dollars. That's nearly six times what a second lieutenant makes in a year." He walked around the damaged airplane with the engineering officer and spoke to him in a low voice.

Turning to the boys, he said: "Now this airplane isn't a total washout, but it'll probably cost maybe three thousand dollars to repair it. At seventy-five dollars a month, your entire paycheck, it would take —let's see—it would take more than three years to pay that back. Anyone who'd cause a loss like that because of negligence, disobeying the rules, would have to be washed out, sent back for reclassification as a clerk or KP helper. Do you agree?"

Mike nodded, his stomach turning to ice. Buddy swallowed hard and, his voice failing, whispered assent.

"It would be an automatic washout if a stunt like that was premeditated. Was yours premeditated? Did you plan all along to fly over that swamp?"

"No sir," the boys chorused truthfully. Mike was about to add that it had happened on impulse when he remembered the unwritten rule against volunteering—especially volunteering more information than was called for—and fell silent.

"All right," the major said. "A truck will be along shortly to take you back to your base. Each of you will write a three-thousand-word essay on safe flying and the necessity of rules to assure it. I want it on my desk in forty-eight hours. Give your essays to Lieutenant Hurd here. That's all."

The boys popped to attention and saluted. What a wonderful, understanding man! Mike thought. The major returned their salute, eyed them for a moment, turned, and got back in the staff car with Hurd and the engineering officer. As they drove away, the major turned to Hurd: "Do those two little turds really have as much talent as you said?"

"Yes sir, I believe they do," Hurd answered.

"Well, under normal conditions I'd wash them out of the cadet corps and let them clean garbage cans in dirty fatigues for the rest of the war. But we've invested about fifty thousand dollars in each of them so far and we have a very bloody business ahead of us in Europe. We're going to need every good pilot we can find. Whether he's a fuckup or not."

The essays were turned in on time, though Buddy wailed like a sick dog through most of the forty-eight hours as he struggled to find the necessary words. Mike pounded out his essay on the operation office clerk's typewriter in four hours and then typed out suggested notes for Buddy to use.

The boys finished the advanced course two weeks before graduation and were granted a series of forty-eight-hour passes to spend in the Albany area. They immediately began planning how to meet some girls.

"I got that old Hawaiian disease and I got it bad, Mike-boy," Buddy complained. "Lack-a-nookie."

"I know," Mike sighed, thinking wistfully of his previous thrice-weekly schedule with Ginny. He hadn't realized how rich and satisfying an experience it had been and he cursed himself for failing to value it at the time.

An opportunity to find out what Albany society had to offer came from a notice posted on the bulletin board. It was an invitation to the graduating class to attend a buffet supper and dance at the Albany Country Club. The town's fathers would be on hand to welcome them and hostesses would be available for conversation and dancing.

"Con-ver-say-shun!" Buddy crowed, broadening his accent for dramatic effect. "Dan-cin'! And, I humbly hope, a *li'l* diddlin' with one of the town's li'l darlin's. Who knows? Maybe I'll fall in luv. Any change at all in m'present condition'll be a major, I mean a *majuh,* improvement."

At the party Buddy was true to his word. He disappeared into the darkness in mid-evening with the giggling, slightly chubby daughter of the town banker. Mike, feeling himself a stranger among the tight-knit clan of southerners, hung around the bandstand.

The band had eight pieces and it was surprisingly good. They played the top pop songs of the day and followed the arrangements of the big swing bands. When they moved from the upbeat tempo of "Chattanooga Choo-Choo" to a romantic ballad, "I Only Have Eyes For You," Mike, standing to the side, unconsciously began singing the lyrics.

The pianist cocked an ear, leaned forward to the leader, and spoke to him. The leader moved sideways, listened, and then motioned to Mike.

"You sound pretty good, kid," he said. "Come on up here and we'll go 'round again." When Mike shook his head, the leader motioned vigorously. "Come *on,* fella," he said, "I'm too hoarse to sing and, besides, what've you got to lose? We're all friends here."

Well, why not? Mike thought. *I've been making a fool of myself pretty regularly over the past few months. Why should tonight be any different?* He climbed up and let the leader adjust the mike to his shorter size as the band swung back toward the opening chorus.

Looking over the heads of the dancers and imagining he was singing beside his mother's piano in the living room in Baltimore, Mike vowed to avoid the amateur's habit of starting off tentatively. As his cue came, he took a deep breath, let a little out, and sang out forcefully in his high baritone:

> *Are the stars out tonight?*
> *Don't know whether it's cloudy or bright,*
> *For I only have eyes for you, dear . . .*

By the time he had sung sixteen bars and was into the bridge, there were three girls standing beneath the bandstand in front of him. Two were leaning away from their disgruntled dancing partners; the third, a bold-looking blonde in a green dress, was standing alone and smiling seductively at him.

Growing in confidence, Mike looked directly at her and sang:

> *I don't know if we're in a garden*
> *Or on a crowded avenue,*
> *You are here, so am I*
> *Maybe millions of people go by,*
> *But they all disappear from view,*
> *Annnnnnd. . . .*

He held the *f* as the band slowed for him and then launched into the final line:

> *I on-ly have eyes for yoooou.*

There was a lively round of applause. From the back of the room came a rebel whoop. Mike laughed aloud when he saw the source: Buddy, hair disheveled and smeared with lipstick, hanging on to the giggling brunette.

The band leader shook Mike's hand and patted him on the back. As Mike stepped down, the blonde walked up to him and said: "That was real nice, real pretty, mister cadet."

She said "mistuh," of course; Buddy couldn't have made the accent any thicker. She held out her hand. "I'm Clarisse, Clarisse Hunnicut. My friends call me Claire. What is yew-er name?"

As Mike introduced himself, the girl gently placed the palm of her hand against his heart. No one had ever done that before; her touch surprised and jolted him. It was as if she had given him an electric shock.

Speaking softly, looking directly into his eyes, and moving close to him—presumably to be heard over the band music—she seemed to be trying to hypnotize him. And, he realized, with considerable success.

Before he fully knew what was happening, they were dancing and Claire was very close to him. He couldn't tell whether the fragrance was from her skin or her perfume. Probably, he thought, it was both. When the set ended, she steered him outside for a cigarette. At the end of the evening, she drove him back to the base in her car, a handsome blue Buick convertible.

"You're a real nice Yankee boy, a real gentleman [it came out 'gennimun']," Claire said when they parked by the gate. "Most Yankees we see here don't seem like our kind of class of people somehow. But you're different, Michael. Would you like to get together middle of the week, maybe? Understan' you finished your course. All you got to do is wait for graduation, I hear."

"A couple of us thought we'd get passes and stay at the Albany Hotel," Mike said.

"Um, that'd be fun for you, I'm sure," she said. "But actually I couldn't go *there*. My family's real well-known around town and if I was seen in the *hotel* my reputation would be in, well, *tatters*, you know. If you wanta stay there that's fine, Michael, but"—she moved in close again and gently put a hand on his bicep in a way that automatically made him tighten it and feel like a fool—"my parents would be pleased if you'd stay at our home for a night or two. We have a nice room for guests. Would you like that?"

Mike mumbled that that sounded fine and they set a date. Feeling such an advance would be welcome, he leaned toward her to kiss her before getting out of the car. She swayed backward and away from him and then moved forward enough to kiss him so lightly their lips barely touched.

The gesture seemed incredibly erotic and in his frustration he felt as if his lips were protruding like a moose's.

"Michael, you're so, so *masculine* you make me feel a little faint," she breathed, both hands on his chest. Her handsomely-rounded breasts, he noted, were rising and falling. On the rise, they seemed to be straining the fabric of her low-cut dress.

"I *have* to hold you off, Michael," she said earnestly, training her large green eyes on his. "I just *have* to. If I didn't, I don't know what would happen. Something very harmful, I'm sure. It's so easy for you men, but"—she shook her head—"not for us women. I know you understand."

Back in the barracks, Buddy listened to an account of Mike's experience with a knowing smile. Occasionally, he chuckled, his shoulders shaking.

"You pore boy," Buddy said at length. "You've finally met a S'uthe'n Belle, a real raised-by-her-mama, finishin'-school, man-eatin' S'uthe'n Belle. That's a very special kind of species, Mike-boy, very dangerous. A man needs a 'structional manual to know how to deal with *her*. See, she wouldn't pay any 'tention to me cause she'd automatically know I know 'bout all that. But you, pore boy, you're fresh meat for the tiger."

He shook his head. "Fresh meat!"

"Are you saying she isn't sincere?" Mike asked in irritation.

"Hmph," Buddy said. "Sincere's not the point. Listen, boy, that girl has been trained to a tee to keep a man off-balance, waitin', hangin', droolin', eventually makin' a complete fool of himself. She'll promise and promise—well, she won't really ever *promise* in so many words, she'll make you think she's promisin'. But she won't *deliver*, Mikey-boy.

"That kind of babe—well, you know all those nasty words: ball-breaker, cock-teaser, all that."

"Ah come on, Buddy," Mike said. "Claire's gotta be like any girl at heart. She's gotta have real feelings, real emotions. Just because she's not an easy lay doesn't make her a manipulative person. If she likes me, who knows what'll happen?" He sighed. "I'd sure like to have *something* happen." He meant sex, of course, but a good deal more than the mechanical act. He was starved for warmth, closeness, the smell and touch of a caring woman.

When they met at her house for dinner three nights later, Claire was captivating in a white dress that dramatically set off her tanned skin, green eyes, and long blonde hair. Her mother, Helene Hunnicut, was a faded beauty with pleasant manners and an air of quiet dignity.

The father, Justin, was a tall, heavyset cotton merchant with a ruddy complexion and a set of strongly-held opinions that he expressed during dinner. His elation over the short-term benefits of supplying cotton to the War Department for the duration was, clearly, offset by concerns over the long-term effects that the war would have on existing differences in class and race.

"It's all very well, *very well*, to talk about the benefits of all this in-migration and out-migration of our work force," he said, pointing at Mike with his fork. "But it could have very serious consequences, very serious ones, when the war is over. They said it in World War One, you know. 'How you goin' to keep 'em down on the farm,' right? Well, add to that our delicate race situation and you got a real peck of troubles ahead. A real peck of 'em." He munched on his food for a while, ruminating, and then pointed his fork again. "Don't get me wrong. This is a good war, a good, clean war. But, afterward—well, we're in for a peck a trouble."

Mike nodded and listened respectfully with the tiniest part of his attention, which was already divided between an excellent roast of beef—the finest food he had eaten in many months—and the rising and falling of Claire's breasts across the table.

After dinner, Mrs. Hunnicut startled him by saying that Claire had told her he had a fine singing voice. She herself was a pianist, a conservatory graduate, and she would play for him if he would sing something afterward to her accompaniment.

"Mother's a real good pee-anist," Claire said enthusiastically, "and you've got a dreamy voice. Say you will, Michael."

So, trapped, embarrassed and, to his irritation, initially shaky, he did. After Helene had competently played a Chopin waltz, they hemmed and hawed over the sheet music in the piano bench and finally settled on "The Nearness of You."

He stood straight, as his mother had taught him, and sang to the wall, shifting his focus to Claire in the last few measures as the lyrics expressed the ambition that was growing within him:

> *If you'll only grant me the right*
> *to hold you ever so tight,*
> *And to know in the night*
> *the nearness of you.*

Claire was like a well-fed cat lying in front of a fire. Her eyes glowed; a small smile played across her full mouth. She did everything but purr and sharpen her claws. Her mother looked up, eyes narrowing, as she sensed the interplay between the two young people. For his part, the father sat quietly, as he had obviously done many times before, and, looking inward, mentally reviewed his sales figures.

Later, Mike and Claire walked hand in hand under the towering oaks that flanked the darkened streets. Little was said. Claire seemed to be relaxed and content within herself. *Was she adding him to her list of acquisitions as her father added up his cotton bales? As she had tallied up many other young males?* He knew he wanted the girl; he burned for her ripe body and he wanted to shatter her obvious confidence that she had assumed control over him. *I'm fascinated by this girl*, he thought, *but do I really even like her?*

Sitting on the swing of her porch, she led him through a recitation of Army life and flight training, as he was sure she had done many times before with other cadets. She oohed and ahhed appreciatively at the proper moments. In the middle of one ooh, he took Claire by the shoulders and kissed her.

She responded instinctively, losing control momentarily and digging her fingers into his shoulders. Then she broke away; her eyes, startled, sparkled with angry highlights. Pressing gently against his chest, she dropped her head for a moment. When she looked up, she was smiling and her eyes were big, beautiful, and opaque.

"That wasn't fair, Michael," she said.

"I guess I could ask 'why not?' but that wouldn't lead anywhere productive, would it, Claire?"

"Oh, it's all just so very confusin', that's all," she dissembled. "And you're here for such a short time, you know."

She glanced at her wristwatch. "Oh my goodness; look at the time. I simply have to have my beauty sleep and you do too, Michael. You have to go back to Turner in the mornin'."

She rose briskly. "Come on, now. Time for bed. I'll see you to your room, like a good escort. The folks have gone on to bed."

At the door of his room, she melted into him and kissed him slowly, running her hands up and down his back. As she did, he pulled her gently into the room and closed the door. Breaking away, she said: "I have to leave, Michael. Please don't make a scene."

"I wouldn't think of it," he said. "I just don't like to kiss a girl in an open doorway. It makes me nervous." He smiled. "One more kiss and I'll let you go."

"Just one more," she said, moving forward. He had remembered something that Ginny had taught him. *If you want a girl to want to kiss you, break it off just before she's ready to. And once in a while, pull away just as she's coming to you.*

As Claire's lips barely touched his, he pulled back slightly. Her eyes snapped open in surprise. "I'm sorry," he said. "I was just a little off balance." She closed her eyes and moved in. As their lips touched, he pulled away the tiniest bit, leading her to lean forward again.

Again her eyes snapped open and, with an uncharacteristic growl, she seized his head with both hands and crushed her lips against his. When he tried to break it off before she did, she held him tight. Finally she broke it off, stared at him and broke into a throaty laugh.

"You beast!" she said. "You horrible beast! Who taught you that trick anyhow, Michael?"

"A girl back in basic," he said. "I guess you'd call her an older woman."

"Hmph. Well, I must say, you're not quite as nice as I thought, Michael. And you're much more dangerous than I thought. And I'm leavin'."

"I want you very much, Claire. And I think you want me," he said. "Come back later tonight. Will you?"

"Who knows what people will do?" she purred. "Who knows?" She ran one long finger delicately down his shirtfront to his belt, then turned, opened the door, and blew him a kiss.

"What do you want from me, Claire?" he asked.

She smiled. "Only your heart and soul, lover." She left quickly, went into her room down the hall, and closed the door.

He splashed cold water in his face and, when that didn't help, undressed, stepped into the shower, and let the cold water run over his body. His erection returned when he was drying himself.

Cursing, he considered masturbating. But the thought made him angry: *that's probably what she wants to force me to do. The ultimate humiliation. So damnit to hell, I won't.* He drank water, thought about flying, tried to count sheep, fell asleep, woke, and thrashed about during the night. It was daylight before he fell into a sound sleep. The sound of a door banging and Claire's parents going downstairs awakened him.

Wearily, Mike went to the bathroom, urinated, washed his face, brushed his teeth, and took a half dozen deep breaths. He was still sexually aroused. Coming to a decision, he cautiously opened the door and peered out. Claire's father was leaving the house and her mother apparently had returned to the dining room for her breakfast.

Mike walked barefoot to Claire's door, opened it slowly and quietly, and crept in. She was asleep on her back, her lips open enough to show the edges of her even white teeth. He carefully pulled back her covers. She was wearing a short silk nightgown. He stripped off his shorts and lowered himself carefully into bed with her.

Ginny had always been exceptionally passionate in the mornings, Mike had found when he was able to stay with her overnight. Maybe this would be true of Claire, too. She woke with a start as he slid his arms around her.

"You fool!" she whispered huskily. "You damn fool!" She pronounced it as a two-syllable word, "few-ul." He smothered her protest with a deep kiss and, pulling her to her side, slid his hand up her nightgown and stroked her back. As he moved to her ear and throat, she spoke huskily. "You sure have a lot of dirty tricks. And you better stop. If you kiss me like that again, keep doin' what you're doin', you and I are goin' to be in bad trouble."

So encouraged, he continued, kissing her deeply again. She groaned and wrapped her free leg around him. When he started pulling up her nightgown, she lifted her hips and then her torso to make it easier.

They kissed each other hungrily and she moaned when he slid down to suck her breasts. She felt for him and took a firm hold. "You don't have a safety on," she said in alarm. "Didn't you bring a safety?"

"A safety—you mean a rubber?"

"Yes, of course. Didn't you bring one? I can't let you make me pregnant, you fool!"

"I'll be careful; I won't come in you."

"You better not; I'll kill you if you do."

She moaned and her eyes rolled up in her head as he slid into her. Her legs wound round him tightly and she dug her fingernails into his back. They moved slowly together, but in less than a minute Mike realized he was losing control. He arched his back and bit his lip.

Claire opened her eyes and, feeling his muscles tense, heaved with all her strength and bucked him off. He came as he fell sideways; semen sprayed over her, the bed, and himself.

"Oh God," she groaned. "What a mess. What a horrible mess."

Chagrined, he picked up his shorts, mopped her belly, himself, and what he could of the sheets. She groaned again, teeth clenched. "*Damn* it all. And I'm so, so much on the *edge*."

He slid his hand down to her cleft and began slowly stroking her. Within a few minutes, she arched her back, came, and mumbled incoherently. After the wave had subsided, she pushed his hand away. He sat up and looked at her. The Southern girl was gone. In her place was a disheveled and angry naked woman.

"You're beautiful," he said.

"Thank you, I'm sure," she said tersely. "Go back to your room now. *Quietly*, for God's sake. I'll have to roll up these sheets and slip them in the maid's laundry *and* put new ones on the bed. Come downstairs in thirty minutes for breakfast. Now go."

Thirty minutes later they met for breakfast. Claire wore no makeup. She was simply dressed in a blouse and skirt and, oddly, looked more appealing than she had the night before. Mrs. Hunnicut had gone to a meeting of the Legion auxiliary. The maid took their order for breakfast and they ate silently.

"I'm sorry it wasn't better," Mike said at length.

"Let's not talk about it," she said, looking at her plate.

"I think we should," he said. "I admit it was dumb of me not to bring something just in case but—why lead me on if you didn't really want it to happen? It's as if you were just trying to put me in my place for some reason—though I haven't done anything to you that I know of that would make you have it in for me."

She looked at him levelly. "Don't be so sure." She toyed with a piece of toast. "I'm sick of you men. You just want the one thing and then when you get a chance to get it—taking me by surprise like that was really a sneaky trick—you really can't do it."

Mike struggled to control his rising anger. He took a few slow breaths and said: "Claire, you really can't expect much when you keep a man waiting all night. *All night!*"

He lowered his voice. "Let me tell you something. A few months ago I had a wonderful relationship with a girl, a woman. I was a very good lover—she called me *divine*—and I was good because she made it possible for me to be good. Hell, she guaranteed it."

Claire looked up at him, seemed ready to speak, and then looked down again. He went on: "But when you lead a man on and then fight him off and keep him dangling and waiting, and play the Southern belle"—her eyes flashed briefly—"and morning comes and he's all pent up—well, you get what you deserve. Which isn't much.

"Fact is, Claire, you're over-armed in the battle of the sexes. You just can't enjoy the pleasure of, well, intimacy with a man and be at war with him at the same time. So you wind up frustrated. And maybe this has happened to you before."

She turned to him angrily. "You just don't understand; you don't understand at all." He noted irrelevantly that most of her accent had disappeared. "We *are* at war. Just look at my mother and father. He bullies her and orders her around and then goes off on his own—God knows what he does on those business trips with his cotton-broker buddies, buys prostitutes, probably—and she sits at home and goes to her little meetings twice a week. Oh, she gets back at him all right, in her own way."

"I can guess what that is," Mike said drily.

She flushed with anger. "Well, I'll be goddamned if *I'm* goin' to live like that. Sit at home and be subservient."

"And that's why you're mad at men."

She looked at him glumly. "That and a pretty rotten love affair, if you really wanta know. It was some time back. He was an officer, an older man. Out at Turner. He was a lot smarter than I was at the time and he took advantage. But I smartened up quick."

"I'm sorry," Mike said. "But I hope those things won't stop you from having a good relationship with a man. But, you know, there's a great big, goddamn world war going on. Instead of spending your time thinking about how to castrate men—now let me finish—why don't you find something useful to do? Not just wrap bandages or whatever. But something you really *want* to do. You're a very bright person. In this big wide world, there must be something useful that you'd enjoy doing."

He laughed mirthlessly. "Of course, who the hell am *I* to be giving advice? I can't get through two weeks of training without fucking up, excuse my language."

Claire sighed and put a hand over his. "You're a nice boy, Michael, and I'm sorry I put you through all this. I know how hard this kind of thing is on a man's ego—and I guess I've learned how to go after that soft spot, haven't I?

"But up to now it seems like you men go out and have these big adventures, flyin' planes and everything, and we women are supposed to sit home and knit and bat our pretty eyes and then flop on our backs when you all come back braggin' about your victories.

"But you're right, Michael. Takin' it out on men isn't goin' to change things. Neither is sittin' around bitchin' about it. There must be *something* a woman can do that's worth doin' and I'll find it. By God, I will."

The searchlights snapped on, blinding her, as Galina glided toward the German lines. The regiment had switched tactics when three of the PO-2s had been shot down by concentrated anti-aircraft fire. Now they flew in pairs. One biplane would bomb the assigned target; the other would attack the flak gun emplacements.

Galina fought down her panic as the flak explosions burst around her. When they reached the target she pulled the release wire and the stick of bombs fell free. She banked sharply away, flooded with relief at the thought that she would be back behind Soviet lines in a matter of minutes.

It was then that she heard a staccato sound and holes abruptly appeared in the fuselage and wing. *A German night fighter!* One had caught Rufa and her navigator three nights earlier and killed them both. Desperately, Galina dived and banked, twisting away to avoid the deadly cannon shells. But there was a sharp explosion and the propeller disappeared.

A stream of light-colored fluid covered the windscreen and bathed the fuselage. She smelled gasoline. Nadia was shouting something in the intercom. There was another, shockingly-loud explosion and she heard Nadia cry out.

Swiveling around, she saw Nadia, her face a grotesque, bloody mask, slumped over her windscreen. The silhouette of the Messerschmitt was visible behind her.

Galina threw the biplane into a reverse bank and began peering ahead, straining to find a place to land. A cloud of smoke drifted by and the Volga reflected the unobscured light from the moon. She was on the wrong side of the river!

The German fighter, unable to maintain a low speed, sped by her. The biplane was losing altitude fast; there was little time for a decision. A patch of ground that appeared to be fairly flat lay ahead. In the moonlight, it appeared to be a pasture. A semicircular stand of trees flanked the northern and western ends of the field.

Galina pulled the nose up to cut the speed and needlessly pulled back the inoperative throttle. The PO-2 hit hard, bounced high, struck the ground again, and nosed over with a heavy crunch that knocked the wind out of her. She unbuckled her belt and fell from the cockpit. Blood was dripping down her face from a cut on her nose.

Galina crawled to Nadia, hanging upside down in her cockpit. The girl's eyes were open and part of her face and head was gone. She was, clearly, dead. Galina felt a terrible sense of loss but there was no time to mourn. Voices shouted somewhere in the near distance. The language sounded guttural; it was neither Russian nor Ukrainian.

Galina crawled into a row of underbrush near the trees and pressed herself into the ground. Gunfire sounded nearby but the voices came no closer. Finally, exhausted, she fell asleep. It was daylight when Galina awoke. She heard Russian voices and, looking up, saw two peasant women picking up firewood. There were huts some two hundred yards away. Someone had come by earlier, Galina saw, and pulled Nadia from the plane. They had laid her out respectfully on the ground, apparently to await burial.

As the women approached, Galina stood up. The heavier of the two women recoiled for an instant and then walked to her quickly.

"You are the pilot!" the woman said. "The *Nyemtsy*, the Germans, are looking for you. Wait here."

Talking animatedly to each other, the women walked away. Within a few minutes they returned carrying a sack. Drawing Galina into a nearby clearing, they opened the sack and dumped a pile of old clothes on the ground.

The older woman motioned impatiently and, understanding, Galina nodded. Hurriedly she pulled off her boots, baggy trousers, tunic, leather jacket, wool socks, and boots—she would like to have kept *those*—and put on the peasant clothes and a pair of wooden clogs. The women picked up Galina's things and stuffed them in the sack.

The old clothes smelled of sweat and soot. Galina tied a scarf around her head and, pulling her Tokarev pistol from the holster she had placed on the ground, tucked it into the folds of a heavy shawl one of the women wrapped around her. The woman picked up her load of firewood and hoisted it onto Galina's back.

What a clever idea! Galina thought. She would become a dirty-faced peasant woman—she stooped and scooped up a little dirt to smear on her face—carrying a load of firewood to her home.

But which way were the Soviet lines? Before she could ask, the peasant pointed down a narrow road that was little more than a path. *That* way. Galina began walking. Heavy gunfire sounded to her left. Perhaps she was skirting the battle. She judged that she must be south of the city and walking eastward.

The path was deserted for the first twenty minutes as she trudged along. But when it curved about a growth of wild shrubs near some trees she recoiled in shock. A German soldier, rifle slung over his shoulder, was leaning against a tree smoking a cigarette. A motor bike was propped against the tree beside him.

He looked up sharply as Galina approached and then relaxed. As she drew abreast of him, the soldier suddenly leaned forward and snatched her scarf from her head. Galina's dark hair tumbled around her shoulders.

The soldier grinned and spoke. Though the words were unintelligible, their meaning was clear. He had found a pretty girl beneath the disguise of the homely peasant woman. He straightened, flipped the cigarette away, seized Galina by her left arm, and began dragging her into the trees.

The meaning of that action was clear, too. Galina struck at his arm, broke away and tripped over a root, falling on her back. As the grinning soldier advanced, she groped for the Tokarev, pulled it loose and, holding it in her right hand, cocked the slide with her left.

The soldier's eyes widened and he quickly unslung his rifle. Before he could lift the muzzle, Galina fired twice. Both slugs struck the soldier in the chest. He staggered back, looked at the holes in the front of his uniform, and collapsed.

Galina rose and walked cautiously over to him. He had fallen on his back but his arms and legs were askew like those of her childhood doll. His eyes were fixed and half-open. So was his mouth. His helmet had fallen off and she noted that he was young, no older than herself. With his blond hair and slim face, he would have been considered good-looking under normal circumstances.

Normal circumstances! There were none. Galina staggered to a tree, leaned against it, and vomited. She had eaten and drunk nothing for fifteen hours so there was little to bring up. She closed her eyes and took deep breaths to calm herself.

This was not at all what she had expected when she applied for service with the air regiment. She had imagined herself flying proudly against the Hitlerites in a clean tunic and white scarf with people applauding and a band playing in the background. Bombs would be dropped—from a distance, of course—on the enemy. But the war would be clean as well as good.

The crash of the PO-2 had brought her, literally, down to earth. First there was Nadia's bloody death in the biplane. Then *this* horror and degradation, shooting and killing at short range a young man who was going to rape her.

Summoning up her courage and waning energy, Galina moved back to the path, picked up her scarf, wrapped it around her head, and then gathered up the firewood and set off down the path again. Fifteen minutes later, the path ended in a small village.

Gunfire sounded up ahead and she saw soldiers running back and forth. She couldn't make out the uniforms at such a distance but she realized she had to be near the front lines. Dropping the firewood, she ran to the right behind a semicircle of peasants' huts.

As she was creeping around the side of one, trying to find out what was happening, she ran into a Soviet soldier who was backing around the corner. Startled, he struck her a hard blow that threw her sprawling to the ground and lifted the submachine gun he was carrying.

"Stop!" she commanded. "I am Lieutenant Flying-Officer Galina Tarasova of the 588th Air Regiment. I was shot down. I am trying to return to my base."

The Russian listened to her open-mouthed and then burst into laughter. "You! A flying officer? A lieutenant? And I am Comrade Stalin!" He scowled. "Who are you and what trick are you trying to pull? Are you a spy?"

"Listen to me closely, comrade," Galina declared, rising to her feet. "If you harm me or impede me, you can be sure that you will be found guilty of anti-Soviet activities and you will suffer the usual punishment for that. Time in a penal brigade, perhaps."

She drew herself erect and pulled off her scarf. "Do I sound like a peasant woman? Do I look like one? I will tell you how I got here and then I will expect you to help me to our lines." She quickly told him of the night flight, the crash, Nadia's death, and the shooting of the German soldier.

Five minutes later, she was reciting the same tale to the captain who commanded the soldier's infantry unit. A broad-shouldered man with a pockmarked face, he listened to her quietly and then said: "Let me see your pistol." He looked it over, smelled the muzzle, and pulled out the clip.

"Two cartridges missing, as you said," the captain said. He handed the Tokarev back to her. "What airplane do you fly?" he asked.

"What is its horsepower and flying speed and what armament does it carry?"

"The PO-2," she answered. "It has a single hundred-horsepower engine. It is not fast; cruising speed is eighty miles an hour, less if there's a head-wind. It has two cockpits; the navigator serves as a gunner and has a 7.62-mm. machine gun mounted on a ring in the rear cockpit. Under the wings we carry . . ."

The captain held up his hand. "All right, all right. Look over there. The river is just around that bend. I'll send a man with you. We run ferries back and forth. Sometimes they're hit by German shellfire. It's risky, but it's the only way to get back. Do you understand?"

"Yes sir," she said. "*Spasibo*. Thank you." She came to attention and saluted.

The captain smiled slightly, drew himself up, and flipped a salute in return. "*Zabud*," he said. "Forget it." His eyes glinted in amusement. "Besides, I'm always happy to rescue a lady."

Galina looked at him stonily. "I seek your help as a soldier, not as a woman, Captain."

The ferry was a motorboat carrying six soldiers. An artillery shell exploded nearby, throwing up a fountain of water, as they reached the middle of the Volga. Galina gasped and crouched. The soldiers swore and ducked. Another shell whistled overhead and struck the bank as they were within a few feet of it. The explosion showered Galina and the others with dirt.

A truck gave her a ride back to the airfield. Major Kravchenko stared at her in amazement as Galina stumbled into the bunker.

"We thought you were dead!" she said.

"Nadia is; I almost am," Galina said. She fainted as she tried to salute.

CHAPTER THREE

THE WARRIORS

Josif Vissarionovich Djugashvili, variously known as Joseph Stalin, the Man of Steel, The Generalissimo, The Great Leader, The Father Of Peoples, lowered himself into his chair in his dining room, leaned toward the polished wood cabinet with the green eye, and turned on his German Telefunken short-wave radio.

It was 1:00 A.M., a time when the air waves were free of static, a good time to hear the Russian language broadcasts of the foreign radio stations to find out what was *really* happening. At this hour the British were reporting that Soviet forces were encircling the German forces at Stalingrad; the momentum was shifting and the Germans faced the prospect of being trapped.

So it might be true after all. He listened to the reports of his generals, of course, but he didn't always believe them. He didn't really believe anyone; that was the way his mind worked and it had served him well through the years that had brought him to the undisputed leadership of the Soviet Union.

So he listened to the foreign broadcasts every night before presiding over his military briefings. The limousine was waiting downstairs to take him the short distance from his *dacha* to the Kremlin. He would let it wait. He wanted the time to savor what lay ahead.

The broad, pockmarked face remained impassive but hatred simmered within him. He was a venomous hater. He had hated many men and some women—he still called his mother "the old whore"— and he had caused the death of millions. But the one he hated most at this time was the man who had so completely unnerved, even panicked, him on June 21, 1941, by launching the massive German attack on Mother Russia.

He was so surprised and unnerved by the attack that, when General Zhukov's telephone call woke him at the Kuntsevo dacha to say that German planes were bombing Kiev, Minsk, Sevastopol, and Vilnius, he, the Man of Steel, found himself unable to speak.

Zhukov kept asking: "Do you understand me, Comrade Stalin? Do you understand me?" All he could do was to breathe heavily into the phone. He remained silent for two hours and fell into so deep a state of shock that he received no one for a week.

It fell to Molotov to tell the people by radio that the Soviet Union had been invaded and to appeal to them to resist. But many did not resist; thousands, particularly in the Ukraine, greeted the Germans with flowers and bread and salt. They, of course, would be remembered.

Stalin was a strong man; he had to have been strong to achieve what he had achieved. But Adolf Hitler had, for a time, turned him into a confused and craven fool. That knowledge burned within him; the only cure for that hurt was the abject humiliation of his nemesis.

And now it was in sight. Hitler had committed another blunder. It was a mistake to have squandered so many troops and tanks and airplanes in an assault on Stalingrad; only the name of the city propelled Hitler's insistence on taking it. It was an even greater blunder for Hitler to order his tank generals to abandon the attack on Moscow in order to fan out and round up millions of Russian soldiers.

That was stupid; there was an inexhaustible supply of Soviet soldiers. By confusing the need to seize territory with the desire to capture soldiers, the Nazi leader had given Stalin the means to victory. Hitler had abandoned the war of the *blitzkrieg*, which Stalin could not win, for a war of bloody attrition, which Stalin could not lose.

And now Hitler would taste the bitter gall of defeat while he, Stalin, would grow immensely stronger.

There was, of course, another reason for the hatred he bore for the Austrian. They were so much alike that the realization made him acutely uncomfortable. Both had been born in modest circumstances in a remote village, though the Georgian's family had been the poorer of the two.

Both boys had been beaten by brutal fathers. Both were thought by many to have been illegitimate. Both had been sullen and rude youths; neither had ever had any close friends. Both were suspicious of others to the point of paranoia.

Both were unprepossessing in appearance. Both were uneducated and uncultured. Both had once aspired to professions; Hitler to architecture, Stalin to the priesthood. Both had become outlaws and had been imprisoned or exiled. Both had ordered the killing of old comrades in arms. Both were the subject of endless speculation at home and abroad by others who couldn't understand how they could have risen so high.

Both, the Generalissimo knew, possessed quick intelligences and superior memories. Indeed, Stalin never forgot nor forgave a good deed. His old tutor, Jan Sten, had worked hard to teach him the principles and rhetoric of Marxism so that Stalin could pose credibly as the leader of a Socialist society. (In repayment, several years later, he had Sten shot.)

Both leaders were regarded by the West as monsters, and mainly for the same reasons—the arrests and murders of the intellectuals, the clergy, the Jews, military officers suspected of disloyalty or excessive ambition—and, in Stalin's case, the starvation of ten or more millions in the collectivization of the peasants.

Both had profoundly shocked their countrymen and foreign followers when they announced the now-shattered unity pact between Germany and the Soviet Union. A despicable British cartoonist had drawn a cartoon that depicted Hitler and Stalin bowing to each other. In it, Hitler said: "The scum of the earth, I believe?" Stalin, bowing, answered: "The bloody assassin of the workers, I presume?"

Yet, despite all their similarities, one all-important characteristic separated the two men, the Generalissimo knew—and it would spell the difference between victory and defeat. Both started out believing they were military geniuses. After making several colossal mistakes —the first being his refusal to believe in or prepare for the German invasion—Stalin began taking the advice of his generals. He remained suspicious of them, but, in military strategy and tactics, he had learned to heed their counsel.

Adolf Hitler never learned to do that. He surrounded himself with sycophants in uniform who nodded and agreed with his every order. The word had been brought to Stalin by German officers who were taken prisoner that Hitler's generals were joking grimly that they needed the Führer's permission to move the sentry from the window to the door.

That difference would defeat the superb German army. The Germans were killing eight Soviet soldiers for every German soldier killed. But Mother Russia always had more men to sacrifice—women, too. Stalin rose to his feet, buttoned his brown tunic with the red shoulder boards, pulled on his greatcoat, and strode to the door.

Aleksandr Yakovlev, designer of the Soviet Union's Yak fighter planes and Deputy People's Commissioner of the Aviation Industry for Development and Research, walked through the small office of the personal bodyguard and into the Generalissimo's second-floor inner office.

In this sand-colored building, which stood near the white brick bell tower of Ivan The Terrible behind the Kremlin walls, the Generalissimo held his nocturnal briefings, conferences, and awesome tongue-lashings.

What, Yakovlev wondered, did Stalin want with him at this godforsaken hour? He had worked hard all day and he was tired. When he looked at the long rectangular table near the left-hand wall of the Generalissimo's office, he knew, and his knees turned to jelly. Beside him, P.V. Dement'yev, chief of aircraft production, became as pale as a ghost.

On the table sat a large piece of cracked wing fabric. It came, Yakovlev knew, from the wing covering of a Yak-9 fighter. A defect had been discovered and defects were equated with sabotage, an offense punishable by death. The designer felt himself fighting for breath; ice seemed to be forming in his stomach and lungs.

The unhappy numbers were emblazoned in Yakovlev's mind. Some four hundred and fifty designers and engineers had been arrested for suspected sabotage; three hundred had survived. The names surged into his mind. The great designer of heavy bombers, A. N. Tupolev, arrested, imprisoned, and later paroled to work under police supervision. K. A. Kalinin, another name from the Soviet pantheon of design geniuses, arrested and shot because his experimental K-4 aircraft crashed on a test flight and killed four Party members. The list included A. G. Kostikov, and that was particularly ironic. The multiple *katyusha* rockets he had invented were creating havoc at this very moment as they landed among the German troops. Yet Kostikov had spent years in prison for suspected sabotage. His talk of multiple rockets had been considered the ravings of a lunatic.

It was grotesque. Yakovlev looked around; the dozen or so men in uniform in the room seemed to be avoiding eye contact with him. And, when they moved around the room, they walked quietly and carefully, as if a careless step would set off a mine.

At 2:00 A.M., the door of the suite burst open and two uniformed guards entered, looked about suspiciously, and then stopped, one on either side of the door. As they came to a halt, the Generalissimo strode in, walked to his desk without looking left or right, picked two cigarettes from a wooden box, tore them apart, and stuffed the tobacco into his pipe.

Only when he had lit his pipe did Stalin peer at the people in the room. When his gaze fixed on Yakovlev, his face hardened. He strode to the long table, picked up the piece of torn wing fabric and brandished it.

"Why did this happen?" he demanded in his coarse Georgian accent. Yakovlev's voice failed him as he tried to respond. With an effort he tried again: "It was a regrettable mistake, Comrade Stalin. We are aware of it."

The answer seemed to infuriate Stalin. "You are *aware* of it? Several hundred urgently needed fighter airplanes have been made with wing coverings that peel away and you are *aware* of it? Are you making airplanes or bananas?"

"As you know, Comrade Stalin," the production manager said placatingly, spreading his hands in a gesture of appeal, "we had to work very quickly to meet the needs for the airplanes at the front."

"The glues and dyes for the wing coverings of the Yak-9 had to be prepared very hurriedly, Comrade Stalin," Yakovlev added. "The defects weren't apparent until frontline conditions exposed them. The aircraft were shipped immediately after assembly from the factory to the front, you see, Comrade. There was no time for the usual inspection."

"No time?" Stalin roared, now in a fury. "*No time?* Do you know that only the most cunning enemy of the *Rodina* (the Motherland) would do such a thing? This is *exactly* what an enemy would do: turn out airplanes in such a way that they would seem good at the plant but no good at the front."

Stalin swelled his massive chest and pointed a thick finger like a gun at the designer's head. "No enemy could do us greater harm. Hundreds of airplanes disabled. This is working for Hitler! Do you

know what a service you have rendered to Hitler? You two are sabo-
teurs!''

That was the dreaded word, the word that had sent hundreds,
thousands, even millions to imprisonment, degradation, and death.
Yakovlev grew dizzy, the room seemed to rock around him. Beside
him, Dement'yev sagged perceptibly.

The Man of Steel stared at them in a gathering silence that seemed
to generate an ominous sound of its own. Yakovlev could see the
wheel turning in the Generalissimo's head. At which place would it
stop? Arrest? Brutal interrogation? Death? Or simply demotion?

Stalin turned suddenly, went to his desk, tore two cigarettes apart
and stuffed the tobacco in his pipe. Then, relighting his pipe, he sat
behind his desk, pulled a pad in front of him, and began drawing on
it. It was his habit when he was thinking. He doodled, often drawing
pictures of wolves in red ink.

Abruptly, he looked up. ''Well, what are you going to do about the
problem?'' he asked the two culprits. Relief flooded through the men.
As Yakovlev opened his mouth to answer, Dement'yev spoke first:
''Comrade Stalin, the problem will be repaired in its entirety within
two weeks. Rest assured, it will be done.''

Yakovlev wasn't sure that was possible but he nodded enthusiastically. Stalin waved a hand in dismissal. ''See to it then.'' As the pair
turned gratefully toward the door, Stalin called out: ''Yakovlev! Why
does the British Spitfire have a greater range than our fighters?''

Yakovlev staggered and turned back. ''With all respect, Comrade
Stalin, it does not. Perhaps you have been told of the Spitfire reconnaissance model. It carries no guns and is much lighter, you see, so it
can carry more petrol and fly twelve hundred and fifty miles, much
farther than the combat version. But the regular version, you see, it
does not . . .''

Stalin leapt to his feet and erupted again. ''Do you think I'm a child
to be so easily misled? Don't presume to tell me what I know! The
Spitfire has a greater range than ours and this is intolerable!''

He pointed to a handsome, broad-shouldered general of about
forty. ''Novikov, step forward.''

The general took two steps forward and stood at attention. Alexander Novikov was commander of the Red Air Force. Talented, ener-
getic, and tough, he had created a new Soviet air doctrine, reorganized the resurgent VVS into mobile air armies under centralized
control, and changed Soviet air combat techniques, mainly by doing
what the British had done—learning from the Germans.

Novikov knew his worth and he knew that Stalin knew it. He also knew that, despite his achievements—or because of them—at some future date he probably would suffer the same fate as previous air commanders of the VVS. Tukhachevskiy, Alksnis, Smushkevich, Khripin, Troyanker, Todorskiy. All, like himself, had been heroes. All, today, were dead by execution.

The thought faded; Stalin was speaking. "This must be heard by all! We will have the best aircraft not only because we must but because it is our heritage! Was not the first airplane invented by Zhukovsky? The first steam locomotive by the Sherepanov brothers? The first radio by Alexander Popov?"

Stalin grew impassioned; he raised his arms and shook his heavy fists. "Did we not lose seventy-five percent of our air force, seventy-five hundred aircraft, between June and September of last year? Have we not replaced that loss by moving fifteen hundred factories and ten million aviation plant workers behind the Urals in a matter of months?"

His voice rose to a hoarse shout. "We are capable of any action, any invention, any sacrifice, *anything* that will lead us to victory! Any of you who slackens in that effort in any way is a saboteur!"

Breathing deeply, the Man of Steel returned to his desk.

"General Novikov," he said. "What is the situation at the front?"

"We are on the offensive, Comrade Stalin," the general answered. "We now have fifteen hundred aircraft at Stalingrad. Since the weather turned colder, the enemy's normal superiority in numbers has been canceled. They don't know how to fly in our weather. Their lubricants freeze, ours do not. We have set up radio stations at the front to guide our fighters. They are two miles from the forward line at intervals of five miles. Each station maintains contact with our fighter pilots in the air and can vector them from one place to another quickly to meet a threat or exploit an opening.

"Our Yak-9 fighter," he nodded toward Yakovlev, "has proven itself a match for the Messerschmitt 109 and even the Focke-Wulfe at low to medium altitudes. By day our Shturmovik tank-killers destroy their tanks and attack their command posts. By night, our women pilots harass the *Nyemtsy* by bombing their positions with the PO-2s. So we are able to bomb the enemy around the clock, twenty-four hours a day."

"The PO-2. Are those the same primary flight trainers we built back in 1929?" Stalin asked.

"Yes, Comrade Stalin, they are. The equipment is very old and fragile. It's the only pre-war airplane we have in combat. But it's still proving useful."

"And the women? They're little more than girls, aren't they?"

"Yes, Comrade Stalin, girls of eighteen and nineteen, seldom more than twenty. But they're all graduates of the paramilitary flying clubs you had the foresight to establish around our cities for young people several years ago. Most of them have been flying this aircraft for at least a year. They perform a valuable service. The Germans call them 'night-witches.'"

"Night-witches." Stalin nodded, visibly pleased by the words, and puffed on his pipe. "Night-witches. My love for children, for the young, is well-known," he said. "But even children, female children, must serve the *Rodina* in this hour of danger. These children, these young girls, are one of the instruments that will lead us to victory."

Novikov smiled and nodded. He would never speak of anything as —what was the French word? *gauche*—as the Christian Bible, but the words seemed eerily relevant. Comrade Stalin doubtless would remember them better than he. Novikov knew the passage was from the prophet Isaiah: *The wolf also shall dwell with the lamb, and the leopard shall lie down with the kid . . . and a little child shall lead them.*

The child, her head resting against the back of the PO-2's cockpit and her eyes closed, felt more like a woman of seventy than a girl of nineteen. Galina Tarasova had flown eight sorties since nightfall and she and her navigator, Valya Budanova, asleep in the rear cockpit, were waiting for the signal to take off again.

Galina had become a combat veteran. She still felt the unavoidable animal panic when the flak burst around them or a night fighter appeared like a black bird of prey. But she had learned to smother her fear and do her job.

Somehow, though, the pride was gone and she wasn't sure why. Killing the young German with the pistol had taken something out of her, she knew. For the rest, she dropped her bombs on the assigned targets with the same professional detachment that a good mechanic brought to her work. The exhortations of the political commissar had become little more than a repetition of meaningless slogans.

Some of her loss of enthusiasm was due, she knew, to fatigue. Other pilots had burned out before her. It was also due to insufficient food—she felt she would have long since starved without the chocolate ration—and to the numbing, paralyzing, forty-below cold. Swaddled in fur socks, fur-lined helmets and coveralls, heavy padded jackets, thick leather trousers, fur-lined gauntlets, and heavy boots, she was still cold.

Galina sighed. There would probably be one more takeoff tonight from the snow-covered field. It wouldn't be long till dawn; the night bombers would go to bed and the day bombers and fighters would begin operations.

"Good morning, Lieutenant," a male voice said unexpectedly. "Or is it still good night? I am not a Greek, but I come bearing a gift."

She opened her eyes and saw that the figure standing below her cockpit was Viktor, a Yak pilot from the nearby fighter airfield and a frequent visitor to the women's night bomber regiment.

Captain Viktor Fyodorovich Markov, thirty, was an ace. He was also a handsome man who was predatory where women were concerned. Though many regarded him as a prize catch, it was often he who did the catching, releasing his prey only after he had taken what he wanted.

That was why Galina's regimental commander, Major Kravchenko, disapproved of Markov. She couldn't legally order him off the 588th's airfield, but she made her disdain for him obvious when they met.

Yet most of the girls liked Viktor. He was not only handsome and dashing; he had a lighthearted way about him, a quick sense of humor, and a talent for self-deprecation. Only one thing seemed to bother him: his inability to create a spark of romantic interest in Galina Tarasova.

Galina saw that his black mustache and eyelashes were filmed with ice, but his smile, as usual, was warm and beguiling.

"Why have you come, Captain?" Galina asked. "What is it you want at this hour?"

"The most unattainable gift of all," he said. "Your love."

"That and two kopeks will get you a ride on the Moscow subway," she said wearily. "Besides, I know you. If you had it, you'd get tired of it. For myself, I'm already tired."

"Ah, but that is why I'm here," the pilot said. He held out a bar of chocolate. "A burst of energy for those darkest hours before the dawn. It is part of my loot from a card game.

"Please accept it," he said, holding it out to her. "You can't believe I think you'd trade your favors for food. It's simply a gift from the heart. If it were spring, I'd bring a flower. Since it's the depth of winter, I offer a chocolate ration."

She took it. "Thank you, Viktor; I accept your gift. But tell me, please, why do you keep trying? Is it manly pride, the desire for still another conquest?"

Markov shrugged and pulled a face. "Perhaps a little. But there's more, Galina, and I confess I don't really understand it. There's something about you that's irresistible to me."

"Why? I'm not big and buxom like—well, you know who. I'm small and thin, I have no experience in love, certainly not the kind of love *you* seem to specialize in. Besides, who can think of love in times like these?"

Markov grinned. "Everything you say is true, Galina, and that makes the paradox. Somehow I'm still drawn to you. Part of it is that angelic face, those compelling eyes of yours—as brilliant and blue as a Messerschmitt's tracers. A romantic analogy, don't you think? Part, perhaps, is a primeval desire to protect you, and that, of course, is ridiculous. But I'm not the only one. What about that huge lout, Petrov, who hangs around you? If I weren't his superior in rank, he'd have chased me off long ago."

"Petrov is a very nice young man," Galina said without conviction. Actually, Petrov Antisferov, a hulking navigator of a bomber crew, was a bore. But she didn't want to hurt his feelings and, so long as he didn't interfere with her, she could hardly object if he often seemed to be nearby when he was off-duty.

"Admit it, Comrade Captain," Galina said, "the kind of love you seek is the kind that's quickly gotten and soon satisfied."

"Correction, Comrade Lieutenant. That may be the kind of love I get; it's not the kind of love I seek." He laughed at himself.

"Have I accidentally said something profound, or is it a new line that I've invented?"

Galina smiled. "You will have to decide. For myself, I don't believe that one can be rationally and truly in love in a setting like this. This . . . *danger*, living on the edge, makes for passion and intensity, or perhaps it's an excuse for it—you know more about that than I do. But *love?* I don't think that's possible. Certainly not for me."

Markov sighed theatrically. "I consider that a great personal loss."

A green flare shot up at the end of the field. Galina reached back and tapped Valya to wake her. Then she squared herself in her seat, adjusted her straps, and started the engine of the PO-2.

Markov waved cheerily and began walking back to the Yak airfield. Soon it would be dawn, time to climb into his long-nosed Yak to hunt and kill Heinkels and Messerschmitts. Viktor Markov was the leader of a free-hunter squadron. He was a free-hunter in the air and on the ground.

* * *

Five thousand miles to the west-southwest near Hendricks Field at Sebring, Florida, two other children whooped and yelled as their four-engined B-17 bomber, stripped down and light in their hands, roared down the Tamiami Trail so close to the ground that the four propellers kicked up dust and rippled the water from the Everglades.

For eight weeks, Mike and Buddy had plodded and droned through days and nights of close formation flying, cross-country navigation without navigators, two- and three-engine performance drills, hooded takeoffs, practice bombing, use of the Norden bombsight, gunnery practice, flying on the Minneapolis-Honeywell autopilot, use of radio equipment—even unheeded instruction in how to change an engine.

Both were chafing to graduate from the seemingly endless succession of flying schools and get into combat. And, when opportunity presented itself, they delighted in flouting authority. As now. It was forbidden to go down on the deck and buzz houses, farmers, animals, and vehicles.

But let's be realistic, the boys agreed. An empty B-17 was remarkably light and maneuverable—almost like a fighter—and they had grown to love the big, graceful bird with its long nose and huge, soaring tail. And when you'd been working your ass off, there was nothing as thrilling as streaking along the ground in the early morning, cutting swathes through the long grass, ripping across the swampland of the Everglades—that thing that happened in the Okefenokee was strictly a fluke that could never happen again—and spooking anything that moved.

"It's such a feeling of sheer power," Mike marveled. "Such a kick. It's almost like being God, just tearing over the landscape this way and—I don't know—just making it your own, owning it, sort of."

"Whoop-to-do!" yelled Buddy. If he had had the words, he would have said that it was an esthetically powerful experience. You shot like a huge bird over the blue of the water and the green of the pastures and the yellow of the fields of grain. You looked straight down on a family of startled birds nesting in an oak tree and then banked over a cluster of toy houses.

And the Everglades! A hundred miles of mangrove swamps and salt marshes. Vast plains of sawgrass twelve feet high with eerie tree islands poking up here and there. Graceful wax myrtles and big willows and cypresses and custard apples. At the edges, fields of sugar cane and vegetables. Alligators in secret ponds. Ghostly mists and sparkling sunlight. And you could thunder across all of this, only a few feet above it, in a matter of minutes. This was *flying!*

And now—oh, my—here came a big truck, a couple of tons, at least. "Let's see if this guy has good nerves!" Mike yelled. "You got it!" He lifted his hands from the controls like a concert pianist who had struck a resounding chord.

Buddy seized the wheel, planted his feet on the rudder pedals, took hold of the throttles, and lowered the big bomber until it was flying only a few feet off the roadway and heading straight for the front of the oncoming truck. As the distance between the two narrowed, the truck driver began jerking his steering wheel back and forth in panic. He couldn't leave the roadway because there was swamp on both sides.

Buddy bared his teeth and settled the B-17 even lower as it roared, all four engines bellowing at full-throttle, toward the windshield of the truck. At the last possible instant, he pulled up over the cab and blasted down the roadway.

"Turn back! Turn back!" Mike yelled. "I can't see him."

Buddy banked the B-17 around sharply and chandelled upward to gain altitude for better visibility. The truck was missing. It just wasn't there. Had the driver driven it into the swamp?

"Do tell," Buddy said, mystified.

"Well, hell, I hope we didn't actually *kill* the guy," Mike said. They were relieved that afternoon when the base commander, a heavyset and balding middle-aged command-pilot colonel named Bachman— informally known as Herman the German—spoke to the pilots in their ground-school class.

"One of you pilots screwed up royally this morning," Bachman said. "I had a call from the Statewide Trucking Company with a serious complaint. One of you drove, I mean *forced,* a two-ton truck off the Trail and into the swamp. It's only by the grace of God that the driver wasn't killed. But he got good and wet and the Army Air Forces are going to have to pay damages for the truck. And we already have a black eye from an incident at another base where the crew actually dropped hundred-pound practice bombs on a county courthouse lawn."

The colonel glared around the room and expelled his breath. "Now look. You men are supposed to be officers—and that means grownups. You've got less than two weeks to go here before you go on active duty. Why screw the pooch now, huh?" Then, flushing red, Bachman lost his temper. "For Christ's sake!" he yelled, his voice rising to a high tenor, "take it out on the Nazis, not on U.S. citizens! All right?"

"Those guys bombed a courthouse lawn!" Mike marveled later. "Why didn't we think of that?"

"Well, it's too late now," Buddy said, "and we'd have to pull a bombardier in on it."

Life became a routine of drudgery again and Mike began to feel lonely and depressed. The feeling was exacerbated by a liaison that Buddy had developed with a red-haired headquarters clerk named Linda. This left Mike increasingly alone in the evenings. Buddy and Linda dated on and off the base; some nights, Buddy confided, they sacked out on piles of blankets in the supply room.

"Sex is a peculiar damn thing," Buddy said reflectively one day at lunch. "There just isn't anythin' else in life where you can get so far behind and then catch up so fast. Right now, it's gettin' to seem like work. I'd almost welcome feelin' horny again."

"You wouldn't like it," Mike grumbled. Finally, he decided to call Ginny. He often thought of the close and richly satisfying relationship they had had back at Augusta. Around nine o'clock that night, when she'd be likely to be home, he got a handful of quarters at the PX, stepped into a phone booth, and dialed her number.

It rang a long time and he was about to hang up when she answered. She seemed out of breath. "Ginny-babe, it's me," Mike said.

"Who is it?" she said.

"It's Mike, Ginny. Mike Gavin."

There was a pause. Then she said, rather tentatively, he thought: "Oh Mike, of course. It's been a long time. How are you?"

"Well, that's why I called," he said. "Because it's been so long. I wanted to talk to you."

There was some noise in the background and she said: "Hold the phone a minute, will you?"

He heard arguing in the background and then she returned to the phone. "Listen, Mike, this isn't a very good time to talk, you know? Maybe we could talk another time, okay?"

This time Mike clearly heard an angry male voice. His spirits dropped. "Yeah, sure, Ginny. Some other time." He hung up carefully. On the way to bed he tried to sift through his feelings. *What did I expect? That she'd remain true to me, wait for me? I didn't ask for that; I didn't even want it. I wasn't in love with her. So she's taken up with another guy. She said she would. So why am I depressed about it? Is every woman I go to bed with supposed to wait around for me? Grow up, Gavin.*

It was all very logical, but it didn't make any difference. He still felt lousy and, though he knew it was nutty, he plunged into an angry daydream in which he imagined going back to Ginny's apartment and yanking the new guy out of her bed and punching him in the nose and kicking his ass out the door and then shaking her until her teeth rattled and then kissing her and stroking every inch of her body as he used to do and . . .

Ah, piss-ant! Mike stayed in a funk for two days and Buddy's humorous attempts to talk him out of it only made it worse. On the third day a miracle occurred. On the bulletin board of the bachelor officers' quarters was a message that Claire had phoned. He was to phone her back.

Claire, he thought incredulously. After the disastrous encounter they'd had at her home in Albany, what could she possibly want? When he got her on the phone, it became surprisingly clear.

"Michael dear," she said, "I'm truly hurt." Her opening salvo threw him off balance and he groped for words, realizing dimly that he was being wound around the girl's shapely fingers.

"I *mean*," she said, leaning on the word, "you haven't invited me to Hendricks for the gala. You haven't even thought about li'l ol' me."

"Wha', what gala?" he said.

"Why your big pre-graduation dance, honey. Next Tuesday night. Didn't you even know 'bout it? My, you *have* been workin' hard."

"Honest, I really didn't know."

"Well, it's gonna happen, Michael, and if you haven't made other arrangements I'd be happy to be your lady fair for the evenin'."

Abruptly, she dropped the Southern Belle manner and spoke crisply: "Michael, I really do want to see you. That little encounter we had a couple months ago—especially, what you said at breakfast—made me realize what a jerk I've been. So I've done something really exciting about it and I can't wait to tell you about it."

"Well, great, Claire," Mike said. "I can't wait to hear about it, and, sure, great, I'll look forward to seeing you. But what sort of arrangements shall I . . ."

"Don't worry about that," she said. "I'll get a hotel room near the base and I'll take care of everything. I'll meet you at the officers' club that night at, oh, eight o'clock. Okay?"

"Okay, great," Mike said happily. "But, Claire?"

"What, lover man?"

"The way we parted back at your house, I didn't think we'd ever get together again. So why . . ."

She laughed. "It's sort of like dropping the other shoe, Michael. You've helped me see some things in a different way. I find that I really like you. And I feel I owe you something"—she paused—"and I always pay my debts."

"That's funny," he said. "My best friend, Buddy, says that S'uthe'n girls promise and promise, but never deliver."

She laughed again and thickened her accent. "Some of those S'uthe'n boys run us gals down somethin' awful jus' 'cause we don' find them irr-ee-sistible." She dropped the accent again. "Why don't we just wait till next Tuesday night, all right? And, Mike, I'll make *all* the arrangements. Just you don't worry about a thing."

The last word came out "thang," of course, but he didn't expect her to sound like a girl from Back Bay, or even Roland Park.

The impending visit was like a shot of adrenalin to Mike but it made him nervous. Since no blood brothers are bonded more tightly than two young flying officers who have lived and learned and sweated together for nearly a year, Mike told Buddy of his humiliatingly brief sexual encounter with Claire in Albany.

Buddy chuckled wryly. "Reminds me of an ol' S'uthe'n sayin': 'If I had to do it all over again, I'd do it all over you.' Now listen, son. Just relax and enjoy whatever comes, ex-cuse my choice of words. You just need to learn a little S'uthe'n philosophy, Mike-boy. Take me, now: the very worst sex I ever had was sen-say-tional."

In an act of noblesse oblige, Buddy gave Mike a duplicate key to the headquarters supply room "just in case." He and Linda had taken a room for the night off the base.

Claire showed up at the officers' club the night of the dance and, as expected, she was gorgeous in a low-cut red dress that revealed the tops of her beautiful breasts and accentuated her tiny waist and long legs. Her blonde hair fell in waves around her shoulders.

"God, you look beautiful," Mike said helplessly.

"Thank you, Lieutenant," she said. "So do you, 'specially in your officer's uniform. And oh, those lovely wings."

Mike had polished his silver wings, gold shoulder bars, and belt brass and shined his shoes until they glowed. He was dressed in his belted Class A jacket and a pair of tailor-made officer's trousers informally known as "pinks."

They danced close to each other, saying little throughout the evening. For a time they sat with Buddy and Linda. Linda clearly felt uncomfortable near the obviously monied and more sophisticated Albany belle, but Claire and Buddy got on famously.

At one point, until Mike complained he couldn't understand what they were saying, they seemed to be competing to produce the thickest and most impenetrable Southern accent.

Finally, the band played "Good Night, Sweetheart," and couples began leaving. "Well, let's see now," Mike said uncertainly when they walked outside. "What would you like to do?"

She looked at him directly, her blue eyes bright and challenging. "I want you to make love to me."

Mike's heart leapt and he had to try twice to answer. "So do I. I mean yes. Do you want to go back to your room?"

She curled her lip. "I don't particularly like the idea of a hotel room, including my own. Isn't there some place we can go 'round here? Your quarters or somethin'?"

"The BOQ isn't such a good idea," he said. "Too many people around and the walls are like paper. I do have another idea; I don't know whether you'll like it or not."

"Try me."

"I have a key to the headquarters supply room. It's a pretty big place and we'd be alone and there are—well, Buddy says—blankets piled around."

"It sounds like real Army and tonight that sounds perfect. Let's go."

They groped their way into the dark supply room. Mike made sure the door was locked from the inside and then wedged a chair against the doorknob just to make sure. As their eyes became accustomed to the darkness, Claire spread out a thick pile of brown Army blankets, found two pillows, and quickly took off her clothes.

Naked, she was silvery, beautifully-formed, infinitely desirable. Mike shucked off his clothes like a bear shaking water from his coat and lay down beside her. They seized each other and began kissing fiercely. He broke free for a moment to ask: "What about a, you know, a safety?"

"I've taken care of it," she said. "Another way. Now come here." He did. It was still too brief an experience the first time but the second time was long and languorous. He groaned and she cried out and said strings of words he couldn't understand. Little by little, passion subsided. They marveled at how slick with perspiration their bodies had become.

"I've never been *this* way," she whispered. "That was wonderful. It was divine. *You* were divine." *There's that word again*, Mike thought. *Do girls only use it to describe love-making?*

Mike found towels and they mopped themselves and then lighted cigarettes, dropping their ashes in a steel helmet. "I feel like I've been in hell for a long time and all of a sudden I've been taken to heaven," he said. "And you're the angel. But you've never told me the big news you said you had."

She smiled and dragged on the cigarette. "Oh, I didn't mention it earlier because, well, I guess I was kind of intimidated by all you men wearing wings and looking like real flying officers, all that. But it *is* important to me."

"Well, what is it?"

"After you left that morning back in Albany, I felt really desolate, absolutely useless. And then I thought: get out of it, *find* something that makes you feel like a real person. Not just wrapping bandages and all that ladies' auxiliary stuff—oh, I'm not putting volunteer work down—but something *real*.

"Then, just a day later, I found out through my dad that Washington is about to invite women to apply for flying duty. He heard it from a War Department bigshot he went to see in Washington about his cotton shipments."

"Women? Flying duty?" Mike said. "I can't imagine . . ."

"Just you wait," she said, putting two fingers over his lips. "It's gonna be called the WASPS—Women's Airforce Service Pilots—and they're gonna sign up maybe a thousand women to ferry all kinds of military planes around the country, from factories out West to bases like this in the East, for instance."

"Great God."

"Yup. Fighters and bombers and transports, in this country and to Canada and even to the Caribbean. But there's one thing."

"What's that?"

"They're only goin' to accept women who have private pilot licenses. Of course you have to pass mental and physical tests . . ."

"You won't have any trouble with either of those, believe me."

"No, and not with the other one either. Ever since you left, for about eight weeks now, I've been taking flying lessons at the Albany airport. I've logged forty hours in a Piper Cub and I'll be taking my check-ride for my license as soon as I get back. I'll pass it and I'll be ready just as soon as they announce the program. I'll be one of the first to get my application in. Daddy's friend says he'll put in a word for me."

"Good Lord," Mike mused. "Women pilots. Imagine. Oh, there's Amelia Earhart and Jacqueline Cochran, I guess, but that's different. What do your parents think?"

"Well, that's what's funny. I haven't exactly been close to my father for some time, as you know, but this has changed all that. He never had a son and all of a sudden I'm the apple of his eye. A new kind of woman, something he's never seen or met before."

"And your mother?"

Claire laughed mirthlessly. "She practically took to her bed and called for smelling salts. Helene is the original S'uthe'n Belle mother; you might say she made me what I am today. Or was. The very idea of her finishing-school daughter doing something as dangerous and dirty—dirty's even worse than dangerous—was almost too much for her. But we've had it out, and now she accepts it. She doesn't like it, but she accepts it."

Claire turned to him and kissed him. "But that's enough talk. Now that I'm the new American woman, I say what I want. I want to make love again. Do you think you could manage that?"

"I'll try," he said. "Believe me, I'll try."

Afterward, they slept. In the morning, the light woke them and, fearing a clerk would start rattling the doorknob any minute, they dressed hurriedly. "What are you doing today?" Claire asked as she was putting on her shoes.

"Oh, I'm scheduled to slow-time a rebuilt engine on one of the B-17s at noon. I'll fly around for an hour or so."

"I wish I could come along," she said wistfully.

"That would be fun, but there's really no way . . ." He paused. "I wish you hadn't said that."

"Why?"

"Because that's what Buddy and I do to each other. One of us makes some nutty suggestion and then it becomes impossible *not* to do it. Lemme think. God, this would really rip it if they found out. Oh, piss-ant. Claire, there's lots of uniforms around here. In those shelves there, see. Quick now. Find a pair of flight coveralls that'll fit —a man's small size oughta do it. Also find a cap and a pair of shoes that'll fit. Just ball them up and bring them along."

She smiled broadly, her eyes glittering. "How are we goin' to do this?"

"Lemme think a minute." He pondered a moment. "Okay, this just might work. I'll walk you back to the officers' club and call you a cab. It'll pick you up at the gate. Get some breakfast at your hotel and change clothes and get a cab back here. Meet me at, oh, eleven-thirty at the entrance. Be dressed in the coveralls." He plucked his gold lieutenant's bars from his jacket. "Pin these on the shoulders of the coveralls. And, ah piss-ant, take my ID card, too. Just flash it at the guard on the way in. He won't look at it close. Just wear your cap down low on your face. Can you get all your hair inside it?"

"If I can't, I'll cut it off. And I won't wear makeup, of course. I'll look awful plain."

"You could never look plain, but that's not our problem. God, if they find out . . ." The thought made his head hurt. He would tell the assigned co-pilot there had been a replacement. No other crew-man was necessary for a slow-time flight.

Smuggling Claire aboard the B-17 was a horribly dangerous thing to attempt. It could wreck his career, get him assigned to a desk somewhere, maybe even get him broken to the enlisted ranks. But if he *didn't* do it, that fact would forever haunt him. As he and Buddy had agreed countless times before in illegal or unwise situations, there was really no choice.

When she arrived at eleven-thirty, Claire didn't really look like a man but, he decided, that was because he knew she wasn't. "Keep your head down," he ordered. "And try to walk like a man. Toe out, toe out, and don't swing your hips, for God's sake. Oh geez."

For an instant, he had forgotten and taken her hand. They walked quickly to the flight line, saying nothing. He pushed her toward the nose of the waiting bomber. Glancing quickly around to make sure no one was looking, he opened the hatch on the underside of the nose.

"Chin yourself up," he said. "Pull up and swing inside." When she got halfway up, he placed his hands on her bottom and pushed. She sprawled in the passageway between the nose section, where the navigator and bombardier normally sat, and the pilots' cabin above.

"Stay where you are till I get aboard," Mike said nervously. The crew chief walked up, head cocked to one side. "Taking it up for a slow-time, Lieutenant? Got a co-pilot?"

"All taken care of, Chief," Mike said. "Have you pre-flighted the airplane?"

"All ready to go, sir," the crew chief said. He looked up toward the cabin, apparently wondering where the co-pilot or mechanic was.

"Let's go then," Mike said. He was supposed to make his own pre-flight inspection but he was too nervous to do it. Grabbing the lip of the hatch, he swung himself up and inside the nose, turning over to land on all fours in the passageway. Quickly, he leaned forward and kissed Claire on the mouth. "Now crawl up into the cabin and get in the right seat. Fasten your seat belt and pick up the checklist you'll find between the seats," he said. "Keep your cap pulled down and don't look around. Just look at the checklist."

"Yes, sir," Claire said meekly. "I'm scared to death."

So am I, Mike thought. But he said, "Everything's Roger."

In the cockpit, he told her to read off the checklist as he flipped the switches.

"Batteries on."

"Batteries on."

"Hydraulic pump auto."

"Hydraulic pump auto."

They continued the ritual. Flaps up. Cowl flaps open. Master switch on. Gyros caged. Bomb bay doors closed. Booster pump on Number One. Throttle cracked. Fuel mixture to idle cutoff. Props high rpm. Mags off. Circuit breaks on. Generators on.

"Starter on for twenty seconds. Ignition. Prime the pump. Claire, prime the pump there. Down there. Come on."

"I'm *trying*, Mike, I'm trying. If you harass me you'll just make me more nervous."

"I know, I'm sorry. I just want to get this big-assed bird off the ground."

"Well, so do I." The Number One engine started with a clatter. Claire caught onto the routine as they started Number Two.

"Number Three is the rebuilt engine I'm slow-timing," he explained. "We've gotta baby it. Pump now." It started smoothly and so did Number Four.

Within minutes, they were rolling toward the takeoff runway. Mike called the tower for clearance as they taxied. "What I have to do is hold the Number Three throttle back about a third on takeoff," he explained. "That's the only time it really'll make a difference."

But he screwed it up. On the takeoff roll, Claire's cap blew off and Mike momentarily goggled at the sight of a woman's blonde hair flying around the shoulders of the co-pilot.

"Oh piss-ant!" he yelled as they neared the end of the runway. "I waited too long!" He slammed all four throttles to the stop for emergency power and they lifted off just in time.

"Wheeew," he sighed. "What a fuckup! Well, so the engine's gonna be fast-timed instead of slow-timed. Gear up. I mean hit that switch there, okay?"

As they climbed for altitude, she leaned sideways anxiously. "Did that hurt the engine?"

"Oh, probably not," he answered. "It seems to be okay; the instruments read all right." He turned to her and grinned broadly as they cleared the area. "Well, here we are. Whattaya say?"

She shrieked with delight, unbuckled her belt, and leaned over to kiss him. "Oh this is fabulous!" she screamed. "Absolutely super, wonderful, fabulous! What are we gonna do now?"

"Well, first, we're going up there." He pointed to a massive castle of puffy white cumulus clouds thousands of feet above them. "We're going to go play in the clouds awhile. It's a real kick and you really can't do that in a light plane. And when we get tired of it we'll go down in the nose and maybe make some more love. We haven't done it for a couple hours. Don't worry. I'll put the big bird on autopilot."

"This is unbelievable," she breathed.

It was. They soared around towering mountain peaks of cumulus, seeing how close they could come without touching them, then dipping the edge of a wing into the wispy substance and circling around it. Spying a relatively flat mass of cumulus, Mike lowered the bomber into it so that only their heads were above it as they tore along.

Claire cried out in delight. She gasped when Mike finally leaned over and said: "You take it for a while."

"Me?" she exclaimed. "I don't know how to fly this big thing!"

"Sure you do," he said. "Flying is flying. You've got a column with a steering wheel on top of it instead of the stick in that Cub of yours. Works the same way except the wheel turns the ailerons. The rudders are just the same, only these are bigger and you have to press down harder. Put your feet on them. You've got a handle here for all four throttles. Okay, you've got it." He lifted his hands and feet from the controls.

"Oh my God," she said reverently. Tentatively at first, and then with growing confidence, she banked the bomber to the left and then reversed and banked it to the right.

"That's good," Mike said. "But pull your nose up a bit on the turns. See." He tapped the altimeter to show her they had lost a hundred feet.

"Oh, right," she said.

"Okay, it's all yours. You want to climb, advance the throttles. You'll get the feel of it," he said. Soon she was playing in the clouds as Mike had done, soaring up and around peaks, plunging into the gray depths of the valleys, dipping one wingtip and then another into the wall of a wispy fortress, exploding through the cotton-candy top of a billowing cloud castle, bobbing up and down like a porpoise atop a massive blanket of alto-cumulus so that their heads alternately disappeared and emerged.

Finally she leveled off. The sky above them was a cerulean blue. Laden with dewdrops from the clouds, the B-17 sparkled in the intense sunlight as if it were encrusted with jewels. She turned to Mike with the face of a delighted child.

"How did I do?" she asked.

"Just great," he said honestly. "I wouldn't have believed anyone could learn so fast. Certainly not a . . ."

"Woman," she said, completing his thought.

"Well, yeah, I guess I'll have to adjust my thinking some."

"You said something about going down in the nose," she said.

"Yeah, let's. Let me set up George here." He swung the B-17 on a due-east heading and began turning the dials of the Minneapolis-Honeywell automatic pilot to order it to fly the airplane straight and level. Then he pulled the master switch and, with minute jerks and corrections, the autopilot began flying the bomber like a reliable but slightly nervous aunt.

He watched the instruments for a moment, made a fine-tuning adjustment, and said: "Okay, co-pilot. Follow me." They climbed down from the cabin into the Plexiglas nose. "This is where the navigator and bombardier work."

"It's real roomy," Claire said wonderingly. "And it's so open, all this glass. The view is—you can see ahead and to the sides and even above and"—she threw her arms around him—"it's all so beautiful." Tears of joy welled up in her eyes. Feeling himself melting into mush, Mike took her in his arms and kissed her softly.

When the kisses became deeper and more passionate, they undressed, positioned the air crew's pillows beneath them, and stretched out together. After they had kissed and stroked awhile, she whispered: "I'll get on top. All right?"

"Anything you want," he said hoarsely.

The experience was surreal, hypnotic. Pinned to ecstasy, she sat naked and erect, a mythic Valkyrie, and rode him through the skies as cloud banks whipped by her, raindrops spattered against the Plexiglas, sunlight dazzled her, and hundreds of miles of blue sky and green earth unreeled before her. Soon, the light changed and she realized half-consciously that they were over water and it was green in the shallows and dark blue with whitecaps in the distance.

The climax boiled up within her suddenly. She screamed aloud and fell against his chest. They rolled over and convulsed frantically together inside the nose while the big bomber, sun-spangled, dew-drenched, cloud-shrouded, soared benignly eastward.

They returned to consciousness slowly. "Have you any idea where we are?" Claire asked at length.

"Not really," Mike said.

"Don't you think we'd better find out?"

"Oh, I guess." He reached for his clothes; she did the same and they dressed and clambered back up into their seats.

"Boy, I'm sore," she said.

"That's what too much flying does to you," he said.

"Yeah, sure," she grinned. "Now how about turning us around? Can you navigate us back?"

"Piece a cake," he said. "We came out on a ninety-degree heading. So we go back on the reciprocal—two hundred and seventy." He turned the autopilot off and banked the B-17 steeply on a reverse course. "You take it."

"Oh, great," she said, taking the controls. "But what about wind drift? Even I know you can get blown off course if the wind's coming at an angle."

"Well, babe, it's a clear day and Florida isn't that big and wide a state, you know. And there are some pretty good landmarks, like Lake Okeechobee, the Glades—hell, if you go too far you hit Tampa-St. Pete and the Gulf. Besides, you can always pick a radio station, set your radio compass on it, and home on in. No sweat."

They found Hendricks without incident. As they entered the traffic pattern, Mike said: "We've come this far; we might as well go whole-hog. You do the approach and land. We've got dual controls; I'll follow you through on mine."

"Jesus, Mary, and Joseph."

"Yep, and St. Christopher, too. We'll go to full rpm now and put the flaps down a third. Now drop the gear. That switch there. Feel the drag? Okay, reduce power a little. Let down at five hundred feet a minute. Gentle turn here. Going to half-flaps. Straighten out on final approach. Full flaps coming down. Hold it at about one hundred ten miles an hour. Settle in a bit now."

"Is this all right?" she shouted.

"It's fine. Flare out a little. Easy. Easy. Let the wheels touch; I'll help you." He pulled his wheel back slightly. The front wheels touched with a squeak. "Perfect. Hold it there; the tail wheel will fall on its own. Great. Now unlock the tail wheel. Down there. *Careful;* don't get the control lock by mistake or it's upsy-daisy. Okay, fine, I'll take it now."

He braked, blasted the port engines, and swung the B-17 off the runway onto the taxiway and perimeter track. When they reached the hardstand, he nosed in, toed down hard, chopped the port engines, and blasted the starboard engines, swinging the ship around in a circle so it stopped pointing outward.

"That does it," he said. He closed the throttles and turned off the switches. "Now we get out of the plane the way we got in, except we just drop from the hatch. Get your cap on tight and, when you get up, just start walking away. I'll have to sign the crew chief's maintenance log; then I'll catch up with you."

When they arrived at the entrance of the officers' club, they stopped and impulsively threw their arms around each other. Seeing a group of officers stop and gawk, Mike deliberately pulled off Claire's cap and let it fall. Grinning, she shook her head and her blonde hair fell around her shoulders.

The knot of men in the doorway froze as if they were looking at an alien being. One of them, Mike saw, was Buddy. His jaw seemed to be hanging down on his chest.

"Buddy!" Mike called. "Go back in and call a cab for the lady, will you? She'll meet it at the gate."

Buddy closed his mouth, surveyed them silently for a moment, and finally said: "Yo." He turned and went inside.

Mike and Claire walked to the gate together, her arm around his waist, his around her shoulders. She gave him back his shoulder bars and ID card. He put them in his pocket. "I'll never forget you, Claire," he said. "Never. This has been a wonderful day. Last night, too. Just wonderful."

"Wonderful isn't a big enough word," she said as they stopped at the gate. She looked at him without speaking for a minute or two. "Last night was wonderful, but today—there can never be anything like that again. Never has been, never will be, for me, for anyone, I think."

She shook her head in wonder. "We don't use the word 'love,' do we? Not when we're goin' in different directions, when we meet on the fly, you might say, when there's a war on."

"I guess I hadn't thought about it."

She smiled. "Maybe someday."

As the cab pulled up, she leaned back and laughed. "One of these days, some man is goin' to tell me how great it's all goin' to be, what a big time he's goin' to show me, how he'll just open the eyes of this naive li'l Albany girl with all he's goin' to do. I'm goin' to say to him: 'Mistah Man, you just don't have a *clue*. If you wanta talk about *big*-time, let me tell you about a young man named Michael. And his big airplane. And the afternoon we spent in it together.'"

She kissed him quickly and started to get in the back seat of the cab. Turning and smiling, she shifted into her Southern Belle accent: "I declaih, Loo-ten-ant Gavin, you sho'ly do know how to show a lady a good time."

When Mike arrived back at the club, Buddy was waiting. "Just what in the livin' hell have you been up to, Mike-boy?"

"Buddy, if I told you, you wouldn't believe it," Mike said. "All I'm gonna say is that there's a new kind of woman out there. Pretty soon there'll be more of them. And, boy, when they come, you better watch your ass. You won't *believe* what they can do."

The instant she pulled the lever to jettison the undercarriage of the experimental ME-163 rocket plane, Flugkapitan Hanna Reitsch knew she was in serious trouble.

Hanna always waited until the Komet was fifty or more feet above the ground before jettisoning the landing gear. At any lower altitude, the wheels might bounce up and strike the bottom of the aircraft. So, as she had done six times before, she waited until the roaring rocket engine had lifted the Komet fifty feet in the air before pulling the lever to release the wheels.

A violent shudder shot through the tiny airplane, quickly increasing to the point that it became almost impossible to control it. Red flares curved up from the ground. As she shot by a transport airplane, she noted that it was pulling its landing gear up and down.

Her landing gear had stuck! It wouldn't release! Clearly, it was hung up, loose, and banging against the bottom of the airplane. In doing so, it was disrupting the airflow over the egg-shaped fuselage and creating a serious turbulence.

Wallowing and shaking violently, the Komet shot up through the clouds. So long as she could control the aircraft, she would burn off the volatile rocket fuel. It wouldn't take long. She thought briefly about leveling off, turning the Komet on its back, and bailing out. *No.* She was wearing a parachute, but a dedicated test pilot simply didn't abandon a valuable aircraft just because there was a problem.

The rocket flamed out and the Komet nosed over and became a glider. Hanna swore to herself. Her mother wouldn't like to have heard her do that, but this really was exasperating. She had hoped that, without the power, the lower airspeed would produce less turbulence.

But it lessened not at all. Now there was the problem of landing. The field was coming up fast and, as usual, there was only one chance to make an approach. The safest way—perhaps the only way—was to come in a bit high and sideslip onto the runway, kicking the Komet straight at the last second.

As she streaked toward the runway, she pressed the tiny left rudder pedal and brought the stick to the right to lean the Komet sideways so that it would present a larger surface to the headwind. This would kill altitude and speed at the same time.

But the action made the Komet shudder violently and, before she could neutralize the controls, it flipped into a spin. Here came the ground! She threw her arms over her face and the Komet crashed heavily onto the runway, somersaulted twice, and slammed to a stop. Dazed, Hanna opened the side door and carefully felt along her chest, arms, and legs.

Her limbs seemed to be intact but, she realized, blood was dripping down her face. She felt her jaws, lips, and cheeks and stopped at her nose—or where her nose had been. There was a deep cleft in it. Above, blood was flowing freely from her helmet.

Hanna heard voices and knew she was being lifted gently from the wreckage. There was the sound of a siren and she realized that she had been transferred to a rolling stretcher and was being wheeled through corridors. She judged she had been taken to the Sisters of Mercy Hospital in nearby Regensburg.

Someone—was it her mother?—was talking to the chief surgeon. The X-ray plates had revealed four fractures of the skull and two in the face, he said. Her nose had been smashed.

But she felt little pain. As she slipped into unconsciousness, Flugkapitan Reitsch consoled herself with the thought that at least she and others like her were ensuring that German soldiers would have the very best equipment with which to defeat the barbarians of the East.

Field Marshal Friedrich Paulus rejected the cup of coffee that his adjutant, Colonel Adam, tried to hand him. Paulus hadn't slept all night. His superb Sixth Army had been defeated and its remnants, three hundred thousand frozen, half-starved, and lice-ridden men, were surrounded at Stalingrad.

The telephone lines and cables had been cut. The Russians had achieved air superiority; Reichsmarshall Göring had promised to defeat the Soviet blockade by airlifting 750 tons of supplies a day into the German pocket, using 375 JU-52 transports, each of them carrying two tons.

It was a very specific plan but, as usual, the Reichsmarshall's boast had proved to be an empty one. Harassed and destroyed by Soviet fighters, impeded by the dreadful winter weather, the transports brought in an average of eighty-four tons a day.

Finally, the Sixth Army had run out of ammunition and food. It was the final humiliation. His soldiers, battered by artillery and pounded day and night by Soviet aircraft, were exhausted. It was really too much, almost an insult, to be bombed twenty-four hours a day. Even if the night bombing was a relatively puny effort, it had been an intolerable irritant.

The costly drive to take Stalingrad—the campaign that never should have been undertaken—had failed. There was no longer any reason to fight and, except for random skirmishes, the shelling and shooting had stopped. Soviet soldiers would be at the door of his command bunker at any moment. There was no way to know whether they would be Soviet officers, approaching formally to receive his surrender, or vengeful, trigger-happy troopers.

Paulus feared the moment that the door would swing open, but he realized that this desperate moment had come because he had feared Adolf Hitler even more. He should have withdrawn when he could, saving the main part of his army even though he would have had to leave their heavy weapons behind.

He should simply have *done* it instead of asking permission. Twice —that in itself had required courage—he had sent coded radio messages to the Supreme Commander asking permission to withdraw to the southwest, make contact with Field Marshal Erich von Manstein's relief force, and form a corridor for the evacuation of the troops.

The Führer's reply to the first message was to promote Paulus from general to field marshal. A week after the second message was sent, Hitler announced that Paulus had been awarded the Reich's highest decoration: the Knight's Cross with Oak Leaves.

Paulus realized finally that these were really posthumous awards, part of the process of building an image of the heroic German martyrs of Stalingrad. Even now, the heroes were eating the last of Stalingrad's dogs, crushing lice, and, if a Russian woman could still be found, raping her in a cellar.

Paulus' suitcase was crammed with heavy underwear. He hoped he would be would be allowed to keep it in Siberia, if that was where he was going. The door of the bunker opened and a voice ordered him in Russian to come out. Paulus rose from his chair, pulled his greatcoat, trimmed with green leather, around his shoulders, picked up his gray rabbit-fur hat, and walked out, head erect.

Five hundred miles to the north-northwest at Tula, just south of Moscow, General Heinz Guderian wondered how a brilliant military position could have been so completely botched in two months' time.

The hard-faced panzer leader who had stormed across the European continent to Dunkirk in ten days was frightened. Not for himself; he had a deserved reputation for fearlessness. For the first time, he foresaw, against all reason, the defeat of the splendid, unmatchable German army—and the defeat of Germany itself.

Guderian had become a thorn in Adolf Hitler's side—more than that, an open sore—because of his harsh and open criticism of the Führer's orders. They had stood, face to face, and shouted at each other while terrified generals and adjutants cowered in the background.

Other generals would have been shot out of hand. Guderian's reputation as the first among military professionals protected him from that—but not from the idiocy of stupid orders.

Maneuver, *Aufstragtaktik,* was a skill at which the German commanders excelled. Yet Hitler, with his repeated orders to stand fast, had denied them this advantage and forced them to fight a war of attrition and materiel that they could not win.

Guderian laughed wryly as he shoved his papers in his map-case. Instead of sitting in a snow-covered bunker and waiting for an airplane to take him westward, he could have been sitting in the Kremlin by now. If Hitler hadn't stopped them at Smolensk on the road to Moscow—*Gott im Himmel!,* they had advanced one hundred and fifty miles in four days—they would have captured the Russian capital before the rains came.

Now they were in retreat, and Guderian, in open rebellion, had resigned his command. He could never have been accused of coddling his soldiers, but the situation had become intolerable.

His soldiers were still in summer denims in thirty-below cold. Hitler had indignantly denied that winter clothing hadn't been sent to the front until the Quartermaster General was called in and had to admit that it was still at the railway station at Warsaw. So his soldiers had to make do with blankets and, sometimes, with fur wraps and other pieces of women's winter clothing that had been sent from home.

By now the ranks were filthy and unshaven; their underclothes were ragged and verminous. The sick had to march up to twenty-five miles a day with the column. There was no soap, toothpaste, needles, or thread. Boots were falling to pieces and there was nothing to repair them with.

Their equipment was becoming useless, too. They had wheels on the trucks instead of the treads Guderian had wanted. Caulking for the tanks hadn't arrived. Nor had the salve that was supposed to stop the telescopic sights from freezing. Fires had to be lighted under the engines of tanks and airplanes to get them started. Even the fuel was freezing.

And, Guderian admitted, the Soviet's equipment and tactics had surprised him. The Russian T-34 tank was better than its German counterpart. The *katyusha* rockets were an unhappy surprise. So were the white-clad Soviet ski troops who swooped out of the white mist like some exotic cavalry from outer space and ambushed the marching German columns.

Further, while he hated to admit it, the Siberian soldiers frightened his soldiers. They had never seen troops who looked like the Siberians, or were as physically strong, or who could march so far and still fight. They had actually marched continuously for four days and then attacked at the turning point of the Moscow campaign.

All of this had to be recorded. Guderian pulled his diary from his map-case and began writing:

Only he who saw the endless expanse of Russian snow during this winter of our misery and felt the icy wind that blew across it, burying in snow every object in its path; who drove for hour after hour through that no-man's land only at last to find too thin shelter with insufficiently-clothed, half-starved men; and who also saw by contrast the well-fed, warmly clad and fresh Siberians, fully equipped for winter fighting—only a man who knows all that can truly judge the events which now occurred.

CHAPTER FOUR

THE MESSAGES

"My ass is busted this time and that's for sure," Mike said after he and Buddy had been summoned to the colonel's office. "But you weren't any part of it and I'll make that clear, don't worry."

"You haven't told me squatly, so I don't even know what it is that I wasn't part of," Buddy said. "Maybe Herman the German wants us for somethin' else."

He did. Colonel Bachman told them to stand at ease and said without preamble: "You men are all through here."

Mike glanced sideways, saying silently *I told you so.* Then Bachman surprised them: "Except for screwing up from time to time—matters of personal behavior, like that business with the truck, I know it was you two—you've done well in four-engine school. In fact, you're my best pilots. So I'm not going to keep you here to finish out the course next week. I'm sending you today, right now, up to Langley on special assignment."

When the two looked baffled, Bachman said testily: "Langley. As in Air Force Base. As in Virginia. Air-sea rescue and anti-sub patrol. Oh for God's sake, get your faces up off the floor. You'll be going off to England to get your asses shot off in due time. I *told* you, this is a special assignment."

"May we ask what it is, sir?" Mike asked.

"No, you may not," Bachman said. "First, I don't know and, second, it's supposed to be secret so I wouldn't tell you if I *did* know. So pack your bags, gentlemen; a transport'll be ready to fly you there in exactly two hours. That'll give you just enough time to get signatures for your clearances. Better get cracking."

He handed each a clearance sheet that had to be signed by the appropriate officers at the officers' club, bachelor officers' mess, billeting office, base finance, signal office, personnel, administration, and organizational command before they left the base.

Mike and Buddy saluted and executed an about-face. As they were leaving, Bachman called out: "Gavin."

"Yes, sir?"

Bachman's heavy face broke into a grin. "Did you imagine that you're the only pilot who's ever smuggled a girl aboard a B-17 here at Hendricks?"

Startled, Mike started to answer, but the colonel cut him off: "Never mind. It's not part of the training course, and it's not recommended, God knows, but it *has* happened." Herman the German smiled broadly. "You might even be surprised at who it's happened *to*."

On the way out, Mike furrowed his brow. Was the colonel saying that *he* had done something like that at one time? That was hard to imagine. He was an old man, practically bald, with wrinkles in his face, probably almost forty years old. Even *thinking* of something like that at his age was ridiculous.

Reichsmarshall Hermann Göring's penchant for exotic costumes was viewed with disdain by the general officers of the Third Reich. So was his obsession with stag-hunting.

General of the Bombers Werner Baumbach understood both reactions as he sat for the first time at the long table at Karinhall, Göring's fabled hunting estate near Berlin, and listened to the Luftwaffe chief talk.

Today, the Reichsmarshall was resplendent in a great leather waistcoat, beneath which he wore a huge snow-white shirt with great puffed sleeves and an open collar. On the pudgy third finger of his right hand he wore a large sapphire ring.

What could the man possibly weigh? Baumbach wondered. One hundred and fifty kilos, three hundred pounds? At least that, probably much more.

Sitting before the man-mountain at the head of the table was a large, intricately-decorated, Bavarian stein of beer. To either side of Göring sat Baumbach and Luftwaffe Chief of Staff General Hans Jeschonnek, both in dove-gray Luftwaffe uniforms.

Looking down on the table from both walls was a veritable museum of stuffed heads of royal stags, elks, and boars that had once strayed into the Reichsmarshall's rifle sights. It was, Baumbach thought, like being in a zoo. But Göring maintained a private zoo of live animals on the estate, too.

Upstairs, the bomber general had heard, was an elaborate model railroad. The more you saw of Karinhall, the more you realized why the Reichsmarshall had so much trouble following through on the projects he initiated or promised to fulfill. He had too many toys and distractions.

For the moment, however, he sounded serious. Picking up a leg of roast venison and waving it in the air, Göring said: "The plans have been made. We're going to bomb America, and very soon."

Baumbach suppressed a smile. He had heard all this before. First it was to be with the Heinkel 177, now universally called "the dead racehorse." The bomber general had to sympathize with Göring on that one because Professor Heinkel repeatedly made the same two mistakes: coupling two engines with one airscrew on each wing and trying to stress the big aircraft for dive-bombing.

"I don't *want* engines coupled together in that way!" Göring had shouted at Heinkel. "They keep breaking down, not to mention catching fire, and they would be practically impossible to repair in the field."

"But it's the only way the 177 can be designed for dive-bombing," Heinkel said. "You can't dive-bomb with four separate engines and propellers. It's never been done."

"But it's not *supposed* to dive-bomb!" Göring roared.

"Well, if it's not going to dive-bomb, we won't have to strengthen the airframe further," Heinkel said.

"Exactly!" Göring yelled. So the 177 was put into production. A squadron was assigned to Stalingrad. The first four caught fire and the rest were grounded with malfunctions. Then the "racehorse" was assigned to submarine escort duty. But its range was only nine hundred and thirty miles. Finally, the 177 was pronounced outdated and work began on the "real" Amerika bomber, the Messerschmitt 264. It would have a range of eight thousand miles, enough to fly from Brest to New York and back; it would be designed with four engines, and it would carry three to five tons of bombs.

But the available engines weren't powerful enough. A light, wood design was suggested and vetoed. Midair refueling at night was planned, but initial experiments weren't satisfactory.

Then there was the A-10, the two-stage version of the V-2 rocket, that would reach America. It had been designed and it was perfectly feasible. But, Baumbach mused, the plain fact was that Germany's production resources were simply too strained to put even the best new ideas to work.

Baumbach wanted desperately to win approval for production of a new radio-controlled missile that could be fired from a bomber. It was called the Fritz X and the prototype had been tested with great success. The descent and direction of the FX could be controlled by a lever in the bomber's cockpit. It was the world's first "intelligent" bomb; it promised to revolutionize naval warfare and the bombing of land targets, too, if only the men and materials would be made available for production in quantity.

Jeschonnek was just as desperate to use all available production capacity to build new-generation fighter planes. With the Reich under continuous attack from the air, the need was critical. But Germany's production capacity was dedicated to a continental land war.

And now Göring insisted on bombing America. The argument for it was plausible, of course. A successful attack would provide a great morale boost at home and it would strike fear and confusion into the hearts of the smug, seemingly-unreachable Americans.

"As I said," the Reichsmarshall continued, munching on his food, "our plans are nearing completion."

"May we ask what you have in mind?" Baumbach asked.

"That's what I called you here to tell you," Göring said, slurping his beer. "We are going to use available equipment. One of you should have thought of this before."

"What equipment, Reichsmarshall?" Jeschonnek asked.

"I don't know why I have to think of everything," Göring grumbled. "It's very simple. We'll use one of our new Blohm & Voss flying boats, the Viking. It can carry forty-two thousand pounds. Most of that will have to be fuel, of course, but there can be as many as five or six tons of bombs."

"But it hasn't the range, Reichsmarshall," Baumbach said.

"It won't need it," Göring answered. "Being a flying boat, it can land on water, obviously. It will do so seven hundred miles off the Atlantic coast and rendezvous with one of our new *Milchkuh* submarine tankers. We have ten of them, you know, and each can carry nearly one thousand tons of fuel. But ours will carry aviation gasoline rather than diesel oil for this project.

"The sub tanker will refuel the Viking, which will then fly on to bomb New York City. We have singled out the Jewish quarter for the attack, though we should hit their tall buildings as well. The Americans won't know what hit them.

"Then the Viking will rendezvous at a second point, refuel again, and fly down to the Panama Canal. We will put the Canal mechanism out of business, absolutely, and the Americans will be unable to move ships from one ocean to another without sailing all the way around the tip of South America. The Viking will rendezvous with another *Milchkuh* off the Canal and fly on home."

Göring took another gulp of his beer and looked appraisingly over the rim of his stein. Jeschonnek began laughing in spite of himself. Baumbach smiled, feeling a strong tickle of interest in the idea. On principle he disapproved of anything that distracted the Luftwaffe from its true priorities. But, he admitted, the plan appealed to him. And it just might work. America's coastal defense had, so far, been amazingly incompetent. But the *ne plus ultra* for making it work was, of course, watertight security.

"It's a fascinating plan, Reichsmarshall," Baumbach admitted. "How far have you gone with it?"

"I've exchanged messages with Admiral Dönitz—coded and secure, of course. He's to tell us when he can get the *Milchkuhs* at the two appointed stations with the fuel for the Viking. You will see to the Viking and its crew. I want this attack carried out without delay."

Admiral Karl Dönitz, *Befehlshaber der Unterseeboote* (BdU), commander in chief of Germany's submarine fleet, looked up from the message he was writing and stared out the window of the chateau that served as his headquarters near the flotilla headquarters on the River Scorff at Lorient.

Dönitz, a fifty-year-old U-boat veteran of World War I, seemed much taller than he was because of his slender physique, erect bearing, and an air of dignity that was heightened by a lean and ascetic face. If it weren't for the uniform, he might easily have been taken for a Lutheran minister.

Dönitz was widely respected for his intelligence, integrity, and iron will. Because of the latter, he was known to his U-boat commanders as The Lion. Today, the Lion pondered his exchange of messages with Göring with mixed feelings.

No one wanted revenge against the Americans more than he did. They had made fools of the *Ubootwaffe* time after time during 1940 and 1941 when they were supposedly neutral in the war between Germany and England. U-boat commanders, spying a smoke cloud or masthead on the horizon, would race to the scene only to find a freighter with a huge American flag painted on the side.

And the Germans knew from radio intercepts that the duplicitous Americans were tipping the British to the positions of the U-boats when they spotted them. This added insult to the injury Germany had suffered when Roosevelt persuaded his Congress to change America's neutrality laws so that any belligerent could sail to U.S. shores to buy war goods.

Roosevelt was laughing up his sleeve when Congress passed *that* one; he knew perfectly well that the only nation able to cross the ocean in surface ships to pick up war materiel was Britain.

Dönitz had enjoyed a large measure of revenge following Germany's declaration of war on America just after Pearl Harbor. Within a six-month period in 1942, the U-boats sank *four hundred* freighters carrying war goods off the Atlantic coast.

The large number of ship sinkings and the tiny number of submarine losses surprised no one more than Dönitz. Who could have guessed the U.S. Navy would be so incompetent at defending its own seacoast?

Still, no U-boat or surface vessel or aircraft had ever bombed or shelled an American city—though their coastal towns and cities were still brightly lighted—and that really was a shame. Göring's plan, if carried out, would remedy that fault, at least.

The admiral sighed. But wasn't this simply a stunt at a time when far-ranging reform was needed? Even the Lion's iron will was insufficient sometimes to keep him from gnawing at the past like a dog at a bone.

He had been forced to start the war with England with only fifty-seven U-boats when he had told the Führer very plainly that a fleet of three hundred was required. Only one-third could be on station at any one time, he had explained. Another third would be coming out or going back to the fortified sub pens, and one-third would already be there undergoing maintenance. Unless, of course, dockyard workers hadn't been pulled off again to work on something else.

With one hundred boats on station in 1940, he could have starved Britain into surrender within a year. Even with a dozen boats attacking British ships, the *Ubootwaffe* had sunk a million tons of shipping in less than a year.

But Adolf Hitler was a land animal who thought only of troops and tanks.

Even today, in early 1943, the *Ubootwaffe* had only a handful of boats on station in the Atlantic. The new seventeen-hundred-ton *Milchkuh* submarine tankers served as a multiplier, of course; by refueling the U-boats they extended the range of the larger ones by eight weeks—though an additional eight weeks at sea drove the unwashed, unshaven, and overworked U-boat crews to the point of exhaustion.

Dönitz picked up his pen and began writing a message for coded wireless transmission to Kapitanleutnants zur See Kraus and Seigel, each of them commanders of *Milchkuhs* at sea. Both had been ashore when Göring's message arrived. Each had been personally briefed on the Amerika project and had—with obvious reluctance—emptied his boat of its cargo of diesel oil, supervised a careful scrubbing of the tanks, reloaded with aviation gasoline, and put to sea.

The message assigned each commander a prescribed naval square of ocean and instructed him to inform BdU as soon as he arrived on station. He would then stand by for a further message giving the time, date, and precise coordinates for the rendezvous with the Viking.

The Lion sat and tapped the message with a finger before handing it to his aide. The cipher security of the Kriegsmarine, he knew, was the tightest and best of any of Germany's armed forces. All used the miraculous Enigma code machine, whose encrypted product was called HYDRA in the Kriegsmarine.

The Enigma machine, the size and shape of a typewriter, had three small wheels or rotors at its back that were rotated each day to different positions dictated by a list given to all cipher clerks and U-boat radio operators. The list provided the settings for a month; for security's sake, the U-boat lists were printed on paper that would dissolve in salt water.

The cipher clerk at headquarters typed the message on a keyboard at the bottom of the machine. A separate alphabet was displayed in tiny light bulbs at the top. Each keyboard letter at the bottom illuminated a different letter in the alphabet above. The letter *B* might illuminate a *P*. But, because the Enigma's three wheels turned eccentrically with each depression of a key, the second time that *B* was tapped it might come out *F*. There was no logical way to predict the progression of letters being transmitted by Enigma.

The Enigma machine defied all basic rules of cryptanalysis. When the coded message was typed, it was handed to a wireless operator who sent it in Morse code to the submarines at sea or to any branch of the service on land.

Every U-boat commander had his own machine. When his antenna picked up the message from BdU, the U-boat's radio operator would translate the Morse code into its letter groups, check his list for the day's wheel settings, turn them to their proper positions, and type out the incoming message on his keyboard. The deciphered message would appear in the illuminated alphabet above.

Enigma's messages were considered undecipherable by all German intelligence experts. And the naval services used a supplementary *Adressbuch* that changed any directional coordinates given in the messages, day by day, by adding or subtracting values to or from the true numbers involved.

Still, Dönitz worried. He worried about security and he worried that he might become paranoid over the worry. But it was an undeniable fact that he had recently lost two boats soon after sending them messages ordering them to new positions. And it seemed to defy the odds of chance that Allied convoys seemed so often these days to be avoiding the ocean squares where he had placed U-boats on station.

When these worries became acute, Dönitz would convey them to the naval staff in Berlin. On occasion, they would send him representatives from the Berlin cipher firms of Heimsoht and Rinke to assure him, once again, that the code was unbreakable. Even if such a technical feat were possible, they said (and they assured him it was not), it would take the enemy so long to recreate the messages—given the machine's use of constantly-changing, random letters—that the messages would be operationally useless.

The experts would smile, spread their palms, and ask: Who could possibly penetrate the intricacies of Enigma and then figure out the changes prescribed by the *Adressbuch* at the same time?

Soon, Dönitz had heard from reliable sources, he would succeed Erich Raeder as Grossadmiral of the Kriegsmarine and become commander in chief of all of the Reich's naval forces. But his heart and, today, his attention, was devoted to his beloved *Ubootwaffe*. And he was worried.

As the German cipher clerk tapped out the Morse message in the communications building next to Dönitz's office, a British WREN—a member of the Women's Royal Naval Service—picked it up from her receiver on the Channel coast southeast of London.

The German clerk's "fist," or sending style, was recognizable but, to make sure, she asked her supervisor for a radio triangulation with the help of two other stations that would fix the location of the transmitter within a dozen miles.

This was accomplished in a matter of seconds. The WREN nodded; the message was from Lorient. She copied out the incomprehensible five-letter groups and handed them to a cipher clerk who encoded them in the prevailing British code and sent the message by teleprinter to a country estate north of London called Bletchley Park.

There, one of the ten thousand men and women who worked twenty-four hours a day in nondescript Nissen huts received the message in the registration room. He copied it and sent it by courier to the intercept control room. The supervisor, after looking at it, decided it deserved priority attention. Copies were made and sent to the crib room in the adjoining hut, where cryptographers searched for repetitive and familiar elements like standard salutations. These they called cribs. Finding a good crib could speed the process of decoding.

A world-class chess player studied the frequency and call sign and compared it against a stack of other messages with the same characteristics that had arrived over the past few weeks. Spotting a vague but promising similarity in the pattern of introductions, he noted it and sent the message text to the cryptographers in Hut Number Eight.

Three hours later, the group, which included a professor of advanced mathematics, an expert on probability theory, and a professional cryptanalyst, gave a courier four pairs of letters that they thought might connect the electrical circuits of the Enigma keyboard with the machine's illuminated lampboard.

The courier took the letter pairings to a hut containing several five-foot-by-ten-foot electromechanical calculators called *bombes*. There, a clerk programmed the letter pairs into a machine by inserting metal plugs with prongs into selected receptacle slots. Then he pulled a switch.

The *bombe*, containing twelve replicas of the Enigma's rotors, churned through 17,576 possible wheel settings. Two hours later the machine stopped. The clerk looked at the three-digit number displayed by the *bombe*, copied it on a piece of paper, and sent it by courier to the cryptanalyst's hut.

The professor of mathematics sat down before a replica of an Enigma machine built by exiled Polish mathematicians using inductive reasoning, set the wheels in the positions specified by the *bombe*, and typed out Dönitz's coded message. As the decoded words appeared in the clear on the lampboard, the watch officer got up and watched.

It had been a productive day. This message would go to naval intelligence for transmittal westward to the Americans to give them the latest information on the planned rendezvous between a Viking flying boat and a submarine tanker. A message received earlier in the day would be sent eastward to tell the Russians of a major counter-offensive the Germans were planning in the Caucasus.

"At ease, gentlemen. Sit down." The speaker wore the eagles of a full Army colonel. Out of uniform, he could have been taken for a university professor. Colonel Horace Sorensen was a tall, slightly stooped man who looked a bit like a worried crane.

Lieutenants Gavin and Bryce sat down carefully in two of the three chairs placed in a semi-circle before Sorensen's desk at the base commander's office in Langley, Virginia. The third chair was occupied by a young civilian dressed in a white shirt, dark tie, and dark blue suit. He had a square face that revealed nothing and black hair that was combed straight back.

"This is Mr. Jones from Washington," the colonel said with a wave of his hand. His inflection made it clear he assumed the name was a pseudonym. The civilian nodded but said nothing.

Sorensen looked at the three for a moment. "Well, let's get to it. You two officers have been recommended to me for a particular mission. You are described as exceptional pilots and your records suggest a certain, ah, inventiveness, which your base commander seems to feel might be an asset to this mission.

"I have no way to judge the validity of that opinion," the colonel said, momentarily appearing even more worried than usual. "But we have to move on this. The matter is top secret." He shuffled the papers on his desk for a moment as if he were reluctant to reveal it.

Finally, he looked at them with an expression that was almost belligerent. "It appears that the Germans are going to try to bomb New York. And then the Panama Canal."

"Good Lord, they can't . . ." Buddy burst out.

"No," Sorensen said. "We intend to stop them. We expect to have the exact date and ocean coordinates at any time now. A flying boat will rendezvous with a German submarine tanker—they call those things milk-cows—in a few days. How we know that is none of your business—or mine.

"Their rendezvous point has been selected at the outer limit of the radius of action of a B-17. A PBY flying boat would solve the problem of flying range, of course, but our PBYs are much too slow for an air-to-air encounter, if that should be necessary, and they're not properly armed.

"So we're using a B-17 with an extra, jettisonable gas tank that's been installed on one side of the bomb bay. We'd already modified that airplane for experimental purposes. It has a 37-mm. cannon mounted in the nose. We won't have 50-caliber machine guns for a top turret or radio operator, nor will we have a tail gun—we need to save weight—but we will have waist guns. Any questions so far?"

"Sir, I assume the flying boat will be our primary target and that we'll attack it on the surface," Mike said. "Ideally, while it's refueling. That cannon sounds great. But what about the bomb load? Or should it be depth charges?"

The colonel's face crinkled unhappily. "We've debated that at some length. If our primary target was the sub, we'd want 300-pound depth charges. We'd *like* to get the sub, no question, but we *must* get the flying boat. It's called the Viking. So we decided finally to carry bombs. We decided on 260-pounders, fragmentation type. Twelve of them, giving us a 3,120-pound bomb load. That's a fairly small load for the airplane, but there has to be a compromise between bomb load and gas."

"We'll probably get just one shot at them anyhow," Mike offered. "And it's a pretty good bomb load for that small a target."

"Yes it is," the colonel said, nodding approvingly. "And you're right; it's logical to think you'll have just one run at them. The sub may crash-dive, and if you haven't gotten him, he'll be gone. That's where depth charges would be nice. But we want you to get them both on the ocean surface, if at all possible.

"If you miss, or don't disable the Viking, it'll take off, or try to. That's where the nose-mounted cannon comes in."

"Can you tell us about the Viking, sir?" Buddy asked.

"It's no piece of cake to attack. It's a very large high-wing cantilever monoplane, about twice a B-17's size and weight, with six thousand-horsepower BMW radial engines and a large single-fin tailplane."

Buddy whistled involuntarily.

"Yes," Sorensen said. "We estimate that it carries about forty thousand pounds and that it may carry six or seven tons of bombs. Even

so, it flies a shade faster than you do, and, if they carry normal armament, it could be a handful. According to G-2, the typical armament
of a Viking is one 13-mm. machine gun in the nose—that's about like
our 50-calibers; a second one in a forward dorsal turret, a third in a
rear dorsal turret, and four laterally mounted guns of slightly smaller
caliber in side windows.

"Further, you'll have to get in close to use the 37-mm. cannon
effectively. It gives you a bigger bang but it doesn't have the range or
flat trajectory of your .50s. So if you haven't put the airplane out of
commission, you'll be taking fire from its guns. And from the sub,
too, if it stays on the surface. G-2 says the sub has two deck-mounted,
two-centimeter anti-aircraft guns. They call them machine guns but
we rate them as rapid-firing cannon. So the sub packs quite a wallop,
even though it's a pretty vulnerable piece of iron, sitting on the surface with all that gasoline inside. Questions up to this point?"

"If they see us comin', they'll out-gun us any way you figure,"
Buddy said. "So we've gotta take them by surprise."

"Exactly," the colonel said. "How would you plan that, Lieutenant?" He pointed at Mike like a teacher testing a pupil.

"Well, first, I'd want to be on the deck, right on the waves, so they
wouldn't see us coming," Mike answered. "Second, assume it's an
early morning rendezvous. Is that logical? I don't know. Maybe
they'd want to bomb at night. I don't imagine there's any real blackout in New York."

"There isn't," Sorensen said disapprovingly, glaring at Jones.

"So they'd have good visibility for bombing and they'd be hard to
detect at night," Mike said. "In their shoes, I'd prefer that. But they
have to have good visibility for the rendezvous on the surface. Assume it's a late afternoon rendezvous, then. We hit them from the
west with the sun at our back. Morning rendezvous, we'd have to
approach at an angle, out of sight, and then turn and come in from
the east, with the sun behind us."

"What's the problem in the morning scenario, Lieutenant?" Sorensen pointed at Buddy.

"We'd use a whole lot more gas, sir. And there's a chance of being
spotted before we're ready."

"All right," the colonel said, making a steeple of his fingers. "I
guess we've got the right men"—he smiled slightly—"or at least as
good as we'll get on short notice. I haven't decided which of you will
fly left-seat, first-pilot. You're rated as even-up."

Mike and Buddy looked at each other. "We can flip a coin," Mike
said.

"All right," Sorensen said. "We'll have defense in depth, of course. A second B-17 will head east off the coast at the time you're supposed to make the interception. We'll give it directions, as necessary, when we receive your radio signal at the interception point. A squadron of medium-range, twin-engine aircraft will take off an hour later from Mitchel Field, New York, and we'll have a squadron of single-engine interceptors sitting on the ground ready to scramble."

The colonel's worried look returned. "But there's a lot of ocean out there and New York's right on the coast. A single airplane might slip through and hit the city before we intercepted it. Particularly at night. So we want to catch it at its most vulnerable moment—at the rendez-vous."

He turned to the civilian. "Do you have anything to add, Mr. Jones?"

"No," the civilian said.

Galina was dreaming. She was trying to get back to the base but the controls of the PO-2 wouldn't work. They kept bending in her hands like soft candy and it frightened and frustrated her, particularly since a loud voice was calling to her. She assumed it was her navigator's voice and she tried to tell her to shut up, but she couldn't seem to make a sound.

The badgering voice became louder and more annoying.

"Lieutenant! Lieutenant Tarasova!" It became louder still, and now she was being shaken. "Galina!" She woke with a start and realized that Major Kravchenko was standing over her bunk and gently shaking her shoulder.

"Comrade Major," Galina said sleepily.

"I know you flew last night, Galina, but a courier has arrived with an urgent message for the Army's divisional headquarters. He was wounded on the way and he landed here. We've taken him to the surgeon. We'll have to make the delivery for him. It's in a town forty miles from here. The message is urgent and the delivery must be made within the hour."

Galina wanted to ask *why me?*, but she had long since learned that asking that kind of question was unproductive in the VVS. So she swung her legs out of her bunk and sat for a moment to clear her head.

"Get some breakfast," Major Kravchenko said. "I'll give you a map with the proper directional markings while you're eating your kasha. Valya will fly navigator for you. You haven't flown in the daytime for quite a while, Galina; remember to hug the ground. It makes you harder to see from above; if an enemy plane should see you, remember that your maneuverability and the lowest possible altitude are your best defenses."

As she was leaving, the older woman turned and smiled: "Make the delivery properly and return safely, Lieutenant. I'll take you off the flight roster tonight. You can get some extra sleep."

It was below the freezing point, as usual, and the wind cut like a razor. Valya, who was barely five feet tall, looked like a small circus bear in her bulky flying clothes. She smiled at Galina painfully with blue lips.

When they snapped the covers from their cockpits, the film of ice on them crackled. The weather was gray with heavy winter cloud cover at medium altitude and an occasional scud of dirty-looking clouds at low altitude. Visibility was several miles, enough to see the town they were flying to, but limited enough to keep the PO-2 from being seen from above at any distance.

Yet the gray-green camouflage, which was effective against grass or even bare ground, created an unwelcome contrast against the snow. But, Galina reflected, you have to make do with what you've got. If that weren't the case, she'd be flying a Yak instead of a ridiculously-old biplane.

But the little engine started up readily, wheezing and popping, and soon they were hedge-hopping across the countryside. Though Galina had once enjoyed this kind of flying, she felt terribly exposed and vulnerable in her old biplane in the daylight.

She occasionally flicked her eyes to the sides, but mainly she had to concentrate on watching the ground ahead because she was flying so close to it. Valya, who was carrying the message in a map case, continually rotated her head to look out for any enemy fighter that might dive on the PO-2 from above or slip in from behind.

They had just reached the town and Galina was looking for a flat place to land when Valya called out, "Messerschmitt! Five o'clock high!"

Galina swiveled around in her seat and peered to the right rear. Here it came! She saw flashes from the ME-109's wing guns and tracers arced toward the PO-2. Galina tramped the right rudder, threw the stick over, and rolled hard to the right, standing the biplane on its wing to turn inside the Messerschmitt. The ugly Maltese cross on the enemy's side was clearly visible as the fighter screamed past her.

Galina banked vertically to the left, straightened out, and depressed the nose to fly straight down the main street of the town. A dozen or so soldiers and civilians on the ground looked at her in surprise. They barely needed to lift their eyes. As she flew down the street, she saw the Messerschmitt make a climbing turn to circle around and dive on her. There was no place to hide. Or was there?

The end of the street was coming up and she heard the PO-2's little machine gun firing as Valya trained it on the enemy fighter swinging toward her tail. Galina had to decide *now*, instantly. She flipped the PO-2 on its side, yanked the stick back diagonally to pull the nose up sharply, kicked the left rudder, and made an impossibly tight ninety-degree bank-and-turn into the side street. As she turned, the wheels barely touched the walls of the building at the end of the main street and then bounced off.

For an instant, Galina thought she would lose control of the biplane. It wobbled for a deadly second and almost rolled over. The wingtip came within an inch or two of the ground. Then, as the ME-109 ripped by her at a right angle, she straightened out, cut the power, pulled the nose up, and dumped the biplane on the ground for a hard, bouncing landing.

Before the PO-2 rolled to a stop, an officer was running to the cockpit, his hand outstretched, yelling for Valya to give him the map case. Valya thrust it into his hands and swiveled around to look up. Here came the enemy fighter again!

Galina waited; there was no point in trying to take off here, even if there was space enough to do it. Nor was there time to climb out of the PO-2. She said a silent prayer. What must be would be. She heard Valya's machine gun chattering and there was a violent explosion.

Parts of the ME-109, burning fiercely, shot overhead and showered the ground ahead of them. Openmouthed, Galina wondered how Valya and her little gun could have made such a miraculous kill. *No!* It was a Yak! Its red star was beautifully visible as it swept by and executed a flamboyant victory roll.

As he came three hundred and sixty degrees through the roll and started a climbing turn to leave the scene, Captain Viktor Markov smiled. The free-hunter had scored another victory in the air. And perhaps it would lead to an even more satisfying one on the ground.

CHAPTER FIVE

THE RENDEZVOUS

KAPITANLEUTNANT HARRO KRAUS was an angry man. Bearded and dirty, his face set in a hard line, he stood on the bridge of the *Milchkuh* in his oilskins as it bucked through the waves of the North Atlantic.

Kraus detested the clumsy submarine tanker and the seven hundred tons of stinking octane gasoline that it carried. It was bad enough to carry diesel oil for the refueling of U-boats that were doing what *he* ought to be doing—sinking Allied freighters with torpedoes.

But the gasoline was far more volatile than the heavier oil and, therefore, much more dangerous. Wherever fumes were present, the flame of a cigarette or spark from a dropped tool could ignite them and blow the boat and its crew to bits.

The burly *Milchkuh* commander accepted danger; if the Americans ever became as competent as the British at attacking U-boats, few members of the *Ubootwaffe* would survive the war. But counterbalancing the danger for most U-boat crews were the joy of victorious combat and the promise of promotion.

Neither reward would be his. Kraus acknowledged, grudgingly, that, from BdU's point of view, he was lucky to be at sea in anything larger than a rowboat. For, on his last sortie—he had sunk a total of seven ships on three previous ones—he had mistakenly torpedoed and sunk a German freighter that was running the Anglo-American blockade.

The ship had sailed, undetected by the British and Americans, all the way from Indo-China. It carried thirty-five hundred tons of desperately-needed rubber and three hundred tons of tin, together with supplies of tungsten, quinine, and hemp. This precious cargo went down with the ship when his third torpedo struck it at the waterline. So, unhappily, did thirty-five German merchant seamen.

"But this is unjust!" he had complained to the court-martial at Lorient. "I had no way to know it was one of ours. It was not in one of the ocean squares we were told might be traversed by a blockade runner. The outline was an American freighter's. And it had an American sort of name—the *Boston*. How could I possibly know?"

Nevertheless, the court-martial found Kraus guilty of negligence. It did not recommend imprisonment or even demotion, but it questioned whether he had the judgment to command a U-boat.

"Look at it this way, Kraus," the Lion said afterward. "You won't have to endure the ignominy of being demoted to second or third in command. You aren't being assigned ashore to shuffle papers. Further, Kapitanleutnant, think where you'd be going if the courtmartial had adjudged you guilty of *gross* negligence.

"You'd be a member of the Wehrmacht by now; very probably you'd be lying in the snow with a rifle on the Russian battlefront. Of course, you can argue that you were the victim of circumstances, that another commander very likely would have made the same mistake. He might have, but *you* made it and you're the one who has to pay. However, I acknowledge the special circumstances and it's because of them that I'm allowing you to go back to sea."

Dönitz's voice softened. "Please remember that, as commander of the *U-425*"—Dönitz avoided the term *Milchkuh*—"you are performing an essential service to the *Ubootwaffe* and exercising your skills of seamanship. And who knows? If all goes well, you may be back in command of a torpedo carrier at some point in the future."

It wasn't in Kraus' nature to think about the future. It was the present that concerned him, and *that* was the clumsy, broad-beamed, 1,688-ton *U-425* he was sailing to ocean square CC5301 to rendezvous with a Viking flying boat—a Viking!—just before twilight the following day at 2100 hours Central European Time. That would make it 1600 hours—four o'clock in the afternoon Atlantic time—on a winter's day in 1943 east of New York City.

The *U-425*'s twin diesels, each generating twenty-two hundred horsepower, churned the *Milchkuh* across the ocean surface at a brisk fifteen knots. He would be at the assigned location on time unless a far-ranging enemy warship or flying boat forced him to submerge.

Underwater, with the diesels turned off and the boat's two five-hundred-horsepower electric motors running silently, the *U-425* would be lucky to make six knots. And the boat would have to surface within sixty-four miles and stay on the surface for seven hours to recharge the sixty-ton batteries that ran the electric motors. Otherwise, the air in the submarine would become too foul to breathe. Most people thought, falsely, that a submarine spent most of its time underwater. In fact, it couldn't. It was, in truth, a surface boat that was able to dive and stay submerged for a limited number of hours.

Life aboard any submarine was crowded, polluted, and smelly. There was no laundry aboard and the bunks were occupied in rotation by crewmen coming on and off watches. The same sheets would be on the bunks for as long as three months.

But opposing this squalor was the specter of life on the eastern front, where a soldier lived outdoors in sub-zero temperatures, ate horseflesh when he could get it, and couldn't thaw his weapons enough to use them properly. Here, at least, a crewman had three hot meals a day and a dry bunk, however odoriferous, to sleep on.

No, Kraus vastly preferred life aboard a submarine—or did before his tragic accident. He swore aloud into the wind and wiped the salt spray from his face with the towel draped around his neck. He had had enough of the North Atlantic for one day. He would go below now and have his supper. His Number One would take the bridge. And, to soothe his angry feelings, the Kapitanleutnant would tell the radioman to play some records—Piaf's "La Vie en Rose," perhaps, and the crew's sentimental favorite, "Lili Marlene"—while the *verdammt* gasoline sloshed around in the *Milchkuh*'s huge storage tanks.

Major Horst von Neumann settled himself in the cockpit of the giant Viking with a feeling of keen anticipation. He was a happy man. If the plan worked—and there was no good reason to think it wouldn't —he would become the first German to strike a blow at the American mainland.

First, there was the little business of rendezvousing with the submarine tanker—that officer had a rotten job, didn't he? Then there would be the great pleasure of dropping his bombs on New York City. He was carrying three tons of hot-burning magnesium fire bombs. They would fall in a shower and they had delayed-action fuses that were timed to explode in three minutes. So he would sweep in low over the city and have the pleasure of seeing all the buildings and lights and people as he roared overhead.

Nor did he see any reason why he couldn't make a wide circle to watch the effect of the explosions. They would create a real holocaust, an even bigger fire than the ones he and his fellow Luftwaffe bomber pilots had ignited on the London docks late in 1940.

Then, while the Americans milled about in confusion, trying to put out the blazing fires, he would fly away in the darkness to rendez-vous farther south with the tanker at dawn. Then he would fly on to the Panama Canal. On the way, his crewmen would pull the arming pins on four 500-pound demolition bombs that were hung on one side of his specially-rigged bomb bay.

The Panama leg of the journey, he knew, would be more hazardous because, by then, even the inept Americans would have their forces alerted. But, by flying outside the range of all but the longest-range bombers and flying boats in a huge ocean, he would be hard to find.

Even if he were found, his Viking would be a formidable opponent with its heavy machine guns and skilled gunners. No American gunner had had the experience of Luftwaffe gunners who had fought through the air battles of France and Britain and even, some of them, on the accursed Eastern front.

So, Neumann concluded, the odds were heavily in his favor. And the rewards that would follow! He had to restrain himself from bouncing in his seat. A promotion to Oberst, certainly. A Knight's Cross, almost sure to be hung about his neck personally by the Führer. He might even be awarded an estate in the eastern lands.

And, meantime, the publicity! He would become a national hero. Children would ask him for his autograph. And *women!* He sighed in anticipation. Like the legendary Adolf Galland, the young General of the Fighters, he would have his pick of the film stars, not to mention the most beautiful daughters of the bankers and factory owners of Berlin. Perhaps, later, he would even marry one if she were rich and pretty enough.

Who could ask for more than that?

Lieutenants Gavin and Bryce were worried. The B-17 was three hours off the coast and heading due east when the weather began worsening. The midwinter stratus clouds offered some concealment from below but, by the same token, made it harder to spot anything on the surface from a distance.

"Piss-ant," Mike grumbled. "Our navigation has gonna have to be awfully damn good if we're going to catch these bastards."

Buddy nodded. He was already out of sorts, having lost the coin toss for the left seat and first-pilot status. But he realized it was a petty matter and he struggled to shake off his irritability.

The bomber carried a crew of six for the mission. Below the pilots in the nose, Lieutenant Henry Zapp rechecked his navigation on the map spread out on his plotting table. A slight and dour young man, he was highly experienced in overwater navigation. It was relatively easy to direct the B-17 to the general area in which the Viking and submarine would rendezvous. But it would require absolute accuracy and a dollop of luck to catch them head-on, particularly with visibility declining. He peered down at the whitecaps to try to determine whether the wind drift might have changed.

Sitting in the nose by the bombsight and in back of the cannon was the bombardier-gunner, Lieutenant Charles McCabe. He had run up the best scores ever recorded on the practice bombing ranges at Hendricks and McDill Fields in Florida and he had worked diligently over the past few months to bring his gunnery up to the same standard. The 37-mm. cannon was new to him but he had fired it intensively on gunnery runs during the previous week.

Still, he wondered uneasily what it would be like to shoot at a real human being. And be shot at. His palms were wet and he wiped them on the legs of his coveralls for the tenth time.

Behind the pilots stretched the bomb bay. A catwalk spanned it and provided access to the radio compartment behind it. There, radio operator Sergeant Thomas Thurston sat and waited for the moment to send the signal back to Langley. He could send and receive Morse faster and more accurately than any other radio operator at Langley, Mitchel, or Westover, and he liked it when his peers called him Thurston the Magician after the vaudeville performer of the same name.

As soon as he had sent the interception signal, Thurston would leave his radio and man one of the waist guns. The mission's planners had cut the crew to an absolute minimum to save gasoline.

The sixth crewman was waist gunner Sergeant Isiah Zimmerman. He was also rated as a radio operator and would handle communications if anything happened to Thurston.

In the cockpit, Buddy turned to Mike and pressed his throat mike against his Adam's apple for clearer transmission. "I've leaned out the fuel mixture as much as I can. Anything less and the engines'll be suckin' air. They're runnin' hot and sound a little hit and miss as it is."

Mike nodded worriedly. The mission had started out as something exciting but it was becoming chancier by the minute. He surveyed the gray, white-capped ocean with dismay. It was so godawful big and bleak! And, with increasing frequency, they were flying through gathering clouds.

A half hour from the assumed interception area, Mike jockeyed back the throttles and let the nose fall. "I'm going to go down to two hundred feet. We've gotta be getting close and we've gotta get under these clouds. It's gonna be easy to miss them in this mess."

"It'll burn up a bit more gas maybe," Buddy said. "But you're right. If we don't find them, the mission's a flop." Much worse than that, he reflected. The damned Viking might very well get through to New York and dump its bomb load.

Like most southern boys of his day, Buddy disliked and resented the idea of high-and-mighty New York. He and his friends called it "New Yawk," and, when they mentioned it at all, made slighting references to the hordes of Jews who supposedly populated and ruled it.

But his year in the Army Air Forces had broadened his view of the world. Mike Gavin had laughingly dismissed Buddy's prejudices as regional eccentricity. That irritated Buddy at first but, as time went on, it undermined his faith in the beliefs with which he had grown up.

And look at the crew aboard today. Zimmerman was a Jew and maybe Zapp was, too, though it wasn't something you asked about. There didn't seem to be anything very wrong or odd about either of them. Further, New York, judging from the one brief look he'd had of it, was a city so towering and glittering that it took your breath away.

He peered out his side window and shook his head. Up high, they had seemed to be flying in a giant bowl of milk with little definition between sky and sea. Down low, the gray waves with their white-caps seemed to reach up ominously toward them. He shivered. It sure wasn't like a day at the beach.

"Herr Kalev," said second-in-command Oberleutnant zur See Otto Schnabel, using the accepted abbreviation for Kapitanleutnant, "it's 2100 hours." It was always German time aboard the submarine.

"Very well, Number One," Kapitanleutnant Kraus replied. He rose from his bunk in his private cubbyhole on the port side of the submarine tanker and opened the green curtain that gave him the only privacy that existed aboard the ship.

"Anything?" Kraus asked, pointing at the radio man and hydrophone operator in their cubicles on the starboard side.

"Nothing, Herr Kalev," Schnabel said.

"All right. Let's take a look." The sub had been submerged at periscope depth and circling slowly for the past half hour, waiting for the Viking to arrive. Simply sailing in a circle on the surface seemed a foolish thing to do, even out here.

Kraus strode to the 7.5-meter-long, high-angle general observation periscope, pressed his eye socket against the rubber housing of the eyepiece, and turned the periscope laterally with one hand as he focused the eyepiece with the other. There was nothing in sight but gray sky, gray clouds, and gray water. And soon it would be nightfall.

Kraus pulled his oilskin over the wool-lined leather jacket he was wearing and stuck his peaked officer's cap on his head. "Let's go up," he said.

"Lookouts to control!" Schnabel yelled, leaning into the bulkhead opening. Four seamen with binoculars hanging around their necks moved quickly below the conning tower.

"Stand by to surface," Kraus said in a loud voice. "Steer up. E motors full ahead. Blow out the main ballast. Surface!"

Schnabel quickly gave a series of orders to the planesman handling the controls. As he did, the planesman called back: "Six meters, five, conning tower clear!"

The hatch was wrenched open and, with the four lookouts behind him, Kraus quickly clambered up to the bridge as the deck of the submarine, dripping water, rose to the surface. Each man faced a different direction and began sweeping the horizon and sky with his 7×50 Zeiss binoculars.

Below, Schnabel gave orders to feed surface air to the diesels, shut down the electric motors, open the ventilators, and use the exhaust to expel the water ballast that allowed the craft to submerge.

On deck, one of the lookouts suddenly hunched his shoulders, pointed eastward, and called: "Herr Kraus!"

Wheeling about, Kraus trained his binoculars at the horizon, then moved them upward to a thirty-degree angle. There it was! A dot had appeared in the sky and it was rapidly growing larger.

"Flak gun crew to battle stations!" Kraus called down the voice pipe. "Bring the blinker light to the bridge." He waited tensely as the men pounded up the ladder and took their positions. It should be the Viking. It was in the right place at the right time. But there was always the freak chance, however unlikely, that it could be a British Sunderland flying boat, a *verdammt* "bee."

Kraus quickly reviewed the admonitions given U-boat commanders by BdU. An enemy aircraft presents the most danger to a U-boat. A surprise attack is most likely to occur on a day like this or on a calm, moonlit night when the submarine's wake creates phosphorescence. Always have the anti-aircraft guns cocked and pointing up, with magazine attached, when on the surface.

If the aircraft is as much as four miles away, you can dive safely. If it's closer, fight it out on the surface.

The aircraft grew steadily larger in Kraus' binoculars. It was definitely a flying boat and, instead of heading directly for the U-boat, as it would if it were an enemy, it approached in a gentle circle, losing altitude at the same time.

"Blink the password," Kraus ordered, keeping his eyes trained on the aircraft. The crewman obediently blinked the word EDEL. Within seconds, an answering light blinked WEISS.

Cheers broke out on the bridge and were quickly echoed below as the word was transmitted that the aircraft was the Viking. Kraus watched in admiration as the huge flying boat, its six propellers turning, glided gracefully onto the surface of the choppy sea.

Now would come the hard part: getting the oddly-matched flying boat and the submarine close enough together and holding them steady enough to effect the fuel transfer.

Major Horst von Neumann blasted the starboard throttles to pull the Viking to the left and taxied briskly through the waves to come alongside the U-boat. Opening his side window, he waved at the bearded U-boat commander standing on his bridge and called to him cheerily.

"Heil, Vier-Zwei-Funf—four-two-five!" he yelled, grinning.

"Heil, Viking!" the U-boat commander answered.

Neumann pulled his helmet off, reached for a large handkerchief, and mopped his forehead and face. He was immensely relieved. He had flown flying boats overwater before but never on a trip this long or to such a godforsaken spot. Somehow the ocean had never seemed as huge or forbidding as today. And he disliked the choppiness that was making the Viking rock back and forth.

He desperately wanted a cigarette, but that was *verboten*. It was no time for luxuries, even small ones, nor for socializing, either. Best to get to business. Seamen were clambering up the bridge of the U-boat to start the fuel transfer.

Neumann shouted to his chief engineer to open the gas tank caps. The fuel transfer would be tricky and it would be dusk soon. But once that was accomplished, he would be on his way again. And soon the Great White Way that he had read about so often and with such envy would suddenly become the Great Red Way.

And Major, no *Oberst* Horst von Neumann would become the Great German Hero. What was it the British said? Piece of cake.

If the visibility were good enough for him to fly at a higher altitude, Mike knew, the B-17 crew would be able to see farther and have a better chance of spotting the U-boat and the Viking. But flying higher would make the B-17 easier to spot from below.

That might have posed a dilemma if the weather allowed any leeway. But the sheets of wintertime stratus clouds had lowered and, by now, he was flying at less than two hundred feet from the ocean's surface.

"Pilot to crew," Mike said. "Keep a sharp lookout. We've gotta be ready to attack any second."

"Bombardier to pilot, shall I open bomb bay doors?" McCabe's question caught Mike by surprise. Momentarily confused, he looked at Buddy, who spread his hands and shrugged his shoulders. They were flying at the outer limit of their radius of action and opening the doors would create extra drag and consume more gasoline. Another goddamned dilemma.

"Hang on a minute," Mike said. It had all seemed so simple when they had met Sorensen. They assumed without much thought that they'd find the target easily and, with the sun at their backs, hit it by surprise. But they hadn't found it, there wasn't any sun, and, soon, they wouldn't have enough gas to get home.

"Navigator to pilot. We're in the rendezvous area and it's forty minutes after the designated time. What'll we do?"

Mike cursed silently. Still another decision! "Pilot to navigator. I guess we'll have to . . ."

"There they are!" The cry came from Zimmerman in the right waist position. "At three o'clock."

Jesus! Mike banked the B-17 savagely to the right and pushed the nose down. There they were, like two toys, sitting right on the surface, maybe a half mile away. Something long—it looked like a hose

—had just been disconnected and the flying boat was starting its engines. The B-17 was dangerously late in finding the target.

"Open bomb bay doors!" he shouted.

"Already doing it!" McCabe shouted back. "Level off, quick as you can."

Buddy pushed the four prop levers to full emergency war power as Mike leveled off at less than one hundred feet. His hand moved, as if on its own, to advance the throttles, but, realizing what he was doing, he snatched it back. The bomb run should be made at cruising speed.

The U-boat and flying boat grew rapidly larger. One man fell from the wing of the Viking into the water. On the submarine, several men sprang to the twin cannons mounted behind the conning tower as others piled down the hatch.

Big red tracers began arcing toward the nose of the B-17. There were several sharp explosions followed by what sounded like rocks hitting the fuselage. Mike heard someone cry out in pain. But he stared straight ahead, wholly focused on the target.

"Bombs away!" McCabe sang out. The airplane, lightened of its bomb load, lifted. Speeding away, Mike tramped hard on the left rudder and pulled the wheel over to throw the B-17 into a tight left turn to see what was happening.

Kraus saw the B-17 at the same instant as the lookout who was facing west. "Enemy aircraft! Open fire!" he yelled. The men at the two-centimeter flak guns turned them quickly toward the low-flying bomber, and began firing.

"Bring up machine guns!" the U-boat commander shouted in the pipe. Two men bounded up the ladder carrying shoulder-held machine guns. Now the Viking was firing, too. Fire and smoke were erupting from the muzzles of its two dorsal-mounted 13-mm. machine guns and from the lighter waist gun.

To the Viking pilot, the decision was obvious and immediate. Though his engineer had just replaced the gas caps and was still outside, Neumann shoved the throttles full forward and began moving away from the U-boat. An instant later the B-17's bombs fell along a line that straddled the submarine but was outside the Viking's new position.

*　*　*

None of the stick of fragmentation bombs hit the U-boat directly, but shards of hot shrapnel sprayed the submarine tanker from one end to the other. Two lookouts on the deck fell dead. Schnabel staggered and clutched his chest. Kraus' cheek felt as if a hot knife had been run along it. Blood began dripping on his oilskins.

"Keep firing!" he yelled to the flak gunners. One began firing at the B-17 again as the second man slumped to his knees.

"What damage?" Kraus shouted.

"The pressure hull has been pierced, Herr Kalev," Schnabel grunted. He was bending over like a man having a heart attack.

Kraus swore. Now he would be unable to dive. It would be a long, dangerous trip back to Lorient, if he managed to down the B-17, or if it left the U-boat to chase the Viking. It would be . . . He didn't get to finish the thought. There was a blinding flash of light and a huge explosion as the submarine's cargo of gasoline ignited.

Sonofa*bitch!*" Buddy yelled as the B-17 flew through the smoke and flying debris. Mike ducked involuntarily as pieces of metal rose around the bomber. He was momentarily disoriented as they emerged from the smoke and he shook his head and looked about frantically for the Viking.

There it was! The flying boat was clearing the water ahead of them and heading due west—and Colonel Sorensen had said it was a shade faster than the B-17. If he didn't catch it now it would pull away and disappear in the gathering darkness. Mike went to full power and pushed the wheel yoke forward. It was no time to worry about gas consumption. He would use his advantage in altitude, gather as much speed as possible, and dive on the flying boat.

In the radio compartment, Thurston tapped his Morse key to tell Langley that the sub had been destroyed but the Viking had survived. Zapp stowed his navigation table and crawled to McCabe's side to help him with the 37-mm. cannon if they got a chance to use it.

Buddy remembered belatedly to ask the crew to report in. When Zimmerman failed to answer, Thurston, having finished sending his message, went back to find him. He found the gunner dead on the floor beside the waist gun. There was a gaping hole in the fuselage. It had obviously been made by the sub's cannons.

The news shook and enraged Mike. The afternoon's exciting adventure had suddenly gone terribly awry. One of his own men was dead—he had never thought *that* might happen—and his primary target, the Viking, threatened to escape and fulfill its deadly mission.

Neumann's mind raced. The U-boat was gone—that was regrettable but inconsequential—and the B-17, which came from God knows where and had found them God knows how, was diving on him from above. The obvious tactic was for the Viking to speed straight ahead toward its destination. That was what he would ordinarily do and that's what the B-17 pilot would expect him to do.

But the two large airplanes were in a most unusual situation—squaring off for the kind of dogfight that only fighter airplanes normally had. The B-17, according to his crew's reports, had a large gun mounted in the nose and machine guns at either side of the waist. But the bomber appeared to have no guns at the top of the airplane, underneath, nor in its tail.

If he could get behind the B-17 . . . Just as the bomber began firing, Neumann swung the flying boat into the tightest possible bank to the left. As he expected, the B-17 zoomed on by. Neumann held the bank, pulling back on the wheel and resisting the Viking's desire to stall out. The flying boat, loaded with bombs and new gasoline, was terribly heavy in Neumann's hands and the Viking turned much too slowly to suit him.

"Bastard! Where is he?" Mike yelled.

"Behind us!" Buddy shouted.

"No, he's not!" Mike yelled, standing the now-light B-17 on one wing and pulling the yoke almost back in his lap. The bomber shuddered at stall point and Mike relaxed the back-pressure a bit and then straightened out to turn inside the Viking.

"Hit him!" he yelled. The B-17 shook with the pounding of the 37-mm. cannon. Now the Viking, beam on, was right in front of him. He pulled up to clear it and thundered over the flying boat, which raked the bottom of the B-17 with heavy machine gun fire. Again, there was the sound of gravel or rocks being thrown against the body of the airplane.

Mike tramped the right rudder, held the wheel over, and pulled the yoke back again to execute a tight right turn. As he did, he saw that the Viking pilot was still banking hard to the left.

If the timing was right, they would meet head-on. And here he came! It would be a game of chicken!

* * *

Neumann's co-pilot had been wounded and a third pilot had moved into his seat. Two other crewmen had been injured, one apparently badly. But all six engines were still running and, as the B-17 swept over him, he saw holes in its fuselage and underside.

Sweating heavily, Neumann leveled out. The lighter B-17 was surprisingly maneuverable; he wouldn't have thought it possible for a four-engine bomber to be so agile. But how good was the pilot? How many missions had he flown?

Neumann would test the American's nerve. He aimed the Viking directly at the B-17. The nose guns of both airplanes began firing. The bomber pilot wasn't going to flinch. Very well!

Neumann noted quickly that he was heading almost due west. He shoved the nose down hard and slipped below the B-17, again calling on his gunners to rake the American with the dorsal guns.

Then, leveling out and flying at maximum power, he headed for the U.S. coast. He would fly low to evade any possible radar—if the Americans had any operating—and use his superior speed to outrun the B-17.

Above, Mike cursed and swung the B-17 around again. He had been outwitted by a more experienced pilot and he had wasted valuable time. The Viking was out of gun range and pulling away. But Mike still had the advantage of height.

Buddy spotted the opportunity immediately. "We've got one shot at diving on him. I don't think he'll try to jink around again."

Mike nodded, pressed the throttles hard against the stops—they were already there—and then had a sudden, crazy thought.

"Pilot to navigator. Is there gas in that bomb bay tank?"

"Navigator to pilot. It's about a third full."

"Can you drop it quick if I tell you to?"

"Sure. But . . ."

"Wait. Pilot to bombardier. When I say 'now,' open bomb bay doors."

"Bombardier. But that'll slow us . . ."

"Do it when I say 'now.' "

"Roger."

Mike pushed the nose down, picking up speed and diving on the Viking. If he missed this time, he knew, the Viking would pull away and disappear in the gloom and he would have to signal Langley that they had failed. Christ, imagine being held responsible for New York being bombed! Imagine *feeling* responsible!

As they neared the flying boat, tracers began arcing up from its dorsal guns and something shattered in the B-17's cockpit. The bomber's 37-mm. cannon began thumping again.

Mike pressed the nose down grimly and yelled: "Open bomb bay doors."

"Doors open." He was directly over the Viking now and almost on top of it but the added drag of the open doors would start pulling him back. "Drop the bomb bay tank!" he yelled.

"Tank away!" the bombardier yelled. The B-17 rocked and some-one cried out again as the Viking's heavy machine guns punched holes in the bottom of the B-17.

There was a blinding explosion that threw the B-17 off on its right wing. Mike and Buddy fought to regain control of the bomber as it tried to roll over and spin. For an instant, he was back in the Link Trainer at Augusta and Ginny was laughing at him. But this was real.

They got the B-17 straight and level just above the waves. Only then did they look ahead, openmouthed, to see what had happened.

Out of the corner of his eye, Neumann saw something unnaturally large falling to his left. An instant later, there was a monstrous explosion that threw the flying boat sideways.

Time seemed to shift into slow-motion and the German pilot watched in horror as the left wing of the big aircraft, its three engines still running, slowly broke away from the fuselage and began spiraling downward.

And then the body of the Viking rolled over and fell. Horst von Neumann cried out in rage and fear as the gray ocean rushed up to meet him.

The tail fin sailed like a huge kite past the B-17. Mike threw the bomber into a circular bank to get a clear view. "The fuselage!" McCabe yelled. "In the water on the port side. It's just going under. We got him!"

Cheers rang through the interphone. They would never be sure whether it was the big cannon or the partially-filled gas tank that blew up the Viking. But who cared?

Mike turned delightedly to Buddy. Buddy's head was pressed back against the seat rest; his face was contorted with pain.

"What is it, Buddy?"

Buddy's voice was a whisper. "Hit my left knee. Smashed it, I think."

"Pilot to radio," Mike said. "Bring up a first-aid kit. Hit the co-pilot with morphine, then dust his knee with sulfa."

"Roger. I've already notified base that we got the Viking."

"Roger. Pilot to crew. Any other injuries?"

"Bombardier to pilot. Zapp was hit in the arm; I've got a tourniquet on it."

They made an emergency landing at Mitchel with one engine out, fifty holes in the fuselage, and, they learned later, only a few gallons of gas left in the main tanks.

Mike and the crew members were whisked to Langley in a waiting transport plane before they could even stretch their legs. Buddy and Zapp were taken to the hospital by a team of medics and Mike was ushered into Colonel Sorensen's office.

Mr. Jones was there. This time, he did nearly all the talking. "I want to make two things very clear to you, Lieutenant," he said. His square face was still impassive and his black hair was still slicked straight back. His voice was low and glacially cold in tone.

"One is that I am speaking for the United States government, for the very highest level of our government. Do you understand that?"

"Yes, sir," Mike said stonily. The man made him angry. He offered no word of praise or even an acknowledgement that the B-17 crew had destroyed the Viking—not to mention the submarine. And he expressed no concern about Buddy, who would soon have surgery to rebuild his shattered knee. (That, at least, was what one of the medics had told Mike on the way down to Langley.)

"Very good," Jones said. "The second point I want to make is that no one—no one at all—is to know about this incident."

That surprised Mike. "But we shot them down. We proved they couldn't come over and bomb us! People ought to know!"

Mr. Jones held up a warning hand. "This is a policy decision." He paused a moment. "I'm not obliged to explain it to you but, since you have a certain legitimate interest, I will. We want to avoid any public panic. If the public even suspects that such an attack on New York or Washington or the Panama Canal is even remotely possible, it will shake public faith in our government's ability to defend the United States. It has been decided not to risk that."

Mike flushed with anger. "Well, I don't think . . ."

"It doesn't matter what you think, Lieutenant," Jones said. "Or what I think. The decision has been made." He pulled a paper from his inside breast pocket and handed it to Mike. "Sign this, please."

"What is it?"

"Your sworn statement that you will be silent about this whole matter from beginning to end. The same statement is being signed by every member of your crew. If you wish to remain on active duty as a pilot, you will sign this. Afterward, if you then speak about any part of this matter to anyone, you will be held in violation of our espionage laws and arrested and imprisoned."

"I'll sign it," Mike said. "In exchange for one thing."

Jones raised his eyebrows. "What's that?"

"A simple thank you."

The smallest trace of a smile flickered on Jones' face and disappeared. "Thank you," he said.

Colonel Sorensen cleared his throat and spoke for the first time. "I will say a hearty thank you, Gavin, and I intend to repeat it to every member of the crew. Hell, I wish we could give you a ticker-tape parade, but we can't." He glowered. "This whole damn business shows us just how goddamn fragile our coastal defense really is! *You* won't get to talk about this—Mr. Jones called it an 'incident'—but I sure as hell will. And I think it'll wake some people up." He glared at Jones. "Particularly in Washington."

Sorensen turned back to Mike. "Now. Orders are being cut to send you where you want to go anyhow. You and the crew. Except for Lieutenant Bryce, of course. He's going to be laid up for a while. Your navigator suffered a flesh wound; he's been judged able to travel. You and your crew are restricted to base today—you need the sack time anyway—and you'll fly a B-17 up to Newfoundland tomorrow; from there you'll fly to Britain and join the 40th Combat Wing. Your group assignment will be made over there."

After Mike saluted and left, Sorensen turned to Jones and growled: "That statement he signed isn't worth squat. We don't have an Official Secrets Act like the Brits."

Jones smiled faintly. "He doesn't know that."

CHAPTER SIX

THE END OF THE BEGINNING

THE AIR IN Casablanca was sweet and heavy and the two Western statesmen sat in their chairs with their military chiefs standing behind them and smiled at the camera.

The tide of war had turned by the beginning of 1943; given the comparative resources of the warring nations, there seemed little doubt now about the eventual outcome.

As Prime Minister Winston Churchill said to the appreciative American President, repeating a happy flight of rhetoric he had concocted for the Lord Mayor's luncheon: "Now this is not the end. It is not even the beginning of the end. But it is, perhaps, the end of the beginning."

The Russians had inflicted a terrible defeat on the Germans at Stalingrad. Bolstered by steadily mounting supplies of materiel, Montgomery had saved Egypt. Allied air and naval forces were building up rapidly in Morocco and Algeria. The Mediterranean was no longer Mussolini's *mare nostrum*.

Soon, the Western Allies would invade Sicily to take as much weight as possible off the Russian armies. The enormity of Adolf Hitler's blunder in invading the Soviet Union and failing to take Moscow when he could have done it was becoming clearer daily.

Churchill and Roosevelt agreed that Hitler's mistake was a godsend. Without it, Germany could eventually have conquered the West.

The leaders were buoyant but one of the men standing behind the President was deeply concerned. General Henry (Hap) Arnold, chief of the U.S. Army Air Forces, had heard something shocking and his normally cherubic face was tense with worry.

As soon as he could, he summoned General Ira Eaker, head of the U.S. Eighth Air Force, and said bluntly: "I'm sorry to have to tell you this, Ira, but the President has agreed to give Churchill our airplanes for night bombing."

Eaker blew up. "Our B-17s aren't night bombers!" he said harshly. "Our crews aren't trained for night bombing. We're trained and equipped for daylight operations, working in formation, hitting targets with precision instead of dropping bombs all over the countryside, the way the RAF does."

Eaker shook his head angrily. "It's a tragic mistake and I won't be any part of it. I'll quit, Hap, and I reserve the right to tell the American people at the appropriate time when that happens."

Arnold, expecting Eaker's response and pleased by it, said: "If you feel that strongly about it I'll arrange for you to talk to the Prime Minister." It was what Arnold urgently wanted; Eaker was a world-famous flier with a glittering reputation. He was also a handsome man with a commanding presence.

Eaker smiled faintly, realizing Arnold had set him up.

Predictably, the chubby little Prime Minister had a large cigar in his mouth and was wearing his zipped-up "siren suit" when Eaker arrived at his villa.

"General Arnold tells me it's been decided to turn our Flying Fortresses over to night bombing," Eaker said. "I think this would be a great mistake, sir. And I've been in England long enough to know that you'd want to hear both sides."

Churchill smiled, pleased and amused at the touch of flattery.

"Sit down," he said, pointing with his cigar to the armchair across from his.

Eaker produced a single sheet of paper from his breast pocket. "What I have to say is written on this piece of paper," he said, handing it to the older man.

That, too, was a subtle touch that Churchill appreciated. As an overburdened wartime Prime Minister, he inveighed unceasingly against subordinates who brought him reports longer than a single page.

The memo summed up succinctly the American case for daylight bombing. The B-17s and their crews were designed for it and had trained for it and carried heavy 50-caliber machine guns whose cross-fire from tight formations provided a deadly defense.

Further, Eaker wrote, with the American Eighth Air Force bombing by day and the British RAF bombing by night, the Germans would be bombed around the clock. Churchill was a masterful phrase-maker and Eaker thought these last words might catch the British leader's attention. They did.

"Around the clock," Churchill said softly. He smiled and looked up. "Your losses in the daytime have been greater than ours at night, and my decision was based on saving your young men. I must say you still haven't convinced me that you can succeed in daylight operations. But you have convinced me that you should have the opportunity to prove that you can."

Churchill nodded. "When I see the President at lunch, I'll recommend that you continue daylight operations."

Eaker, his face breaking into a broad smile, rose, thanked the Prime Minister effusively and left. Churchill smiled and closed his eyes, already formulating the words he would use to the House when he reported to Parliament on the Casablanca conference.

"The British will bomb at night and the Americans by day," he would say. "We shall bomb those devils *around the clock*."

Abruptly, his mobile face drew into a scowl. But what would the West's glacially unfriendly ally, Stalin, say about the Casablanca meeting? That we were doing too little, planning to invade Sicily with a modest force when we should be invading massively across the Channel?

The Soviet regime was indistinguishable in many ways from the Nazis' in its cruelty, barbarity, and suppression of human rights. But the role of the Soviet Union was crucial to the defeat of Adolf Hitler. Churchill had told his private secretary that, if Hitler invaded Hell, the Prime Minister would at least make a favorable reference to the Devil in the House of Commons.

Yet one nagging question grew steadily larger. What would happen after Germany was defeated? Would the West then have to contend with a greatly strengthened and equally dangerous dictatorship?

The Soviet mind defied understanding. Churchill bit his cigar in frustration and pondered a comment he had made earlier on the radio: I cannot forecast to you the action of Russia. It is a riddle wrapped in a mystery inside an enigma.

Galina Tarasova was neither riddle, mystery, nor enigma. She was an ailing girl warrior who had smiled through her fatigue when her comrades had pooled their chocolate rations to make her a cake for her twentieth birthday.

Shortly afterward, Major Kravchenko sent her home on leave for a week to recover from a bronchitis that had been making it impossible for her to fly without falling into coughing fits.

Galina hitched a ride on an Army truck from the airfield to the nearest provincial railway station. There, she sat all night waiting for a train to Moscow that would carry passengers. From the Moscow station she took a tram that was packed with Muscovites. Like many others, she hung from the door, her musette bag slung over her shoulder, until she arrived in her apartment district and could drop off and walk the rest of the way.

Galina could hardly believe the changes that had occurred in Moscow. She had been brought up to revere the symbols of nationhood and the things that had been done to them amounted almost to desecration.

Artists had painted the Kremlin walls to make them look like rows of houses. The beautiful domes of the Kremlin's cathedrals were covered over with wooden planks. Lenin's tomb was obscured by sandbags. Dummy factories had been built in some areas of the city to confuse bomber pilots.

Galina, looking at the camouflage with an expert pilot's eye, found the alterations incomprehensible. There was no concealing the curves and bends of the Volga or the layout of the main streets. Any pilot could use the Volga to check his daytime position and at night the camouflage wouldn't be seen.

The city and the people seemed far shabbier than they were when she had left to join her regiment. Paint was peeling from the walls of buildings and the streets were full of potholes.

And, though she knew she should have expected it, it surprised her to find a population of exclusively old people. The few young people to be seen were, like herself, home on leave.

Almost all of Moscow's citizens were dressed in old clothes and patchwork garments of one kind and another. She expected that, of course; clothing materials went to the armed forces and so did most of the available food. Almost nothing was on display in the gastro-noms. That situation should improve in the spring and summer as farmers planted new crops—assuming, of course, that the Germans continued to retreat.

The stucco on her apartment block was cracked and broken but, as she moved slowly up the stairs to her family's two-room flat, the old corridors and the smell of cooking cabbage made it seem achingly familiar and home-like.

Her mother, Vera, screamed when she opened the door, and threw her arms around her. Her younger sister, Yevgenia, ran from the other room to see what was happening.

"Galishka!" her mother cried. "I'm so glad to see you." Her eyes narrowed with alarm and she held Galina at arm's length. "What has happened?" she demanded. "Are you wounded?" Then her brows drew together reprovingly. "Why didn't you let us know you were coming?"

Galina laughed. "I'm on a week's leave. I've had a cough and I'm tired, that's all. I haven't been wounded. If I had tried to write, you still wouldn't have got the letter. So I just came."

Her mother's face knotted with concern. "Oh, but you're so thin," she said. "And you look so, so boyish. Older, too. Where is the little girl who left?"

"Some of her is still here," Galina said. A small hand was tugging at her trousers and she bent over to embrace her sister. "My, but you've shot up, haven't you, Zhenya? How old are you now? Thir-teen? No, you're fourteen."

"Galishka, Galishka," her sister murmured, burying her head in Galina's shoulder.

Galina's father, Vasily, a foreman in a clothing factory, was at the front supervising the delivery of new uniforms to an infantry divi-sion. The mother and her two daughters lighted candles and had a supper enlivened by Galina's gift of *kolbasa* sausage and two choco-late rations. Yevgenia's eyes widened with delight when she saw the chocolate.

"What can we do for you while you're here, Galishka dear?" her mother asked. "You look so tired. Are you really all right?"

"I'll be all right after I get some sleep, Mamenka," Galina said. "Lots and lots of sleep."

She slept nine to ten hours every night and within three days Galina's cough began to subside. She spent the days assuring her mother that she was all right and that her flying wasn't unduly dangerous. She also was forced to tell her sister, over and over again, what it was like to fly the PO-2 and to bomb the Nyemtsy.

Of course, she left out the parts about fear and blood and death. Yevgenia was entranced. "Oh I *wish* I were older," she said wistfully. "Then I could join the Moscow sports flying club, as you did, Galishka, and go on into the air force, just like you."

Standing nearby, her mother recoiled. Galina looked up and smiled at her reassuringly. "All in time, Zhenya," she said to her sister. "Right now you're needed here to take care of Mamenka and defend Moscow."

As the days went on, Galina grew restless. It seemed like weeks since she had flown and she wondered what was happening at the front. Were her friends still alive and unwounded? She knew it would break her mother's heart if she left early, but she found herself counting the hours till she could return to the regiment.

She missed her comrades. An unbreakable bond of friendship and loyalty had developed among them and she felt an irresistible need to be with them. She didn't miss combat. It was ugly and frightening. But walking the razor's edge between life and death was the common experience that bound them together.

Mike was one of three pilots ordered to fly B-17s from Newfoundland to Valley, Wales. He was given a new co-pilot, a broad-shouldered, Irish six-footer named Jack Gillen.

Mike knew it was irrational but it grated on him that his co-pilot was taller than he was. It ought to be the other way around, he told himself. Gillen had washed out of fighter training and had been transferred to a bomber group as a co-pilot.

But he seemed a nice enough guy. Gillen accepted his transfer without complaint and he willingly took orders from Mike as airplane commander. Mike felt himself lucky to be able to take Zapp, McCabe, and Thurston along as a skeleton crew. They were not only high scorers in their respective skills; they had been tested in battle.

All had signed the pledge of secrecy about the sub/Viking encounter and were tight-lipped about it. Mike suggested that, for now, they try to forget it. "It's best we don't talk about it even to each other, particularly now that we've got a new man aboard," he said. "We'll get proper recognition for what we did later on when the brass decides it's okay."

Mike wondered if the brass had notified Zimmerman's parents that he had been killed in a training accident. But he and the others were sent packing before he could ask.

The trip across the Atlantic was uneventful except for a few hours of worry that began after daylight when Mike saw one of the other two B-17s crossing his path from left to right and apparently flying a very different compass heading.

"Pilot to navigator. Is that guy on the wrong course or are we?"

"Navigator to pilot. I've re-checked course three times. I say he's wrong."

"Roger." But Mike continued to worry until they saw land. When they did, the cloud cover was heavy and low and there were few landmarks to help them find Valley. Finally, Mike told Gillen to call Darky, the ingenious network of low-powered British radio stations that had saved thousands of pilots from running out of gas and crashing.

Each station had a listening radius of only three miles, so any airplane that called a station was near enough to help.

Gillen switched the radio to the Darky frequency as Mike began to circle. As prescribed, Jack called Darky three times. It was like a magical incantation. Darky, in the clipped voice of an English WAF, answered.

"B-17 circling. Who are you and what is your destination?"

"Darky, this is B-17 letter G for George, a heading for Valley, please."

"G for George," the voice replied in a moment, "this is Darky. Turn to seventy degrees and fly for three minutes. At that time you will see a flare."

"Thank you, Darky, G for George, out."

In exactly three minutes, a green flare shot into the sky. Under it they found the Valley runway. A heavy, cold wind was blowing and the sky was a dreary gray, but Mike was elated when they trudged into their barracks, dumped their duffel bags, and were given mugs of hot tea by an orderly.

He stretched out on his bunk and grinned as McCabe stoked the potbellied stove in the center of the barracks. This was the real thing at last, by God! Soon they would be sent to an honest-to-God professional Eighth Air Force bomb group, they would get Eighth shoulder patches for their jackets, and in maybe just a few days they would take off in the finest airplane in the world, the B-17 Flying Fortress, to bomb Germany. *What a kick!*

*   *   *

The two American generals bent over a chart. The sun had set and Hap Arnold bent the goosenecked desk lamp to focus the light on the paper. He traced one of the curves on the chart and looked up at Ira Eaker.

"Statistics make things look even worse than you think they are," he said. "Look here. Just to round things off, suppose you have a hundred-plane force flying thirty missions. If you average a five percent loss on each mission—that doesn't sound like much these days—the average B-17 crewman's chances of surviving his combat tour are twenty-two percent. Hell, that's about one out of five."

Eaker nodded grimly. "Yes, and there's something else here, too. Look at the difference that even a small rate of attrition makes. Take your hundred-plane force and spread it over sixty missions. Over that time, a one percent difference in the loss rate means a twenty-five percent difference in the number of aircraft surviving."

The two middle-aged officers looked gloomily at the paper for a moment and then Arnold pushed it away. "Right now, our two goals —hitting the Germans where it hurts and minimizing our casualties —they look a mite incompatible."

"Yeah, they do," Eaker said. "And we're on probation, too. Churchill said he'd agree to give us a chance. But if we don't get the job done, or we start taking too many big losses, he'll swing the other way."

"He won't have to," Arnold said shortly. "Roosevelt is too sensitive a politician not to respond to congressmen and parents who react to bad losses. He'll shut us down. Or we'll be ordered to stick to soft, close-in targets. Either way, we won't get the job done."

Arnold stared at his fellow general. "What it comes down to is our ability to survive in the air, fight off the German fighters, right? How do we do that?"

"Well, right now we're doing okay until we reach the German border and our fighter escorts have to leave and turn back," Eaker said. "Then we take a clobbering. So we need to improve the B-17's defensive ability and we need to extend the range of our escorts. We're making some progress with both, as you know."

"But not fast enough," Arnold said. "Meanwhile, we've wasted too much time and equipment fooling around with screwy stuff that didn't work."

The two men brooded silently over their recent failures. The Eighth Air Force had developed a gunship version of the B-17 called the YB-40. Heavily armed and without bombs, it was meant to present such overwhelming firepower that it would serve the same purpose as escorting fighters.

But the YB-40 was so heavy that, once the B-17 group had dropped its bombs, making the weight of the individual airplanes much lighter, the YB-40 couldn't keep up with the formation. Either it fell behind and was heavily attacked by packs of enemy fighters or the whole formation had to slow down and expose the group to danger over a longer period of time.

The second failure was the experimental GB-1, the glide bomb. For months, Washington had been urging the Eighth to avoid heavy concentrations of anti-aircraft guns and reduce its losses by finding a way to "stand off" and bomb.

The supposed answer was the GB-1, a two-thousand-pound robot bomb with a small wing, twin booms, and a tail surface. They tried it out over the city of Cologne. Each of fifty-five B-17s released two robots from brackets beneath the wings from a distance of twenty-five miles. Not one struck the city. They wandered all over the countryside. German anti-aircraft gunners were overjoyed; they thought they were shooting down the Fortresses.

Eaker broke the silence. "A lot of our problems with the B-17 really haven't been the result of technical incompetence. No one really anticipated the humid ground conditions in England and those forty-below temperatures up at altitude.

"So things that worked perfectly in the States didn't work here. The supercharger regulators failed at altitude. The brushes in the generators wouldn't work up there. The ball turret froze; so did the guns, not to mention the gunners standing in those open windows with winds of one hundred and fifty miles an hour. Cartridge cases from the ball turret guns tore up the rubber de-icer boots. Until we got the problem with the radio gun straightened out, we had radio operators shooting off their own tail fins."

Arnold chuckled wryly. "And then there was that damn-fool problem we had with the bomb bay doors freezing up. We tried every damn thing you could think of. They always opened and closed fine on the ground."

"Yeah," Eaker said, "it took a Brit to tell us what was wrong."

Both men laughed. The RAF officer told them that they had encountered the same problem and were at a loss to solve it until they found that crewmen aboard the Lancasters were peeing in the slit between the bomb bay doors up at altitude. The wet doors were freezing shut.

"If it weren't wartime, Congress, not to mention the War Department, would cut us off at the knees," Arnold said. "The B-17E model saw a big fat two weeks of service in the theater. The F model is a whole lot better, and it bloody well ought to be, because, as of today, every airplane coming off the line gets fifty-nine different modifications."

"We're not through yet," Eaker said. "The new G model will have enclosed waist gun positions and the windows will be staggered so the gunners aren't always backing into each other. The G model'll also have what we need most right now—twin 50-calibers in a chin turret under the nose. We're taking a terrible beating from fighters attacking us head-on."

"You're making modifications in the field now, aren't you?" Arnold asked.

"Yeah, sure," Eaker said. "That was happening before we ever ordered it or even approved it. The crews were pulling that dinky 30-caliber gun out of the nose and installing either one or sometimes two 50s. But the bigger nose guns made it hard, sometimes impossible, for the bombardier to use the bombsight."

Eaker sighed heavily. "So now we're fabricating a 50-caliber nose-gun installation kit over here for delivery to the bomb groups. It does the job better than those jerry-built mounts. We're also providing armored glass for the windshield and side windows."

Arnold nodded. "There's one big thing we musn't lose sight of, Ira. Even with all this patchwork, we've got a weapon here—God knows it's still imperfect—but it's the answer to a critical need. Hitler said he had created a Fortress Europe, but Roosevelt answered that the fortress didn't have a roof on it. No disrespect to the Brits, but they can't bomb with any precision at night. The B-17's the answer. Hell, if the Germans had a four-engine bomber like it, England would be a wasteland and we wouldn't be able to operate out of our bases." Arnold frowned. "When do we get the new G model?"

"By September, the production people say. Then, by December, they promise, we'll start getting the long-range P-51, the new Mustang model. External gas tanks and a considerably lower gas consumption than the P-47. The P-51 will have legs long enough to escort the bombers all the way in and all the way out."

"That'll make a helluva difference," Arnold said.

"It surely will. We'll be able to hit honest-to-God strategic targets in Germany, start killing the Luftwaffe, and keep our own losses to a politically acceptable level."

"Until then . . ."

"Until then, Hap, we hang on and hope for the best. Maybe the Germans'll make as many dumb mistakes as we do."

Thirty-year-old Adolf Galland, General of the Luftwaffe Fighters, the adored black-haired hero for whose favors women threw themselves at his feet, sat unhappily on the terrace at the Wolfsschanze.

Adolf Hitler had named his East Prussian headquarters near Rastenburg the Wolf's Lair. It was well-known that the Führer privately liked to call himself by the nickname "Wolf."

As the sun set, the surface of the little lake below turned blood-red. It was an appropriate color, Galland thought. German armies were retreating in Russia and North Africa and now B-17 bombers were penetrating the Reich by daylight. Just recently, fifty-five unescorted heavy bombers had attacked Wilhemshaven and lost only three from their formation.

Worse was coming, Galland knew; it was only a matter of time until the B-17s would be raiding deep into Germany with long-range escorts. That would be a disaster unless the Luftwaffe was given a much larger number of fighters for defense.

Adolf Hitler was contemptuous of the very concept of defense. He believed only in attack. But the raid on Wilhemshaven by the B-17s had attracted his attention enough to summon Galland.

The sun had disappeared and the lake, like the pine forests around it, turned black. Galland was in nearly total darkness when the Führer's aide, a colonel, appeared and raised his arm stiffly. Galland threw his fragrant Brazil cigar over the terrace railing—the Führer hated any form of tobacco—and rose, tossing the colonel a casual military salute.

Inside a dimly-lit reception room, an SS officer asked him to remove his gun belt and leave it behind. As he did, the SS man snapped to attention and Galland turned to find the Führer walking toward him with his hand extended.

They walked into an inner office and Hitler waved the fighter pilot to a chair. Galland was shocked at how the Führer had aged in a year's time. His skin had become leathery and sallow; his eyes muddy.

"I have only a few minutes to spare but I wanted to talk with you," Hitler said in his metallic baritone. "These new raids into the Reich by the American daylight bombers. What will it require to stop them, stop them completely?"

"Mein Führer, our Luftwaffe day fighter force must be substantially enlarged," Galland said.

"Enlarged by how much? Do you have to outnumber the enemy?"

Galland was relieved that he had done his homework. He knew the figures exactly. "Sir, these bombers are more heavily armed than any combat airplanes in history, and they fly in tightly-packed formations. A force of only thirty-six Boeings presents us with as many as four hundred and sixty-eight heavy-caliber machine guns, each of them with a range of one thousand yards.

"Further, these Boeings are extraordinarily rugged. At this time we estimate that it takes as many as twenty 20-mm. cannon shells to down one of them. For each unescorted bomber, I will need three or four single-engine fighters."

Hitler stared into the distance and pursed his mouth. "And if you had such a number of machines available, what results could I expect?"

"We will stop the daylight raids absolutely because of losses unbearable to the enemy."

"And what of the armament of your fighter, the ME-109? I am told that some of you prefer the 20-mm. cannon firing through the propeller hub. Others say they prefer two machine guns mounted on the wings. Which do you prefer?"

"I prefer we have both," Galland said.

Hitler smiled slightly. Galland hesitated. "There is one additional factor I should bring up regarding the number of fighters we need, mein Führer."

"What is that?" Hitler said.

"When the Americans start coming with long-range fighter escorts, I will need, in addition, one single-engine fighter for each enemy fighter."

Hitler's face flushed angrily. "The issue of enemy fighter escorts for the bombers does not arise," he said harshly. "Reichsmarschall Göring has assured me that building fighters with that great a range is not technically possible. As to the other matter, we shall have to see."

Hitler's good humor had vanished and, with a wave of the hand, Galland was dismissed. The plain fact of the matter, he mused as he left, was that Adolf Hitler didn't understand the uses of air power. He thought of airplanes only as flying artillery; the Stukas had fulfilled that role brilliantly until they were challenged, over Dunkirk, by British Spitfires.

There they learned that even the best Luftwaffe fighter pilots couldn't defend the Stukas. The Stukas had to dive through ten thousand feet, dive brakes open, at one hundred and twenty miles an hour, to drop their bombs. They were easy pickings for the Spitfires, no matter how many Messerschmitts were around.

Now Göring, Galland's mentor and once his idol, had become a serious liability. He was, of course, frantic to regain the Führer's favor. Göring had boldly declared a year ago that "if any enemy bomber penetrates the Reich, you can call me Meier."

But the penetrations had been made and it was obvious that more were to come. And even the humblest German knew of Göring's passion for stag-hunting. Göring had become so obsessed with it that he had a servant blow a hunting horn at Karinhall to call guests to meals.

So it was inevitable that any German air-raid siren that sounded was now called "Meier's Hunting Horn." Galland hoped it wouldn't become Germany's death knell.

Mike stared almost straight up into the morning sun as the group thundered across the Channel for the marshalling yards at Hamm. Flying in the hole, as the position was called, was a terrible assignment.

In the hole, the pilot nominally became leader of a V-shaped, three-plane flight. In reality, he was simply a necessary piece of a complex puzzle. The eighteen-plane group comprised three squadrons of six bombers. The squadrons were staggered in high, center, and low positions facing toward the sun.

The lead bomber of each squadron was flanked by wingman number two and wingman number three. Directly beneath the leader and just behind him flew number four, the man in the hole. To hold his position, the pilot leaned back in his seat and looked straight up at the tail of the leader. Two wingmen flew formation on number four to complete the squadron box of six airplanes.

The leader's belly gunner looked down and grinned sympathetically as Mike stared up into the sun, tears trickling from under his sunglasses and over his oxygen mask. When the sun grew higher, the tears would freeze.

Occasionally he shot a glance from side to side to ensure that his wingmen were in place. He would have enjoyed the mission if it weren't for the discomfort of flying in the hole. The last six weeks had been a time of gnawing frustration.

Because it was the policy of the 205th bomb group, the one to which he'd been assigned, he flew co-pilot on his first mission. It had been an uneventful raid on the harbor at Wilhemshaven and Mike sat, bored, with little to do except raise and lower the wheels and flaps on command and adjust the manifold pressure.

He had heard that one of the groups had been hit by fighters and had lost three planes, but the 205th hadn't been attacked, though the flak bursts that rose over the target were momentarily scary.

Then the worst weather in a decade had swept over the island and the continent, shutting down all air operations on both sides. The final aggravation was a bad sinus inflammation that the maritime climate created. For six weeks, Mike did nothing but attend meetings, fret, and pace about the rain-soaked field.

The weather still hadn't cleared over the continent but it had improved enough to allow operations to resume. At the 2:00 A.M. briefing, the air crews were told by the base commander, Colonel Mitchell Robinson, that Hamm was a significant target.

"Our target is the marshalling yards," Robinson said. "A major part of the output of the Ruhr industries funnels through here. So if you knock out their transportation system at this point, it doesn't matter what they make in the Ruhr factories. They can't get the stuff to where it's needed."

Robinson unzipped his A-2 leather jacket and took a wide, resolute stance. "There's another important point to be made. This target lies within the outer ring of Germany's defenses. We're pointing a dagger at the heart of the monster for the first time. So what you do today, how well you do it, is very important."

Robinson's voice dropped in volume and the men leaned forward to hear him. "They know this better than we do, of course. So you can expect them to do everything they can to stop us. We'll face heavy flak and, no doubt, a large force of fighters.

"The lead teams have already been briefed. A main force of seventy-one B-17s, four groups, will head northeast over the North Sea on the route to Bremen and Wilhemshaven. Approximately halfway between England and the coast of Holland, we'll swing to the southeast and head for Hamm. Meanwhile, a decoy force of fourteen B-24s will move in at a lower altitude to lure the fighters away from us."

It might have worked, but the weather screwed up the mission. As they moved over the North Sea, heavy clouds moved in and blotted out the sun. At first, Mike was grateful, but soon the murk became so heavy that Robinson's ship above him and his flanking wingmen melted into indistinct gray shapes.

Mike's heart began to pound. This was much worse than the sun;

straying in one direction or another in dense fog could produce a disastrous collision. Others were thinking the same thing.

"Radio to pilot," Thurston called on the intercom.

"Pilot."

"Pilot, the 93rd just called the wing leader. They can't see; they're turning back to home base."

"Pilot to radio, roger." Piss-ant, Mike growled to himself. The defection of a whole group seriously weakened the defensive cross-fire ability of the remaining groups. But there was worse to come.

"Radio to pilot."

"Pilot. What now?"

"Pilot, sorry to say, but the other two groups have abandoned the primary target due to weather. I say again, the other two groups have abandoned the primary. They're going for a secondary or target of opportunity. Radio, over."

"Pilot to radio, roger." Mike turned and scowled at his co-pilot. Gillan pressed his throat mike. "Want me to take it for a while?"

Mike nodded. Gillen put his hands on the wheel and feet on the rudder pedals and said: "I've got it." Mike lifted his hands high from the controls and began rotating his stiffening neck. Robinson hadn't changed course but, obviously, he knew that the other groups had pulled away. Surely he wasn't planning to go on alone against heavy opposition with just one group of airplanes.

A moment later Robinson's voice came over the group channel.

"Blue Leader to group. The weather is improving ahead. We're staying on course. Close in now, close in."

The bombers drew closer together. The clouds began to thin and watery sunlight filtered through the mist. Mike looked out his side window. A lower layer of clouds swirled away and the windows of Hamm winked up at him in the sunlight. With them, abruptly, came four greasy-looking black puffs of smoke and a series of cracking sounds. Mike flinched and clucked respectfully. The German 88-millimeter gun was the best single weapon on either side.

Within seconds, the sky ahead was heavily dotted with black blotches. Mike called to his co-pilot and took back the controls. Robinson began turning toward the target. Mike felt the extra drag and swirl of sub-zero air as the bomb-bay doors opened.

A series of explosions buffeted the bomber and there was the sound he had first heard in the Viking encounter; it was as if someone had thrown a handful of stones against the airplane.

"Bombs away!" the bombardier cried, toggling his bomb load on the leader's drop. Mike's airplane, together with Robinson's above him and the wingmen to his sides, rose as if they were on an invisible elevator. The B-17 became light in his hands.

There was another series of explosions and the airplane lurched. When would Robinson turn off the goddamn target? Now. Robinson was turning left and nosing down at the same time to pick up speed and get out of the flak. Mike banked carefully to hold formation with him. Heavy cloud cover would be welcome now.

They were sliding downward toward a cloud bank at nearly two hundred miles an hour when the fighters hit them. Six of them came, line abreast, from a cloud bank on the starboard side.

"Bogies at . . . !" The waist gunner barely got the first words out when they struck. There was a heavy banging sound to the right as a cannon shell landed and the inboard starboard engine began windmilling and throwing oil. A flicker of flame appeared beneath the engine cowling.

Mike pressed his throat mike. "Close the cowl flaps on Number Three engine and hit the fire extinguisher. Then feather it." Gillen swiftly closed the cowling and yanked the fire extinguisher and the fire went out. He hit the feathering button for the engine and the propeller stopped windmilling and turned edgewise on its hub to present the smallest possible wind resistance.

Mike advanced the throttles on the three working engines to hold his position in the formation. Straggling and spreading out now would turn the group into a gaggle of individual planes. It would be like throwing pieces of meat to a school of hungry sharks.

"Keep your eye on the cylinder-head temperatures," he told Gillen.

"Bogies at twelve o'clock, level!" McCabe yelled from the bombardier's position in the nose. Four shark-like fighters screamed at them, head-on, their cannons and machine guns winking. The B-17 shook as the top turret and jerry-rigged nose guns fired at the fighters. The 109s swept past overhead and the ship shook again as the belly and tail guns followed them.

The bomber wallowed in Mike's hands. "Pilot to crew!" he called. "Report damage."

"Engineer to pilot; a piece of the rudder is gone. Pretty big piece."

The airplane was becoming hard to control. The only saving grace was that the group had dropped its bombs and was in a fast glide. Soon they would be out of fighter range. But not yet.

A cry from the left waist gunner signaled an attack from that direction and an instant later there was a crashing sound as a cannon shell plowed through the nose. Voices cried out. Gillen called for a damage report.

"Navigator to pilot." Zapp was breathing heavily and his voice was shaky. "Shell exploded over our heads. Dented McCabe's helmet; I think he's okay, just dazed a bit. Explosion knocked me back, broke my table. No structural damage I can see."

"Take his gun position," Mike ordered.

"Number five is pulling away," the left waist gunner said.

Mike glanced sideways. His left-hand wingman banked slowly away as if the pilot intended to go home by himself. Several seconds later, the ship exploded in an orange fireball that showered debris over the surrounding airplanes.

More cries of approaching fighters, more firing. An ME-109 began streaming black smoke and the pilot ejected. Mike saw him tumbling through the formation, knees clasped to chest, like a circus acrobat. Another B-17 was hard-hit. Gillen, looking to his right, saw a gunner jump from the open side window. He was swept back into the tail fin, hit it hard, and fell away, unconscious or dead. His chute didn't open.

They were over the North Sea before Mike realized the fighters were gone. When they had descended to ten thousand feet, they pulled off their oxygen masks. They were safe now if they could get home. Gillen tapped the instrument panel. "Engines are getting real hot."

Mike called the leader and was given permission to leave the formation. He decided swiftly to accept the risk of going home instead of landing at the 25,000-foot emergency runway near the coast. The hydraulic system was intact and the flaps and wheels came down without incident. They found the field and landed under a broken cloud layer, quickly taxiing off the 6,000-foot runway to make room for other B-17s coming in behind them.

Back at the hardstand, Mike bent momentarily over the control column and drew a dozen slow, deep breaths. If every raid into Germany was going to be like this one, flying twenty-five of them would be a long, hard, and very dangerous journey.

Throughout the spring of 1943, Mike flew on missions to Kiel, Bremen, Wilhemshaven, Emden, St. Nazaire, Antwerp, and Huls. He was promoted out of the hole to fly deputy lead for the squadron and, once, for the group. Designated as a member of a lead team, he was granted permission to eat in the senior officers' mess.

The food was the same as in the junior officers' and non-coms' messes, but it was prepared with greater care. The oatmeal was cooked through and the eggs weren't burned. There was even a sauce, from time to time, on the meat generally known as filet-of-gray.

More tangible evidence of his new status was a pair of silver first lieutenant's bars and a copy of the official promotion order that the operations officer had placed on his bunk.

The twin recognitions of service were stimulating, but not nearly as exciting as the arrival of the new P-51 Mustang fighter on the base. Mike wasn't flying that morning; he flew in rotation with other members of the lead team. The field was empty except for a few B-17s parked on the outer hardstands; the group had taken off hours earlier for a target in Germany.

He was in the control tower examining the controls for the British DREM airfield lighting system when the P-51 flew into the traffic pattern. The appearance of something as exotic as a Mustang—and apparently a new model at that—was exciting in itself. But Mike's adrenalin began pumping when he heard the pilot's voice requesting landing instructions.

Mike cocked his head to one side. There was something familiar in the timbre, in that accent. Recognition exploded within him like a bomb. Mike ran down the tower stairs and out onto the tarmac as the Mustang taxied up and shut off its engine.

Out of the sleek Mustang climbed 1st Lt. Harrison Bryce in a crushed cap and leather A-2 jacket.

"Buddy!" Mike yelled. Grinning broadly, Buddy strode to him and they threw their arms around each other and banged each other on the back. "What in the living hell are you doing here?" Mike demanded. "And in *that* airplane!"

"Ain't it a beauty? Listen, I'll tell you all about it. I missed breakfast. Can we go someplace and get somethin'?" Mike took him to the senior mess and spoke quietly to the cook. Within minutes, the noncom brought out a plate of fried eggs, toast, and a pitcher of coffee.

Mike poured condensed milk in their coffee mugs. "Okay now, how'd you get here? How's your knee? And what in hell are you doing flying that Mustang? And what is it exactly?"

Buddy chuckled and chewed on his toast. "Well, the last time we saw each other I was being wheeled away to the hospital, right? Turned out the head orthopedic surgeon, he did a fine job of rebuilding the knee joint, was a good 'ol boy from Ol' Miss.

"Nobody would tell him how I got shot up, and I was afraid to say anythin' so he got real curious and called an old buddy of his in Washington, a brigadier named John Sloane."

Buddy laughed. "Another good 'ol boy, from Charleston, my own state. Well, General Sloane got into the confidential files and found out about the Viking deal. And he just had to come see me and talk about it. Hell, he's a general, right, so I told him about it. Maybe I even built it up a little teeny bit. You don't mind my sayin' I was the first pilot, flyin' left seat, do you, son?"

Mike laughed and shook his head. "I don't mind."

"Didn't think you would," Buddy said. "So General Sloane, well, he's been Air Corps for a long time between wars and now he's too old to fly combat, but he loves to talk about it. And I sort of became his boy. 'Bout the fourth time he came to see me he said he was going to England, he'd be stationed at Wing and he could use an aide. Wanted somebody he felt comfortable with, somebody he could trust. Home folks."

"So he offered the job to you."

"I grabbed it. Otherwise, I'd be pushin' papers in some training command and, when my knee got better, checkin' out junior bird-men. No thank you. So I came over with my man."

"What exactly do you do?"

"I don't exactly do anything," Buddy said. "I go where the general goes, I light his cigars and pour his drinks, doncha know. I play bridge, took some lessons so I could play partners with him, we play for money against the hotshot colonels. Sometimes I fill out some forms, help win the war."

"But what about that airplane outside?"

"That Mustang, Mike-boy, is General Sloane's pride and joy. It's closer to him than any wife he's ever had, and he's had a few. He flies it around like a toy. Why he hasn't killed himself yet I don't know, because it's an unforgivin' bitch of an airplane. At first he wouldn't let me touch it, but I pissed and moaned so much about it he finally let me check out in it. I've flown it maybe a dozen times. I checked the Wing roster and found you weren't flyin' today, so here I am."

"That Mustang looks a little different than the ones I've seen. Is it?"

"Indeed it is," Buddy said. "It's a spanky-new P-51C; there's only a couple of them right now. The conversion was made over here by Rolls-Royce. It's got the new British Merlin engine, liquid-cooled, twelve-cylinder, fifteen hundred and twenty horsepower with a two-stage supercharger and a four-bladed Hamilton Standard prop. It'll go over four hundred, straight and level."

"Good Lord."

"And there's a lot more. It carries six, not four but six 50-calibers in the wings. And even bigger news, Mike-boy, is those streamlined racks under the wings. They can carry two 500-pound bombs, or—and it's the big 'or'—two big drop-tanks of high-octane gasoline.''

"You mean . . .''

"I mean it's your new long-range fighter escort. This baby will escort your ol' bombers all the way into Germany and all the way out again. They'll burn gas from the wing tanks on the way in, then drop them for combat, and still have internal fuel to come home on. North American's producin' this model in Texas right now. The engine's bein' made by Packard under a license from Rolls-Royce. It'll be over here in quantity before the end of the year, they claim."

"That will be a life-saver, literally," Mike breathed. "The fighter escorts we have now must turn back at the German border and then it's—well, it's bad." He looked wistfully at his friend. "Boy, I wish I could take a spin in that Mustang."

Buddy smiled. "I wish you could, too, son. But if anything happened to that bird, you know what'd happen to me. I'd be on my way to Biloxi . . ."

"Shoveling shit."

"You said it. So you see why I can't . . ." His voice faltered and a look of distress spread over Buddy's face. "Ah, hell," he said at length, "we've gone and done it again."

Mike grinned. "You mean . . ."

Buddy shook his head disconsolately. "I mean it's been our half-assed, pointy-head philosophy from the beginnin' never to say no, hasn't it? If it's against the rules or just doesn't make good sense, we have to go on and do it, don't we?"

"So you'll check me out in the Mustang."

"Yeah, I s'pose I will."

"When?"

Buddy sighed windily. "Well, it might as well be now."

Out on the tarmac, Mike walked admiringly around the Mustang. It was long-nosed, sleek, and deep-chested, with a plexiglas blister over the cockpit.

"There's a checklist there in the cockpit," Buddy said. "But lemme give you some doo-nots before anythin' else. When you run the engine up before takeoff, do not go over forty inches of manifold pressure or the tail'l come up and you'll nose over and smash the engine and I'll be on my way . . ."

"To Biloxi."

"Right. Next thing: do not jam the throttle forward on takeoff; you'll lose control and go ass-over-tin-cup. On takeoff, this big-ass engine will try to turn you off the runway to the left. Do not expect to control the torque by holdin' down the right rudder. You're not strong enough; nobody is. You crank in about six notches of right-rudder trim beforehand, take it out afterward. And do not try to force the tail up when you take off. You'll pitch over. Let it come up by itself.

"One good thing: it takes off and lands at about the same speeds as the B-17—about one hundred on takeoff and one hundred and twenty or so before touchdown. Same drill on landin'; half flaps, then full flaps. And you can't see out the front when you're taxiin'; you're sittin' even further back than in the B-17. So taxi like a snake. Takin' off, you have to watch the edge of the runway till the tail comes up and you can see what's ahead."

Buddy waved toward the cockpit. "You might as well climb in. Don't step on the flaps, please."

Mike settled himself in the cockpit, adjusted the rudder pedals, moved the control surfaces to make sure they were free, checked the gas, secured the shoulder harness, and put on his earphones, pulling one off the ear nearest Buddy, who had climbed on the wing and was standing beside the cockpit.

"There's the checklist for startup and warmup," Buddy said. "I'm gonna get down now and pull the prop through a few times to give you some lube. Just take your time. Oh, and one thing, please do *not* dive over five hundred miles an hour, Mike-boy. You could pull the wings off and kill yourself. If that thought doesn't stop you, just picture me back in Biloxi with a shovel."

When Buddy had manually turned the prop a few times and stepped back, Mike ran over the checklist for the third time and turned the mixture control to idle cutoff. In quick succession, he made sure the flaps were up, pushed the prop control full forward, cracked the throttle open, flipped the battery switch on, turned on the fuel booster pump, hit the primer switch for four seconds, engaged the starter, let the prop blades swing through a few revolutions, and turned the ignition switch to on.

The big engine came to life like an angry monster roused from sleep. It clattered and barked alarmingly, far louder than the twelve-hundred-horsepower engine of the B-17. But in a moment it settled into a steady, menacing rumble. He ran it up slowly to one thousand rpms, watched the gauges, and signaled to Buddy to pull the chocks from the wheels.

Then he called the tower. "Mustang to tower. Request clearance to take off, over."

The controller, who obviously had been watching him closely, responded immediately. "Tower to Mustang. Cleared to take off on Runway Twenty-seven. Happy landing. Happy takeoff, too."

Mike taxied out to the end of the runway, set the parking brake, checked the magnetos, set the fuel booster pump on emergency, and cranked in the proper degree of trim. Then he swung onto the runway, made sure he was aligned with the edge of it, and slowly opened the throttle, advancing it till it showed sixty-one inches of manifold pressure.

The engine came to full voice like a hungry lion greeting an unlucky tourist. The sound was immense, bloodcurdling. Mike's heart began beating heavily and he broke into a sweat. But he concentrated closely on keeping the Mustang straight with little touches of his feet on the rudders.

He was relieved when the tail rose and he could see ahead. At 100 miles an hour, the Mustang bounced gently and took to the air. He held the nose down until he had picked up speed and then angled upward, setting the power at 46 inches and 2,700 rpm.

He climbed through a thin overcast at 200 miles an hour and headed for 10,000 feet. He leveled off, adjusted the throttle to cruise at an airspeed of 325, and pulled the nose up slowly to feel the stall point. It announced itself satisfactorily, buffeting a bit before the airplane fell off on one wing. It recovered quickly when he relaxed the back pressure on the stick.

Had his long days in the heavy bomber made him too heavy-footed to do aerobatics? He would find out. He depressed the nose, pulled it back up to the horizon, and kicked the Mustang through a snap-roll to the right. It wallowed coming out. Sloppy. Do it again. He did; it was better. The third time it was perfect.

Then a snap-roll the hard way—to the left. He kept doing it until it was right. Then slow rolls in either direction. A barrel-roll. He pushed the nose down into a screaming dive and pulled up into a half-loop, rolling out on top in an Immelmann. The G-forces squashed him down hard; he judged he had pulled six or seven Gs, at least.

Mike pulled the Mustang through three complete loops, then, flying level, turned it over to see how long it would fly upside down before the engine choked for lack of fuel.

Happy and wet with perspiration, Mike hunted for cloud banks to play with. He exploded through a towering castle and circled tightly around its imaginary battlements. The sunlight fell in shafts through rents in a higher cloud bank and he flew through one of the holes, bathing the airplane and himself in golden light. *What a wonderful kick!*

He checked his watch. Twenty minutes had gone by. Buddy would be worrying. Time to give him a wake-up call. Mike spiraled the Mustang quickly down to five hundred feet, assured himself that the traffic pattern was empty, then shoved the stick forward, advanced the throttle, and screamed low over the field. Where was Buddy? There. He banked to sweep over him and soared upward into a victory roll.

That had been too tame. Approaching from the opposite direction, he flattened out a few feet off the ground and, as Buddy turned, screeched over his head. Buddy dived into the grass at the edge of the tarmac. Mike looked up just in time to see the tower in front of him and swerved away, missing it by half a dozen feet. Out of the corner of his eye, he saw the soles of the controller's shoes as the man bailed out of his seat in the tower.

Pulling up and around the field, Mike called the tower for permission to land and heard a gasping, affirmative response. He put the booster pump on emergency, set the gas mixture to auto-rich, waited till his speed fell below one hundred and seventy, and dropped the landing gear. He let the flaps down halfway, eased the throttle back, set in nose-up trim, turned on final approach, and dropped full flaps.

As he crossed the boundary marker, the airspeed dropped to one hundred and twenty and Mike held the Mustang level, closed the throttle completely, and eased the stick back slowly as the airplane began to settle. In a moment, the wheels touched and the tail slowly descended. He kept the airplane straight with touches of rudder, watching the runway at the side until he had slowed enough to pull off on the perimeter track.

The cooling engine made plinking sounds as he climbed out of the Mustang and walked over to Buddy. "Thank you, Buddy-boy," he said. "That was great."

"Great for you, maybe," Buddy grumbled. "You made me get grass stains on the knees of my new pinks. And I think I'll get a friendly mechanic to check the rivets and change the plugs before I fly that bird again."

Later, over a beer at a pub in Bedford, Buddy confided that his luxurious lifestyle was wearing thin. "Sloane's a good ol' boy and all that, but I don't want my future son to ask me later on: 'Daddy, what did you-all do in the war?' and I'd havta say: 'Why, son, I lit cigars and poured drinks for General John Sloane.' Course I could just have my records switched with yours and take credit for all your missions."

Buddy smiled thinly and shook his head. "No. Sooner or later, I gotta get outa this comfortable featherbed and do some serious work."

"Could you get in a fighter group?"

"I don't know. Maybe. Funny thing, though; it sounds crazy, I know, but you 'member that ol' song about when you fly the big bomber you're carryin' the war to the enemy. Right into the heart of darkness, all that whoop-to-do. Flyin' fighters is fun, but it's kinda playboy stuff. I'm beginnin' to think I've bought that ol' pitch. So maybe, soon as I can rev up the willpower, I'll kiss the General goodbye and wangle a transfer into a bomb group."

"You'll be a credit to your race," Mike said, raising his beer mug.

Reichminister of Armaments Albert Speer and Reichminister of Propaganda Joseph Goebbels disliked each other. It wasn't simply that they were competitors for the favor of Adolf Hitler; they had little in common and distrusted each other. The tiny Goebbels was a fanatic Nazi. Speer was ambivalent in his beliefs; he had become Hitler's architect and now, because of his organizational talents, his chief of arms production.

But on one topic, the increasing menace of the American bomber raids, the two ministers saw eye to eye.

"It's not simply a matter of production losses, at least not yet," Speer told the slight, dwarf-like man in the latter's Berlin office. "It's the diversion of our production that concerns me most. As of today, this air war is costing us the equivalent of ten thousand heavy guns and six thousand medium-heavy and heavy tanks that could make a great difference, perhaps a decisive difference, on the Eastern front.

"We have nearly twenty thousand anti-aircraft guns stationed here in our homeland; with them we could nearly double the anti-tank defenses in the East. We talk about the Americans and British opening a second front. But they've already done it in the skies above us. Every square meter of our territory is the front line, and defending it requires thousands of guns, millions of rounds of ammunition, and nearly a million men. This is very serious."

"Have you expressed your views to the Führer?" Goebbels asked.

"Yes, I have."

"What did he say?"

"As I remember, he said, 'Oh, you'll set it right.' "

Goebbels nodded. "I agree that the situation is growing serious. It may become more so. I'll help to the degree that I can."

After Speer had left, Goebbels opened his diary and looked at the entry he had made in it on May 8: "Wegener told me about the day raids on Bremen by the American bombers. These were very hard indeed. The Americans drop their bombs with extraordinary precision from an altitude of eight to nine thousand meters. The population has the paralyzing feeling that there really is no protection against such daylight attacks."

CHAPTER SEVEN

THE BIGGEST BATTLE

To THE GUARDS standing at their assigned positions in the pine forest, a shaft of sunlight and a touch of warmth would have been welcome. But the gray drizzle suited the Supreme Commander's mood perfectly as he left his concrete bunker in the Wolfsschanze for a private walk.

He could no longer abide the company of his generals or the stifling closeness of his staff headquarters. The air of the East Prussian woodland was sweet, but Adolf Hitler was as oblivious to it as the sound of the forest floor crunching beneath his feet.

At this time two years ago he would have been found at the Berghof with its breathtaking mountain vistas, broad terraces, teahouses, and bowls of flowers. Then, all was sunlight and beauty—the verdant landscape sparkling, pretty women casting him admiring glances, his dog walking faithfully at his side.

Today, there were only black forests, raw concrete, and a persistent decline that was sapping his spirit. The loss of Stalingrad still ached in his heart. Nothing of value had been extracted from it. He would have been able to make a national hero, a martyr, of Paulus, if the overrated Wehrmacht general hadn't turned back from the threshold of greatness and surrendered.

North Africa was gone, the Western Allies were masters of the Mediterranean, Mussolini had become a weakling and wanted peace with Russia, the unspeakable round-the-clock bombing by Britain and the Americans was smashing German factories and cities and eroding the strength of the Luftwaffe.

But worst of all was the humiliation of being beaten by the Asiatic beast, Stalin. He muttered in anger, startling a guard who snapped to attention until he had passed. As he tramped from one guard sector into another, telephones rang the warning that the Führer was walking through the woods.

It was clear, Hitler told himself, that a dramatic victory, an overwhelming demonstration of German power, was needed. It had to be in the East and it must shine out to the world like a beacon. Liking the sound of the words, he repeated them.

He had decided where the victory would be won and he had given it a name. It would be called Zitadelle and it would happen at a city in the Ukraine, three hundred miles south of Moscow, called Kursk. He had selected it because, at that point, the Russian lines bulged obscenely to the west. It was a big bulge, measuring one hundred and fifty miles long and one hundred miles wide, in the middle of the long Russo-German front stretching from Leningrad in the north to the Sea of Azov in the south.

Cutting it off would destroy a powerful Soviet Army group, straighten out German lines of communication, reestablish German superiority in arms, and—most important of all— give Generalissimo Stalin, the cunning shopkeeper from the Caucasus, a bloody nose.

It was growing dark in the forest and the Supreme Commander felt a prickle of apprehension. Even surrounded by hand-picked SS guards, he was a vulnerable target for an assassin in an isolated place like this. Or did his fear spring from the darkness itself? Could the iron-willed leader of the Third Reich possibly believe that some unearthly demon might emerge from the shadows?

The thought was absurd, childish, but Adolf Hitler had always known that his hold on the German people was at least partly based on his intuitive ability to tap into the vein of mysticism that ran through the German people. Ogres and *doppelgangers* were part of that mysticism.

He shivered and turned back toward the bunker. Resolutely, he focused his mind on Operation Zitadelle. His most talented planner,

General Erich von Manstein, had agreed in March that excising the Kursk salient made good military sense.

Manstein said if the attack was to be made it should be launched within weeks. But, over Manstein's protests, Hitler said it would have to wait till June, when the new Panther and Tiger tanks came off the production line. Then, of course, it began to rain heavily, and it turned out that the Panther's performance was poor and its treads weren't designed for the Russian terrain.

Hitler fell into one of his foaming rages over that but had to postpone the attack again. Then—he snarled with anger to think of it—his armies were delayed in building up their force and supplies for ridiculous lengths of time by the *verdammt* partisans who operated behind the lines, blowing up bridges and rail lines, and by that absurd air regiment of girls—imagine it, girls!—who bombed the Wehrmacht's railway yards and ammunition dumps at night from their tiny biplanes.

Never had the proud German army had to defend itself against such an annoying—and, it had to be admitted—effective little weapon.

But all that was in the past. At last, everything was ready. It would be the kind of battle of annihilation described by Germany's World War I genius, von Schlieffen—one in which the enemy was destroyed by swift and ruthless attacks on the flanks. One army group would strike from the north; another from the south. The pincers would neatly cut the bulge into a bleeding stump.

To win his victory, Hitler would commit nearly a million men and three thousand tanks and assault guns, two-thirds of the divisions and equipment available on the Eastern front, together with two thousand aircraft. All were in place at last.

Because of the agonizing delays, his faint-hearted generals—Heinz Guderian, Walter Model, even Manstein—had grown pessimistic over the chances of success and counseled him to cancel Zitadelle. That was to be expected, of course. His generals were a chicken-hearted lot.

Of course, Hitler had to admit, Guderian couldn't in honesty be called chickenhearted. But he was stubborn and impertinent. He had actually had the temerity to challenge his Supreme Commander's choice of Kursk for a major showdown.

"Why there?" Guderian had demanded. "What's the point?"

"For political reasons," the Führer's aide replied.

"What political reasons?" Guderian barked. "Nobody ever heard of the place. And after this long, highly visible buildup of ours, all these delays, it's become a terrible gamble."

"It is a gamble," Hitler admitted. "Whenever I think of it, my stomach turns over."

"Then cancel it," Guderian said.

But he didn't. Adolf Hitler imposed his iron will upon the generals, Guderian included, and, he told himself, he would soon impose it upon the enemy. Kursk would be the biggest land and air battle in the world's history and he would win it. It was his destiny.

He began to walk faster. He would issue Operation Order Number Six, confirming the day and hour for the attack. And he would get out of this frightening forest.

At Bletchley Park, the duty officer scanned the latest series of decoded Enigma messages that had been sent to German field commanders, placed them carefully in an envelope, sealed it, and handed it to a waiting courier.

"These latest *billets doux* should liven things up a bit for Ali Baba, don't you imagine?" the duty officer said to the head cryptographer in the hut. Ali Baba was the name they had given to Stalin.

"Assuming we're giving them to him," the cryptographer said.

"Oh, I should think so," the duty officer said. "After all, he's grinding up Adolf's troops for us. The more the merrier."

The clock struck 3:00 A.M. in the Generalissimo's inner office in the Kremlin. Stalin, his pockmarked face impassive, sat silently at the head of the long table as his generals, some of them struggling to keep awake, waited for him to speak.

Stalin had listened with apparent interest when the British military mission in Moscow told him and his staff of the impending attack on Kursk. They named the day that the German attack on the Russian positions would be launched. But they refused to say how they knew all this.

When they had left, he chuckled contemptuously. He had known about Hitler's plans within a few days of the time they were first formulated. The Soviet spy ring known as Lucy, which was based in Switzerland and had contacts within the German high command, had kept Stalin informed almost daily of the Citadel battle plan as it developed.

He might have been wary of the Lucy reports, considering them an enemy trick, if air reconnaissance and reports from partisan groups hadn't confirmed the Hitlerite buildup. As far back as April, he had studied analyses of the German attack plans by his deputy commander-in-chief.

Stalin broke two cigarettes apart, stuffed the tobacco into his pipe and relit it. "I want an up-to-date report on the status of the Kursk preparations," he said. "General Zhukov."

When the Generalissimo called upon Zhukov, the generals noted, his voice lacked the harshness and impatience that he customarily displayed to other military leaders. The officers moved aside respectfully and Marshal Georgi Konstantinovich Zhukov stepped forward.

Stocky and heavy-featured, the forty-seven-year-old deputy commander of the Soviet military forces looked as if he had been born in his army uniform. Like Stalin's, his brown tunic was decorated with red trim and had gold epaulets on the shoulders with a large gold star and insignia identifying him as a marshal of the Red Army. The left side of his chest glittered with medals and ribbons, and down the sides of his trousers ran a red stripe.

Zhukov was held in fierce respect by the officers and men of the Red Army. He was also deeply feared because he was completely intolerant of failure and lacking in compassion. Any officer who lost a battle, for any reason, could be expected to be demoted and sent to a penal brigade—if not immediately shot—and used as cannon fodder. Many had died after being ordered to walk through mine fields in order to clear them.

Georgi Zhukov had no concern whatever for human life. He didn't care how many of his men died in battle so long as it ended in a Soviet victory. Recognizing the superiority of the Germans in maneuver, Zhukov smothered them with massive frontal attacks. It had been particularly effective since the German generals had been ordered by Hitler to stand and fight. In any such battle of attrition, the force that is superior in numbers must win.

To assure victory, Zhukov stationed machine gunners behind his infantry to keep them from retreating. Faced with mine fields and lacking a handy penal brigade, he simply ordered the infantry to advance as if the mines weren't there. He told Stalin that the losses were roughly equivalent to those his forces would suffer in battle anyway.

For these qualities, Stalin treasured him and treated him with respect, sometimes even a deference, that he showed to no other person. But Stalin's respect was based on Zhukov's demonstrated abilities even more than his character. For the stocky marshal was no mere iron-willed brute. Stalin had plenty of those.

Zhukov had studied in Germany with General Hans von Seeckt before Hitler's rise to power. As an observer, he had studied German, Italian, and Russian tactics in the Spanish civil war. He had gone to China as part of a mission attached to Chiang Kai-shek and examined the techniques of the Far Eastern armies. And he knew his military classics from Caesar to Clausewitz.

Using these strategic and moral resources, Zhukov had won the first victory of Russian arms over the Germans at Yelnya in a savage, bloody battle and then stepped in to turn defeat into victory at Moscow and Stalingrad. In each battle he commanded more than a million men in twenty or more armies.

Now he stepped forward and briefed Stalin without notes.

"Comrade Stalin, we will face the enemy with 1,300,000 Soviet soldiers, 20,000 pieces of artillery, 3,300 tanks and assault guns, and 2,900 combat aircraft. We are, by our estimates, 1.4 times superior to the enemy in men, 1.3 times superior in tanks, and nearly 1.6 times in aircraft, though the aircraft disposition is asymmetrical to the enemy's."

Stalin nodded and puffed on his pipe. "All right," he said mildly. "What of your defensive preparations?"

"We have constructed six major defensive belts with a depth of 190 kilometers," Zhukov said. "We have dug 5,000 kilometers of trenches, thousands of individual tank traps, and an elaborate system of defensive emplacements fashioned from earth and wood. They have been placed in echelon formations along the anticipated corridors of the German advance. In addition, we have laid 400,000 land mines.

"We have set up anti-tank zones and strong points with massed artillery and anti-tank weapons along directions from which we expect the enemy tanks to come. They have been established to provide frontal, slanting, and flank fire.

"To accomplish this, we organized a *levée en masse*, approximately 300,000 civilians, including men, women, and children. Thousands we gathered from the towns and villages around Kursk. The rest we brought to the area, together with our supplies, in several hundred thousand railway cars. To make this possible, we laid railroad tracks throughout the salient."

"What is our weakest point?" Stalin asked.

"There is no weak point as such," the marshal said. "The point of greatest danger is the right flank at the foot of the bulge. If the Hitlerites were able to drive northward through that area they would cut us in two. Our anti-tank defense in that zone is now thirty-five kilometers in depth. We have established nests of anti-tank guns and mortars throughout that sector so that an average of ten anti-tank guns will be directed at each approaching enemy tank.

"Every division, brigade, and company has been given rigorous training in its own sector. Each knows the geography, the possible points at which the enemy may strike; each knows who will fight alongside him and where command posts and replacements have been located. Mortar teams have practiced and adjusted their fire into specific zones. We have made a topographical survey of the ground and set up guide posts. We know the maximum loads of all bridges and the depth of each ford. Codes and signals have been arranged to keep our forces in close touch with one another."

Stalin tore more cigarettes apart, reloaded his pipe, and relit it. *The marshal is very good*, he conceded. *Almost too good. If we win, he will become even more popular. Later, it will be wise to exile him to the countryside and keep him out of party affairs. And, perhaps, make sure his name doesn't appear in the children's history books.*

"What is your strategy, your disposition of troops?" Stalin asked. He knew the answers, since these issues had been hammered out in earlier meetings; but he wanted every general to be crystal-clear on what was expected.

"Comrade Stalin," Zhukov answered, "we have divided the salient into separate fronts. The central front is commanded by Marshal Rokossovsky. To the north is General Popov's Bryansk front. The Voronezh front covers the southern flank of the salient; it is commanded by General Vatutin."

As each name was called, the general nodded or bowed slightly.

"Within the bulge, we have placed two-thirds of our artillery and tanks to stop the thrusts coming from the north and south. Marshal Rokossovsky made the suggestion, which I accepted, to locate a large strategic reserve directly east of the central front. We call it the steppe front; comprising five armies, it is under the command of General Konev.

"This reserve force lies at the heart of our strategy. We will not attack first. As soon as the enemy commits himself and his jumping-off places are identified, we will strike him with all available artillery, mortars, and air power. We will yield ground only as and when it is patently impossible to hold a position any longer, and then only to predetermined locations.

"As the enemy thrust loses its steam, and we have smashed his armor and exhausted his troops, we will counterattack and break out of the salient at five points to roll the enemy forces backward. For air combat dispositions and tactics, I call upon Air Commander Novikov."

Novikov stepped forward and jerked his head in a quick bow to Zhukov. Then he turned to Stalin. "Comrade Stalin, for the initial phase of the battle of Kursk we will utilize two air armies with an operational strength of 1,880 combat aircraft. If we count those assigned to the steppe front, the number rises to 2,900. To accommodate them, we have built 154 airfields, all well-camouflaged, together with fifty visible 'dummy' airstrips to deceive the enemy.

"But these numbers tell only part of the story, Comrade Stalin," Novikov said. "We now have new machines with excellent performance. The radial-engine LA-5 rivals the Focke-Wulf 190 in all respects. It will appear for the first time at Kursk. The new Yak fighters are excellent at low and middle altitudes. And the tactics we have adopted, using the Okhotniki, the free-hunters, in *para* and *zveno*, two- and four-plane formations, have proven very effective."

Novikov didn't concede that these tactics had been copied from the Luftwaffe, but he knew that Stalin knew it. It was no reason for shame; the British, and now the Americans, he heard, were doing the same thing.

"What is the status of our ground-attack aircraft?" Stalin asked.

"We have 940 Shturmovik anti-tank airplanes available for this battle," the air commander said. "To enhance their firepower, many have been fitted with the NS-37, the new 37-mm. anti-tank cannon. The Shturmoviks also will carry the RS-82 and RS-132 rockets against the German tanks. To protect our pilots, the new model Shturmoviks provide 7 mm. of armor plating in the front, 12 mm. of armor at the rear of the cockpit, and 52 mm. of bulletproof glass for the windscreen. They will be a major surprise to the enemy."

Impressed despite himself, Stalin raised his heavy eyebrows and emitted a large cloud of tobacco smoke. "What of the bombers?" he demanded.

"Comrade Stalin," Novikov replied, "intelligence estimates that the enemy will confront us with 1,200 bombers, most of them operating by day. By contrast, we will put up 940 bombers, an only slightly smaller number. Of that number, 500 are day bombers and 400 are night bombers."

Stalin narrowed his eyes in the manner that always gave him a decidedly Asiatic appearance. "Are you speaking of the so-called 'night-witches'?" he asked.

"Yes, Comrade Stalin, I am," Novikov said. "At this time they are flying the only pre-war aircraft in the VVS, the PO-2. And I say without reservation that their work has been of great importance. At first, to be candid, we thought of them mainly as nuisance-makers, a way to keep the *Nyemtsy* from getting any sleep at night. But they have rendered an invaluable service by bombing command posts, railway yards, ammunition depots, and troop emplacements, as well as performing courier duties and even, with some modification, serving as ambulance planes. They are, I must say, not only dedicated, but fearless."

Lieutenant Galina Tarasova checked her stopwatch. "We should be over the target in one minute," she said into her interphone.

"That's correct," Valya said from the rear cockpit. "We should see some sort of lights."

A VVS general had come and addressed them three days ago. It was essential to disrupt the enemy buildup around Kursk, he said, and the army was counting on the night bombers to do it under cover of darkness. The day bombers were trying, but they were taking very heavy losses and, so far, they hadn't been successful.

The regiment was given a series of key targets to attack, night by night. Tonight it was a huge ammunition dump the enemy had established at the eastern edge of Bryansk. It held an almost unbelievable twelve hundred tons of ammunition. The air crews were given its position and, to find it on a dark night with a complete blackout on the ground, they would depend on the partisans to mark it for them.

Her face smeared with lampblack, Sergeant Olga Perminov, twenty-three, led her all-female team of partisans as they crawled through the underbrush toward the wire ringing the enemy's ammunition dump. They traveled slowly because they were heavily laden with equipment: rifles, grenades, and knives for self-defense; a radio transmitter and receiver; and a heavy, battery-operated, high-intensity light for flashing signals.

Perminov's team was one of four approaching the dump from different directions. They had already penetrated the Germans' outer defensive ring by killing two sentries.

One was killed by a whipcord-lean, seventeen-year-old girl using a wood-handled strangling wire that she threw over his head and yanked tight against his throat while she shoved her knee firmly into the small of his back. The second sentry had his throat cut with a razor-sharp knife wielded by a thirty-year-old mother of two.

Both women had lost close relatives in the war. Both, like Perminov and the others, were dedicated nationalists and Communists. They hated the Germans fiercely and had killed many of them, in addition to derailing trains, laying mines and booby traps, stringing wires to decapitate motorcycle riders, cutting phone lines, poisoning water supplies, even creeping up on tanks from the rear and jamming bottles of explosive fuel into their exhaust pipes.

The women partisans were treated with great respect and some wariness by their male comrades.

Perminov stopped, listened carefully, and squinted through the gloom. They were only a few yards from the wire. She motioned silently for the two women carrying the light to come forward, then checked her stopwatch. Exactly one minute. She punched the stem and, with hand motions that had become familiar to the team, motioned the others to take flanking positions. They quickly moved laterally, rifles at the ready. One girl turned backward to keep watch to their rear.

Perminov put her hand on the shoulder of the girl holding the light toward the sky and peered closely at the stopwatch. "Now!" she said. The light flashed upward. Perminov looked around quickly. Similarly thin shafts of light appeared to the north, south, and east. The target was bracketed. She heard Germans shouting. They would be on her position very soon.

"There it is!" Valya shouted.

"I see it!" Galina replied. She cut the engine of the PO-2 and began gliding silently into the ring formed by the four lights. She could clearly hear shouting and small-arms fire below and then several large searchlights snapped on and flak guns cracked.

The biplane rocked and Galina fought to level the wings for the bomb drop. She yanked the wire and the bombs fell free. There was a shattering burst of flak that threw the PO-2 sideways, but she managed to throw the plane into a tight, diving turn. As she streaked away, she noticed that two of the four lights on the ground had vanished. The sky was full of red tracers and explosions from larger guns.

As she turned, the PO-2 that had been behind her was briefly parallel to her. Abruptly it exploded into a ball of fire. Galina cried out in fear but her emotions dissolved in an immense explosion that erupted behind her. An earthquake rocked the ground and even seemed to make the sky itself shudder and shake. Night turned briefly into a hellish daylight. Before it faded, the PO-2 crews saw debris of all kinds—pieces of buildings, wheels of trucks, guns, bodies of men—soar high in the air.

Galina returned to consciousness with Valya standing in the back cockpit and leaning forward to shake her by the shoulder. "Galina! Galina!" she screamed as the ground came up.

Galina pulled the stick back by reflex and shoved the throttle forward. The stick was very heavy in her hand and she expected momentarily to crash. But the little biplane's nose came up and the PO-2 skimmed over the tops of trees, brushing through the topmost branches of several.

She felt dazed and deafened, but realization began to dawn that they had hit their target and blown it up. The *Nyemtsy* had suffered a major loss. They would toast each other in vodka when they reassembled at the airfield.

On the way home, Galina's biplane was passed by a massive formation of large aircraft that was flying several thousand feet higher and on a roughly similar compass heading. What could they be? she wondered. The PE-2 day bombers didn't fly at night. The planes had been too big to be fighters. Then it struck her. They were Germans, probably twin-engine JU-88s, on their way to bomb Russian targets.

The next morning, officers on each side surveyed the damage. The Germans had lost the ammunition dump at Bryansk, together with a railway depot and two key rail lines. They had killed a few Russian women partisans, but that was small consolation.

The Russians had lost the Kursk rail terminal, which they needed to resupply their troops. A huge civilian labor force of men, women, and children cleared the debris and restored the broken lines within twenty-four hours.

Despite their elaborate defensive preparations, the Russians were caught by surprise. It had been confirmed by two prisoners, German sappers, that the official hour of the attack would be 3:00 A.M., July 5.

But General Hermann Hoth, commanding the Fourth Panzer Army, decided not to wait that long. He smashed into the Russian lines twelve hours earlier, tank engines roaring, treads clanking, and guns booming. Striking sharply northward, his target was the Russians' most dangerous defensive point, the underbelly of the Voronezh front at the bottom right of the bulge.

A second surprise was the way he did it. Instead of following the familar German *blitzkrieg* pattern of striking fast with tanks and motorized infantry and then fanning out to encircle the enemy, he advanced in a new *panzerkeil* formation.

The *panzerkeil* was a succession of armored wedges, one behind the other, that spread out in the rear to form the base of a huge spear point. New, heavily-armored, fifty-six-ton Tiger tanks formed the leading edge of each wedge. Each Tiger carried an 88-mm. flat-trajectory gun in its turret.

Behind the Tigers clanked new medium-heavy Panther tanks and older Mark Fours. Behind the tanks came infantry with mortars, grenades, and automatic weapons.

Each wedge was theoretically able to punch a hole in the dense Russian defenses. If it stalled, another wedge would move up, and then another, to create a slow but irresistible momentum. Meantime, German artillery shells whistled overhead. The barrage was followed immediately by Stukas that dived, screaming, ahead of the armored wedges to drop bombs on Russian positions while twin-engine Henschel anti-tank planes armed with new, high-velocity 30-mm. cannons fired on enemy gun emplacements and tanks.

By nightfall, the panzer wedges had crunched through the first Soviet defensive belt, rolling over anti-tank emplacements, punching holes in surprised Russian tanks, sending enemy infantry fleeing to cover, and seizing three villages. Reaching a stream, Hoth called up the elite Gross Deutschland division.

Now, after a breather, they would ford the stream and smash through the second line of defenses at the official starting time of 3:00 A.M. They would drive north toward a point at which Hoth's force would link up with Marshal Rokossovsky's armies moving eastward. When the two met, a big piece of the bulge would be neatly snipped away.

By the light of a naked electric bulb, General Nikolai Vatutin peered at the map on his portable table as his officers reported from the front. He looked up and nodded.

"No need to panic," he told the tense-faced men. "None at all. The enemy has punched through the first defensive belt and inflicted some damage. But, in an important way, this action has been a positive one, don't you see? Now we know exactly where the main force of the enemy is located. He has compressed his forces tightly into this sector"—he traced it on his map—"and made it very vulnerable."

Vatutin stood erect. "This is a great opportunity and we must act quickly. Bring up everything, do you hear? *Everything*. Our heaviest guns, massed artillery, self-propelled pieces, the *katyushas*, everything. When they are in place, we will smash them with an artillery barrage of the like the world has never seen. The heavy guns aren't much use against rolling tanks. But against stationary tanks . . ." Vatutin smiled, leaving the rest unsaid.

He held up a hand. "Wait. We will hold two hundred guns in reserve. When the enemy recovers enough to start counter-artillery fire and we know precisely where *their* guns are, we'll use the reserve artillery to zero in on them. Now move."

Three hours later, the Russian barrage began with a sound like a huge door slamming shut in the sky. Then other doors slammed, shells whistled like banshees in their flight, and the *katyushas*, massed rockets fired from layers of launching racks on hundreds of trucks, took off with the sound of giant bedsheets being ripped apart by an invisible hand.

The shells from the Russian guns plowed up great geysers of earth along with German tanks, personnel carriers, self-propelled guns, convoys of trucks, guns, and infantrymen. The *katyushas* landed with the explosive force of a fleet of battle cruisers, stripping orchards bare and turning the night into fountains of flame and flying shards of steel.

German soldiers caught in the open were flayed where they stood. The veterans dived for ravines and ditches. Some quickly dug themselves underground. The fortunate ones were already in freshly-dug bunkers.

After an initial period of confusion, the German artillery began to reply. When it did, the two hundred guns that Vatutin had held in reserve launched its shells against the German artillery.

The duel of thousands of guns went on for hours. While it did, Hoth's veterans reorganized themselves to strike across the stream and continue their advance. They had been under artillery fire before and, though it had never been as heavy as this, they knew how to function.

And then the weather betrayed them. It had been hot and humid all day and now a thunderstorm exploded to add to the din. Gale-force winds arose, lightning crackled, and rain began to pour down. Within minutes, a flash flood turned the stream into a raging river and the ground beneath the German tanks and trucks melted into a soft, sticky bog. Vehicles with wheels sank into the mud and had to wait, while their drivers cursed, for vehicles on treads to pull them out.

Walking outside in the rain, Vatutin laughed aloud and shook his fists toward the sky in exultation. Communist philosophy said there was no God, but this turn of events could convert the most hardened atheist. He ordered his heavy guns and tanks brought up closer so that, when the storm ended and dawn came, the Germans would find their way slowed by a still hard-running stream, muddy banks, and, waiting on the far side, a massive and deadly force of Soviet steel. The Germans would have only two choices: stand and die, or run.

Captain Viktor Markov cursed aloud as, flying high cover for four hundred Russian bombers, hordes of Messerschmitts and Focke-Wulf fighters swarmed into the scene. The Red Air Force, it seemed, was still too raw and incompetent to beat the Luftwaffe, or it was just unlucky.

He and his wingman banked over and dived to fire at one and then another enemy fighter. The first caught fire and the pilot bailed out. The second blew up. As Markov pulled up, his wingman collided head-on with a Messerschmitt and both planes fell apart and began tumbling to earth.

Markov looked up from the disaster, aghast, and slammed stick and rudder to the side to avoid a collision of his own. By now, the sky was filled with nearly a thousand airplanes that were swirling in all directions. He had never seen so many airplanes at one time and it was disorienting. Machine gun bullets stitched a line in his wing and he rolled over to avoid an enemy he couldn't see. Pulling around, he found a Focke-Wulf crossing in front of him. With a touch of the rudder, he led him perfectly and hit him with a burst that killed the pilot.

But the Russian bombers were in disarray. Many had been shot down, their formations had been broken, and their bombs were falling at random over the countryside. Some had turned tail for home. Regardless of the covering Russian fighters, the Luftwaffe had smashed what was to be a major surprise attack.

Air Commander Novikov had known exactly when a large force of German bombers would take off from five airfields in the Kharkov area to knock out the Russian air bases. To preempt it, he had ordered a precisely-timed strike against the German airfields. It would deprive the German army of important air support and leave the VVS bases intact.

But the Freya radar stations installed by the Germans picked up the incoming Russian formations. General Hans Seidmann, commander of the Luftwaffe forces, was thunderstruck. This meant that the Russians knew exactly when the Zitadelle battle was to begin. But this was no time to reflect on that.

After a moment's hesitation, he ordered every available fighter aircraft to scramble from its airfield. "Don't worry about air traffic rules!" he shouted to his subordinates. Tell them the enemy's coming! Get the fighters in the air now, immediately!"

Seidmann decided to keep his bombers on the ground for the moment. In the air, they'd be picked off by the Russian fighters. On the ground they'd be sitting ducks, of course, but that was a necessary risk. If the Luftwaffe fighters did their job, the Russians wouldn't get to the airfields.

The German fighters taxied hurriedly around the bombers and headed for runways, taxi strips, and open spaces—any spot with enough space to allow a takeoff. Disregarding the wind direction and sometimes narrowly avoiding crashing into each other, they took to the air, formed up in their two- and four-plane sets, and headed for the approaching Russians.

Minutes later, Seidmann ordered his bombers to reform on the ground and take off. They would skirt the ongoing air battle and head for the Russian airfields to carry out their initial bombing plan. As soon as his Messerschmitts and Focke-Wulfs had destroyed the Russian bombers, they would land, rearm, and overtake the German bombers to protect them from Russian fighters.

As soon as he had given the order, Seidmann watched, openmouthed, at the biggest air battle that had ever taken place.

Markov spotted the German bombers getting away and, shouting in anger and frustration, banked sharply to dive on the leading formation. Just as he had turned on his back, there was a loud explosion in front of him and his engine shattered. Before smoke poured out to obscure his view, he saw his propeller spin away like a child's toy.

Grimly, Markov pushed the Yak into a steep dive to try to put out the fire and elude pursuit. His wings buffeted as the heavily-multiplied force of gravity tried to tear them away. Cannon shells from a pursuing Messerschmitt ripped the fabric away from part of the left wing.

Turning eastward into the Russian lines, he streaked for a cornfield he saw between two thick stands of trees. Dropping his flaps but keeping his wheels up, he flattened out and slowed, knowing that, for a few seconds, he was a fat target for the German fighter.

But he had no option. Cannon shells thumped through his right wing, breaking it partially away from the fuselage as the Yak crunched and slid through tall stalks of corn.

While the plane was still moving, Markov yanked the canopy open and plunged to the ground. Cannon shells plowed up the corn around him and he ran as fast as he could through the stalks to the shelter of the woods. As he did, panting and wheezing, the Messerschmitt pilot who had been trying to kill him gave up the chase and streaked away.

Markov leaned against a tree to catch his breath and wipe the sweat from his face. Then he checked the compass he always carried in the pocket of his flight jacket and started walking due east. When he got back to the base, assuming it was still there, he would climb into another Yak and go find Germans to kill. Meantime, he knew in his heart that, even with the advantage of surprise, the VVS had been beaten once again by the detestable but admirable Luftwaffe.

It was like a scene out of the Middle Ages. Great blocks of infantrymen marched to battle in formation. All that was lacking were knights on horseback. To replace them, and to remind awestruck Kapitan Bruno Meyer that it was really the twentieth century, hundreds of Russian T-34 tanks clanked forward in formation.

Meyer, leading a formation of Henschel 129B tank-killers, radioed his base at Mikoyanovka and recommended urgently that the entire force of sixty-four fighter-bombers take off at once to attack the Russian armor.

Despite all resistance and obstacles—massed artillery barrages, *katyushas*, tank traps, anti-tank nests, Russian tanks, infantry, and bad weather—Hoth's Fourth Panzer Army had ground northward for a distance of twenty-five miles. But their dramatic advance had made them increasingly vulnerable to counterattack. They had taken heavy losses and their right flank was exposed.

And now a massive Russian force of tanks and infantry was moving up to attack the German panzers on the flank. Fifteen minutes after Meyer's sighting, a heavy force of Henschels, augmented by squadrons of Focke-Wulfs, rolled down from above in tight formations to blunt the Russian counterattack.

The Russians were without air cover; their fighter aircraft had been vectored elsewhere. Meyer pushed his stick forward, advanced his throttles, and led his formation in a low-level attack on the Russian tanks. Machine guns chattered vainly from the tanks and infantry units. Meyer pressed his firing button and pilots flying in echelon formation behind him did the same thing. A first salvo of 30-mm. cannon shells punched through the sides of the tanks and nearly a dozen burst into flame.

Blasted heavily in continuing air attacks, the leading tank brigade wandered out of its formation. In the confusion, some tanks blocked others; some blundered into nearby swamps. Circling around, the Henschels continued their attack on the tanks as the Focke-Wulf fighters swarmed down against the infantry. The fighters fired into the masses of infantry with their cannons and, even more devastating, with fragmentation bombs that exploded in circles of flying steel.

Twenty minutes later, the field was littered with bodies and shattered and burning tanks. The survivors of the Russian counterforce fled to the cover of the forests.

Ten minutes afterward, a handful of Yaks appeared on the scene to find the German planes gone. Assigned to combat on a distant battlefield, they had been called too late to ward off the German air attack. Viktor Markov cursed in frustration and banked away so violently that his wingman was left behind and had to shove his throttle to the stop to catch up.

Next morning, the rising sun revealed a fiery landscape that might have been transplanted from the bottom region of Hell. To Viktor Markov, ranging above in his Yak, the entire earth seemed to be burning.

He wanted his revenge but, for the moment, the scene was intimidating. It was shortly after dawn on July 5 that Wehrmacht General Walter Model's panzer army began rolling eastward.

As the armored wedges ground slowly ahead, they were met by a howling, booming concentration of shellfire from heavy guns, *katyushas*, and mortars. Nests of 76-mm. guns called *pakfronts* poured an unprecedented volume of steel and fire into the approaching Tigers and Panthers.

When German infantry was sent ahead to clean out the *pakfronts*, they were met by deadly fire from nests of machine guns and mortars that were dug in around them. Around the nests were layered perimeters of mines.

At his command post, Model shook his head in reluctant admiration. "The bastards have tricked us," he told his officers. "Our sappers quite naturally staked out corridors for us that had the fewest mines in them. It seems there was a reason why they had the fewest mines. They knew we would come that way. It was precisely those corridors that the bastards had zeroed the guns of their *pak-fronts* on."

Clearly, Model thought to himself, he had underrated the Russians. He still considered them barbarians of somewhat inferior intelligence, but, very obviously, they possessed a considerable talent for misdirection and concealment. And, he had to admit, they were surpassingly brave.

The heavy explosions had set the surrounding fields of wheat and corn ablaze. The smoke mingled with the black oily smoke from burning Tiger and Panther tanks to form a dark haze over the battlefield. The lighter Panthers were supposed to combine the best features of the German and Russian tanks but there hadn't been time to put them through field tests. Now they were finding that their fuel systems had been inadequately protected. Under heavy shellfire, they caught fire. Soon, scores of Panthers were burning fiercely.

Even the vaunted Tigers were being shattered. A Tiger tank could withstand the power of a single 76-mm. gun—the caliber used in self-propelled artillery and in the T-34 tanks—but not the hellfire produced by a concentration of 76-mm. guns firing at point-blank range.

But behind the Tigers came rolling the Ferdinands, seventy-ton, self-propelled, long-barreled 88-mm. guns that blasted the *pakfronts* into rubble while Russian 76-mm. shells bounced off their 200-mm. armorplate. Like fearsome prehistoric beasts, the Ferdinands, dubbed Elefants by the German troops, rumbled forward, ripping open the Russian T-34s with their high-velocity, flat-trajectory 88s.

Irresistibly, the Ferdinands led the Tigers and armored personnel carriers through the *pakfronts* and T-34 hulks past the first belt of the Russian defenses. But the still-withering fire from tanks and surviving *pakfronts*, now directed at the Tigers, Panthers, and personnel carriers, succeeded in slowly separating the Ferdinands from the other German forces.

Above, at the leader's radio signal, a group of heavily-armored IL-2 Shturmovik tank-killers dived to attack the Tigers and Panthers from the sides at low level with their 37-mm. cannons.

A second signal came over the radio and Markov rolled his Yak into a shallow dive, aimed for the infantrymen pouring out of shattered personnel carriers, and dropped his load of six fifty-six-pound fragmentation bombs. Then he and his wingman pulled up, circled around, came back, and began pounding cannon shells and machine-gun fire into the remaining carriers and soldiers who were running from ones that had been disabled.

A two-plane set of Focke-Wulfs zeroed in on one Russian Shturm-ovik and hit it repeatedly from the rear with cannon shells. The lead pilot, a colonel, noted irrelevantly that the Russian pilot was flying in his underwear.

The colonel cursed aloud as the shells simply bounced off the 12-mm. armor plating at the rear of the Shturmovik's cockpit. Hearing his complaint, his wingman responded with words that would make it into the history books.

"Herr Oberst," he said, "you can't bite a porcupine in the ass."

Below, the mammoth Ferdinands, now a separate force, continued to inch forward. But disaster struck them when they rolled over deep, zig-zag ditches that had been dug in their path. For out of the ditches rose fanatical teams of tank destroyers.

If they had been opposing the Tigers made by Henschel, the teams would have instantly been cut down by machine fire from the sides of the tanks. But, despite the loud protests of German tank genius Heinz Guderian, the Ferdinands and the Tigers made by Porsche were designed without such secondary armament.

Now Russian teams of men and women, moving beneath and be-hind the Ferdinands' huge 88-mm. guns, lugged flame-throwers up to their sides. In one squad, a nineteen-year-old Russian private named Natan Yershov ran forward with the flame-throwing appara-tus and a twenty-year-old corporal named Jenny Yeromin clambered aboard the Ferdinand, pressed the nozzle against the behemoth's ventilation slit, and shot a long burst of flame inside.

Screams came from inside the Ferdinand and it stopped dead in its tracks. The same fate met the other giants as tank-destroying squads climbed over them.

Weary and shocked by the spectacle, Markov flew back to his field, had his Yak gassed and rearmed, and went back to the battlefield. He had made three sorties by nightfall. By then the Germans had lost hundreds of tanks and, though he had become certain that they were being stopped, he felt slightly sick at heart.

He enjoyed an honorable contest at arms, but this was more than that, even more than war. It was carnage.

Night-witch Galina Tarasova continued her night-bombing sorties during the Kursk battles. One air strike by her regiment destroyed the Seshchinskaya railroad station near Bryansk as well as blasting a major highway that ran beside it.

Another tore up a main railroad line carrying supplies to three

German armies and ruined a million food ration packages. A third knocked out a double-span bridge that had been critical to German resupply efforts.

But on the morning of July 12 she was pulled out of bed for emergency daytime duty. She listened to Major Kravchenko's briefing with a sense of dread. The last time she had been called for daytime service was the day she and Valya were nearly killed by the Messerschmitt. The experience still frightened her.

She had been saved by Viktor Markov who, later, had mistakenly thought that his action might melt her reserve in the way he found most satisfying. He was clearly crestfallen, yet amused, when she rejected his advances once again.

"Surely this ranks with swimming the deepest ocean or climbing the highest mountain," he complained. "How more dramatically can I show my love and my sincerity?"

"I don't think that the word 'love' is a synonym for passion or conquest," she replied. "And I won't embarrass you by examining the word 'sincerity.' Further, Comrade Captain, do you usually request some sort of payment when you save a comrade's life?"

"This is what comes of being attracted to a Moscow intellectual," Markov sighed. "It wouldn't be the same with a girl from the Ukraine."

Galina enjoyed her verbal exchanges with Viktor. She was never certain whether his persistent but gentle advances were simply a game that he liked to play, or whether he genuinely cared for her. If it were peacetime she might be tempted to find out.

"Galina!" Major Kravchenko said. "Are you listening? Rub the sleep out of your eyes and listen to me."

The mission was simple and dangerous. She would fly an ambulance plane into the Prokhorovka sector on Kursk's southern front and land on a road marked by a sheet bearing a large red star. As she approached it she would see a pair of green flares.

Waiting for her there was a badly wounded general, a member of General Vatutin's staff who merited special treatment. Soldiers would load the general aboard the converted PO-2 and she would fly him to a hospital unit behind the lines that could perform the complicated surgery he needed.

There would be no navigator or rear cockpit gunner. She would have to fly solo. In the ambulance model of the PO-2, a hinged side door behind the pilot swung open to accommodate a stretcher within the fuselage. There was no rear cockpit at all.

"So you will be unarmed," Major Kravchenko said. "Simply hug the ground and come back as fast as you can. Yak fighters in the sector have been alerted to look out for you and provide cover—if you need it—and if they see you, of course."

She flew at treetop level, and sometimes lower, all the way to Prokhorovka. The booming of guns, howling of rockets, and screaming of diving aircraft grew steadily louder as she approached the area. She cringed in horror when she came up over a hill and saw what lay before her.

More than a thousand tanks, roughly half of them belonging to each side, faced each other while German ground-attack Stukas and Henschels fired in low-level passes at the Russian T-34s and Shturmoviks fired at the Tigers and Panthers.

Above all of them, opposing fighters who were trying to protect their ground-attack airplanes swirled in violent aerial combat.

To Galina, both earth and sky were full of booming, barking, and screaming weapons of all kinds. In her old PO-2 biplane, she was a mouse amid a horde of snarling lions and tigers.

The air was heavy with smoke and haze and it was becoming difficult to see, particularly at ground level where she lacked the altitude to scan the area. Finally, she managed to orient herself on her map by landmarks Major Kravchenko had marked for her. Turning on the prescribed compass heading, she punched the stem of her stopwatch, flew for two minutes, and looked for the green flares.

There they were! And beside a narrow dirt road she saw soldiers spreading out a large sheet bearing a red star. She cut her power, circled sharply, crossed her controls, and sideslipped onto the road, dumping the biplane on the ground and stopping within a few feet of the sheet.

Immediately, one man ran forward and opened the side hatch of the plane while two others picked up a stretcher with a man on it and placed it in the ambulance compartment. A Russian non-com with a medic's armband pumped his fist to tell her to leave quickly. She held the left rudder pedal down and blasted the little engine, swinging the PO-2 in a circle. Within seconds, she was airborne and hedgehopping cross-country to get out of the battle area as fast as possible.

Hoth had taken heavy casualties, reorganized and bolstered his panzer forces, and decided to go for broke.

"If we can punch through the remaining Russian defenses at this point, this critical point," he told his staff as they pored over the maps, "we can wheel around behind the Russian lines, link up with Model, and break the salient open. We will have won."

Leading the attack in the morning was the Second SS Panzer Corps under the command of General Paul Hauser.

On a hill overlooking Prokhorovka, General Pavel Rotmistrov, commander of Russia's Fifth Guards Tank Army, recoiled in surprise at the sight of the Tigers, Panthers, and armored personnel carriers rolling toward him. He had thought it was he who would be making a preemptive attack.

To make it successful, Marshal Zhukov had released to Vatutin almost all of the uncommitted mobile reserve. Vatutin had planned to use the First Tank Army, but its commander had dug his tanks into the ground with only its gun turrets showing. So he called upon Rotmistrov, who had commanded his tanks at Stalingrad with brilliance against Hoth's attacks.

And now, instead of attacking as ordered, they would be defending. Or would they? A decision had to be made within minutes, perhaps seconds, but Rotmistrov took the time to ponder two things.

Looking at the sky, he saw dust rising thickly from the dry earth beneath the German tanks. Soon, combined with battle smoke, it would isolate the battlefield from air support of either side. It would soon become a battle of armor against armor.

The two sides were approximately equal in strength—each had about eight hundred tanks and self-propelled guns—but there was one significant imbalance. If the German tanks were allowed to stand off and fire their big 88-mm. guns, they would quickly wreck the Russian T-34s.

The T-34s could win such a battle only if they could get in close before they were decimated. At close range the 76-mm. guns of the T-34s could punch through the Tiger armor. And, thank the gods of battle, the T-34 was nearly twice as fast as the Tiger. They would travel even faster rolling downhill at full speed.

Rotmistrov turned and shouted the order. "Attack with everything now! At full speed! Get in among them and kill them!"

Minutes later, the Russians charged down the hill like the horse cavalry of another time. German 88s stopped a few T-34s on the way down, but the main force of the Russian armor was in amongst the Tigers before the surprised tank commanders could react. The battlefield quickly became a discordant symphony of banging tank guns, exploding tanks, grinding gears, and roaring engines. Flames and smoke filled the valley as the tanks wheeled and turned to attack each other like armored medieval knights. When a Tiger caught a

T-34 in its sights the Tiger blasted it into wreckage in seconds. But, just as often, a T-34 slipped sideways, avoided the big 88, and punched holes in the Tiger at short range with the 76-mm. gun.

Soon, crewmen from the tanks scurried from their burning vehicles and ran for cover. There was little to find, and many were caught by machine-gun fire or crushed by tank treads. One Tiger commander blasted a T-34 in front of him and, when the tank commander opened the hatch and tried to get out, cut the Russian officer down with an automatic weapon.

But, as the officer's cap fell off, the German noted with surprise that the tank commander had been a woman.

By the day's end, each side had lost half of its force in the biggest tank battle of all time. At nightfall, the Russians pulled back, leaving the remnants of the Second Panzer Corps in charge of the field. But, Hoth grimly concluded, it was a Pyrrhic victory, if it could be counted a victory at all.

For, he knew, the Russians could replace their missing tanks and crewmen and he could not. If it were to be a war of manpower and reserves, and apparently it was, the Wehrmacht must lose.

Galina was shaking with strain and fatigue by the time she had delivered the general to the surgical unit and flown back to her own airfield. A Henschel had twice fired at her on the way back but she had eluded it by moving down even lower and turning tightly around stands of trees and hills to mask the biplane from the German's sight. Finally, a pair of speeding Yaks appeared and forced the Henschel pilot to abandon his efforts to swat the annoying fly.

When she landed and stumbled out of the PO-2, she was soaked with perspiration. She would go to the spigot in the hut beside the bunker and give herself the best possible body wash, even though the water was cold. Then she would ask Viktor, if he was on the ground and she still had the energy to look for him, if he would allow her to empty the hot water from his liquid-cooled Yak's radiator into a bucket so she could wash her hair.

Tomorrow, or perhaps the next day, the bath train would come and she could take a real shower. She wanted that even more than chocolate.

CHAPTER EIGHT

THE MEETING

Sitting in his office at High Wycombe, General Ira Eaker looked at the figures and shook his head. The news was good and bad. During the last week of July 1943, Eighth Air Force groups had fanned out to strike accurately at seventeen industrial targets in northwest Germany. That was good.

In the process, they had lost eighty-eight bombers and nine hundred men; another dozen airplanes had to be scrapped. That was bad. And, it appeared, worse was on the way. On July 28, one group lost fifteen of its thirty-eight bombers to an unusually diverse and damaging attack that might provide a pattern for future encounters.

German ground and air defenses used not only the highly-accurate 88-mm. flak guns and fighters armed with cannons and machine guns, but new air-to-air rockets and even aerial mines.

The rockets were a particular concern. One blew a B-17 into two others, bringing down all three. Eighth Air Force claimed they shot down three hundred German fighters during the week, but intelligence officers quickly discounted the claims.

"Any gunner who fires at a fighter and sees it smoking thinks he's the one who got it," Eaker told his staff. "But there might be thirty or forty gunners firing at that same fighter and every one of them thinks it's his kill. At most, that kill should be credited to one or two. But which one or two?"

Now it was August, and Buddy Bryce had wangled a transfer into the 205th Bomb Group to join Mike Gavin. Mike asked him how he managed to persuade General Sloane to let him go.

"Oh, ol' John pissed and moaned somethin' awful," Buddy said. "Who was he gonna talk to if I left? There was nothin' but Yankees around. But I kept thankin' him for all he'd done for me and told him he had inspired me to try to do more.

"That kinda confused him for a while, but he finally realized things just weren't gonna be the same between us if he hung onta me. What really bent his skull was my request to transfer into a bomb group 'stead of fighters. But he knew 'bout the Viking deal, of course, and when I told him you were here, he understood. And here I am."

"Well, it's great," Mike said. Before the next raid was called, he went to operations and asked if Buddy could be assigned as his co-pilot on Buddy's first mission. It was still the group's policy to require a new pilot to fly co-pilot at least once before assuming first pilot's duties.

It was August 17 when their mission was called. In the briefing room at 3:00 A.M., the group operations officer, visibly conscious of the drama involved, solemnly pulled back the curtain covering the big wall map and revealed a long skein of red yarn stretching deep into Germany. It zig-zagged from leg to leg, leading finally to the initial point of the bomb run—a location picked for its sharp radar image—and to a large blob designating the target.

Colonel Robinson moved to the center of the stage. "The target is Schweinfurt," he said. "It's very important, a ball-bearing production center."

A groan rumbled from the aircrewmen sitting in rows in front of him. They groaned at any mission that promised to be a long one. Some jiggled their knees nervously. Some wiped their faces. Others lighted up the Camels and Chesterfields that the cigarette companies sent them every week and added to the cloud of smoke that was gathering under the low ceiling.

Robinson unzipped his A-2 jacket, took a wide stance, and held his hand up. "Okay, quiet down. This is an important one and we've gotta do it. Look: the Germans can make all the tanks and guns they want, but if they don't have ball bearings, all that military equipment will be useless. And the Schweinfurt factories make about fifty percent of all their ball bearings. So we've got to do our part for the guys on the ground.

"The First and Second Divisions will hit Schweinfurt; the Third will head south for Regensburg to hit the Messerschmitt factory there. Maybe that'll dilute the fighter attacks a bit, no way to tell. The weather will be good, so you'll have no trouble seeing the target.

"The brain trust will give you the details in a minute—altitudes, checkpoints, target blowup photos, the works. Afterward, navigators will pick up maps and flimsies, bombardiers will go over target info with the group bombardier, co-pilots will go to equipment and pick up evasion kits. Radio men are checking out the day's frequencies, call signs and wireless codes. The gunners are being briefed separately. Take the trucks to the hardstands at 0400. Takeoff at 0500.

"To wind up, I'll just emphasize that this is an important target. I don't want any dubious aborts. Stay in close, tight formation. Stay alert. Keep the radio chatter down. And you pilots: provide stable platforms for the bomb drops. I'll be leading today. So, good luck and good hunting. And, as Wing always says, if I've left anything out, you may rest assured."

It was Robinson's standard closing line and it always produced laughs, chuckles, and a few catcalls. The crewmen had come to expect it; it had become an incantation of good luck.

In the equipment room, Mike and Buddy, along with the others, dressed for the mission. They placed their wallets in their lockers, pulled on their long underwear—it might be eighty degrees on the ground at midday but it was forty-five below upstairs and the heaters seldom worked—and then donned wool OD shirts and trousers, two pairs of sox, silk and wool, and, finally, coveralls, fleece-lined boots, lined helmet with oxygen mask snapped to one side, and medium-weight alpaca-and-wool B-10 flight jackets.

Mike handed Buddy an escape kit stuffed with silk handkerchief maps of France and Germany, a phrase book in both languages, emergency rations, and various European currencies. He pulled his rubber Mae West inflatable jacket over his head and indicated that Buddy should do the same. Finally, each man took two pairs of gloves, one rayon, one leather, from his locker. The leather would be worn over the rayon.

At sub-zero temperatures, a control column wheel quickly transmitted the deadly cold through ordinary gloves. And even if the cabin heater raised the temperature, the two pairs of gloves would minimize the blistering and callusing of hands that had to wrestle with a thirty-five-ton load for eight hours without benefit of servo assist.

Obviously intimidated by the lengthy ritual, Buddy looked ruefully at Mike. "Well, I guess this is the big casino, isn't it?"

"Yeah, I guess. You feel okay?"

"Funny thing," Buddy chuckled drily. "I was just thinkin' how nice it'd be right now to be sittin' in one of General Sloane's soft armchairs and listenin' to him talk about Georgia Tech football. I wouldn't even mind poppin' up to light his cigar. By the way, how many raids did you say you've flown so far?"

"Twelve," Mike answered. "This'll be the thirteenth."

"Oh peachy," Buddy said. "Sure glad I asked."

The act of running through the checklist in the familiar environment of the B-17 cockpit settled Buddy's nerves. "Well, fuck-it-all," he said when they had finished, "I wouldn't wanta live forever anyway."

The summer sun was up and a low fog had dissolved when the green light blinked from the Van Aldis lamp in the doorway. Waiting at the end of the runway, Mike tramped hard on the brakes, holding them down, and slowly walked the throttles to the fire stop. Buddy reached across with his left hand and blocked them open so Mike could put both hands on the wheel.

The B-17's four Cyclone engines bellowed and shuddered and tried to break free. When the engine roar reached a scream, Mike released the brakes and the bomber lunged forward. With Buddy calling out the speed, Mike had elevator control at sixty and pushed the wheel slightly forward to lift the tail. At one hundred, with red warning lights coming up, Mike lifted the heavy airplane from the ground.

In unusually clear skies, the B-17s circled around the Alconbury radio beacon until all of them were locked into a box formation of three squadrons. Then, following Robinson's lead, the group slowly turned toward the Wing assembly point around a buncher beacon twenty miles away.

Again, the group began circling. Soon, a second group appeared and slid into trail behind the 205th. And then a third. Massively, the combat wing turned toward the divisional assembly point at the coast. Two hours after takeoff, more than three hundred bombers thundered over the English Channel, flying eastward into a blinding sun.

Within a minute of the time they reached the French coast, a group of P-47 Thunderbolt fighters swept across the bombers to announce their protective presence. Leading the high squadron in Robinson's group, Mike turned to Buddy and gave him a thumbs-up. Buddy pressed his throat mike. "Whoop-to-do," he said.

A few flak puffs came up as they moved deeper into the continent but no enemy fighters appeared. When they neared Aachen, barely one-third of the way to their target, the P-47s, having used half their fuel, peeled off and headed for home.

Buddy made a kissing motion with his glove against his oxygen mask to bid them a reluctant goodbye. Mike hunched his shoulders involuntarily. He knew what lay ahead.

General of the Luftwaffe Fighters Adolf Galland stared across his desk at his close friend, fighter ace Colonel Johannes Steinhoff. Early observations from air and ground had been radioed into his Berlin office. The indications were clear; the Boeings were coming in force today and their penetration would be a deep one.

It had been a terrible three weeks. Two Royal Air Force raids in three nights had created an unimaginable catastrophe at Hamburg. The bombing had set off fires that created volcanic updrafts, sucking in surrounding, super-heated air and producing something never seen or heard of before—a firestorm.

Whole apartment blocks were consumed by it; scores of thousands died in them or were roasted alive in the underground air raid shelters that ordinarily protected them. Casualty reports counted at least forty thousand dead; the final toll might rise as high as eighty thousand.

Armaments Minister Speer said flatly that, if a defense couldn't be found against Allied bombing, the Reich's production capacity would be entirely destroyed within four months. Luftwaffe Chief of Staff Jeschonnek called a meeting of all air commanders to find a solution to the desperate situation.

"I told them exactly what I thought," Galland said. "The British nighttime raids are terrible, of course, obscene, killing so many people. But from a military point of view, it's the daytime American raids that concern me most. We need to hit these Boeing formations with heavy concentrations of fighters. But our fighters are being dispersed all over the Reich. Some have been pulled off for night-fighter duty. Now they've discovered that the Focke-Wulfs make good ground-support aircraft for troops. So we've become too thin where we need it most."

The air commanders had pumped Luftwaffe Reichsmarschall Hermann Göring full of enthusiasm to carry their plan to Hitler: make the defense of the Reich the highest Luftwaffe priority and concentrate German resources toward that goal.

But Göring returned, weeping, actually weeping, from his meeting with the Führer. Hitler had shouted that defense was ignoble. Terror would be met with terror. All Luftwaffe resources would be concentrated on bombing England.

"So now, all the Reischsmarschall can offer is the order that our fighter pilots fly at least three sorties against the bombers each time we engage them," Steinhoff observed.

"We'll have to do it to multiply our effectiveness," Galland said. "But that's easier said than done. It's a question of how much a single pilot can take, first of all. But, beyond that, it's a matter of organization. The pilots can't simply fly back to home base; the distances may be too long. They have to land at airfields all over the place. And then who's in charge?

"I've come up with the only solution I can think of. I've sent out the order that, when they disperse to land and refuel, the senior pilot present will act as commander of all those present. When the fighters have been refueled and rearmed, he'll lead them back to the attack on the bombers, using the Reich fighter radio channel to guide him."

"Very good. I think we also need to emphasize our new tactics," Steinhoff said. "Frontal attacks, wingtip-to-wingtip, are giving us our best results."

"Initially, yes. Hit them hard, line abreast, in multiple waves. Go after the lead formations. The strength of the Boeings is in the crossfire their formations create. Break up the formations and we can pick them off."

"Another suggestion."

"Tell me."

"Tell the pilots they have to close in within two hundred meters. It's very hard to do with fifty or sixty heavy machine guns firing at you. Sometimes I feel like shutting my eyes and throwing my arm over my face, but it's the only way. Bore in close before you fire."

Galland nodded vigorously. "Well put. I'll see that the group commanders tell them that at the briefings. We're assembling three hundred fighters, every airplane I could lay my hands on, over Frankfurt. We'll see if we can't teach the Amis a lesson today."

Turning to the phone, Galland made a series of short telephone calls. Afterward, he stubbed out his cigar and rose. "Shall we go and help?"

"After you, General," Steinhoff said. The two men rose, picked up their leather jackets and peaked Luftwaffe caps, and walked outside to the three-seat Fieseler Storch waiting in the nearby athletic field. Galland told the pilot to take them to the FW-190 base at Staaken.

Ten minutes after their P-47 escort left, the B-17s were hit by waves of Messerschmitts and Focke-Wulfs. They slashed through Robinson's group in company-front formation, wingtip-to-wingtip, flashes of light winking from their noses and wings.

Instantly, the bomber radio channel became a babble of cries, shouts, and curses. The bombers shook with the vibration of their 50-caliber machine guns. Spent cartridges clattered to the floors of their fuselages and the smell of burning powder filtered into oxygen masks.

In the lead group, one B-17 slowly wandered away and fell into a lazy, deadly spin as crewmen struggled against the twisting forces to bail out. Another bomber disintegrated in an orange and black explosion. A Messerschmitt, trailing black smoke, plowed into a third B-17.

Mike had never seen the Luftwaffe attack with as much vigor. It was as if the fighters had become a school of sharks that smelled blood and had gone into a feeding frenzy. After the initial waves of frontal attacks, the fighters attacked wildly from all directions—beam-on, from the tail, in steep dives and vertical climbs. And they screamed in closer than they had in the past, firing point-blank at the bombers with cannons and machine guns.

Now, the B-17 waist gunners warned, a line of twin-engine ME-110s was approaching from three o'clock. Rockets swooshed from their wings to explode in and around the bomber formations.

Breathing hard, sweat running down inside his chest in the ice-cold cabin, Mike shot a glance at Buddy in the co-pilot's seat beside him. Buddy was hunched over like a man with acute indigestion. Mike felt a flicker of pity for him; the co-pilot had the hardest job. Unless the pilot was killed or wounded, or he had to man a gun position, there was nothing for the co-pilot to do but sit and endure the attacks.

But he wasn't catatonic. There was a heavy thud somewhere in the rear and the ship lurched. "Co-pilot to crew," Buddy snapped. "Report damage."

"Left waist to co-pilot. Cannon shell through the fuselage behind me. No structural damage I can see." At Buddy's order, the crew checked in, from nose to tail, to report everyone unhurt and alert.

As they neared Schweinfurt, a heavy flak barrage erupted and turned the sky in front of them a mottled black. Sharp cracking sounds burst around them and there was that ugly noise that sounded like gravel being thrown against the fuselage.

To Mike's surprise, the German fighters continued their attacks amid the flak barrage instead of peeling off and waiting for the B-17s to come off the bomb run. Seeing them continue, Mike felt a prickle of fear. These men had become fanatics!

They turned off the IP onto the bomb run. "Full RPM," Mike said. Buddy shoved the prop levers to emergency war power. The heavy rumble of the engines became a discordant roar.

"Bomb bay doors open." As the doors dropped open, icy air swirled through the cabin and fuselage. The flak barrage became a lunatic symphony of fire, sound, and smoke. More stone-like objects struck the airplane.

Now, long pink rocket trails were arcing up from the ground.

Mike realized that he had become relaxed, even passive. He admired the beauty of the scene—the arcing pink trails, the orange and red shellbursts, the flashing of airplanes moving past at high speed, the ground winking and glistening below.

It was really very beautiful but, oddly, the color had washed out of the scene; it had faded to black and white and seemed a trifle fuzzy.

Buddy struck him in the shoulder and peered into what he could see of Mike's face. Then Buddy plugged an oxygen walkaround bottle onto his mask and moved out of his seat. He reached down to Mike's left and twisted the oxygen system's dial, blowing emergency oxygen into Mike's mask.

As the oxygen flowed into Mike's lungs, the color returned to the scene and sharp focus returned with frightening clarity. His breath came short and his heart began to bang.

Buddy detached the walkaround bottle and plugged his mask back into his oxygen system. "That last flak burst knocked your demand valve shut. You're on the emergency system now. Breathe a bit and let me take it."

Mike lifted his hands and feet from the controls and slid his seat back. Buddy peered sideways to hold station with the lead squadron. It was only seconds now.

"Bombs away!" Thousand-pound bombs fell in streams from the bomber force, wobbling downward and disappearing from view.

An instant later, the intercom barked. "Bombardier to pilot. I've got a red light here."

"Pilot to radio," Mike said immediately. "Check for a bomb hangup." A red light went out on the bombardier's display panel each time a bomb left the bomb bay. But one light was still on. A live thousand-pound bomb could blow up the airplane and others nearby if the fuse propeller spun loose in the gale-force winds that swirled through the bomb bay and the bomb's nose touched anything on the way out.

Thurston plugged in an oxygen walkaround bottle, left his radio position, and moved into the narrow catwalk of the bomb bay. *There* the bastard was, as big as a man and a million times more dangerous. The fuse was still attached to the nose. He could go back, get a screwdriver, and try to release the shackles holding the bomb. But it would take too long.

Holding onto the catwalk bracing, he began kicking and tramping on the bomb's cylindrical shell. It was a frightening thing to do and he shouted and swore inside his mask to deny his fear.

Twisting in his seat, Mike watched him nervously. Would the damn thing go off? If it fell free now, would it hit another airplane below? They were turning off the target now and other airplanes were closing their bomb bay doors.

With a mighty kick, Thurston dislodged the big bomb and it fell free. Turning around, Mike exhaled heavily. The moisture from his breath leaked from the sides of the oxygen mask and froze in a strip on his side window. He became aware that sweat was freezing on his chest and inside the mask. He tapped the point of the mask to break the ice free.

"I'll take it now," he told Buddy, putting his hands on the control wheel.

There was an enormous explosion and the bomber slewed violently sideways as a fighter slashed past them. Two cannon shells caught Thurston just as he was moving back to his radio table and flung his body against the fuselage wall.

The new left waist gunner, a boy named Schneider, called to say that Thurston had had it. There was nothing to do for him. Then, shouting incoherently, he turned back to his guns to fire at a fighter coming beam-on.

The fighters harried and battered the bombers all the way back to Cologne. There, fresh squadrons of American P-47s flashed onto the scene and engaged the Luftwaffe planes in violent combat. Soon, sliding downward in a gentle glide, the B-17s were over the Channel and heading home.

Over the field, there was nervous confusion as exhausted pilots in disabled airplanes and those with wounded aboard fired red flares to alert controllers and ambulances and then jockeyed for landing positions.

At the hardstand, the men in the cockpit and nose dropped out of the nose hatch onto the tarmac. The others left by the door at the rear of the right side of the fuselage. Mike and Buddy watched broodingly as Thurston's bloody body was lifted out the door onto a stretcher held by medics. His blood had trickled down the floor of the fuselage before it froze; it was visible on the boots of the waist gunners.

"Lordy, Lordy," Buddy said quietly to Mike as they stood in a line outside the crew interrogation room and drank whiskey out of paper cups. "All the raids aren't like this, are they?" Buddy's eyes were fearful and the words came out pleadingly.

Mike shook his head. "There've been bad ones, all right, but today was the worst. The worst yet. We sure as hell need those long-range P-51s to escort us in and out."

"They're supposed to arrive pretty soon. That P-51 is the finest fighter plane there is. It'll make all the difference, Mike."

"It can't come too soon. We need the help bad."

General Ira Eaker looked at the reports and groaned. Eighth Air Force groups had made numerous strikes on the ball-bearing factories at Schweinfurt and on the Messerschmitt factory at Regensburg; that part of it was good. But the cost was too high, nearly five times too high. Sixty bombers had gone down with their crews and another fifty or so needed major repairs. Seventeen of them had to be junked.

In crews alone, they had lost nearly twenty percent. That was unacceptable.

He knew how Washington would react. The deep penetrations—the strikes on Germany's most productive targets—would be stopped for the time being. They would lose valuable momentum. And there would be another debate over the feasibility of daylight bombing.

In Adolf Hitler's Germany or Josef Stalin's Russia, bomber missions of this kind would continue, regardless of human and materiel losses. Both were dictatorships and dictators placed a small value on human life.

But England was a democracy, just as America was, and the British kept on with their night raids, flying their cumbersome, virtually unarmed Lancasters over Germany one at a time and suffering casualty rates of sixty percent or more. In fact, he had been told that no Lancaster crew had ever finished a thirty-mission tour. Were the British that much tougher a people?

Or was America so isolated from other nations, geographically and culturally, that even a total war was viewed differently? Eaker sighed. He was sure of one thing only. He needed the new, long-range P-51s to escort the bombers in and out and he needed them now. Nothing would be able to match them.

At an airfield at Intersburg in East Prussia, Adolf Hitler watched expressionlessly as the German superplane, the world's first operational jet fighter, the Messerschmitt 262, whistled, low-level, across his field of vision at more than five hundred miles an hour.

Near him, Adolf Galland watched nervously. He had test-flown the fantastically-fast propellerless aircraft in May. It was the answer to a heartfelt prayer. With it, in even modest numbers—one hundred or two hundred of them— the Luftwaffe would rip through the bomber formations and break them up with rockets and cannon fire.

When the Americans' long-range fighter escorts arrived—Galland knew they would eventually arrive—they would be powerless to prevent the carnage. The wonderplane was twice as fast as the Messerschmitt 109, some one hundred and twenty miles an hour or more faster than the fastest American fighter.

Compared to the German jets, even the newest American prop-driven fighters would be left wallowing in the sky like balloons.

Beside Hitler stood Göring, enormous in peaked cap and greatcoat, and Willi Messerschmitt. Abruptly, the Supreme Commander turned to Messerschmitt and asked: "Can this aircraft carry bombs?"

Messerschmitt paused and said: "Yes, mein Führer. Theoretically, it could carry two five hundred kilos."

Göring opened his mouth and closed it. Galland scowled. Göring knew that the ME-262 had no bomb sights or fixtures for carrying bombs, couldn't dive steeply without loss of control, and burned too much fuel for low-level attacks— never mind the trouble that bomber pilots would encounter trying to fly a tricky, super-fast fighter aircraft. Messerschmitt's answer was careful, theoretical, and deceptive. Göring's failure to respond was cowardly.

Hitler's response came fast and harsh. "For years I have been waiting for you to give me a *blitz* bomber which can reach the target in spite of enemy defenses. You haven't done it. In this aircraft you present to me as a fighter airplane I see the *blitz* bomber. You will convert this airplane into a bomber. It will be my revenge weapon against the coming invasion. At last I have the *blitz* bomber!"

He waved a hand contemptuously. "Of course none of you thought of that!"

Galland's heart sank. This was throwing pearls before swine. With

Hitler a madman, Göring a coward, and the new jet racehorse hitched to a plow, the Amis must inevitably win the air war. Foreseeing defeat and frustrated by Göring's bullying, Galland's friend and chief of staff, Jeschonnek, had shot himself a few days ago. Ernst Udet, one of Germany's most famous aces, had done the same thing earlier for much the same reasons.

To Galland, suicide was an alien concept. But he could resign.

A pale sun filtered through the clouds gathering around the Berghof as Flugkapitan Hanna Reitsch walked into the room with the big window where the Supreme Commander invited his guests to tea. The shafts of sunlight peeping through the cloud banks lent a striking beauty to the countryside around Berchtesgaden.

It was hard to think of war in such a place, on such a day. The thought crossed her mind that coming to retreats like this might be one of the reasons why the Führer's decisions seemed sometimes to be at odds with reality. Better he should stay at the Wolfsschanze; better still, he should visit his troops and bases in the field and learn about the war firsthand.

For now, Adolf Hitler was acting the gracious host. He rose and shook hands courteously with his famous woman test pilot. If all of his generals and his Luftwaffe commanders were as brave as she, he reflected, the war would be won.

As he presented her with a certificate to confirm her award of the Iron Cross, First Class, he told her so.

"Thank you, mein Führer," she said, inclining her head in a small bow. "Make I take up another matter with you?"

He waved her to an armchair and they sat silently for a moment as a servant brought a tea tray and sweet cakes. She suppressed a smile. It was well-known that Adolf Hitler loved sweet cakes. He had them morning and night; he must, she thought, ingest a good deal of sugar in the course of a day.

"What would you like to talk about, Hanna?" he asked.

"Mein Führer," she said, "I have been talking with many of my friends—my former colleagues in the flying club, the glider pilots, Luftwaffe pilots, some of our technicians in aeronautical research— and I've found we are in agreement on a concept I wish to propose to you."

"I'm always interested in your views," Hitler said. "You've earned the right to my attention."

"Mein Führer, the air war is not going well. Every day that passes brings a further drain on our resources. Our towns and cities are crumpling under the Allied air attacks, our transport system and production centers are being systematically destroyed."

Hitler's voice acquired an edge. "I don't believe that things are quite as serious as all that, Hanna. What is your point?"

"I believe that the war must be brought to an early end through a negotiated peace, mein Führer. But to prepare the ground for negotiation, it is necessary to considerably weaken the enemy's strength."

Hitler hesitated. "I agree with your comments. I would like to see the war end tomorrow, and it's well-known that I've always been willing to negotiate. I made such an offer to England after Dunkirk, but the drunkard Churchill refused to accept it. I agree, too, that we must weaken the enemy. What do you propose?"

"Mein Führer, given present conditions, I believe it can only be done from the air. We must deliver a series of suitable projectiles into the center of key targets, striking generating stations, waterworks, air bases, key production centers—and, in the event of an Allied invasion—at naval and merchant shipping. At present, we cannot penetrate to such targets with guaranteed accuracy."

The Supreme Commander raised his eyebrows and tapped two fingers against his uniformed thigh. Seeing these early signs of impatience, she hastened to get to the point.

"Mein Führer, as you know, some of our Focke-Wulf and Messerschmitt pilots are ramming the American bombers in their aerial encounters. We also have one-man torpedoes and frog-men in our naval forces. These are unselfish sacrifices, made individually and in random fashion."

She took a deep breath. "What I propose, what many of us are willing to embrace, is formation of an elite group composed of men who are ready to sacrifice themselves in the conviction that only by this means can we save our country."

"I have often called upon our soldiers to sacrifice themselves," Hitler said, frowning. "In what way would this be different?"

Hanna Reitsch pulled a piece of paper from the pocket of her uniform and handed it to him. On it was typed two sentences:

> I hereby voluntarily apply to be enrolled in the suicide group as pilot of a human glider bomb. I fully understand that employment in this capacity will entail my own death.

"We ask your permission to begin experimental work on this project," she said. "It's possible we could use the jet-powered ME-328 that's being developed at present. Or, better, we might use a piloted version of the jet-propelled V-1 flying bomb. This would achieve an accuracy and therefore a striking power that would be impossible under any other circumstances."

"A suicide group?" Hitler asked incredulously. "Have you talked to any of my staff about this?"

"I've talked to the deputy Luftwaffe chief, Field Marshal Milch," she said.

"What did he say?"

"He said that such an idea is contrary to German mentality."

"He was right." Hitler pondered. "Also, public opinion must be considered. Of course, sacrificing onself for the future of the Reich is justifiable and admirable. As you said, such sacrifices occur every day on an individual basis and sometimes at the company or squadron level. But to formalize it this way—that's a different matter."

He shook his head. "If and when such an action becomes necessary I reserve that decision to myself."

"Of course, mein Führer," Hanna Reitsch said, falling back to her second line of attack. "But if and when you make such a decision, the suicide attacks should be ready to begin at once. Therefore, what I ask at this time is your permission to begin our experimental work with the right aircraft and to proceed with recruitment and training."

Hitler looked at the five-foot-tall pilot for a moment and grunted in exasperation. "All right, Hanna, all right. Go ahead, then. Just don't worry me further about this while you're developing this program."

A broad smile crossed her heart-shaped face. "Thank you, mein Führer."

Eaker was right. The protests over the heavy losses at Schweinfurt forced the Eighth to fly shorter, easier missions over the next few weeks. The 205th bomb group made a successful attack on a Focke-Wulf workshop at Villacoublay and, a few weeks later, on German air bases at Amiens and Romilly-sur-Seine.

In September, the Eighth regained its boldness and struck Stuttgart with 262 airplanes, losing 45. Then, to dramatize the value of fighter support, 195 bombers, accompanied by a fighter escort, hit aircraft plants in Belgium and Holland the following day. Not one bomber was lost.

Wing and group commanders were anxiously awaiting the arrival of the new B-17G models with the chin turrets and staggered waist gun positions. And they yearned for the long-range P-51 escorts they had been promised.

But they couldn't simply sit on their hands and wait. It was time for the Eighth to stick its neck out again.

By now, Buddy had acquired a crew from a wounded pilot and was flying his own plane. He had had the name *Carolina Baby* painted on the side of the nose; beside the name was a painting of a shapely, scantily-clad girl.

Mike picked up a replacement radio operator named Michaels; Jack Gillen was his regular co-pilot again. He had learned how to smother his fear on the missions. There was always the moment of animal panic when heavy flak burst around him or a German fighter bored in and fired at the windscreen at close range.

But he had developed a technique of "pressing down" on his fear, as he explained to Buddy. The only aftereffects of the missions were headaches, sometimes severe, that came on when he was safely home and had showered and changed.

Wartime life had almost become routine. He had installed a paper lamp at the head of his bunk in a corner of the barracks. He had his own battered bureau for his clothes. In the top drawer he kept fresh eggs that he bought from a nearby farmer.

The transatlantic mail delivery had improved. His mother wrote him regularly and he faithfully responded, though he had to struggle to find something to say beyond the statement that he was well and comfortable and hoped she was the same and that she had an ample supply of students.

One day, to his surprise, a letter came from Claire. It was heavily censored but he welcomed it nevertheless.

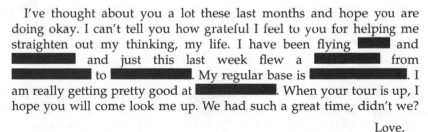

Dear Michael,

   I've thought about you a lot these last months and hope you are doing okay. I can't tell you how grateful I feel to you for helping me straighten out my thinking, my life. I have been flying ▆▆▆▆ and ▆▆▆▆▆▆▆ and just this last week flew a ▆▆▆▆▆▆ from ▆▆▆▆▆▆ to ▆▆▆▆▆▆▆. My regular base is ▆▆▆▆▆▆. I am really getting pretty good at ▆▆▆▆▆▆. When your tour is up, I hope you will come look me up. We had such a great time, didn't we?

                                                          Love,
                                                          Claire

By October, Mike had flown seventeen missions and, halfway through his tour of duty, was beginning to think about what he'd do when he returned to the States. Unless, of course, he volunteered for special duty with the weather force to enjoy the fun of flying speedy airplanes again.

That speculation ended on October 9. When the operations officer drew back the curtain in the briefing room at 2:30 A.M., the crewmen gasped in dismay and wonderment. The red yarn stretched farther than it ever had before, all the way up across the North Sea and the Baltic—even past Germany, it appeared.

Sitting at the end of the second row of seats, Mike and Buddy looked at each other in surprise. "Lord and Aunt Lucy," Buddy exclaimed. "Wherever are we goin'?"

Colonel Robinson strode to the center of the stage and told them. "It's called Gdynia," he said. "The Gulf of Danzig. It's in Poland. Yes, gentlemen, Poland. The target is the port of Gdynia itself, the docks, the naval ships that operate out of there, and the submarine pens. It's the longest raid that the Eighth has undertaken to date. So it's a historic mission for us.

"We've had some short milk-runs lately but this will show the Nazis that we're back in business. The Russians, too. G-2 says the Russians have pushed within a few hundred miles east of there.

"Basically, we take the yellow brick road to Kiel, as we've done before," he continued, tapping the map with a pointer. "We cross the North Sea and Frisian Islands and the Schleswig-Holstein peninsula here, except we swing north of Kiel and into the Baltic to the Gulf of Danzig and the target. The trip's mostly over water.

"But the water's cold this time of year, so stay out of it. Sweden's back over your left shoulder if you want to be interned for the duration and miss all the fun. The Russian lines, as I said, are straight ahead and a little farther.

"But we need these airplanes, gentlemen, so hit the target, defend yourselves from the fighters, and come back. And if I've left anything out, you may . . ." The rest of Robinson's standard closing line was lost in groans and jeers.

In his cramped office after the briefing, Robinson talked to his adjutant, Major Ed Carlino. "The Germans have taken a page right out of Napoleon's tactics at Waterloo," he said. "If you remember your history, Ed . . ."

"I don't," Carlino said, "but I'll play straight man. I always do. What did Napoleon do?"

"He sent his cavalry against the British infantry to make them form up into their famous squares," Robinson said. "Cavalry couldn't penetrate the British square and the cavalrymen would get cut down by the British rifles if they persisted. So they didn't. But the cavalry hung around to keep the British in their tightly-packed squares.

"Then Napoleon ordered his artillery to fire on the squares. Imagine what those cannon balls did to the troops standing shoulder to shoulder, several ranks deep. But if they deployed out of those squares to avoid the artillery, the cavalry would attack the lines of infantrymen and cut them down."

"Very clever. What's the parallel?"

"The parallel is that the fighters are attacking us to make us close into the tightest possible formations. Then the rocket carriers, the ME-110s, line up and shoot rockets into the formation. When we're tightly packed into our box formation, one well-placed rocket can bring down two or three of our planes."

"What's the solution?"

"The real solution is to get long-range fighter support to knock out the ME-110s and keep the fighters off our backs. Until then, the best thing I can think of is to stay in tight formation—we can't survive without it—keep a close eye on the ME-110s, and, when they line up to fire the rockets, drift the formation to the right or left to spoil their aim and make them miss."

Robinson expelled a long sigh. "It's not anything sensational, but it's all there is right now."

"Yeah, but don't forget one thing, Colonel," Carlino said.

"What's that?"

"Napoleon lost at Waterloo. It was Wellington who won."

"Good thought. Maybe you should call me Duke from now on."

"Happy to, your Highness."

Takeoff was routine except for the moment that could never be routine. It was a gray morning; a heavy cloudbank hung over the field and extended all the way up to ten thousand feet. The trip up through the clouds was, as usual, wet and dark, like riding up a bumpy mountainside in a truck in the middle of the night. The B-17 bounced and jolted in the turbulence and water spattered over the windscreen.

The four 1,200-horsepower engines drank the moisture without concern. Near ten thousand feet, the dark clouds began to boil and streaks of purple and red appeared. And then the B-17 exploded silently into the brilliant upper world like a huge marine creature rising from the sea. Water dripped from the airplane, the drops sparkling in the sunlight. Mike and Jack put on their sunglasses and, as pilots always did at that moment, unconsciously smiled at each other.

Below them stretched an infinite ocean of billowing white. Above, the azure blue of the sky was etched with traces of cirrus formed by ice crystals. The spectacle dwarfed in its magnificence anything that men could see on the ground. And center stage was held by the huge, blazing sun that beckoned them eastward.

The clouds below them broke as they passed over the Frisian Islands. Flak bursts began probing for the formation as they moved over Schleswig-Holstein and became steadily thicker. And then the fighters came, line abreast, wave after wave, attacking head-on. As the first wave screamed through the formation, cannons firing, Mike and Jack ducked involuntarily and the nose guns of the bombers chattered, shaking the ship. An instant later, the tail gun fired at the fading fighters.

And then there was bedlam. Gunners began crying out, reporting bogies coming from all directions—four o'clock, nine o'clock, six o'clock. The chatter and curses saturated the interphones as well as the bomber channel. Dark blotches filled the sky as bombers and fighters caught fire or exploded, leaving long trails of black smoke hanging in the air.

Aboard the lead ship, Robinson struggled to maintain order.

"Leader to group. Get off the air. Maintain radio silence. And stay in formation. Close up. Low group, close up."

In his airplane, flying the deputy position on the low group leader, Mike pressed his throat mike to his larynx and yelled angrily, "Pilot to crew. Shut up! Just shut up, damnit! No point calling in to report fighters if they're coming from everydamnwhere. If you need to call in, somebody's hurt, keep it short. And keep your gun bursts short, goddamnit. You're wasting ammunition!"

Mike realized his anger was a defense against the fear that threatened to envelop him. But it worked, and the things had to be said even if they were overstated.

Tracers drifted lazily past the cockpit like big red globules. They would seem pretty, Mike thought, if you didn't know what they were —and if four invisible and deadly pieces of lead weren't hiding between each two you saw.

"Right waist to pilot."

"Pilot."

"ME-110s lining up at three o'clock. They'll have rockets."

"Pilot, roger."

The lead squadron began drifting to the left and the low squadron banked to follow it. The action was perfectly timed; the first salvo of rockets exploded well to starboard. Now the bomber group swung back on course. Another flight of ME-110s jockeyed into position to fire and again the B-17s drifted leftwards to spoil the attackers' aim.

This time two rockets exploded within the group. One B-17 blew up in a huge explosion of black and red and two others staggered away, one catching fire and spiraling downward. The third struggled to stay in formation, though one engine began windmilling and gaping holes appeared in the fuselage.

The third time the ME-110s prepared to fire, Robinson drifted the group to the right. The rockets exploded ahead of them.

"Turning on the IP," McCabe said. "Bomb bay doors coming open." There was the familiar drag, the swirl of cold air. Flak bursts shook the plane.

"Bombs away!"

The group turned right off the target and nosed down to pick up speed. The airplane became light in Mike's hands. "Thank God!" he said to himself.

There was a huge crashing sound and a blinding light. He tried to say something but the words wouldn't come. It was dark for a minute and then he realized he was arguing with his father and he didn't like it, so with an effort of will he thought of his mother. He was standing by the piano, singing while she played. It was one of those nice summer afternoons.

What was the name of the song? Oh yes, it was that pretty thing by Rachmaninoff, "In the Silence of the Night." That was the English name of it, anyway. He didn't know what the Russian was. It was a hard bitch to sing; the tessitura was high and there was that big *F* sharp.

His mother said: "Drop your jaw on that high note, Mike, don't raise your head. Remember what we talked about: you don't think 'up' to reach a high note, you think 'down.' And the *F* is on the word 'song'; sing it as an *ah*. Think *ah*. Keep the vowel open. Now do it again. From the beginning of the measure."

It went very well that second time; he hit the *F* sharp on the nose and held it and the sound rang through the room. He loved that ringing sound when he could produce it, the ringing overtones that the Italians called *squillo*.

The singing lessons were hard work but they were so peaceful and satisfying. Maybe it was the deep breathing, all the oxygen you took in, but afterward there was that special feeling of well-being, almost a high, as if you'd taken a drug or drunk something that produced a feeling of euphoria.

Except for people who kept shaking you and trying to interrupt. Angrily, he swung his arm to keep them away, but they kept talking and bothering him.

"Mike! Mike Gavin! Lieutenant! Wake up! Please wake up! We need you!"

He opened his eyes reluctantly. His vision was slightly blurred, he had a terrible headache, and his ears were ringing. His stomach contracted. He was in the cockpit of the B-17 and Zapp, Zapp the navigator, was sitting in the co-pilot's seat. He had his right hand on the control column and he was peering sideways and shaking Mike's shoulder with his left. He wasn't wearing an oxygen mask.

A moment of panic washed over Mike and he struggled to speak. "What? What's going on? How'd you get here?"

"You were out cold," Zapp yelled. "Concussion. Cannon shell exploded. Wrecked damn near everything."

"Where's Gillen?"

"We dropped him out."

"You *what?*"

"Had to," Zapp gasped. "He was hit bad. Couldn't stop the bleeding. He was conscious. Latched on his chest chute, put the ring in his hand, told him to count five and pull it. He said okay. So we dropped him out the hatch. His only chance—to get medical attention down there. He'd bleed to death here."

"Oh God," Mike said. "What else?"

"Look."

Mike pulled himself up in his seat and flinched in horror. Both port engines were dead. Either Gillen or Zapp had feathered the props. The cowlings were black and oil was smeared over the wing. There was a large hole in the left wing. Zapp or Gillen had trimmed the airplane hard to the right to keep it from drifting out of control to the left. The B-17 crabbed through the air at an awkward sidewise angle.

Mike looked at the instrument panel. Most of the engine and flight instruments had been smashed. He looked outside. The sun was still ahead of them, though higher. And it had moved slightly to the right. He estimated they were flying on a course of fifty or sixty degrees. They plunged through a cloudbank and out into the open again. The ground was much closer; he judged they had descended from their bombing altitude of twenty-seven thousand feet all the way down to eight or nine thousand. He pulled off his oxygen mask.

"I crawled up here after we got hit; neither of you answered,"

Zapp said. "Gillen managed to trim things up though he was bleeding bad. I would've turned left to Sweden except I knew better than to turn into the dead engines—I washed out of pilot training, you know, but I did remember that. And there was a lot of fighter activity over the Baltic."

"Good job, Zapp, holding on like this. But you could've turned right, all the way around."

"Couldn't. Right aileron's jammed. We had multiple hits."

"Did you try to skid it with the rudder?"

"No."

"Any idea where we are?"

"We're well east of Gydnia, couple hundred miles east anyway. We've been going downhill. You were out quite a while and I lost track."

Mike looked down. There were flashes of fire and billows of smoke on the ground up ahead. They stretched across a long, irregular line. Ground fighting. He looked at Zapp's anxious face. He was waiting for a decision. *Concentrate*, he told himself. *Do something*. But what?

Try to skid around one hundred and eighty degrees and get to Sweden and be interned? It would be too risky now to turn back over water, even if he could. And the thought of internment was repulsive. Try to get back to England? Impossible; even if they could traverse that long distance without being pounced on by fighters, their fuel would run out long before they reached the Channel. Two overheated engines burned a lot more gas than four working ones.

Go as far as possible and, when the time came, put the wheels down, land and become a German prisoner? *No*. Then *what?* Try to make the Russian lines and be repatriated, somehow, to England so they could return to the 205th?

Zapp yelled suddenly and pointed to the left. Two long-nosed fighters with stars on the side flashed by. "What was that? They had a star on the side. The RAF planes have stars on the side."

"There're no British planes out here," Mike said. "And they didn't really look like Spitfires." The fighters flashed by again. The stars were red. *Russian fighters*, he marveled. He had never expected to see one.

They were looking him over. One of the fighters slowed and crept up on the left. He could clearly see the pilot surveying the damage to the bomber and shaking his head. The pilot looked over and pointed straight ahead. Mike spread his hands helplessly in answer. The pilot's finger jabbed ahead vigorously and he sped ahead, apparently to lead them.

The inside starboard engine quit with an audible bang and flames began flickering from the cowling. Mike swore, reached to the feathering buttons and hit the third from the left. Nothing happened. He hit the fire extinguisher. Nothing happened. *Does anything still work on this wreck?* The flames expanded and began licking over the wing. An explosion was imminent. The B-17 sagged and began losing altitude.

Mike hit the alarm bell and shouted through the interphone.

"Fire aboard! Bail out! Bail out now!" It wouldn't matter now which side of the battle line they came down on. Right now it was life or death.

"Should I stay with you?" Zapp yelled.

"No, get out! Quick!"

The crewmen began tumbling out of the B-17 and chutes blossomed below. Zapp climbed out of the co-pilot's seat and slid through the entrance to the nose. In a matter of seconds, he was gone, too.

"Is anybody still aboard?" Mike yelled. There was no reply, only the rasping of the one remaining engine. A plume of flame burst from the starboard engine and streamed back alongside the fuselage. The B-17 was in a shallow dive. It was time to go.

Mike pulled his chute from beneath the seat, snapped the clips on the rings of his chest harness, and slid into the nose as fast as he could. The B-17 began to wander off to the left and turn. In a second it would start spinning. No time to think or get scared.

He threw his left arm over his face, jumped from the hatch, counted a long five, and pulled the ring. There was an instant of panic when nothing happened and then the chute opened, snapping him brutally backward and bashing his arm into his nose. It began bleeding.

There was a loud explosion above him and the B-17, flaming, broke into a dozen pieces. Mike ducked his head and said a quick prayer that a flaming piece wouldn't hit him or set his chute afire. Thankfully, the burning debris fell past him.

The sound of gunfire made him aware that the ground was coming closer and he realized that he was being blown sideways. Looking down, he saw blotches of red, puffs of smoke, and what appeared to be zig-zag lines of trenches.

The battle line seemed directly below him. He looked up at the sun to orient himself and pulled on the shrouds, partially collapsing one side of his chute to pull him eastward. In a moment, he was skidding over a stand of trees. A heavily-trampled cornfield lay ahead. In the distance was a small village.

Men were crawling through the cornfield, he saw, as the ground came up. He landed heavily on his back and shoulders and the chute billowed over his face. Quickly, he unsnapped the harness and fought free. An unshaven soldier in a baggy brown uniform was standing over him with a cocked rifle.

"*Nymets!*" the soldier snarled, bringing his rifle to his shoulder.

"No!" Mike shouted, knowing he was being called something undesirable. "American! *Amerikanski!*" He didn't know whether the word was properly said but it sounded Russian enough. The man hesitated, lowered the rifle slightly, and appeared trying to think what to do.

"*Amerikanski!*" Mike repeated, rising to his knees. The rifle came up again and Mike sank back down. "Look!" Mike called, pointing to the inside pocket of his jacket. Carefully, he reached inside and pulled out his red escape packet. By now a second soldier had arrived and was looking at him with intense interest.

The first soldier extended a hand for the escape kit, lowered the rifle, opened it, and tried to read one of the silk maps. Then, with the second soldier covering Mike, the first one dropped the kit and started thumbing through the multilingual phrase book. He shrugged his shoulders and spoke rapidly in Russian to the second man.

They engaged in heated conversation for a moment, pointing occasionally to Mike, until a third man—a sergeant, judging from the stripes on his sleeve—swaggered authoritatively forward, took in the scene, grabbed the escape kit and phrase book, scrutinized them quickly, and stared at the American on the ground.

Then, wheeling, he barked orders harshly to the two privates, who hastily retreated. The sergeant thought for a moment, unslung his rifle from his shoulder, and barked at Mike, motioning for him to get up. When Mike rose, the Russian bobbed the muzzle upward to tell Mike to raise his hands.

"*Amerikanski!*" Mike offered. The Russian shook his head, shoved Mike by one shoulder to turn him around, and jabbed the gun in his back to get him moving. Within a few minutes, Mike found himself shoved into the back of a truck with a canvas top. It was a Chevrolet, Mike noted with surprise.

It had become dark. There were three soldiers in the truck. One, apparently, had been wounded. He had his arm in a sling and groaned intermittently. One man held an automatic weapon pointed at Mike. The truck bounced and jounced over uneven dirt roads for what seemed like hours.

Mike's head ached horribly but he finally fell asleep. He woke once when a hard bounce threw him to the floor. Since there was plenty of room and the man with the gun didn't voice an objection, Mike stretched out on the long seat that ran along one side of the frame, hooked an arm over a support, and fell into an exhausted sleep.

Someone poked him hard in the back and he awoke to daylight and a gray landscape. It was cold and he shivered. His head still ached but his vision had cleared. They were parked in front of a small building. It looked like it might have been a village hall or a school-house. He was pushed inside and the man with the gun pointed to a bench and motioned for him to sit.

A soldier, apparently an orderly, entered the room and handed the man with the gun a tin cup of tea, a thick slice of black bread, and a long piece of sausage. Mike looked inquiringly at him and the man with the gun spoke to the orderly in Russian.

A moment later, the orderly returned with tea, bread, and sausage for Mike. The man with the gun nodded and motioned for him to eat. *"Khleb,"* he said, pointing to the bread.

"Khleb," Mike repeated.

"Da," the Russian said, and took a bite. Then he pointed to the sausage. *"Kolbasa."* And to the tin cup of tea. *"Chay."*

"Kolbasa," said Mike, finding the words familiar. *"Chay."* His grandfather had used them years ago, he remembered.

"Da, da," the soldier said, obviously pleased with his tutorial. Mike found that he was ravenously hungry. He devoured the sausage and bread quickly and closed his eyes blissfully as the sugared tea warmed his stomach.

Eying him with amusement, the soldier, having finished his food and tea, detached a canteen from his belt and took a swig. *"Voda,"* he said.

"Vodka?" Mike asked disbelievingly.

"Nyet, nyet," the man laughed, shaking his head. *"Voda, voda."*

"Water," Mike said. The soldier smiled. Mike remembered that he had a flattened pack of Camels in the inside pocket of his jacket. The sergeant who had searched him had missed it. "Cigarette?" he asked.

The Russian frowned and cocked his head. Mike motioned to his pocket and, while the man watched him suspiciously, pulled out the pack. He tore it open, pulled two cigarettes halfway out, and leaned forward. "Cigarette?" he asked.

The Russian's eyes widened. *"Tabachok,"* he breathed in wonderment. Quickly, he took the two protruding cigarettes and looked longingly at the pack. Mike shook out another half dozen cigarettes and handed them to him.

The soldier nodded gratefully and carefully placed all but one of the cigarettes in an inside pocket. He looked at Mike inquiringly. *Why aren't you having one?* Understanding, Mike pulled a cigarette from the pack and placed it between his lips.

The Russian found a match and leaned forward to light Mike's cigarette. Then he lit his own, puffed contentedly, and closed his eyes. Mike noted that he held the cigarette between his thumb and index finger.

A door opened and a voice barked. The soldier opened his eyes, leapt to his feet, and motioned to Mike to stand up. A tall Russian, obviously an officer, made a summoning motion with his hand and said in excellent English: "Come in."

Mike entered the room. At one end was a battered desk. There was one chair in front of it. Sunlight filtered through the dirty window behind the man sitting at the desk. He was short, bald, and bull-necked. His uniform had shoulder boards with a badge of rank on them. At a guess, Mike took him for a major or colonel.

The tall officer moved to the side of the desk. Mike noticed that the man's tunic fit better than anyone else's he had seen. There was a definite elegance about the officer's carriage and manner and he was movie-star handsome with his black hair, black eyes, and mustache. Something like—what was his name, that old silent star?—Jack Gilbert. Or maybe Gilbert Roland.

"I am Captain Viktor Markov of the VVS, the Soviet Air Force," the man said. "And this is Colonel Rakov of the Fourth Guards Tank Army. We wish to ask you some questions. What is your name and nationality, the name of your air group and division, and how did you arrive where you did?"

Standing before them, Mike cleared his throat. "I am Lieutenant Michael Gavin, serial number 0-812813. I am an American."

Markov translated quickly for the colonel, who nodded and kept staring at the American. "The name of your group, also the type of aircraft you flew," Markov demanded.

Mike began to answer and then paused, thinking.

"Why do you hesitate?" Markov asked suspiciously.

"We are instructed, if we are taken prisoner, to give only our name, rank, and serial number."

Markov translated for the colonel and looked up again. "You refer, of course, to being taken prisoner by the enemy. But we are not your enemy. If you are really an American, the Soviet Union is your ally. You are actively supporting us at this time with American equipment —tanks, Aircobras—you call them P-39s—trucks and medical supplies. So that restriction should not apply in this case."

Mike pondered. "Well, that's true," he said at length. "All right. I'm a member of the 205th Bomb Group in the First Division of the Eighth Air Force. We are stationed in England, in the Midlands. I am a first pilot, or was, on a B-17."

There was another exchange in Russian. "The Flying Fortress, I believe you call it," Markov said. "Describe it, please. In some detail."

Mike shrugged. "A four-engine bomber, four 1,200-horsepower Wright Cyclone engines, General Electric turbo-superchargers, a crew of nine, thirteen 50-caliber machine guns, a bomb load capacity that usually ranges from 6,000 to 8,000 pounds, depending on the type of bomb. We operate normally at 25,000 to 28,000 feet. In box formations."

The description evidently produced intense interest on the part of the Russians, particularly for Markov. In answer to subsequent questions, Mike described the Gdynia mission, the heavy damage to the bomber, and his bail-out into the Russian lines.

Markov considered the answers for a moment. "The colonel is not fully convinced that you are who and what you say you are. You could as easily be a German—you would call it a 'plant'—sent to spy on us. He directs me to ask you further questions stemming from my knowledge of your country. For example: what is the name of the professional baseball team of New York City? Where do oranges come from in America? Who was your, ah, third President of the United States?"

"The Yankees, California and Florida, and Thomas Jefferson," Mike answered promptly.

"Very well," Markov said. "Then tell me: who is the leading U.S. female you call a pin-up girl? Who is your leading heavyweight boxer?"

"Betty Grable and Joe Louis."

"Very well. If you were a German you would, of course, know about the two matches that your Joe Louis had with Max Schmeling. But who was the very clever boxer who very nearly knocked Louis out but was himself knocked out, ah, near the end of the match?"

"Billy Conn," Mike said. "It was the thirteenth round. Conn was ahead on points and got too cocky. Louis hit him with his Sunday punch and that was all."

Markov smiled. "His Sunday punch. Yes." The Russian talked animatedly to the colonel who shrugged and held up a finger. Markov turned back to Mike. "The colonel is still not fully convinced. He says every military service has an official song. What is the name of yours? He wants you to sing a few lines."

"Now?"

"Now."

Mike cleared his throat. "It's called 'Wild Blue Yonder.' I think I can remember the words, I hope." He took a deep breath and began to sing:

> Off we go, into the wild blue yonder
> Climbing high into the sun,
> Here they come, zooming to meet our thunder
> At 'em boys, give her the gun . . .

The colonel waved his hands for silence and waited till Markov translated. The he rolled his eyes and stuck out his lower lip.

"The colonel says the words are silly," Markov said, smiling slightly.

"Everyone's entitled to his opinion."

"Really?" Markov said, his smile growing wider. "How . . . *American* of you to say that." He turned to the colonel and then back again. "The colonel would like you to sing part of a marching song. You must have a marching song."

Mike shrugged. "Our marching songs were in the cadets. They were mainly informal. We made them up to keep cadence. I'll sing you a bit of one."

"If you please."

Mike took a deep breath, began marching in place, and sang an anthem-like marching ditty that was popular when he was a flying cadet:

> My eyes are dim, I cannot see
> I have not brought my specs with me
> I have . . . not . . . brought my specs with me.

Mike launched into a second verse as the colonel's face crinkled in puzzlement. Markov, now grinning broadly, translated. "He says the song makes no sense. What does it refer to?"

"The song refers to the Quartermaster Corps. The department that issues our supplies and equipment—or is supposed to."

The colonel listened to the explanation, frowning. Abruptly, his face cleared and he began to laugh and pound the desk. He leaned back, laughing heartily and turning red. Finally, he finished, smiled broadly for the first time, displaying a glittering steel tooth, and spoke.

"The colonel says he believes you now," Markov said. "He says no German could possibly make up such a song." Markov paused. "I don't think a Russian would, either. He also says that, from what the words say, every army must be the same."

Markov's smile faded. "Now we must decide what to do with you."

"Repatriate me, send me back to my bomb group."

Markov smiled faintly and shook his head. "Not possible at this time. As you've seen, our resources are strained. Our roads are not what they should be; our communications are, ah, incomplete. As you would say, there's a war on."

The colonel, Mike noticed, was leaning forward now and staring intently at his face. Markov spoke to him briefly and turned back. "The colonel has one more question. What is your extraction? We know that all Americans come from some other country, or their fathers or grandfathers did. The colonel is interested in knowing."

"I had a Russian grandfather, as a matter of fact. His name was Gavronov. Gregor Petrovich Gavronov."

Markov's eyes widened in surprise. When he translated, the colonel banged the flat of his hand on the desk.

"He said he knew from your face that you were Russian. What is your patronymic?"

"My patronymic. My father's first name was Stephen. Stepan. Mine, as I said, is Michael. Mikhail."

"So," Markov said, turning to the colonel and pointing to Mike. "Mikhail Stepanovich Gavronov." The colonel nodded vigorously. *"Da! Da!"* he said.

"Well," Markov said. "This changes things a bit. You are an American of Russian descent. An experienced pilot. We have, you know, foreign pilots here as volunteers. There is a French air regiment; its name is Normandy-Neiman. They fly our fighters. Also the First Warsaw Air Regiment, a Polish group. But they are, as you might say, closed corporations—for their own nationals only. And, after all, you have Russian blood. Perhaps you could come with me."

Markov turned back to the colonel and spoke briefly. The colonel nodded, made a shooing motion with one hand, and bent over the papers on his desk. "He says he has work to do and we should leave now. You can come with me, he says, if I assume full responsibility. Are you worthy of that trust?"

Mike stared at the taller man. "Yes, I am. But I'd like to know where we're going—and where we are, for that matter."

"We're in a village named Veliklye Luki. Don't try to pronounce it. It happens to be the westernmost point of our counter-offensive at this time. We'll be going south. Into the Smolensk region. By the Dnieper River; that's the general battle line all the way up and down the front."

On the way south in the back of a truck with other soldiers, Markov said: "Would you like to fly with us?"

"Until I can be repatriated, why not?"

"Why not. The question is: what kind of aircraft? You are accustomed to flying heavy bombers."

"I can fly anything," Mike said. "Not long ago, I was flying our newest fighter, a prototype. It's the new P-51C Mustang. We'll be getting it soon to escort our bombers—all the way in and out. It'll make a helluva difference."

Markov's eyebrows rose sharply. "The Mustang? Surely you joke." He looked skeptical. "Tell me, please, the specifications and performance of the airplane. Also, the starting procedure. And how it handles."

Mike described the Mustang in detail. By the time he finished, Markov was clearly impressed. "Well then, we shall see. At this time we have what you might call a mixed air regiment; actually, it's part, or parts, of three air regiments. We have had some losses. One is the night bomber regiment. One is the Yak fighter regiment, my own. The third flies Shturmoviks, our ground-attack aircraft. We should be able to find a spot for you in one of the three aircraft."

"All right," Mike said. "Except I hate night flying, always have. Now I have a question of my own, Captain. How come you speak such good English? It's not even British English. It's real American English. If I didn't know better, I'd think you were an American from —well, I don't know where—you don't even have a regional accent."

Markov smiled. "Thank you. The answer is simple. In 1933, Comrade Stalin decided to renew relations with the Western nations. Germany was already becoming a threat to peace."

"So he put world revolution on hold for a while, is that it?"

Markov's face acquired a pained expression and he looked at the others in the truck before answering. "The words are your own and I would advise . . . At any rate, my father became part of the Soviet diplomatic service. He became second secretary for our new Washington embassy. I was a teenage lad in your nation's capital city; our instruction at that time was to mingle with . . ."

"The natives?"

"In a manner of speaking. At any rate, I picked up English rather quickly. That, of course, was how I happened to be here. My superiors detached me from flight duty when a translator was needed to interrogate the foreign flier who claimed to be an American."

"So how did you become a pilot?"

"It's obvious you're an American, Lieutenant. No Russian would ask so many personal questions. But all right. After two years of duty in America, my father was recalled. I went to university for a time. But then, well, there were *questions* concerning one of the diplomatic officers who had been abroad. It became, um, *appropriate* to, I should say, demonstrate that two years out of Mother Russia hadn't . . ."

"Corrupted you?"

"*Changed* us. So I applied to the Military Theoretical School for Pilots in Moscow. I was accepted for training, and here I am."

At the 205th base at Whitwick Green, thousands of miles to the west, Lieutenant Buddy Bryce paced the perimeter of the airfield in a damp, chilling wind.

Five new B-17Gs—complete with remotely-controlled Bendix chin gun turrets; staggered, enclosed waist gun positions; and a new tail gun with a reflector sight and wider range of fire—had been delivered to the base that day. Operations had assigned one of the new models to Buddy, partly as a reward for his crew having shot down two Focke-Wulfs on the Gdynia mission.

But none if it mattered right now. Where was Mike? *Where in hell are you, damnit?"* he yelled into the wind. His ship hadn't blown up or anything, so far as anyone knew. A couple of gunners said during the post-mission interrogation that they had seen his B-17 get hit and slide out of the formation. Nothing more.

Buddy felt a gnawing anxiety. It was like a rat in his stomach. He had never lost a friend, a real friend, before. Mike couldn't have gotten himself killed, could he? Not Mike-boy. Buddy wasn't so sure about his own survival. But Mike? Buddy always thought Mike would live forever.

CHAPTER NINE

THE NIGHT-WITCH

THEY WERE WALKING along a path through a wooded area when Viktor Markov slowed his pace and frowned. "It occurs to me, I may have missed the obvious. I was concentrating on whether you could be a German agent. It never occurred to me, with your face and background, that you could really be a Russian, someone . . .

"Sent to spy on you? Inform on you?"

A look of irritation crossed Markov's face. He started to say something, but stopped.

"If that were the case, it's too late to do anything about it, isn't it?" Mike said, grinning. "I'd have written you up; you'd be a marked man by now. So why worry?"

"Why worry," Markov said drily. He smiled faintly. "No," he said at length, "either you're a complete innocent, the kind of young American I remember, or you're a consummate actor and a very clever man."

"I'm not *that* clever," Mike said.

Markov smiled. "I don't think you are; no disrespect. With your innocence, your openness and, um, impertinence you could only be what you say you are."

When they arrived the previous evening, Markov took Mike to an old, weatherbeaten house, once the dacha of a minor party official, now the barracks of the Yak regiment. It was made of wood planks— Viktor said all dachas were supposed to be made of wood—and it had intricately carved window frames that had been painted white. The house lay within a stand of white-barked birch trees that gave it natural concealment.

In the barracks, Markov scrounged a uniform, toothbrush, and razor for the American and took him to a nearby bath house where an orderly handed him soap, threw buckets of warm water over him, and gave him a rough towel to dry himself with. Afterward, Markov presented him with a new pair of long johns which, Mike noted with surprise, tied at the wrists and ankles.

Mike winced at the appearance of the Russian uniform. It was so foreign—baggy brown trousers, a shapeless tunic that buttoned down the front and had officer's shoulder boards, cheap-feeling black leather boots, a soft cap. Should he be wearing another country's uniform at all, even for a short time? He stowed his own clothes under his bunk; later, if he flew, he'd at least wear his own coveralls and heavy jacket.

"I don't know whether I really should be wearing your uniform," Mike said. "Even if I should, does it have to be so baggy-looking?"

"That depends on how much charm you can exert on our female comrades," Markov said, smiling. "They have a sharp eye for fashion and some of them are fine seamstresses. They embroider flowers and other designs on their collars and caps and take in their uniforms. Perhaps one will take pity on you."

"I notice your uniform fits very well," Mike observed.

"As I said, one needs to exert some charm."

When he had dressed, they ate bowls of thick cabbage soup with steamed potatoes and slabs of black bread and drank the ubiquitous tea. Before showing Mike to an extra bunk that had been set up in Markov's tiny room, the Russian pulled a vodka bottle from the chest in which he kept his clothes, produced two small glasses, and offered a toast to their meeting.

The Russian laughed when Mike choked on the fiery liquid. "Now I'm fully convinced," he said. "No Russian would choke on vodka. He'd only ask for more."

In the morning, they walked through the woods to an adjoining airfield. Mike marveled at the way the Russians had strung camouflage nets over buildings and any airplanes parked in the open. Most planes, he saw, were either hidden beneath trees or in revetments concealed by the netting. There was nothing whatever like that on the bomber bases in England.

"I'm taking you to the night-bomber field," Markov said. "I think we should start there. Are you up to flying this morning?"

"Sure," Mike said stoutly, exuding more confidence than he felt.

They rounded a stand of pine trees and walked up to a line of light biplanes, obviously very old, that were parked, wingtip-to-wingtip, beneath a canopy of gray-green camouflage nets.

Markov walked up to one of them and patted the fuselage.

Mike said: "Are you kidding? Is this what you want me to fly? The biplane trainer I flew in primary was a better airplane than this."

There was an angry sound nearby. It was followed by a rapid exchange of Russian. Mike turned and saw three girls in flight coveralls. The one in the center, he saw, was very pretty. Her face was flushed and her eyes were bright with anger.

Markov grinned. "You've put your foot in it already, Mikhail. I think you've offended the pilots, particularly Galina here. This is her airplane."

"She flies missions?" Mike asked incredulously. "*Girls* fly combat missions? And they do it in these airplanes?"

The girl in the middle, who couldn't have been more than nineteen or twenty, said tartly, "Yes we do, nearly every night."

"Every night?" he asked, parroting her answer and feeling stupid doing it. He realized with a shock that she had spoken in English. The other two girls, obviously oblivious, smiled at him in a friendly fashion.

"Every night," the girl repeated.

Markov intervened. "This is a PO-2 night bomber. It is not, obviously, a great four-engine Boeing, a *bombardirovshchik*. But it serves. There is a machine gun on a ring in the rear cockpit for the navigator. Underneath, you see, are racks for small bombs. In the cockpit is a wire pull to release the bombs. These women fly every night; sometimes with as many as twenty airplanes, flying in train, to bomb German positions and emplacements."

Mike looked closely at the biplane. It was never intended for combat. Wood and fabric from front to tail. A wooden prop. A tiny, air-cooled, five-cylinder engine in front. It probably generated 110 horses, if that. Hell, he thought, my Stearman primary trainer had 220 horses. It was a B-17 compared to this tinker-toy.

"What was this airplane designed for?" Mike asked.

"It's a trainer, or was," Markov said. "However, we use *all* our resources. We've built twenty thousand of these PO-2s over the years.

Since 1929, as a matter of fact. They've been our basic trainer in our paramilitary flying clubs, where these women and many of our men learned to fly.

"In combat, we've found our women—the night-witches, the Germans call them—to be very effective, very useful indeed." He smiled and repeated the last words in Russian.

"*Spasibo*," the women chorused with mock humility. The pretty one continued to stare angrily at Mike.

Markov motioned to her. "Lieutenant Galina Ivanova Tarasova, I will introduce you first, since this is your airplane and you speak English. This is Mikhail Gavin; he is an American. He speaks no English but he had a Russian grandfather. His Russian name is Gavronov. His father's name is Stephen in English, so his patronymic is Stepanovich. Mikhail Stepanovich Gavronov. Mikhail is a pilot. He was shot down in his four-engine Boeing. We have no way to repatriate him for the moment, so he has volunteered to fly for us—which you should recognize he is not required to do."

Markov patted the fuselage of the PO-2. "So I need to find out how he flies. He is accustomed to flying a very heavy airplane and this is a very light one, so the contrast will make a good test, I think, of how quickly he can adapt to our aircraft. I will give chase in my Yak and observe what he does."

"You suggest he fly in *my* airplane, my *Ved'ma?*" Galina said.

"What is *Ved'ma?*" Mike asked.

"The Russian word for 'witch,'" Markov said. He turned back to the young woman. "That was my request and your major asked me to use this one, since it's already been refueled."

"Suppose he crashes it?" Galina demanded.

Mike flushed with anger. "I won't crash it," he said. "I can fly anything, certainly an old crate like this."

Galina bristled angrily and Viktor held up his hands in supplication. "Please, comrades, let's be friends," he implored.

"Let's fight the Hitlerites, not each other. Mikhail, listen, please. Galina will instruct you. When you take off, I want you to climb to two thousand meters—that's, um, about six thousand feet. I will intercept you in my Yak. You are not armed, I am. Don't try to leave the area and go anywhere."

"I have no intention of trying to go anywhere," Mike said. "I wouldn't know where to go if I did. Besides," he said, staring boldly at Galina and deliberately looking her up and down, "I may even learn to like it here."

She blushed and seemed to grow even angrier.

"Oh, well said, Mikhail, well said!" Markov said sardonically.

"Galina, please explain the instruments and controls to Mikhail." He pointed aloft. "I will meet you up there in ten minutes." Markov walked away.

Galina stepped forward. "Very well," she said crisply. "Climb up here, please. This is the starter switch, the throttle, the rudders, you can see. It will take off in a very short distance, what you would call about fifty miles an hour. Keep the nose down until you pick up flying speed. You will see this is a very maneuverable airplane. Be sure not to stall at low altitude. It lands very easily. But notice the landing gear; the wheels are close together. You must keep very straight so that when you touch down you don't circle . . ." She groped for words.

"Loop?" he asked. "You mean ground-loop?"

"Yes. Ground-loop."

"You speak very good English, almost as good as Captain Markov," he said. "May I ask why?"

"No, you may not," she said, "but I will answer this one question. In my second university year, I was placed in a special language course, an experimental course, to study English. I also had a foreign friend who spoke the language well. We spoke only in English for many months. Now I think that is enough information about myself. We are here to talk about the airplane only."

"Thank you, Miss, may I call you Galina?"

"You may call me Lieutenant Tarasova or Comrade Lieutenant," she said.

"Thank you, Comrade Lieutenant." he said. "And please accept my apology if I was rude a bit ago. The whole thing caught me by surprise. The airplane, you, the idea of women flying combat; we don't have anything like that at all. I don't know anybody else who does. So I'm sorry if I offended you." He cleared his throat. "Also, if I may say so, you're very pretty."

"Get into the cockpit, please," she said. He climbed in and settled himself. "No parachute?" he asked.

"No," she said curtly. The question seemed to make her angry again. "Fasten your safety harness."

Some safety harness, he thought, when you don't even have a parachute. But he obediently secured the straps across his shoulders and snapped them into a large ring that was attached to the lap belt.

The engine started easily but it made a curious popping sound.

"Does this engine sound normal?" Mike shouted.

"Yes," she shouted, "perfectly normal. Mind you take off into the wind. And please remember this is my airplane." She turned on her heel and walked back to her friends.

He advanced the throttle slightly, looked for the wind sock, and, rumbling across the grass field, lined up facing the wind. He held the brakes, pushed the throttle cautiously forward, and ran up the engine until the little aircraft shuddered and bucked.

When the brakes began to slip, he released them and slowly moved the throttle all the way to the stop. The PO-2 moved forward, bounced a few times and, to his surprise, became airborne almost immediately.

As the girl instructed, he held the nose down till he picked up ample flying speed. Then, yielding to his habit to thumb his nose at authority, he pulled the nose up sharply, at the same time banking sharply to the left, and executed a steep chandelle, a climbing turn, away from the field.

As he did, he looked down and saw the girl flap her arms in alarm or disgust. Probably both, he thought.

He began climbing in long, shallow spirals. When he reached two thousand meters, he leveled off. As he did, a Yak fighter screeched by him at least three times the PO-2's speed.

Let's see if this thing's a hawk or a turkey, Mike decided. He advanced the throttle and pushed the stick slightly forward, putting the airplane into a shallow dive. When the wires and struts began keening, he pulled the nose up past the horizon, yanked the stick back toward his right hip, and kicked the left rudder. The little biplane flipped over neatly into a 360-degree snap-roll.

As the horizon rotated, he shoved the controls back in neutral, stabilizing the airplane barely in time to keep it from slewing awkwardly in the air. Heavy-handed and heavy-footed, he thought.

He put the PO-2 through four snap-rolls, gradually reacquiring his lightness of touch, and then went through the same maneuver in slow motion. The aircraft rotated slowly on its axis rather than snapping around. The next time, he executed the same slow roll but stopped at each of eight points through the circle.

As he leveled out, the Yak pulled up beside him, wheels down; the flaps were partly down. Mike admired Markov's airmanship, mushing through the air at such a slow speed. The Russian stared at Mike appraisingly for a long minute and then, seeming to come to a decision, retracted his wheels, milked up his flaps, and shot away.

Mike saw the Yak make a climbing turn to the right and then swing around sharply. Mike realized that Markov was about to make a simulated attack on the tail of the PO-2. He smiled and waited; it was

Captain Redman all over again. He turned in the seat and looked back. The speeding Yak grew larger rapidly. When Mike judged that Markov was within extreme firing range, he reversed his controls and skidded the little airplane violently to the left.

The Yak screeched on by. Mike caught a glimpse of Markov's startled face as the Russian realized he had missed what should have been an easy target. Mike leveled out and flew straight ahead, assuming that the Russian would swing about and attack from the front.

He was right. The Yak came screaming toward his nose. Mike went to full throttle and put the biplane in a shallow dive, a hardly discernable one, that allowed the PO-2 to pick up speed. Just as the Yak closed in for the kill, Mike pulled the stick back in his stomach, soared upward in a half-loop, and rolled out on top in an Immelmann. Markov sped by beneath him. Mike smiled to himself and leveled out.

When the Yak started a beam-on attack, Mike flipped the PO-2 on its back, pulled the stick back, and dumped the biplane into a near-vertical dive. Unable to slow the Yak enough to follow the PO-2, Markov flew harmlessly by again. At three thousand feet, Mike leveled out and waited.

At length, the Yak pulled up alongside, wheels and flaps down. Through the fighter's perspex canopy, Mike could see Markov's angry face. The Russian jabbed a finger downward sharply, pulled up his wheels, milked up his flaps, and banked away.

Mike banked, pulled his throttle back, and spiraled down toward the field. As he leveled out on the approach, he realized he was too high and that the biplane would float past the field before it settled in. That would be embarrassing. He pushed the stick to the left, held right rudder, and forward-slipped the biplane sharply—nearly sideways—to lose altitude quickly. It shuddered at the strain but held steady.

Just before touching the ground, he moved the controls into neutral, held the nose off, and let the front wheels kiss the ground in a soft landing. The PO-2 rumbled through the short grass to the line of parked airplanes. He swung the little craft around in a circle with a blast of the engine and a sharp tap on the brake and cut the engine. It pinged musically as the hot metal began to cool.

The three women, standing close to where he had left them, were watching silently. He released the safety harness and climbed out of the airplane.

"It handles very nicely," Mike offered, trying to make up for his previous comments about the PO-2 and looking directly at Galina. "It's a very smooth-flying aircraft."

She looked at him coolly. "Yes, it is. I'm relieved to see that it's still in one section—one piece."

"It was a pleasure," he said. "Thank you." She shrugged and walked around the aircraft, checking the tautness of the struts and running her hands across the fabric to find any tears the aerobatics might have created.

Mike leaned against the fuselage and waited. Five minutes later, Viktor arrived, a sardonic smile on his face.

"I was pretty angry at you," the Russian said. "Making me look a fool. It was my fault, of course. I shouldn't have expected you to simply sit there." He shrugged and stuck out his lower lip. "Coming down, I had a chance to think. You seem a pretty good pilot, Mikhail, you have good instincts, reactions. So maybe you can handle something a little faster."

"Whatever you say," Mike said. Then, raising his voice so the girls would be sure to hear, he added: "This is a very nice airplane, though. I know these women pilots can do a very good job in it. I'm sure they do."

"A little international diplomacy, eh?" Viktor said, grinning. "Very good. We can use some of that. But I think we will introduce Mikhail to something different. If the comrade lieutenants will excuse us."

"Oh yes," Galina said witheringly. "We'll be happy to." The other two responded in Russian and one openly winked at Markov.

Mike bowed slightly toward the women as he and Viktor walked away. "Well, you put your foot in it back there, all right," Viktor said. "If you had any hope for that young lady, I'm afraid you've stamped it out."

"You told me her name," Mike said. "But who is she?"

"She's a fine pilot," Viktor said. "She flew many missions in the battle of Stalingrad. Very rough, very tough. Many of the girls were killed or wounded. She flew night and day, she bombed troops and depots and rail centers; she even blew up an ammunition dump at one point. She's a very fine pilot, a fine woman."

He sighed. "There are some negatives, however. She's a virgin— some call her the Virgin of Vladimir, after the famous Russian icon that was used to frighten our enemies. I can see you don't know the history. Never mind. But saying she's a virgin, which is unquestionably a fact, isn't necessarily a compliment. This is, after all, wartime. Every day you fight and live is a day you don't die.

"So why be so selfish, eh? Many of the girls would like to share themselves with us. A few manage, though their commander, Major Kravchenko—you'll know her when you see her, she's the big, broad-shouldered Russian one with the braids—Kravchenko acts like a giant hen guarding her chicks. She shoos the men away from their quarters every night—they're living in an old *shkola*, a schoolhouse—and she makes a nightly bed-check on the girls."

Markov shook his head gloomily. "I managed a half-hour under a wagon with one of the girls a week ago—I'm too much of a gentleman to mention her name—but it's ridiculous, really, to treat us all like children. Particularly under these circumstances.

"But I drift from the subject, Lieutenant Galina Ivanovna Tarasova. Many men have tried, believe me. None, I will swear on my mother's grave, none, including myself—and I have had a modest number of conquests, if you will permit me a small statement of fact—none has succeeded. She saves herself for her mission and"—he shrugged—"for some future hero."

"Maybe I'll be that hero," Mike said.

Markov raised his eyebrows. "What resolution! What optimism! I hope you can apply those same qualities to your flying, if we can discuss that now. We'll catch a ride to the Shturmovik field; it's very close by."

"To the what field?" Mike asked.

"The Shturmovik. Our ground-attack airplane. It's been very successful. Very. It's heavily armored, and heavily armed. The new model has a 37-mm. cannon firing forward. It also carries rockets and as much as five hundred kilos, one thousand pounds, in anti-tank bombs."

"Wow."

"Yes, wow. Technically, it's the IL-2, named for the designer, Ilyushin. It's a low-wing, cantilever monoplane, metal and wood construction, a two-seater. The rear-seat gunner has a 12.7 Berezin machine gun. About the same as your caliber fifty, I think."

"The engine?"

"The engine of this new model has 1,750 horsepower. Twelve cylinders, liquid cooled. Top speed is rated at 448 kilometers, about 280 miles an hour."

"Not very fast."

"Not very. But remember, this kind of aircraft attacks tanks and guns. At low-level, perhaps ten meters, thirty feet. The pilot needs time to acquire his target. It still would be faster, but there is very heavy armorplate below, in front, and particularly behind the pilot. Oh, I should add that the landing gear is very rugged. This airplane operates off grass fields and some of our Shturmovik pilots are—well, I admit, pretty raw. Some of them don't land as much as just drop the airplane from above when they want to come down."

"You want me to try it out."

"Why not?"

"Why not, indeed."

When they arrived at the field, Mike looked the airplane over with keen interest. Heavy, rugged, very plain, spartan even, a vehicle made for service. Short-term service, most likely. Markov spoke for a few moments with a major who at first seemed surprised and then, shrugging, appeared to acquiesce.

"He says okay," Markov said. "In fact, this is a good time for this experiment, this orientation of yours. We've just arrived in this area and we're still setting up. We're not due for action till tomorrow or perhaps the day after.

"Very well now. This is very much like any airplane of this type. The controls and instruments are the same. There is no night-flying apparatus here. It's all very simple. The major asked me to impress just one thing on you. This airplane may seem quite heavy in your hands, at least at first. And it's a bit sluggish on takeoff. Don't try to hurry it. And, please, when you get aloft, no tricks or stunts. This is not an airplane for aerobatics."

"It doesn't sound like much fun."

"*Fun?*" Markov said exasperatedly. "We're fighting a *war*." He flapped his arms. "Oh, I know what you mean. Never mind. Just take it around for ten minutes or so, all right?"

Markov was right. Mike thought the Shturmovik would never leave the ground. Just as he was running out of field, it did, but reluctantly. He held it flat for a longer time than usual, then gently moved into a climbing turn. To his surprise, the IL-2 was quite maneuverable, though heavy to handle.

At five thousand feet, he checked its stall characteristics. It took a long, somewhat scary moment to recover when it fell off on a wing and started to spin. As bad as the old Vibrator, but a lot heavier. Obviously not an airplane for aerobatics.

But hell, or whoop-to-do, as Buddy would say. He dived, pulled up, and slammed the controls through a snap-roll. He was halfway around again before he could stop the roll.

Piss-ant! he yelled. Maybe it was all that armorplate. It spoiled the flight characteristics. Angrily, he tried it again. It was better the second time but it still wallowed badly. A third time was very little better and he abandoned the effort. The damned thing just won't do stunts, he concluded. Landing was easy but rough; the plane wanted to land as soon as he closed the throttle. He opened it again slightly to round out, but he still banged onto the grass harder than he wanted to.

Markov had red spots on his cheekbones when Mike walked up to him. Mike, seeing his displeasure, held up his hands. "I'm sorry," he said. "I know you told me not to do stunts. I just got curious, I . . ."

"Lieutenant, I've been very generous with you, very sporting," Markov grated. "At the moment I'm inclined to hand you a rifle and send you to the infantry. Now listen, please. If I'm going to fit you in somewhere here, you *must* accept my orders, the orders of any superior officer. This is not America. And I'm surprised that American pilots are so undisciplined."

"Most really aren't," Mike said, abashed. "I understand; I'll shape up." *Boy, it's a good thing Buddy isn't here,* Mike thought. *The two of us would drive this guy crazy and, no doubt, wind up somewhere a lot worse than Biloxi.*

"All right," Markov said, calming down. "What do you think of the airplane?"

"It flies like a truck. Even a B-17's lighter in the hands, a lot lighter. At least when it isn't fully loaded. It might be fun to fire that big cannon but, geez, it's really not flying. How about a spin in one of your Yaks? That's more my style."

Markov looked at him for a moment. "Well, perhaps we can do that. As the old British expression goes, in for a penny, in for a pound." They walked out to the roadway and hailed a truck driving in the right direction.

When they arrived at the Yak field, Mike frowned. "I thought you said you were just setting up here, that this was a new base."

"We are. It is."

Mike pointed. "Then how come you've got a concrete runway? And those revetments or berms or whatever you call them. They didn't get there overnight."

"But they did," Markov said, "or nearly so. Obviously, you don't understand the kind of people we are, Mikhail. We don't have a great deal of your technology, but we have an enormous supply of people. Labor. And Soviet people are accustomed to manual labor."

He indicated the length of the runway with a sweep of his hand. "A large force of civilians—many of them women and children— leveled this field, first with shovels and hoes and then by dragging heavy logs across it. With the help of a few horses. Afterward, trucks brought in these prefabricated concrete sections. A few winches, ropes, and pulleys and the combined strength of many hands and backs—that's what put them in place.

"They'll keep us out of the mud. If one block cracks in the cold, we replace it. And, as you see, the blocks were painted to make them appear to blend into the surrounding earth. This runway was put in place in three days, from beginning to end."

"Good Lord," Mike said. "At the 205th we had a plane hit the trees on takeoff. It blew up and caved in the end of the runway. A British team of workers piddled around for six weeks without getting it fixed—it was our long runway and we needed it. Finally, our adjutant kicked them off the field and got some Navy Seabees in to do the job within ten days or so. But *three* days . . ."

"You have a good deal to learn about us, Mikhail," Markov said. "About the way we use our resources, including the girls we were talking to." He frowned. "I must stop using that word 'girls.' I've found they don't like it. They're women. Call them that. Better still, call them Comrade Lieutenants."

"Which raises the question of what I should call *you*," Mike said. "Comrade Captain, or Ace, or what?"

Markov smiled and smoothed his mustache. "You see, you're learning discretion already; that's good. If we're around others, particularly the men, call me Comrade Captain. If we're alone, or in a strictly social setting, say, with the girls—I mean the ladies, the *women*—call me Viktor. I'll call you Mike or, around Russians, Mikhail. For now, however, let's concentrate on aircraft rather than protocol."

Mike walked around Viktor's Yak fighter. The airplane was long-nosed, like a shark, and had a fuselage of metal. The wings, Viktor told him, were made of Siberian pine and covered with fabric. The fuselage was sleek, the tail was short and stubby. A 20-mm. cannon was mounted in the propeller shaft. Two synchronized 12.7-mm. machine guns were mounted on the engine. Viktor stroked the nose of his Yak with the same affection a horseman would show to a prize stallion. "This is the Yak-9," he said. "The engine is liquid cooled, twelve cylinders, twelve hundred horsepower, a three-bladed metal airscrew, as you can see, with hydraulic pitch control and constant-speed governor. The speed, by your method of figuring, is three hundred and seventy miles an hour, about the same as a Messerschmitt or Focke-Wulf. A match for the ME-109, not quite a match for the Focke-Wulf at altitude. At medium altitude, a better rate of climb. And, at our preferred altitude, the Yak is more maneuverable than either aircraft.

"So we try to get the enemy into a turning battle between the ground and, perhaps, fifteen thousand feet. Now I will check you out. Not in my airplane, thank you. This one beside it. It's a good bird. The pilot is no longer with us. He was wounded. He managed to land the aircraft before he—well, you understand."

He went over the instruments and controls with Mike. "So," he said afterward, "let's fly. I want you to take off and fly around a bit—you know the drill. Become familiar with the stall point, the handling; go ahead and wring it out. Take, let's say, twenty minutes. Then I'll come up and join you. Let's say at ten thousand feet. You'll get on my wing and stay there, no matter what I do. Do you think you can fly this airplane?"

"I can . . ."

"I should have remembered," Markov said. "You can fly anything."

Mike grinned. "Right. Also, by now I've had maybe five or six hundred hours of practice, flying formation."

"So many?" Victor said. "But not in an airplane as quick and light as this one. We'll see."

Mike shrugged into the parachute harness he found in the Yak's cockpit. "I see there's a parachute."

"Of course. What did you expect?"

"The girls—I mean, our female comrades—don't have any in those biplanes."

Markov looked embarrassed. "Yes, that's regrettable. Perhaps it's the fact that the Yak is a much more modern, more sophisticated aircraft. We have more instruments, we fly higher. We have to have radio contact with the ground and each other, for example. Also, we must have oxygen. The night bombers fly lower, so they don't."

"The Yak costs more than the PO-2 to produce," Mike said.

"Of course."

"So it's not as expendable. But the pilots are. I think my country values people, individuals, more than yours does."

Markov shook his head irritably. "Mike, keep such opinions to yourself, if you please. You might say them to the wrong person. Let's fly, not talk."

Mike was delighted with the Yak. It didn't have the raw, intimidating power of the American P-51, but it was quick, fast, light, and very maneuverable. A tricky little beast on takeoff; not very forgiving, but that was all right. It would be fun to fly it in combat.

He was sweating lightly when Viktor joined him at ten thousand feet. The Russian waggled his wings and Mike slid his Yak into formation with him. At first, Viktor's movements were slow and gentle —a bank to the right, a bank to the left, a climbing turn. Mike easily kept station with him.

Without warning, Viktor turned his Yak on its back and went into a steep dive. Caught by surprise, Mike slammed his throttle forward, yanked the stick over, stamped the rudder, and caught up with him. Now they were in a series of tight turns. Mike had to reduce power and pull the nose up to stay on his wing. He felt the Yak beginning to shudder; in a second it would stall.

But Viktor, sensing the critical moment, flattened out. Relieved, Mike pushed the throttle open again and closed on him. For minutes on end, the two fighters climbed, dived, and corkscrewed. In their maneuvers, they ranged from ten thousand feet all the way down below one thousand.

Finally, Viktor leveled off and pointed down. Mike landed a few seconds behind the Russian and they taxied up to the revetments and swung around. The engine pinged and ponged as Mike climbed out. Sweat was running down his face and he mopped it with a handkerchief.

"So what do you think?" Viktor said as they walked away.

"It was a helluva kick. What do *you* think?"

"I think you're a very promising pilot, what you'd call a natural," Markov said. "We'll have to meet the major, he's a good friend of mine. I'll recommend you for my wingman."

Major Valentin Borisenko was a jovial, broad-shouldered Russian with a square jaw, alert brown eyes, and a ready laugh. It was obvious that he and Markov were fast friends.

"So," Borisenko said when the three met. "This is your protégé." He knew only a few words of English, so he spoke in Russian with Viktor once again acting as translator when Mike was part of the conversation.

Borisenko raised his eyebrows when Viktor told him he had been testing Mike's flying abilities. "I wondered where you were," he said. "Well, actually I didn't wonder. Quite naturally, I thought you were hanging around the schoolhouse trying to catch a night-witch out in the open."

"Not with Major Kravchenko around," Markov said. "Can't you get her transferred?"

"I have a better solution, Viktor," Borisenko said. "Why don't you transfer your attentions to her? She's a big, fine, broad-beamed Russian woman, not like those skinny-assed little girls of hers. Take her to bed, Viktor, and you'd have the run of the henhouse."

"I'll make any sacrifice for the Motherland but that," Viktor answered. "Even Comrade Stalin wouldn't ask that of me." They burst into laughter as Mike sat uncomprehendingly, smiled politely, and looked from one to the other.

After another exchange in Russian, Viktor turned to Mike. "Forgive us, Mikhail; we had some logistical matters to discuss. I've told Major Borisenko that you're a good pilot and he says it's okay for you to fly with us if the political commissar doesn't object. I'll take you to him later. For now, the major would like to hear about the P-51. Please repeat what you told me about it."

Borisenko listened to the story with intense interest, asked him questions about the B-17 and bombing tactics, and about his training. "How many hours did you spend in training?" he asked.

"Officially, twelve hundred," Mike said.

"So many?" Borisenko asked. He spoke rapidly to Markov. "Our pilots receive only a fraction of that number," Viktor said. "How many hours did you spend in ground school and in flight training?"

"Four hundred hours in each."

"How did you spend the other four hundred hours?"

"Screwing around, filling out forms. Waiting."

Viktor translated and the two men laughed. "He says all air forces must be alike," Viktor said.

"Then we had an extra nine weeks in four-engine school," Mike offered. "I flew about four hundred hours in the B-17 before we got into combat."

Hearing the translation, Borisenko rolled his eyes. "What resources you must have, to spend that long." He looked from Viktor to Mike, reached into a drawer, and pulled out a bottle of vodka and glasses. *Good Lord*, Mike thought, *you have to have a strong head and an iron stomach to survive out here.*

Borisenko raised his glass in a toast. *"Na zdorov'ye novogo tovarischa,"* he said.

"To a new comrade," Viktor repeated.

The meeting with the commissar, a thin, bookish individual named Spirin, was considerably more formal. Viktor had warned Mike beforehand to curb his tongue and avoid offering any political opinions.

"Why do you want to fly for the VVS?" Spirin asked.

"We have a common enemy, the Germans, the *Nyemtsy*," Mike said. "Eventually, of course, I want to be repatriated. When you can arrange it."

"Have you been active in political affairs in America?" Spirin asked.

"No, I haven't. I'm a bit young for that."

"In the Soviet Union our young people are politically responsive at a much earlier age."

"Not in America, at least not at this time."

"What, exactly, are your political views?"

"I don't have any, really. I believe in democracy, freedom. In individual rights." Viktor frowned slightly at the last comment.

"In the Soviet Union," Spirin said primly, "we consider individual rights subordinate to the national interest."

"Well, if you're talking about unity, I guess it's the same in the United States right now," Mike said. "We're all united in the war effort, to beat the Germans and Japanese."

"There is a fundamental difference in our systems, however," Spirin said. "Your system is based on capitalism, ours on socialism. Comrade Lenin said the two systems must inevitably come into conflict and that only one can survive."

"I wouldn't know."

"But what is your opinion? You must have one."

"No disrespect to Comrade Lenin, but I think maybe the contrast he drew is too sharp a one, at least under present circumstances."

"Explain, please."

"Well, I'm no expert on this, understand. But I've noticed that the farmers around here seem to have private plots of their own, and I've seen them loading the stuff into wagons. They must be taking it to market somewhere. Isn't that capitalism, at least in a small way? Our farmers do that. And your utilities—your gas and electric plants, for example. They're owned by the government, aren't they?"

"The people."

"Okay, the people. Well, some of ours are, too. We call them cooperatives. One's called the Tennessee Valley Authority, as I remember. And even the ones that're privately owned are regulated by the local governments—what they can do, how much they can earn, all that. And the post office. That's publicly owned. Businesses are privately owned but they're regulated; so are working hours and minimum wages. Maybe that's socialistic up to a point. Certainly, the army is a socialistic organization, if you want to call it that."

"Do you want to call it that?"

"I'm really not concerned with labels. I just think the people need to be in charge—*really* in charge—and I think it's pretty hard for that to happen under *any* system. Either because the handful of people who're supposed to represent them take the power away from them, or the people go to sleep and let them. But that doesn't concern me right now. I just want for us to win this war, and I'll do what I can to help—at home, here, wherever I can."

Afterward, Viktor complimented him. "You were very good. You walked on thin ice for a minute or two there, but you didn't sink. Now we can concentrate on the important things—flying and night-witches. And one important thing we've neglected: shooting."

For four long days, Mike flew his Yak to a gunnery range east of the base. There, he fired at target drogues towed behind PO-2s and at ground targets. He was surprised at how poorly he did at first; he had been a good shot with rifle, pistol, and with a shotgun on the 205th's skeet range. But he improved quickly.

On the fifth day and evening, bad weather rolled into the area and all flight operations were shut down. At lunch—sausage, pickled mushrooms, bread, and fruit—Viktor told him there would be a party that night at the schoolhouse that the night bomber regiment used as barracks and headquarters.

"We'll have music and dancing and conversation. Girls, of course. I think it's all right to say 'girls' under such circumstances, don't you?"

For a moment, Mike remembered the day at Albany when Buddy spotted the country club invitation on the bulletin board. "Conver-say-shun!" he'd crowed. "Dancin'!" It had been so very long ago. He wondered if Buddy was all right and what he was doing.

"It sounds fine," he said to Markov.

The party was in full swing when they arrived that evening. The women had pushed their bunks against the walls and created a large open space. Adjoining rooms created more space for dancers or conversation. At one corner of the main room was a makeshift jazz band —a battered, slightly out-of-tune piano played by a woman, a man with a guitar, another with a saxophone, still another with an accordion, a girl who played drums.

Candles flickered on small tables set against the walls. In the center of the room, young men and women pilots, navigators, and mechanics from the mixed air regiments swayed together, clearly enjoying the physical contact that ordinarily was denied them.

Mike halted at the doorway in surprise. He could hardly believe what he was hearing: they were playing "In A Little Spanish Town." A moment later they swung wildly and erratically into "Tiger Rag" and the dancers began singing along with it. *Hold that tiger! Where's that tiger?*

For a moment, Mike felt an acute sense of disorientation. He had imagined they would be playing and maybe dancing gypsy songs or some mournful Russian ballads. But old American pop music?

Viktor motioned him to a door set on trestles that was being used as a buffet. On it was a bowl filled with what turned out to be a punch made from vodka and fruit juices. An assortment of ill-matched glasses and tin cups were placed beside it. And there was a platter of small sweet cakes created, apparently, out of pooled rations.

A cup of the punch made Mike feel a little less out of place. The second one dissolved his feeling of shyness. The band struck up "Down Mexico Way" and a nice-looking young woman came up to him, spoke in Russian, and, seeing that he didn't understand, held out her arms, inviting him to dance. Unable to talk, they smiled at each other. Then she put her head on his shoulder, drew close, and they swayed together on the now-crowded floor.

Across the room, he saw Galina; it was as if her face somehow stood out in relief. Her blue eyes were large and luminous; they seemed to catch the candlelight in a way that others didn't. Near her was a large, brooding figure he hadn't seen before; a man who acted as if he were some sort of bodyguard.

Apparently sensing Mike's stare, Galina looked up, locked eyes with him, and then looked away. Mike had been beginning to feel warm; the girl he was dancing with was pressing close to him and seemed to be offering more than a fox-trot. But, and it irritated him to realize it, the sight of Galina drove away any thought of taking his dancing partner somewhere for a carnal embrace.

When the tune ended, Mike thanked the girl in English and excused himself. She looked surprised for an instant, but smiled and left him for someone else. Mike picked his way through the crowd and walked over to Galina. The band struck up another ballad as he arrived by her side.

"May I have this dance?" he asked. She looked at him coolly and seemed on the point of refusing. But then she shrugged and walked with him to the dance floor. Mike noticed that the large man in the background scowled, started to step forward, and then backed up again.

Mike realized with a shock that the little band was playing, or trying to play, "I Only Have Eyes For You," the same pop ballad he sang at the Albany Country Club the night he met Claire.

As he took Galina in his arms, Mike said: "Oh but I know this song. The last time I heard it was back in . . ." He winced and stumbled. Instead of going to a b and b flat at the end of the first eight bars, the band had dropped off mistakenly to what sounded like an e and an *a*. He couldn't be sure of *where* they'd gone; he knew only that it was wrong; it spoiled the song.

"What is the matter?" Galina said. "Are you ill?"

"No," he frowned. "Excuse me. It's just that they did it wrong. The tune. They played it wrong just now."

She looked at him disdainfully. "You are an expert on music as well as airplanes?" she inquired.

By then they were dancing at arm's length and he had lost the rhythm. He felt his cheeks grow warm. "I don't pretend to be an expert on anything. It's just that I know this song; I've sung it many times, and it surprised me when . . ." He winced again; again they had mangled the melody at the end of a passage. "There they go again; that's wrong."

Galina flushed angrily. "So the ignorant Russians have made still another mistake, Mister *pokazukha*, Mister hot-shot?" She seized him by the hand and began pulling him to the corner where the band was playing. Before he realized what was happening, she had spoken in rapid Russian to the saxophonist, who looked surprised, bent and spoke to the piano player, and then motioned to Mike to join them.

"What are you doing?" Mike shouted to Galina. "What did you say to them?

"I said they were playing the song wrong and you had sung it many times and you were going to show them how it should be done. So go and do it." She shoved him in the back and he nearly tripped over the saxophonist. By then the band had stopped playing and Mike was standing in front of them, feeling like a complete fool.

The saxophonist smiled sardonically, bowed his head, and held out his hand in invitation. For an instant, Mike thought of bolting for the door. But then he grew angry. If he did, he would feel like a coward as well as a fool. *Damn her.* He should show her; he would show them all.

The pianist struck a few chords as an introduction. Mike turned, took a deep breath, and launched into the song:

> *Are the stars out tonight?*
> *I don't know if it's cloudy or bright*
> *Cause I only have eyes for you, dear*

He came in firmly on the *b* and *b* flat on the last two words. Out of the corner of his eye, he saw the saxophonist raise his head in surprise and then nod vigorously. Mike moved into the bridge with the band players following him cautiously. At the end of the bridge, the pianist shouted "Aha!" when she realized where the melody was going. Moving into the final eight, the saxophonist demonstrated that he knew now what to do. He began weaving the sweet, grainy sounds of the sax around Mike's voice in a blues-like obbligato.

By the time they had reached the last few measures, they were all together and the audience had moved close to the band and was swaying with the song. Mike's anger had dissolved; now there was only the music and, across the room against the wall, Galina's eyes.

> *You are here, so am I,*
> *Maybe millions of people go by*
> *But they all disappear from view,*
> *And . . . I only have eyes for you.*

The band ended with a loud thump, a "button," his mother used to call it. The audience burst into loud applause and shouts. The saxophonist rose and shook his hand. But, true to the lyrics, Mike had eyes only for the blue-eyed girl across the room. She had lost her hostile look; it had become an appraising one.

The saxophonist was trying to say something to him. Mike shrugged and pointed to Galina. The sax player motioned urgently for Galina to come over. Again she approached and, again, Mike noted, the large man who had been standing near her scowled angrily.

Galina and the sax player spoke briefly. "He wants you to help him write down the melody and English words of the song," she said. "When they stop for a moment . . ."

"Take a break."

"A break? Yes, I see. He also asks what other American popular songs you could teach them. The American music they know is very old, he says." She said the last grudgingly, obviously annoyed at the admission.

"Ask him if they know, 'I Can't Get Started With You,'" Mike said.

She spoke to the sax player. "He says he thinks he's heard it; he'd like you to teach it to him."

"If they could take a break, I could go over it with him and the— the comrade playing the piano. Would you mind standing by to translate?"

She grimaced. "Oh, very well," she said at length. "It would be proper first to introduce you to each other." She made the introductions; the sax player was Lieutenant Boris Gusarov, a fellow Yak pilot. The woman was Nadia Chuikov, a night-witch navigator.

A third member of the band brought them tin cups of vodka and Mike hummed the song as Boris scribbled the notes on a piece of staff paper. Nadia copied them on another piece and began noting chord progressions.

By the time they had finished, voices were calling for music. Boris nodded and picked up his sax. "He says he's ready," Galina said. "He asks if you'll sing it."

"Oh boy," he said. "I don't want to have people thinking I'm a big party hog or something."

"You're not very big," she said.

"Thanks. That makes me feel better."

The piano and sax played an introduction while the accordionist and guitar player listened, coming in when they thought they could predict the flow of melody. Mike turned toward the dancers, looked squarely at Galina, and began singing:

> *I've been around the world in a plane*
> *I've settled revolutions in Spain,*
> *The North Pole I have chartered*
> *But I can't get started with you . . .*

Spots of color appeared in Galina's cheeks and she looked down and then, as if unwillingly, up again. As he sang, Mike's peripheral vision caught Viktor Markov off to one side, holding a long-haired blonde close to him. Viktor was grinning; his eyes glittered in the candlelight. At the end of the number there was a big round of applause. Boris shook hands vigorously with him again and several girls looked appraisingly at the young American.

Galina began walking away and Mike caught up with her. "We didn't finish our dance. Let's do it now." She hesitated, nodded, and, as the band struck up again, let him take her in his arms. "Well, it seemed to work out all right," he said.

"You did very well, I admit it," she said. "You also seemed to attract the attention of a few of the girls in my regiment."

"Maybe so," he said, "but I only have eyes for you." She looked at him quizzically and dropped her eyes.

As the tune ended, Major Kravchenko walked to the center of the room and clapped her hands for attention. She smiled, made an announcement in Russian, and pointed to the door.

"What did she say?" Mike asked.

"She said it's midnight and the girls have to go to bed. It's time for the boys to go to bed, too, she said. In their own barracks." She detached herself from him.

"I wish I could walk you home."

"I'm already home."

"I know. Would you take a walk with me another time, perhaps tomorrow or the next day, when we're not flying?"

"Why do you want to walk with me?"

"For company. I could learn to speak a little Russian, maybe. Maybe you'd like to learn a bit more English—American English, the way the language is actually spoken."

Galina considered and then nodded. "The idiom. On that basis, perhaps."

"Good. I'll come by and see if you're, uh, available. So, for now, I guess, it's goodnight."

"Goodnight."

Outside, he was joined by Viktor. "Well, you made quite a hit in there. With Galina, I don't know how much, but certainly with others. Though you, what is your expression, cramped my style a bit."

"How was that?"

"I had persuaded the young lady I was dancing with . . ."

"The blonde."

"The blonde. I had persuaded her to leave the party with me, it isn't very cold outside yet, and I thought we could find a nice spot . . . But you began singing and she said she wanted to stay and listen. You sang too well."

"I'm sorry."

"There's always tomorrow."

A deep voice spoke harshly in Russian. Mike looked to his right and saw the big man who had hung around Galina at the party. He was scowling at him. The man spoke again, glared, and walked away.

"What did he say?" Mike asked Viktor.

"He said you should leave Galina alone. Go back where you came from, or something like the American expression."

"Who *is* that guy?"

"I'd be careful of him, if I were you. His name is Petrov Antisferov. His name's not important. What's important is that he's very big and strong, and he's smitten with Comrade Tarasova."

"He hasn't . . ."

"Of course not. She tolerates his hanging about the way he does out of kindness. He's not a very attractive sort of person. He's a navigator for a PE-2 dive bomber regiment some miles from here. He comes here when he can, simply to be near her. Take care, Mikhail. Not every Russian is as civilized and well-behaved as I am."

The Soviet generals were drunk—uproariously, helplessly drunk—at the Kremlin party following the foreign ministers' conference. Josef Stalin watched them with contemptuous amusement. Beside him, British minister Anthony Eden, frail and aristocratic, as far out of his element as a pedigreed cat among mongrel dogs, looked at them uneasily.

"Do your generals get drunk in public like this?" Stalin asked Eden in mock concern. Eden opened and closed his mouth like a stranded fish. The diplomatic service had not equipped him to deal with people like this.

Stalin beckoned to Lavrenti Beria, the faintly menacing head of the NKVD. When Beria obediently advanced, Stalin chucked him under the chin.

"This is my Himmler," Stalin said. "Have you met my Himmler? He looks like Himmler, doesn't he?" Again, Eden's mouth opened and closed. Clearly enjoying the embarrassment of the two men, the swarthy Georgian dictator motioned to his dignified foreign minister, Vyacheslav Molotov, often called The Hammer.

"Molotov," Stalin demanded, "I've been wanting to ask you. That curious non-aggression pact you signed with Hitler in 1939. Just why did you do that? Tell us." As Molotov uncharacteristically began to stutter, Stalin threw back his head and laughed.

He's confident now, Eden thought; he smells victory and he's indulging himself. But, good heavens, he's a sinister person. And this visit has proven very difficult, particularly having to drink all these toasts in vodka.

In the past, it had always been possible to simply touch one's lips to the glass as a courtesy. One didn't have to actually drink all the liquor that was offered. With this man, however, it was different. He was the head of state and he was a terrible bully. He actually, literally, stood by and forced one to drink it down.

And here it came again. Stalin took two glasses of vodka from a waiter's tray and handed one to Eden. Each time Stalin drank, he threw his head back and flexed his knees like the caricature of a German baron. And, each time, he placed his hand on Eden's shoulder and made him flex his knees, too.

Soon they were bobbing up and down together. Eden felt a complete fool. Soon he would be as humiliatingly drunk as the Russian generals. He simply didn't understand these people.

Before they went to bed, Viktor and Mike checked the assignment board in the briefing room at the barracks. Their names were listed for flight duty the next morning. Mike was assigned as Viktor's wingman. He studied the way his name appeared in the Cyrillic alphabet so he would recognize it in future.

He slept poorly that night, waking often, and, when asleep, dreaming of flying with Viktor or sometimes with Galina. At dawn, an orderly pounded on the door and was heard calling the others. Breakfast was tea and a kind of porridge; it was filling but not anything, Mike concluded, he would pick from a menu.

"We will fly in *zveno*, four-plane, four-finger formations," Viktor said. Each *zveno* is made up of two *paras*, two two-ship formations. We are free-hunting today; others will fly cover for our Shturmoviks.

"I want you to stay on my wing and a little behind me, as you did the other day. Your first reponsibility is to protect my tail when I attack. If an enemy airplane gets behind me, tell me which way to break. If, afterward, you turn to attack, I protect you. But, mainly, your duty today is to stay with me. All right?"

"All right."

"If we become separated and you have to fight, try to remember a few things. We're best at low to medium altitudes. Our rate of climb is better than the Focke-Wulf within this range and we can out-turn either the FW or the Messerschmitt. Try to make the enemy turn with you. But watch he doesn't catch you from above."

"All right." Mike felt a little shaky; his stomach was tight but his knees seemed loose. He had flown twenty missions of tough combat by now, but always as the pilot of a heavy bomber being attacked by German fighters. He had never flown a fighter against a German fighter.

It had snowed the night before and the whiteness of the ground made a sharp contrast to the heavy stands of dark evergreens that dotted the area. It also reflected the morning sun so strongly that it was blinding to look at the ground for long; the eyes could have trouble adjusting to the sky at a moment when sharp vision spelled life or death.

Ahead, the Dnieper River shone like silver. Fighting was still going on at various bridgeheads as the Russians moved steadily westward, exerting pressure with their superior numbers like a heavy wrestler grappling with an agile but smaller man.

For the moment, it appeared that the struggles were localized, the prelude to a big drive that hadn't yet materialized. Where fighting was going on, the snow was dirtied by shellfire, smoke, and debris.

"*Smotri!*" The word rang sharply through the earphones. Look out! It was one of the first Russian terms Mike had memorized. Markov broke sharply away from the other *para* and Mike, intensely alert, followed him as he banked sharply and climbed.

Mike realized he hadn't seen the two Focke-Wulfs that were trailing a Shturmovik below. That was bad enough, but now he was comfused. Why are we climbing away from them? he wondered. Following Markov, his Yak was streaking nearly straight up. Then they were inverted and pulling nose-down above and behind the Focke-Wulfs.

In that instant, Mike understood. Traveling faster than the Germans, the Yaks would have overshot them unless they had chopped their throttles and, if they could have slowed in time, put down partial flaps. But a mistake in timing would have left the Yaks lagging and unable to accelerate if the FWs succeeded in reversing their positions and turning in behind them.

Through the looping barrel-roll maneuver, the Yak pilots retained their speed as well as full control of their aircraft and came down behind the enemy fighters in firing position.

Viktor's guns fired in two long bursts and the leading Focke-Wulf caught fire and fell away. Mike wanted to shoot at the wingman, who broke left. But his orders were to stick with his leader. He wobbled momentarily, lost pace, and had to jockey his throttle back and forth to regain his position on Markov's wing.

Before his mind could assimilate what had happened, they were attacking a flight of twin-engine bombers with Maltese crosses on them. They slid entirely through the formation at high speed. As they did, Mike saw tracers arcing toward the bombers but couldn't immediately tell whether they were from Viktor or another Yak.

But a Heinkel 111 crossed in front of him and, at the right instant, he pressed the firing button atop the stick. And found he had forgotten to take off the safety catch. "*Piss-ant!*" he yelled. Another Heinkel spiraled down in a slow spin, trailing black smoke. Now a second *para* was attacking the bombers and the Heinkels scattered like geese. Viktor dived on one and walked his cannon shells along the top of its fuselage and into the cabin. The Heinkel exploded and the Yaks flew across the debris.

A pass at a lower level dislodged a Messerschmitt from the tail of a Shturmovik. And then, with gas running low, it was time to go home. They eased into the field for a landing, taxied to their revetments, swung around, and cut their engines.

"How was your first taste of combat?" Viktor asked as they alighted from the Yaks.

"What combat?" Mike asked. "You did fine; all I did was sit there like a jerk and watch."

"Sometimes that's what a wingman does. Today I wanted you to stay close and become familiar with vertical movement, the sort of thing you didn't do when you were flying straight and level in large formations. We'll go out again after we've been refueled and had something to eat. Tomorrow, if all goes well, I'll take you up over the field here to practice dogfighting, one against one. How much did you think you saw?"

"I was confused. Things happened so fast and, as you say, I'm not accustomed to trying to shoot somebody while we're climbing up and down the sky."

The afternoon mission was uneventful; another *para* caught a Henschel making ground attacks on Russian positions and two Messerschmitts fled the scene when they saw a four-finger *zveno* approaching at a higher altitude.

At sundown, the Yak pilots drank shots of vodka and ate a supper of wild hare, steamed potatoes, and cabbage—there always seemed to be cabbage—and talked volubly. Picking up only a few words now and then and not wanting to drink more vodka, as the others were doing, Mike fell asleep on his bunk.

When he woke, it was late at night. In the bunk nearby, Viktor was asleep and snoring. Mike got up, padded to the latrine outside, and looked up. There was a new moon and the stars were twinkling in a velvet sky. Without conscious thought, he pulled on his trousers, boots, and heavy jacket and set out on the path to the night-bomber field.

As he reached the edge of the night-bomber field, he heard the snik of a rifle bolt and was challenged in Russian by a woman's voice. Groping for a reply, he said: "*Tovarishch*, friend." He cautiously walked a few steps forward and realized the sentry was the girl he had first danced with at the party.

"Hello," he said. "Uh, *zdravstvuy*, hello."

She smiled. "*Zdravstvuy.*"

"I'm taking a walk." She shook her head uncomprehendingly. He pointed ahead. "Galina?" The girl jabbed a finger at the sky.

"She's flying?" he said. He walked ahead. "Okay?"

She nodded and he walked around the edge of the field. Oil drums were burning to mark the landing area. A PO-2 had just landed and was taxiing to its parking place under a net. A young woman wearing a leather helmet was standing nearby. In the background Mike recognized the large man. Antisferov.

"Galina?" Mike asked the woman. She pointed along the landing strip. He understood; she would be approaching soon. Another PO-2, its engine popping, landed and taxied up. He peered at the cockpit as it passed. No.

Then came a third. As it taxied by, he recognized Galina's face inside the helmet. He walked toward the plane as it turned. So, he saw, did Antisferov.

He approached as Mike neared the plane, and called to him menacingly. Galina's voice, sharp and angry, intervened, and the man flinched and moved backward. Then she was standing in front of him, oil smeared over her cheeks. Her eyes were hollow and tired.

"Why are you here?" she demanded.

"I couldn't sleep. I decided to walk on over to see if . . ."

"If? If what?"

"If you were flying. If you were all right."

"All *right?*" she said wonderingly. "What is *all right?*"

"Well, safe."

She laughed harshly. "*Safe.* How foolish. Go back to your barracks. Go to bed. *Dobroy nochi.*" She walked away. Deflated, he turned and left.

The next morning he was grumpy at breakfast. "Don't they have anything but this?" he asked, pointing at the unappetizing porridge.

Viktor sighed. "Mike, Mikhail, last year at this time we were living on one meal a day. Things have improved a lot, thank God, so don't complain. Our people are still very short of food in Moscow." His eyes darkened. "I worry about my parents there."

"I'm sorry," Mike sighed. "I'm just a little out of sorts this morning."

"I woke in the middle of the night and you weren't there," Viktor said. "Did you go to the PO-2 airfield?"

"Yes."

"And . . ."

"She told me to go away. And that big jerk, what's-his-name, was there. He gave me some flak again."

"Rejected and threatened all together, eh?"

"Something like that."

"A real shot in the arm, as you would say. But if you don't mind, we'll concentrate on business today. We're not on the mission board so I'm going to drill you in some dogfight maneuvers. All right?"

"Great."

It was one of the toughest mornings of Mike's life. Whatever he tried to do, Viktor outmaneuvered him. He would get on Viktor's tail and, in what seemed like a few seconds, their positions would be reversed. They got into a tight-turning contest. The circles grew steadily smaller and tighter and Mike stalled out.

When they matched up again, Mike thought he had outsmarted Viktor by using a variation of the trick Viktor had used to get above and behind the Focke-Wulf on their first flight. At that time, Viktor had pulled up into a high barrel-roll—Viktor called it a yo-yo—to come down behind the FW without losing speed.

On this occasion, Mike was chasing Viktor through a long turn but lagging behind and unable to turn hard enough to point the nose ahead of Viktor without losing altitude. So he tried a low yo-yo, plunging down and in front of Viktor and then pulling up into a barrel-roll to come out directly behind his mentor.

For an instant, Mike thought the trick had worked. But, sensing or seeing what was happening, Viktor had banked hard, nose down, and turned tightly. Mike looked about desperately for his opponent; he had lost him. No, Viktor was sitting, grinning, on Mike's tail.

"*Piss-ant!*" he shouted in frustration. On the ground, he was disconsolate. "I guess I'm a real flop as a fighter pilot," he said gloomily. "Better hand me that rifle and point me to the infantry."

"Oh, let me borrow your quaint expression, piss-ant," Viktor said, laughing. "Actually, you did very well. A poor pilot would have lost his nerve and accelerated out of those tight turns. You kept your nerve, even to the point of stalling. And going to that low yo-yo, which I hadn't even taught you, was inventive. Since you hadn't used it before, you couldn't be expected to know the defense against it. We'll talk through the maneuvers again at lunch, and then we'll go up and do it again."

It went better in the afternoon. The third time up, Viktor showed him how a good wingman would weave from one side to the other, depending on which rear quadrant he should be looking toward to spot a suspected threat. And he showed him how to switch from protector to attacker upon his or Viktor's call. If he had the better opportunity to shoot, he would take the leader's position and Viktor would, for the moment, become the wingman.

A moment of high glory, followed by depression, occurred the following morning when he and Viktor were ranging behind the bridge-heads hunting for enemy aircraft. Streaking out of the sun, a Focke-Wulf dived toward Viktor's tail.

"Break right!" Mike yelled. Unhesitatingly, Viktor rolled his Yak to the right. As the Focke-Wulf turned to follow him, Mike pulled behind the FW, pressed the firing button, and blasted the German with his cannon and two machine guns. A piece of the wing fell from the FW and the fuselage tumbled away.

"Break left!" Viktor called. Mike stamped the rudder and threw the stick over as a second FW shot by. Seconds later, with Viktor behind him, the German exploded in an orange and black cloud.

Mike realized they had flown into a hornets' nest. The air suddenly swirled with airplanes and he and Viktor became separated. Mike saw an FW settle in behind a Yak from another *para* and called: "Break right!" The Yak pilot, obviously failing to understand, stayed on course and the FW's cannon smashed the Yak's engine. The Russian pilot bailed out and the FW flew away before Mike could react.

As suddenly as the fight began, it was over. Mike found Viktor several thousand feet above him and slid into position behind his wing. Later, in Borisenko's presence, they reviewed what had happened.

"The major compliments you, as I do, on warning me promptly and then shooting down the German," Viktor said. "You saved me and scored your first kill. Though he says you should have been more watchful and realized that the Focke-Wulf pilot who attacked me would have a wingman—the one who tried to attack you.

"The bad thing is that you were unable to warn the other Yak pilot properly because you called to him in English and, quite naturally, he didn't understand you. Major Borisenko says you need to learn some Russian quickly—starting with the expressions we use commonly in the air. I'll write them down for you phonetically, but you need to learn more than that so you truly understand."

"I will," Mike promised.

The next day, finding he wouldn't be flying, Mike set off for the night-bomber field and, walking to the schoolhouse, asked a young woman who was entering if Galina was there. A moment later Galina came out.

"Yes?"

"Would you walk with me?"

She looked at him for a moment. "Very well." She went back inside and reemerged in her padded flight jacket. They began walking around the perimeter of the field. They walked without speaking for several minutes. She was the first to break the silence.

"You have been flying?" she asked.

"Yes. It's been—a new kind of experience for me. Being the hunter instead of the hunted. But I shot down a Focke-Wulf yesterday. He tried to ambush, surprise Viktor."

"Oh? I congratulate you," she said. "I think I envy you, too." The last sentence was said in a low voice as if to herself. "Then it was a very good experience."

"Not entirely." He told her of his failure to warn his fellow Yak pilot because of the language problem. "I need to learn as much Russian as possible, as quickly as I can. Would you help me?"

She shrugged. "I'm not a language instructor."

"But there isn't one here and you obviously have a very good ear for language. Or you wouldn't speak English as well as you do. I don't want to impose on you, but . . . well, it would help me a lot, help me to be a better pilot. In a common cause."

She nodded. "Very well. On that basis I will try to help you." She thought for a moment. "I have a grammar-school text on the Russian language at the barracks."

"I don't know your alphabet; that Cyrillic looks like Greek to me."

"In a sense, it is. But it's simpler than your English alphabet. I can show you. I won't be flying tonight; several of your people will be coming to visit, to talk with friends. If you wish to come over in the evening I'll spend an hour with you—on our language."

"Perfect. Thank you."

That evening, the classroom that had served as the dance floor had reverted to its natural state as a barracks. And, Mike noted, as a barracks for women. It was much cleaner than the men's. Rows of wooden beds ran along either side of the room. On each bed two blankets had been neatly folded.

At the end of each bed, an old ammunition box served as a table. On most tables sat a small handmade box; a few were open and women's items like lipstick, powder, mirrors, and needles and thread were visible. On the wall on pegs or crude wooden hangers were uniforms. Behind them, in a few instances, peeped party dresses, blouses, and underwear.

The old piano sat in a corner. Atop it, peering suspiciously at the male guests sitting with the women on their beds or in a few ramshackle chairs, was a large orange-colored cat. Nadia, the navigator who had played the piano in the band, was quietly fingering a few chords.

Many of the women were wearing dresses, some of them in bright colors. Seeing them in party dresses and makeup, it was hard to believe these same females climbed into the cockpits of ancient bi-planes and flew through flak to bomb Germans.

Galina wore her wool uniform and no makeup. She didn't want to give the brash young American any ideas. She had mixed feelings about him. On the one hand, she found him rather exotic and, there-fore, interesting. On the other hand, he was crude and culturally ignorant, as you would expect someone to be who came from a crass and materialistic culture. But he was also oddly innocent, so unlike the subtle and worldly Russian men who approached her from time to time.

Like Viktor, for example. Viktor and Mikhail were as unlike as any two men could be. And yet they had become fast friends. What was it that formed the bond between them? Men were sometimes hard to understand. Both had expressed an interest in her, of course. Viktor, because he was attracted to any woman who seemed hard to get. Mikhail because—why? Several of her comrades had smiled sensu-ously and said they would like to know him better. They were, well, "looser" than she, and one or two were more generously endowed, in a physical sense, than she. Yet Mikhail seemed to prefer her company.

Was the American more like Viktor than appearances suggested? Was his innocence a pose? She was interested, though she resisted admitting it, in learning from Mikhail what America and Americans were like. And she was flattered that he had turned to her for help in learning Russian. But she would be on her guard.

When he arrived, she motioned him into the adjoining room that was used for briefings and was furnished with a desk and several chairs. "It's not quite so noisy in here," she said. "It will be easier to sit and work."

She began with the Cyrillic alphabet. After repeated alterations through the centuries, it had settled into thirty-two characters. The written language was first called Old Church Slavonic. The alphabet, adapted from the Greek, was first formalized by Cyril and Methodius, two brothers from Macedonia. Eventually, it acquired the name of the more scholarly brother.

"So your language came from Greek and mine came from Latin," Mike said. "The Greeks and the Romans. First the Romans conquered the Greeks and then the Greeks, through their culture and their beauty, conquered the Romans." He looked at her levelly.

"Let's get on with the work," she said. "You need to become famil-iar with our alphabet as quickly as possible so you can begin to acquire a vocabulary. Without that, all I can teach you are a few terms phonetically and a few basic rules of grammar to commit to memory. Be careful of one thing: some of our letters look like yours, but they're not. Don't let that confuse you."

An hour and a half passed quickly. By then, Mike's head was swimming with alien symbols, words, and rules and he became distracted by singing that had started in the next room. "I think that's enough for tonight," Galina said. "Would you like to spend a few moments with the others?"

"If you'll be there."

"I have no place else to go."

The pianist, laughing, was accompanying two women, apparently a pilot and navigator, who were singing and dancing an original song. From the gestures, it appeared that the pilot was afraid to fly and the navigator couldn't plot a course.

A moment later, a girl with a high soprano voice sang what was clearly a patriotic song. She stood erect, her eyes shining and face flushed, like a heroic statue in a park. The group joined her in the last chorus and there was thunderous applause. One of the women pointed to Mike and spoke to Galina in Russian.

"She says she's enjoyed your American popular music, but it's too bad you don't know any Russian songs."

"Tell her I do, though."

Galina looked at him skeptically. "Do you really? If I say that, they may challenge you."

"Well, I do. Why would I say I do if I didn't?"

"I don't know. Sometimes I think you could be, what is it, shamming, perhaps."

"Bluffing? No. You have a suspicious mind, Comrade Lieutenant."

"Very well." Galina spoke to the girl in Russian and several looked quizzically at the American.

"Tell them I used to sing a beautiful song by Rachmaninoff," Mike said. "It's called 'In The Silence of the Night'."

Galina frowned. "The translation for that is *V nochnoy tishine*. Oh yes, that's a well-known song. But it's not . . ."

"Not from Tin Pan Alley. Never mind."

"Do you know our song in Russian?"

"No, just in English."

A rapid exchange took place. The pianist, who joined in the conversation, nodded. "They ask if you'll sing it. In your language, of course."

"Oh hell. It's a difficult piece, classical as you say, and I'm not warmed up."

"If you refuse they'll think you were telling a lie. Nadia says she played it for singers at the conservatory. She agrees it's a difficult song, to play as well as to sing. She'll try if you will. She asks what key you sing it in."

He sighed. "D. D major."

Nadia considered the answer, struck a few chords, and nodded, looking at Mike. *Here I am again,* he thought. *the party hog. But they asked for it, probably to call my bluff. So here we go.* He stood, as his mother would want him to, took a deep breath, let a little out, and began in full voice. It sounded gravelly at first, but his throat soon cleared.

> *Night may enthrall me long,*
> *In her mysterious silence . . .*

Soon, he forget where he was. Looking inward, he was standing by his mother again. Realizing that he missed her and had no way to contact her to tell her he was alive, his voice faltered for a moment. The pianist waited expectantly. He took another breath, nodded to her, and picked up the song at the beginning of the measure as she followed.

When he approached the climax, he concentrated on what his mother had said. *Drop your jaw, Mike. Don't think up for the high note; think down. On "song," for the high note's sustained vowel, sing "ah." Keep thinking "ah" as you sustain the note.*

> *For with thy name I'd turn that silence into*
> *song. . . .*

He hit the F sharp squarely, let it ring through the room, and then came down to the end:

> *Ah, with thy magic name,*
> *Turn silence into song.*

The crowd sat silently for a moment. The fact that the young American had a nice voice and could sing his country's popular songs for them had been a pleasant surprise. But this was something else. Here was a young man from an alien nation, a capitalist nation, who not only knew the classical music of a Russian composer but was able to sing it clearly and sensitively.

Finally, a shout came from one of the men—Mike recognized him as Boris, the saxophone player at the party—and the rest began clapping and stamping their feet. When they stopped, one and then several spoke to Galina.

"They thank you for singing our music and singing it well," she said. "Several who spoke know that I've undertaken to tutor you, help you, in learning our language. They suggest that, when your study has progressed, you sing this same song and perhaps one or two others of ours in the native Russian. As a test."

"I'll try."

When he returned to the Yak barracks, Viktor listened to his description of the evening with a look of assumed seriousness. At the end of Mike's story, he produced the trusty vodka bottle and two glasses and poured a drink.

"I think I will have to revise my opinion of you, Mike," he said. "All of this time I'd thought I'd come to know you, your character and personality, rather well."

"Haven't you?"

"It appears I haven't. You look and act so, so fresh-faced and innocent, like someone who's a bit lost. I hadn't realized you were capable of such low cunning."

"Cunning?

"Oh yes. For my part, I've tried to woo Galina with my devil-may-care, swashbuckling pose, the sort of approach that's worked so well with other women. And I've been miserably rejected. Meantime, you've played the oldest trick in the world, appealing to her mothering instinct, persuading her to help the lost boy learn the language, to spend time with you, actually making her responsible *for* you."

"I hadn't thought about it that way."

"If you've done it intuitively, without conscious thought, it's all the more serious; it suggests that duplicity is part of your character." He laughed wryly. "This is a double blow to my ego, you understand. To be rejected by a maiden and then outsmarted by a boy."

Viktor drank his vodka, poured another, and looked into his glass. "There is an old Russian saying—it probably comes from our people of the desert in Uzbekistan—about a camel who asks permission to put his nose under a man's tent to get warm. It's only the nose, and the tent's occupant doesn't object. But, after a time, the entire camel is inside the tent."

"We have the same saying."

"Do you really? How strange."

"Viktor, I admit that I'm interested in Galina. She fascinates me. But I turned to her, well, just automatically; she speaks English very well."

"I don't?"

"Of course you do. But you're very busy, and I . . . well, it just seemed the natural thing to do."

"A convincing explanation."

"She has the most beautiful, most expressive eyes."

"She was probably swaddled for a long time as an infant."

"Swaddled? What do you mean?"

"Mike, you know so little about us. It's the custom; when Russian infants are born, their *babushka*, their grandmother, swaddles them, bandages them from head to foot, their feet together and their arms at their sides. They are bandaged, immobile, in that way, for many months."

"Like a mummy?"

"Yes, like an Egyptian mummy."

"Why do they do that?"

Viktor shrugged. "It's simply the custom. The point is that the eyes of the infant are virtually the only part of the body that can move freely. We believe that's why Russian women have such expressive eyes. Surely you've heard the Russian song 'Ochi Tchornia,' dark eyes."

"Yes, of course. But her eyes aren't dark, except when she's angry."

"A detail. We're flying tomorrow. Time for bed."

In her bed in the schoolhouse, Galina tried to sort out her thoughts about Mikhail. She had decided earlier that he was crass and ignorant, though he seemed sincerely to want to learn the language. But his knowledge of the Rachmaninoff song, and his—it had to be admitted—highly sensitive interpretation of it confused her. She hadn't mentioned it to Mikhail, of course, but she was still affected by an incident that had happened at the university two years earlier when an American, supposedly a good Communist, had arrived for a stay.

He not only expected to go to bed with all the female students as if it were his due; he was unbelievably crude and gross in his behavior. He had actually taught one beginning student, a girl, to say "I would like to fuck you" when she thought she was saying "I am glad to meet you."

Galina was outraged when she learned of it and told a young male friend, an Englishman, who was helping to augment her classroom study of his language. The English youth hit the American in the jaw and knocked him down a flight of stairs. The university provost expelled both young men. Ever after, she had held a grudge against Americans, believing them all to be the same. Her first meeting with Mikhail seemed to confirm that belief.

Now, his actions had proven her wrong. She hated to be wrong; even worse, to be confused. And she was both. She punched her pillow angrily. He wasn't important enough to cost her her sleep, so why was she awake? It was irritating; *he* was irritating, like a pebble in a shoe.

CHAPTER TEN

STRAIGHTEN UP AND
FLY RIGHT

"Now LISTEN, SON," the voice said through the scrambler telephone. "Just listen to 'ol John Sloane, y'hear? You've been buildin' up a real good record. I know, I've been checkin' up on you. You got twenty-one missions now, you're a captain, you're flyin' some squadron leads for your bomb group, Buddy. And now you've got those fine, long-range P-51s to escort you all the way in and all the way out—*all the way*, son."

"It's really turned things around, General," Captain Buddy Bryce said. "No question; it's all gonna be downhill from here on."

"If it wadn't, I wouldn't be tellin' you to sign up for a second tour, son. The 'ol Luftwaffe ain't washed up yet, by any means, but the odds are gettin' better and better for you. You fly just five more missions when you finish the first twenty-five—just *five more*, son—and they'll be puttin' you in for major. They don't, I *will*. I got ways. Get you a regular squadron leader job, fly some deputy group leads, then

217

group leads. What I want, Buddy, is to get you command of your own bomb group."

"A *group?*" Buddy said incredulously.

"Why'n hell not? Don' look like that Colonel Robinson of yours is gonna stand down anytime soon—though he oughta. So you get that oak leaf on your collar and I'll set about gettin' you switched to another group. Maybe the 300th. They got hit pretty bad a few weeks ago and they're short of command staff jus' now."

"I was thinkin' of signin' up for another twenty-five anyway," Buddy said. "Sorta see if I can see the end of what we started." *And be in the right place if and when Mike pops up, escapes or whatever.*

"Good, good," Sloane said. "We need as many S'uthe'n boys as possible in command of those bomb groups. Figure on stayin' in after the war, son. Get you a bird colonel's rank before this thing winds up, even if they bust you a rank or two in the regular peacetime Air Force —we're gonna be a *separate* branch of the service, the U.S. Air Force— you'll be a general like me with all the perks before you retire. And the South shall rise again!"

"Be like a Confederate air force, General, is that it?"

"That's right, son, but we won't call it that. Jus' you stick with 'ol John, Buddy, you'll be in deep clover."

"Whatever you say, General."

"Good, good. Now, next page. There's nothin' new 'bout your friend, Mike Gavin. He coulda bought it, of course, you got to accept that. But the chances are good that he's sittin' in a squarehead POW camp. Hold onto that thought. I'll keep checkin' for you."

"Thanks a million, General."

"Don' mention it, son. Jus' remember now; I'm too old and lame to go out and do all those great things you're doin.' So you do 'em for me. You're my boy. Jus' remember our motto."

"The South shall rise again."

"It shall indeed."

Buddy hung up the phone and sighed. Old John was laying it on pretty thick these days. He had come to think of Buddy as a son or as a champion to send into battle, as a medieval earl or duke once sent his favorite knight. John was a blowhard, an Army version of Fred Allen's Senator Claghorn. But Buddy had grown fond of the older man. John Sloane had been immensely helpful. He checked periodically to see if there was anything new on Mike and, at Buddy's request, he had located Claire and allowed Buddy to make a transatlantic phone call to her from his office at Wing headquarters.

She had been surprised and pleased to hear from Buddy and

shocked to hear that Mike was missing. He asked her to telephone Mike's mother in Baltimore and try to comfort her. By now, Laura Gavin had received the War Department telegram saying that Mike was MIA.

Buddy was thunderstruck to hear that Claire had actually ferried new P-51s from Texas to East Coast bases for overseas deliveries. Congress wouldn't let the WASPS fly the planes overseas. Buddy had expected her to be ferrying transports; she had done that, too. *But P-51s! M'God, what are these women gonna do next?* It was almost scary to think about.

Of course, that kind of thinking hadn't arrived in the UK theater yet. The English girls barely drove cars. And they still jumped when a man said "frog." But they were so sweet. They had the nicest, milkiest skin—no freckles or bumps like some of the American girls had. And the ones he had met were always ready for love.

Well, whoop-tee-do, he thought unenthusiastically. You could get sick eating too much ice cream. And he still couldn't get used to not having Mike around. What was that Yankee doin' right now, do you suppose? Probably sittin' on his bunk in a POW camp somewhere in Germany, eatin' a chunk of Kraut sausage, bored out of his skull.

Mike was never bored when he was with Galina. He was happy or angry or depressed, but never bored. It was a foggy morning with zero-zero visibility and they were walking in the woods. By agreement, they talked in English on the way out. Walking back, they would talk as much as possible in Russian.

"You were flying yesterday?" she asked.

"Yes. Did you fly last night?"

"Yes. We bombed a group of tanks and trucks that the partisans had located for us. They were poorly concealed; the *Nyemtsy* don't understand camouflage as well as we do. So the mission was successful. Do you have more than one victory now? In your Yak?"

"Yes. I have three; the last one was just plain dumb luck. I hit a Messerschmitt as he passed in front of me."

"I congratulate you; you seem to be learning very quickly."

"I've been out ten times. Viktor says when you've flown ten sorties and survived, you're as good as the average German pilot. Of course, their average is going down. Sometimes I think I've become pretty good. But sometimes I do something dumb and feel like a real klutz."

"Klutz? Is that a German word?"

"It's just an American expression. It means a 'jerk.' "

"Jerk? You have peculiar expressions."

"A fool. A *durak*."

"I see. And your relations with the Russian pilots? Are they good?"

"With Viktor, very good. And I've become good friends with Boris Gusarov."

"The saxophone player."

"Yes. He's a real good guy. I'm teaching him some new American pop songs—'Flat Foot Floogie,' 'Straighten Up and Fly Right,' 'GI Jive,' all those."

She wrinkled her face. "Flat Foot?"

"Floogie. It doesn't mean anything. It's a nonsense song."

"We don't have nonsense songs."

"Don't you? All that heroic stuff—'our wings of steel will crush the Fascist beast'—that's pretty nonsensical, isn't it?"

She looked at him coldly. "Those are patriotic sentiments. Perhaps you don't love your country as much as we love ours."

"We express it differently, that's all. But this raises an important point. I can say anything to Viktor and, I hope, to you. Almost anything to Boris. With the others I have to be careful not to pop off, say something I shouldn't. I'm not used to pussyfooting around."

"I can hardly understand what you say sometimes, Mikhail. Pop-off, of course, is a well-known Russian name. But pussyfooting? What can that possibly mean?"

"It's just an expression, the popular idiom; it means, oh piss-ant, it means . . ."

"Pees-ann. You've said that many times. What is pes-ann?"

"It's not pees-ann, it's piss-ant. It means, oh, let's see, it means 'nuts.' Uh, like you'd say *Chert voz'mi!* The devil take it! But it's not an American expression you would use, piss-ant."

"Why not?"

"Well, it's not nice."

"If it's not nice, why do you say it?"

"It's nice enough, I mean it's okay, it's normal for someone like me to say it. Not for someone like you."

"Is it only for Americans to say?"

"I don't mean that. I mean it's just that . . ."

"You mean it's only for men, is that it?"

"Well, it's mainly a man's expression; it just wouldn't be nice for . . ."

"For a woman."

"Well, yes, for a woman."

"What is so different about a woman, Mikhail, especially at this time? Don't we face the same risks, endure the same hardships, go on the same missions, eat the same food?"

"Yes, but . . ."

"But men can still do things that women cannot. Men can even say things that women cannot."

Mike shrugged helplessly and spread his palms.

"You're as bad as the Russian men, Mikhail, just as bad. Blind and narrow-minded."

"Narrow-minded? Me?"

"Yes, you. And I will say pees-ann if I wish. I'll say it now. Pees-ann! Pees-ann!"

"Well, if you just have to say it, you might as well say it right. It's not pees-ann, it's piss-ant. But you still shouldn't say it."

"What I am saying sounds fine to me. Pees-ann!" She glared at him, thrust her hands in her pockets, and walked resolutely back to the barracks, leaving him angry, frustrated, and depressed.

When she reached the barracks, Galina pulled off her jacket, threw it on her bunk, and plopped down.

"What's the matter, Galina?" Valya asked.

"Oh, it's that American. He makes me so angry. All those men make me angry. They're so smug. They can say what we can't. They can do what we can't."

"But we've come farther than ever before in history, Galina. We're flying combat alongside them, aren't we?"

"Because they need us so badly. Even then, they give us old, decrepit training planes. Though I do love our *Ved'ma*. But in every other way it's always the same. If they swear and curse, that's fine. If we do it, we're not *nice*."

Valya smiled. "But Galina, some of these things we're breaking down. The relations between women and men, for example. Many of us have declared our freedom from the old taboos. And aren't you being a bit inconsistent? Many of the girls have decided they have the same right to physical pleasure as the men. But you're still . . ."

"The icon. I know what they call me. The icon, the virgin, the ice maiden. But that's different, Valya."

"How different?"

"In a matter like that, I believe, we're equal only if both parties think we're equal. If we do these things and we don't think cheaply of *them* but they think cheaply of *us*, it's not really equality, is it?"

"What the other person thinks deep down inside is something we seldom know, Galina. All I know for certain is that we face danger every day and it seems, excuse me, shortsighted not to take advantage of any pleasure or joy we can find."

"I understand that, and I admit I'm inconsistent. But isn't it true that, for most of these men, participating in sex is a matter of scoring a new victory, making a new conquest, something to boast about?"

Valya shrugged. "Yes, I suppose that's true."

"And isn't it also true that most women want something more than simply submitting, even if the experience is pleasurable? Don't we want some mutual feeling of respect, of love?"

"Respect, yes. *Love*—well, if we're lucky."

"I'm not really a cold person, Valya, regardless of what the others may think. I've had a sheltered sort of upbringing, yet I feel—*stirrings*. But then they come close and I'm repelled by the hot eyes, the hot hands, the wet lips—like hungry wolves who see a deer. And that vacant-eyed, slack-jawed look they get sometimes when they come around you."

"Even Viktor?"

"Viktor conceals it better than most."

"Do you see that look in Petrov?"

"Oh, Petrov. He's like a big dog, a bear; he hangs around when he can get here. He's harmless, and I'm touched sometimes by his devotion, but I'm going to tell him not to come."

"Mikhail doesn't have that look, does he?"

"No he doesn't. At least not yet."

"I think he respects you."

"Yes, I think he does. I'm sure he does. He also irritates me. Perhaps it's because he's so open, or seems to be. With him, nothing is hidden."

"He's with you a great deal these days."

"Yes, he is. First it was to teach him Russian and help my English, this American English. Now we're taking walks, long walks, almost every day." She brooded for a moment. "Sometimes I wonder if he's really as innocent as he looks. Sometimes I feel that he's wormed his way into my life in a way I don't quite understand. And that, somehow, I've become *responsible* for him. I don't *want* to be responsible for someone else."

"Does he . . . stir you, Galina?"

"No. I'm not sure. Sometimes there's *something*. His hair is too long; sometimes I feel like cutting it for him. His uniform jacket is too baggy. And I sometimes wonder if he really knows enough Russian to talk to his comrades when he's flying. But I'm flying, too, so why should I be concerned for him?"

"He comes and stands at the edge of the field every night we're flying, I'm told. To see that you're down safely."

"I knew he did it sometimes. I didn't know he does it every time."

"If I become too personal, tell me, Galina, but, we're friends and . . ."

"You're my navigator, Valya. In the air and"—she laughed—"on the ground, too, it seems. What are you trying to say?"

"I just wanted to ask: do you feel—what is the right word?—do you feel *tender* toward Mikhail?"

Galina sighed. "Tender? Perhaps; I don't know. Why I should feel that way, any way, I don't know. He's certainly not handsome."

"Oh, but he's very interesting looking with those brown eyes . . ."

"They're hazel."

"All right, hazel. And that brown/blond hair. And compact body. I can tell you that he stirs feelings in some of the girls. They'd be happy to have a relationship with him if he'd show any interest in them. And he has a beautiful voice. When he sang that high note near the end of the Rachmaninoff—that ringing sound—I have to tell you I practically creamed my pants."

Galina clapped her hands over her cheeks and giggled. "Oh, Valya, what a thing to say! You're terrible!" She shook her head.

"But he does have a nice voice." When he sang that high note, Galina admitted to herself, it sent shivers through her. Something definitely stirred within her. But she had always believed that the man who ultimately stirred her would be a truly handsome Russian man. Like Viktor. But Viktor, inexplicably, didn't stir her.

Still, Mikhail is not handsome, she thought, and he shouldn't delude himself into thinking that he is. She would set him straight on that at the earliest opportunity.

Adolf Galland, General of the Fighters, sat in the cockpit of a Focke-Wulf 190 at twenty-five thousand feet and watched the parade of American bombers from a respectful distance of seven or eight miles. On his wing, in a second FW-190, was Oberst Hannes Trautloft, Inspector of the Day Fighters East.

Galland had sneaked away, as he had been doing with increasing frequency, to fly sorties of his own. Impulsively, he had invited Trautloft, who was supposed to be inspecting airfields, to go with him. Sitting in an office trying to deal with self-defeating orders from the Reichsmarschall, his onetime patron and friend, was too maddening to endure for long.

The sight before them was depressing. Sightings, reported by radio, estimated the size of the B-17 force at eight hundred. Group after group, wave after wave of the bombers droned on toward their targets with thousands of tons of death and destruction in their bomb bays.

And over them, to right and left, vapor trails streaming to mark their paths, flew vast packs of escorting Mustang fighters.

Where was the Luftwaffe? Galland switched his radio to the command wavelength. The German fighters had just landed after attacking the B-17 force and were being gassed and rearmed to take off again. Galland shook his head disbelievingly; the armada passing before him showed no sign of damage or distress.

At this moment, he estimated, there were seven American fighters for every German fighter in western combat. Further, increasing numbers of the German pilots were boys with only fifty or sixty hours of training. They had had little to no instrument training and they were flying ME-109s and FW-190s that had become obsolete.

The American Mustangs were better airplanes and their pilots, he had been told, received several hundred hours of training before being sent into combat. By any measure, the struggle had become unequal.

Adding to Galland's burden was a chain of destructive events. One was Göring's suicidal order to Luftwaffe commanders to ignore the fighter escorts and go after the bombers. When the pilots obeyed, the American pilots simply jumped on their tails and shot them down. Part of every *Geschwader* should be devoted to a force that did nothing but attack the American fighters, Galland said. But Göring would hear none of it, despite the hard evidence of how well the Luftwaffe could do when it was allowed to.

On the previous October 12, before the long-range American fighters arrived, the Luftwaffe won a resounding victory when the Amis had attacked Schweinfurt for a second time. The Americans lost so many B-17s on that raid that they called that day Black Thursday and, once again, lost air superiority and stopped virtually all long-range bombing.

Until now. With the arrival of the long-range Mustangs, the tables were turned again. That couldn't be helped, perhaps, but there was a remedy: more sensible tactics—and, most important of all, the German wonderplane, the jet-propelled ME-262.

That, he knew, would make a difference! When the sleek jets flashed through their formations, the Mustangs would flap around like frightened geese and the bombers, failing even to see the attacking jets, would go down in flames.

Yet the wonderplanes, nearly a year after the prototypes were tested, were still sitting fallow as the bomber command, following Adolf Hitler's order, tried to convert them to bombers and retrain bomber pilots to fly them.

And now word had come of a new and ominous event. General James Doolittle had arrived on January 6, 1944, to take command of the U.S. Eighth Air Force. Galland had followed Doolittle's career with great interest and respect. Doolittle was not just another general with wings on his jacket. He was a legend, a man who had been a penniless orphan in Alaska and grown up to excel at many things— as a scholar and strategist; a daredevil on motorcycles and in airplanes; an acrobat and wing-walker; winner of the coveted Schneider and Bendix racing cups; the only man ever to have flown, won with, and survived flying the treacherous, virtually unflyable BeeGee racer; the commander of the B-25 twin-engined U.S. Army bomber squadron that somehow took off from the pitching deck of an aircraft carrier in the Pacific in 1942 and actually bombed Tokyo, though every bomber but one on that mission either crashed or crash-landed.

When he arrived in England, Doolittle immediately had made his goals clear. The bombers of the Eighth would destroy Germany's transportation system and oil refineries. By doing so, all the new tanks and airplanes and guns made by the ingenious Speer in underground factories would be useless. They would have neither fuel to run them nor highways nor railroads to travel upon.

And, by attacking such targets, the bombers of the Eighth would force the Luftwaffe aloft to combat them so that the swarms of new-generation Mustang fighters could kill off the German pilots.

The Luftwaffe would have to accept the challenge to try to protect what was left of Germany. But the German fighters would have only occasional chances to smash the bombers as bloodily as they had done in the past. Now the old ME-109s and Focke-Wulfs would be met by large numbers of the superb American fighters.

Once Doolittle's program had achieved clear air superiority, the coming Allied invasion of the continent would be assured of success. His program burst into malignant bloom in late January. Eight hundred bombers, the largest number yet assembled, attacked Frankfurt. And in one week of February, a thousand American bombers accompanied by seven hundred fighters—*seven hundred!*—attacked multiple targets throughout Germany and ran the Luftwaffe ragged.

In desperation, Göring had recalled several groups of Germany's already-outnumbered fighters from the Eastern front to try to slow the Allied avalanche in the West. At that point, Galland knew the war was lost. But he was still pugnacious enough to want to fight. As he did now.

The idea of two German fighters daring to attack any part of the American armada droning by was ridiculous, he knew. But so was sitting up here and watching.

"Hannes!" he called to his wingman over the fighter channel. "Let's get one!" He shoved his throttle forward and banked toward a bomber that was straggling behind the last formation. Galland streaked to within a hundred yards of the B-17's tail and fired his cannons at the bomber. Metal flew from the bomber's engines and a wing caught fire. The pilot jettisoned his bomb load and the B-17's crew began bailing out.

As Galland watched, the radio crackled: "*Achtung,* Adolf! Mustangs! My guns are jammed! I'm beating it!"

A burst of machine gun tracers flashed around Galland's fighter and he pushed the nose down and dived at full power to escape. Tracers struck his cockpit. Diving for the ground with four Mustangs in pursuit, he pulled a desperate trick that had saved his life in the Battle of Britain. He punched the firing button and fired his cannons and machine guns straight ahead.

The Mustangs sheared off as the blue smoke from the FW-190 blew backward. Was another German behind them and firing at them? Did this audacious German pilot have a new kind of gun aboard that fired backward? They didn't know, but why take a chance?

On the way home, Galland brooded over what he had done. It had been rash, even stupid to make that attack. It was one thing to die when there was some reason for the sacrifice. It was quite another thing to die for no good reason at all.

He had already lost two brothers in the Luftwaffe, and several of his oldest and best friends had been shot down and killed. He wanted the rest, wherever they were, to stay alive.

At that moment, Mike Gavin and Kapitan Otto Ritter, a seasoned Luftwaffe pilot, were doing their best to stay alive by trying to kill each other in a furious dogfight over the Eastern front line sixty miles west of the Dnieper.

The instant Mike started the attack on the Focke-Wulf, he knew he had made a mistake. Viktor had warned him repeatedly about acting hastily. "There's a vital difference between acting quickly and acting in haste," Viktor had said. "Learn it if you want to survive."

He still hadn't learned it. He and Viktor had become separated in a melee of opposing fighters that were trying to protect their respective ground-attack airplanes over the front. Flying at an altitude of seventeen thousand feet, Mike spotted what he thought was an easy kill.

The Focke-Wulf was moving several thousand feet below him and passing from left to right. Mike briefly considered a diving side-on attack but, realizing that the German would quickly turn onto the tail of his Yak if he missed, opted for a high barrel-roll that would loop around behind the German while preserving his speed.

Hastily, he pulled up, rolled on his back, and came down the roller-coaster in a steep dive. *Too steep,* he realized too late. His nose was too low and, when the German saw him and pulled the FW's nose up, Mike overshot him. The German promptly rolled over to close on Mike's tail for a killing cannon-shot.

Peering frantically behind, Mike pulled his nose up vertically and climbed into another barrel-roll. The German, diving fast, overshot just as Mike had done. Mike rolled down into a dive to get behind the FW but the German pulled his nose up again. Cursing, Mike overshot him again.

Now the German was diving onto his tail again. Once again, Mike pulled his nose up into a vertical climb. As he did, he belatedly remembered Viktor's warning to avoid getting caught in the maneuver called the vertical scissors. But he and the German were locked into it now and, each time they went through the maneuver, passing each other vertically, canopy to canopy, so close they saw each other's face, they lost altitude.

By now they were only a few thousand feet from the ground and continuing to sink. Then Mike remembered Viktor's second warning: "If you do get caught in the scissors, you have to stay in it. The first man who tries to break out gives the other a clear gunshot."

"But suppose you get too close to the ground?" Mike asked.

"Too bad," Viktor said. "It depends on whether you want to be killed by the Fascist or the ground. For myself, I'd prefer the ground."

The German was pulling out of his barrel-roll to regain the tail-shot position. Desperately, Mike pulled up vertically again. His airspeed had diminished along with the altitude and the Yak was close to stalling. When he rolled over this time and let the nose drop, he needed all the space available between himself and the ground to regain control of the Yak.

Barely clearing the treetops, Otto Ritter had to make an instantaneous decision. One more maneuver of the scissors would very probably take his Focke-Wulf into the trees. If he somehow managed to clear them, the Yak would almost certainly crash. But that was small comfort when his own chance of surviving another climb, roll, and dive was so poor.

Ritter made up his mind. He was, after all, a Luftwaffe ace with sixteen kills to his credit. Few, if any Russian pilots, were that good. With his superior skill, he would surprise the Russian. He would quickly break off the engagement, escape, and live to fight another day.

Ritter slammed the Focke-Wulf into a tight and level turn over the treetops. Mike was caught by surprise, but his conditioned reflexes acted for him. He automatically yanked the Yak into the tightest possible turn to get inside the curving course of the FW and intercept it. The Yak shuddered as he brought the nose up to maintain his skimpy altitude. The nose wallowed around and edged just ahead of the Focke-Wulf.

As the German crossed his nose, Mike pressed the firing button. The Yak's cannon thumped and the two machine guns stuttered. The German exploded in a red and black cloud. Mike flew blindly through it, pulling up just in time to avoid hitting the top of a tall pine tree. A stream of light flak curved up at him.

Turning sharply in the opposite direction, he looked up and back. It would be ironic, after his desperate struggle, to be picked off like a sitting duck by another German. He caught his breath when he saw that there was an airplane above him. But, instead of a Maltese cross, it bore a red star.

"Desna Two, this is Desna One," a voice said. "Return to position."

Gratefully, Mike shoved his throttle forward and climbed into position on Viktor's wing. When they landed, Mike's Yak was nearly out of gas and he was exhausted.

"You seem to do well in spite of yourself," Viktor said as they walked back to the briefing room to report to Borisenko. "But there's an old Russian saying that you should commit to memory. It goes: *Netu starykh khrabrykh pilotov.* You cannot be an old and bold pilot. Not one and the same."

Mike nodded. "We have the same saying. 'There are old pilots and there are bold pilots. There are no old, bold pilots.' "

"Is that so?" Viktor said. "It's odd how many Russian sayings you Americans have taken from us. The next thing you'll be telling me is that you invented jazz."

* * *

Flugkapitan Hanna Reitsch crawled into the cockpit that had been carved out of the body of the V-1 flying bomb. It had taken the matchless German scientists and their assistants just four days to convert the jet-driven missile that would soon terrorize Londoners into one that could be flown and aimed by a human pilot.

Now, if ever, was the time to use it. Conditions were deteriorating rapidly. The American bombers were pulverizing German cities and industries by day while the RAF smashed them by night. The Luftwaffe was shrinking day by day. And everyone knew that the invasion of Europe was coming.

In the East, the seige of Leningrad had been lifted, rail lines were open between Leningrad and Moscow, and German Army Group North had been pushed back into the Baltic states. To the south, the Red Army had begun an offensive aimed at destroying the German Eighth Army in the Ukraine.

Meantime, one stupid mistake after another had delayed the training of the suicide group. First there had been the resistance of Field Marshal Milch and the Führer's refusal to commit himself to the project. Then the odious Himmler had gotten himself into the act, proclaiming that the suicide group should be made up of criminals, deserters, and others who could volunteer to die to regain their honor.

That was unbelievably stupid! Only the best-trained and most skilful pilots would be capable of carrying out the task of flying the bombs into invasion ships and key enemy installations.

Then they were told the original group could begin training with the experimental twin-jet Messerschmitt 328. Explosives were to be placed in the aircraft's tail to turn it into a flying bomb.

Soon afterward, the Air Ministry suspended work on the ME-328. Other priorities, they said. Finally, the legendary paratroop colonel, Otto Skorzeny, had come to their rescue. He had heard of the suicide group from Himmler and he had promptly suggested using a piloted version of the V-1 "buzz-bomb."

For the moment, any recommendation by Skorzeny counted for a great deal. With ninety of his elite troops in gliders, he had rescued the deposed Italian leader, Benito Mussolini, from a mountaintop hotel in Abruzzi where the new Bagdolio government had imprisoned him. Greatly impressed, Adolf Hitler had impulsively invested Skorzeny with unspecified "full powers."

Waving the decree, Skorzeny ordered the V-1 program engineers to give Hanna whatever she wanted. And they obeyed. The piloted V-1 prototype was given the code name of Reichenberg and placed on the secret list. It had a small cockpit behind the missile's stubby wings. A stick, rudders, and landing flaps were provided. Cushioned skids were installed for landing.

The final version would have no flaps or skids, of course, because it would not be landed.

Already, two fine pilots had crashed trying to fly the V-1. Both were alive, though badly injured. So, once again, it was up to the Luftwaffe's diminutive female test pilot. She would determine whether even skilled pilots could take off in the flying bomb, control it in flight and, because it was necessary for training, land it.

For her attempted flight, the V-1 had been placed on a set of rails that inclined upward at a shallow angle. Hanna had had a sack of sand placed in the front of the craft to simulate the explosive charge that the real thing would carry.

Now all was ready. She adjusted her helmet, strapped herself in tightly, and lifted a hand to give the signal for takeoff. It was, she knew, very much like climbing onto a large firecracker and telling someone to light the fuse.

A technician sitting at a nearby console depressed a button. The crude jet engine ignited with a thunderous roar and the V-1 shot off the rails like a bullet, squeezing her hard against the back of her seat.

Aloft, she saw immediately that the V-1 required an exquisitely sensitive sense of touch. No pilot of average skill would be able to control it. It would take the very best. She made gentle climbs and dives and reached five hundred miles an hour in level flight while banking gently to right and left. Now would come the hardest part: landing the missile. She approached the field, let down properly, and felt the sack of sand slide forward.

The craft nosed down. She pulled the stick back to force it up. The elevator wouldn't respond. She tried again. No response. Her heart began beating faster and she struggled to stay calm. The earth was coming up fast. Nearing the ground, she yanked the stick back with all her strength, thrust it forward, then yanked it back again, porpoising along the landing strip.

The sand shifted slightly, the nose came up, and the bottom of the V-1 slammed into the ground. It skidded wildly, slewed, and stopped. The engineers came running toward her from all directions. Hanna unbuckled her harness, got out winded but unscratched, and walked around the V-1. The hull was splintered and the skids were smashed.

"Get another one ready for me," she said to the chief engineer. "I'll fly it tomorrow. This time, put a water tank in the hull and fit it with a drain plug that I can open from the cockpit. I'll release the water before landing."

Awed by the courage and skill of the tiny woman, they had the craft ready the next morning. All went well until Hanna tried to move the lever to release the water at eighteen thousand feet. It wouldn't budge. The drain plug had frozen to the tank.

There was no time to descend to a lower altitude and fly around in the warmer air till the ice melted. The V-1's fuel was exhausted and the craft was nosing over into a dive. She yanked repeatedly at the lever to break the plug free and release the water. With it aboard, the V-1 was far too heavy to land. It would simply crash.

Skilful as she was, all she could do was yank on the lever like a moron. At no more than twenty feet from the ground, the drain plug broke loose and the water cascaded out. The V-1 soared briefly upward, giving her just enough time to flatten out for a rough but safe landing.

Flying the V-1 was very difficult, she concluded, and the mediocre pilots among the volunteers would have to be weeded out. But it could be done. The time had come to activate the suicide group and she was confident that, by now, the Führer would agree. Personal survival was unimportant compared to the survival of the Fatherland.

She knew by the pressure being exerted from both East and West that the enemy held the same beliefs. Personal considerations had no place in the struggle that lay ahead.

Galina was on the night-flight roster and, knowing it, Mike couldn't sleep. So, as he had done a dozen times before, he got out of bed, put on his trousers, boots, heavy jacket, and fur-lined cap, and trudged over to the night-witches' field.

The PO-2s were landing, one by one, as he arrived. Using the rudimentary Russian he had learned, he determined that she hadn't landed. He moved to the edge of the strip and waited. In the flickering light of the oil drums, he saw a large figure.

It was Petrov. Mike was surprised and annoyed. He thought the lout's PE-2 twin-engine bomber unit had been transferred elsewhere. The big man stiffened as he recognized the smaller American.

"*Doloy!* Go away," he said harshly.

"*Nyet,*" Mike said curtly.

Petrov strode angrily to Mike and seized him by his collar. Mike struck his hand away. Petrov pushed him. Mike staggered back, recovered his balance and, as Petrov pushed him back, Petrov swung a clumsy punch at Mike's head. Mike sidestepped and hooked sharply to the larger man's stomach.

Petrov bent at the waist as the blow forced the air from his lungs. Then he pulled himself erect, bellowed angrily, and charged the smaller man. Mike sidestepped nimbly again and threw a straight right-hand punch to the side of Petrov's jaw. Petrov staggered, shook himself, and came charging back.

"*Perestan!*" a woman's voice shouted. "Stop it!" Glancing quickly to the side, Mike saw that it was Galina. Her face was streaked with oil and she was, clearly, very tired. But her eyes were angry. She spoke quickly in Russian and then in English. "The next one who strikes will leave immediately. I will never speak to him again."

Mike looked at her, stood erect, and dropped his hands. Petrov's heavy fist crashed into his jaw and the ground slanted up and struck Mike in the back of his head. He was dimly aware that Galina was shouting and that Petrov was protesting. Hearing Petrov's bass tones, it occurred irrelevantly to Mike that, with proper training, the big lout might develop a fine singing voice.

He tried to push himself up but he became dizzy and sank back again. Galina dropped to her knees and peered at him closely in the flickering light.

"*Ty durak,*" she said. "You're a fool, Mikhail. Such a fool." Shifting expressions of concern and irritation crossed her face.

"You have no need to be here. I've told you that before. Are you all right now? Do you need to go to the infirmary? Is your face broken?"

He moved his jaw from side to side. "I don't think so. Just help me up. I think I can stand up now." She pulled him to his feet. He felt a trifle unsteady and held onto her. She raised a hand to the spot on his jaw that was already swelling. He winced slightly but stood stock-still, enjoying the contact. It was the first time she had touched him. Slowly, carefully, he put his arms around her and drew her to him.

They stood together silently for a moment. Finally, she said: "Go to bed, Mikhail. You mustn't come here every night. You need your sleep."

"Will you walk with me tomorrow?"

"Perhaps. I don't know."

"I'm not flying; I'll come by in the afternoon."

"Very well."

Mike's jaw ached painfully, but he went to sleep happier than he had been in a long time.

* * *

Mike and Galina didn't walk or even talk together for three days. The morning after his fight with Petrov, all flight operations were suspended. The mixed regiment was to pack up and leave immediately. Transport planes and trucks arrived to carry away all ground personnel and equipment—airplane parts, machinery and tools, ammunition and food stores, and medical supplies. Briefings were held for regimental commanders and flight leaders to tell them where to fly their airplanes.

"What's going on?" Mike asked Viktor.

"We're moving southwest. Apparently we've launched a big offensive, so big that Marshal Zhukov is leading it, to drive the Fascists out of the Dnieper bend. They say we'll be at the Rumanian border within a few days. And the word is that Vatutin's made a big breakthrough west of Kiev."

"Kiev?"

"The capital of the Ukraine, Mike. Very important. They say the front there is one hundred and eighty-five miles long. They say twenty-two German divisions are being pushed back to the Polish border. We're winning. There's really no question about that now."

"So where are we going? Is the mixed regiment staying together?"

Viktor smiled. "Yes, for now, at least. The night-witches will be there soon after we get there, don't worry. We're taking over some fields and underground bunkers the enemy have evacuated in their retreat. They're near a town named Zhitomir. That won't mean anything to you, or to me either. But we'll have some good navigational landmarks—watermarks, really—for our work in that sector. Attacking the Fascists, we'll have the Dnieper at our backs, the Bug River south of us, and the Dniester in front, to the west of us. Soon our ground forces will be across the Dniester."

Soon, they were. Stalin received a report that ten German divisions had been trapped in the Ukraine. His generals claimed that they had killed fifty-five thousand Germans and taken eighteen thousand prisoners. The Soviet dictator turned on his Telefunken short-wave radio to see if any of the foreign-language broadcasts would confirm the claims.

A little bad news was mixed with the good. The able Marshal Vatutin had been ambushed and killed on the First Ukrainian Front by Ukrainian nationalists; some were fighting for the Germans, some for the Russians.

A few weeks later, Russian troops surged to the Rumanian border at Yampol on the east bank of the Dniester. And forty thousand Germans were trapped at Skala. Stalin laughed heartily at the statement Hitler made to his generals when the German defense line in the Ukraine was split in two. That action, the little Austrian claimed, had "exhausted and divided" the Russian forces.

Meantime, a host of little and big events illuminated the landscape of the biggest war in world history:

• Reichsmarschall Hermann Göring, caught in the open during an air raid, sat, bemedaled, in a state of monumental embarrassment among ordinary Berliners in a Berlin bomb shelter while the bombers he had said would never reach Berlin dropped a thousand tons of bombs on the city. The Americans and British were now bombing Germany's capital around the clock and "Meier's hunting horn" sounded the alarm night and day.

• Despite the large fighter escorts given the bombers, General Doolittle concluded, the bomber losses were still remarkably high. On March 4, 1944, 660 bombers hit Berlin and 69 went down; that was more than ten percent, not counting the loss of eleven friendly fighters. One bomber wing of three groups was virtually torn apart.

• The RAF was hit even harder. On a nighttime raid on Nürnberg, a British force of 795 lost 95 Lancaster bombers and had 71 damaged. The losses forced the RAF to temporarily suspend long-range bombing. You had to hand it to the Luftwaffe. It was dying but, Doolittle thought, when it massed its remaining fighters to attack, it was still a deadly and determined force.

• After four months of heavy air attacks by American bombers and ground assaults by soldiers from fifteen nations, incredibly stubborn German troops were finally driven out of the shattered Benedictine monastery atop Monte Cassino, opening the road to Rome. Twenty thousand men were killed taking the hill and one hundred thousand were wounded.

• Just north of Palau in the Pacific, the American submarine *Tullibee* torpedoed and sank itself. Navy commanders refused to believe it until the only surviving crewman testified that the torpedo ran in a circle and struck the boat.

• Luftwaffe General of the Bombers Werner Baumbach groaned and shook his head in despair. It had been nearly a year—a year!—since German scientists had revolutionized the science of bombing. Released by a bomber pilot in the Mediterranean from a distance of several miles, the Fritz X radio-controlled bomb—scientists called it a "smart" bomb—had sunk the Italian battleship *Roma* south of Sardinia as it tried to escape to the Western Allies.

Any rational military organization would have turned itself upside down to exploit such a scientific breakthrough. Not the Luftwaffe. General though he was, Baumbach was unable to get an audience with Reichsmarschall Göring to tell him about the success of Fritz X and show him the film that had been made of the event.

Admiral Dönitz was amazed by the story and demanded to know why the "smart" bomb wasn't being used. When Baumbach confessed his inability to contact Göring, Dönitz sighed deeply and said: "Where is the Reichsmarschall stag-hunting this week?"

Still, limited production of the Fritz X proceeded. But, when Galland was replaced as chief of the fighter arm, the Reichsmarschall ordered that all guided missile production be stopped so that the technical personnel could be transferred to accelerated fighter production.

Baumbach protested, without result, and went to the factory warehouse to rescue the missiles stocked there. There were scores of them and eighty percent were ready for use. He was too late. When he arrived, he found they had been broken up.

• In the Hague, six of the RAF's marvelous new twin-engine wooden Mosquito bombers made a precision strike on Gestapo headquarters and destroyed the files of Dutch men who were to be deported. Another RAF aerial strike breached the walls of Amiens prison in France, allowing seventy members of the resistance, who had been sentenced to death, to escape.

• Though the Third Reich was slowly dying, the SS bureaucracy methodically went on with its work. Greek Jews were rounded up in Athens and sent to Auschwitz. A month later, the first batch of 380,000 Hungarian Jews were dispatched to the same concentration camp for extermination.

• By now, Germany's engines were beginning to run dry. Thousands of American B-17s and B-24s struck synthetic oil refineries in Zwickau, Merseberg, Brux, Lutzkendorf, and Bohlen. Production Minister Albert Speer gloomily pondered the reports. He had done a brilliant job of dispersing the aircraft industry. Despite the heavy bombing, fighter production had risen.

The reason was simple and, to anyone who understood the problems of industrial production, staggering: twenty aircraft plants had been turned into more than seven hundred. Airplanes were being made underground, in camouflaged buildings, even in wooded areas throughout Germany. But what good was it, after all, when the huge oil refineries that supplied their engines had to be located above ground, and they were being systematically destroyed?

Conditions were bleak and grim. The impending defeat of the Third Reich hung like a specter over the German people. Ordinary discourse seemed to have disappeared from daily life.

"You are not handsome, Mikhail."

Galina's words, spoken as they walked through dense woods near her new airfield, startled Mike. "I never said I was handsome."

"There would be no use in your saying it, because you are not," she said firmly, looking straight ahead.

"But I didn't say I was."

"Well, you're not."

He pondered for a moment and asked: "Am I ugly then?"

She shook her head. "No, you are not ugly. You are . . . something in-between."

"Am I maybe homely-handsome?"

"That's another American expression I don't understand. No, you look"—she paused—"somewhat like an animal, perhaps."

"A wild animal, like a lion or a boar?"

"No, a smaller one."

"A harmless animal, like a deer, maybe?"

"How harmless, I don't know."

"But friendly."

"Friendly, I suppose. Like a mastiff, perhaps. One who seems lost. I speak of the look you have in your eyes sometimes."

They walked in silence for a while before she spoke again. "Now Viktor, he is handsome. The way a handsome Russian man should look. Very dashing, Viktor."

"Then why aren't you with Viktor instead of me?"

"I don't want to be with Viktor. Saying that Viktor is handsome doesn't mean that he attracts me."

"Do I attract you?" She stared ahead as if she hadn't heard the question.

"So you don't feel love for anyone, Galina."

She bridled. "I feel love for my country. That is the love I feel."

"That isn't the same thing, Galina."

"For me it is."

"I speak of a personal, intimate kind of love. I picked up that book by Aldington you had in your bunker. Have you read it?"

"He has many impractical theories. He doesn't follow Soviet principles."

"But what he said about love was very interesting, I thought. He said that love, the personal kind of love, is like a flower. It can't be given to a country or a crowd. Only to another person."

Surprised, she looked at him. "You remembered that? You are a romantic, Mikhail."

"Maybe. But don't you agree that Aldington is right? Personal love is something we can offer only to each other."

She looked ahead again and dug her hands deeply in her pockets.

"This is not the proper time to think about that sort of thing," she said.

"It seems to me that, when you don't know how much time you have, it's the best possible time. Wouldn't it be foolish, and sad, too, to miss a chance for love? Not the casual kind of fling . . ."

"Fling?"

"Attraction, relationship, the kind of thing that some of our comrades enjoy. But love, real love; why would any of us want to shut that out?"

They neared the entrance to her bunker. "I'm not prepared to talk about such things," she said.

"You only wanted to tell me I'm not handsome."

"Well, you are not."

The once-matchless efficiency of the German general staff had dissolved into divided authority and confusion. And, Inspector General of Armored Troops Heinz Guderian thought as he stared across the table, he knew who was to blame.

Adolf Hitler stared back sullenly. He held a deep, if grudging respect for Germany's tank warfare genius, as well as for his toughness in debate. But he hated the confrontations that the hard-faced Guderian forced upon him.

After the loud and bitter arguments they had had earlier over strategy, weapons, and the lack of winter uniforms on the Eastern front, Hitler had fired Guderian. But the man was too good a general to sit idle. So he hired him back to oversee the panzer divisions, though this blurred still further the lines of authority that already crisscrossed at headquarters. And here, apparently, was another confrontation.

"We have only ten panzer and panzergrenadier divisions to use as our principal reserves against the coming Allied invasion," Guderian said. "Now I've discovered that they're to be stationed very near the coast. If they're disposed in that manner, they can't be withdrawn and committed elsewhere fast enough if the enemy lands somewhere we don't expect."

"We know where the enemy will land," Hitler grated. "He'll land in the coastal area near the Somme. He must take a beachhead as close as possible to his principal point of embarkation."

"That's staking a great deal on faith," Guderian argued. "And it fails to utilize our greatest skill, the use of mobile tactics, *Auftragstaktik*. We need to move the panzers farther back so they can be directed quickly to the place they're needed."

The two men looked at each other silently. *He has no conception of mobile tactics,* Guderian thought. *That's what's killed us in the East. He's still a trench-warfare corporal reliving World War I.*

A look of irritation crossed Hitler's face. "The present arrangement of the panzers is the one suggested by Field Marshal Rommel. I don't want to give contrary orders over the head of the responsible man on the spot, certainly not without hearing his opinion. Go to France and discuss the matter with Rommel."

Guderian hedge-hopped to Rommel's headquarters at La Roche Guyon in a long-legged Fieseler-Storch the following day. One had to be very careful with enemy aircraft overhead everywhere these days. He had known Erwin Rommel since before the war. Rommel had had a distinguished career capped by exploits in North Africa that had won him the nickname of the "Desert Fox." In Africa, Rommel had outwitted and outfought the British until, starved for lack of supplies and greatly outnumbered in men, weapons, and aircraft, he had had to abandon the fight. Now he was head of Army Group B in France.

The man was upright, brave, and gifted. But, it turned out, the African experience had infected him with an unshakable conviction.

"We will never again be able to move large formations of troops," Rommel declared. "I learned that in Africa. The enemy's air superiority became so overwhelming there, and is so overwhelming here, that any effort to move our forces in the way we used to will be crushed."

"We'll move them at night," Guderian said. "Otherwise, what's the use of having motorized reserves at all?"

Rommel shook his head. "It's simply impossible. Just look up and you'll see what I mean. Even during our training exercises, I wonder how long it will be before they attack us instead of overflying us, the way they're doing now. What I want to know is: will we be getting more panzer divisions to reinforce what we've got?"

"Not enough to help very much. We 'loaned' two SS divisions, the ninth and tenth, to the Eastern front, as you'll remember. Even though they're badly needed there, particularly now, you'll get them back when the invasion begins. That's all, except for three divisions that are being kept in southern France against a separate Mediterranean landing there, though it may be hard to move them up in time if the main attack is where you think it will be. And Army headquarters, OKW, has three reserve divisions of its own. They are under the direct control of the Führer."

Rommel sighed. "Then we'll have to make do with what we've got. We've done what we can to defend ourselves. We've placed obstacles underwater along the coastline to impede the landing crafts. We've planted long stakes in all the terrain available for airborne landings to skewer gliders and paratroops. We've created extensive minefields. And any troops who aren't actively engaged in training are busy digging defenses."

"How much freedom of action will you have?" Guderian asked.

Rommel shrugged. "Technically, I'm subject to the orders of Field Marshal Rundstedt, of course. He's Commander-in-Chief West. But the Führer retains direct command of my army group. So, in the end, we're all subject to his wishes. What's happening in the East?"

"Nothing very good, I'm afraid. The Russians are pushing us back along a long front. It looks like they'll have all of the Ukraine back in their hands soon. And they've greatly increased the number of aircraft. It's almost hard to believe, when you consider the fact that we knocked out three-quarters of their air force in 1941, that they outnumber us now. Further, the quality of their aircraft and their pilots has improved a great deal."

"You really think we're better than they are now?" Mike asked. He and Viktor were sitting at a table in the abandoned, half-shattered church that now served as their combination mess hall and briefing room. Their sleeping quarters were in an underground bunker, entered by a metal door, surrounded by bricks and sandbags, that protruded from the surface.

Viktor squinted and thought before he answered. "Um, obviously we outnumber the Fascists now—in planes and pilots. And, as our skills have improved, theirs have declined. We've killed off so many of them. They seem to have sent some of their best men back to the West, too. So, overall, I suppose we're better."

"When you say our skills have improved, are you talking about individual flying ability or tactics, or both?"

"Both, really." He lowered his voice. "But give credit where it's due. We learned from them. First in the tactics. We used to just form up in circles when we were attacked and fly 'round and 'round till we were picked off. Or just corkscrew away—they called us 'crazy Ivans' —and try to escape. We knew so little.

"But we watched them and we learned and, when we did, we taught it to our trainees. We may not be as inventive as some, but we're quick to learn and then to improve on what others have done. It's one of our national traits. You've probably heard the old Russian saying: 'Give us a flea and we'll shoe it.' "

Mike rolled his eyes. "Another old Russian saying? What in the world does it mean?"

Viktor sighed theatrically. "Your cultural ignorance is embarrassing sometimes, Mikhail. Well, one of our tsars, I think it was Nicholas, was given a marvel of the metalworker's art when he journeyed to England. The marvel was a tiny steel flea that could dance. You had to look at it under a magnifying glass to see it dance. So the tsar kept it as a memento of his trip.

"But the next tsar discovered it and found it annoying. The mechanical marvel made him feel inferior; it seemed an insult to Russian craftsmanship. So he sent it to one of our greatest metalworkers and ordered him to shoe the flea. As you'd shoe a horse."

"Did he?"

Viktor grinned sardonically. "He did. Of course, the flea no longer danced. That's the trouble with making too many improvements."

"Is that story really true?"

Viktor shrugged. "Perhaps. There's another Russian saying; it comes from Soviet Central Asia; it's a thousand years old. It says: 'Half of this is true; half of this is probably not true . . . Don't hold it against me if I add something or miss something. I'm telling you the way I heard it.' "

Mike grinned. "I'm beginning to think I should believe only what I see. And what I see are big open fields of stubble along with your forests. It must be quite a sight in the summer, here in the Ukraine."

"Oh, it is. Immense, waving fields of grain. This is the breadbasket of the nation, you know. Retaking it will mean a great deal in building up our food supply."

"And, no matter where I look, I always seem to see an onion-bulb steeple somewhere on the horizon. I don't think I've ever seen as many churches as I have here. And your government disapproves of religion. You go to London or pretty much anywhere in England and you're conscious of their chimneys. Hundreds and thousands of chimneys. Here, it's churches. In the land of atheism. It doesn't make sense."

Viktor smiled. "When you insist on things making sense, it's time to drink a hundred grams of vodka. The Ukraine is a special place. In normal times, they claim the borscht is so thick you can stand a spoon in it. Their skulls are thick here, too. There's an old story about the two Ukrainians who are waiting for a train. The bell rings and one says: 'That's not our train.' A few minutes later, the bell rings again and the Ukrainian says: 'That's not our train.' Then the station-master comes and pushes them onto the train just as it's leaving the station and the Ukrainian says: '*This* is our train.' It's also said that, in the Ukraine, the men are beaten by their wives."

"That's ridiculous."

"Oh, I don't know. Doesn't the Comrade Lieutenant Tarasova beat *you* once in a while?"

Mike grimaced. "Verbally, I suppose she does. But she seems a little less cold to me than she did before."

"And what will you have accomplished if and when she finally warms up to you, I wonder? Will you have simply shod the flea? For myself, I don't like training virgins. No disrespect to the lady, but you might find, if she eventually falls into your arms, that it's a rather chilly experience. Like making love to an icebox."

"It's too bad you can't meet my old friend Buddy," Mike said. "He has a lot of sayings, too. He says that the worst sex he ever had was sensational."

Viktor frowned, translating, and then exploded into laughter. "Oh, that's very good! Wonderful!" he shouted, pounding the table. "I must tell Borisenko! He'll love it! By day after tomorrow, it'll be an old Russian saying."

Mike stood by her bunker in the cold and waited. One of the women pilots came past, smiled, and went in. A few minutes later, Galina, bundled up in her heavy jacket, fur cap, and boots, came out.

"You want to walk again, is that it?" she asked.

"Yes."

They set out together. For the first few minutes, neither spoke. Then Mike said: "You are not beautiful, Galina."

Startled, she said: "I have never said I was beautiful."

"It wouldn't do any good to say it because you are not," he said coolly.

He glanced at her. Abruptly, she broke into giggles. "I see," she said. "You are getting your own, pulling the wool, whatever it is you say."

"Something like that." They walked along silently for a moment and she erupted into tinkling laughter. He had never heard her laugh before.

"No," he said with assumed seriousness. "Your eyes are too large for your face and your nose is little more than a snub, a button. And one of your bottom teeth is crooked. And, frankly, you're not very, how shall I say, *ample*. Very nice in the hips and legs, from what I can tell with all these clothes. But not ample."

"Is there more?" she asked, smiling.

Her smile created a surge of emotion in him. "Only one thing."

"What is it?"

"I was lying."

"Hmph. Sometimes I think you lie a lot." A pause. "What were you lying about?"

"When I said you weren't beautiful."

"But I'm not. You said very clearly that I'm not. My eyes are too large, my nose is too small, my tooth is crooked, my breasts are too small. Are these things no longer true?"

"They may be true, but it doesn't matter, because you are beautiful to me. That means one of two things."

"What could it mean?"

"It means that you really are beautiful, by any standard. Or it means that you're not beautiful but you make me think you're beautiful because you're a witch. Not just a night-witch, but a true *ved'ma*."

"You talk nonsense, Mikhail," she said with unaccustomed softness. "I'm not beautiful."

"Then you're truly a witch and you've cast a spell over me." He stopped, turned to her, and held her by the arms. "When I look at you, Galina, Galishka, Galya, I see the most beautiful woman in the world."

"Thank you, Misha," she said softly. "I don't believe you, but I thank you."

"I've been trying to translate some Russian," he said. "From one of Viktor's books. I found a poem, a very old one, he says, from Central Asia. The words are:

> *Lips like cream.*
> *A pistachio nose, almond eyelids.*
> *Coral toothed, fairy faced,*
> *little mouth beautiful as a thimble.*

"That's how I see you." He drew her to him gently. "I want very much to kiss you, Galishka. Very softly. Please don't pull away." He kissed her slowly on the mouth. She stiffened at first and then seemed to melt into his arms. Afterward, he held her close. He could feel her struggling to regain control of her breathing; it was as if she had been running.

"You do that very well," she murmured. "You must have had experience."

"I have inspiration," he said. "I love you, Galina. I hope you're beginning to love me."

The words stung her like an electrical shock. She pushed herself back and looked at him with wide, anguished eyes. "Oh Misha, Mikhail, this is craziness, insanity. There is nothing for us together, you must know that. You are American, I'm Russian. We don't believe in each other's philosophies and, even if we did, we could never be together. I could never come to America and, even if I could, Russia is my country, my home. And this is no place for foreigners even if you wanted to stay. We have no future together."

"Galishka," he said, trying to draw her back to him, "how can anybody predict the future in a situation like this? All we can expect to have is each other. Isn't that enough for now?"

"No," she said resolutely. "I don't think so. At least I don't think I think so." She clapped her hands to her head. "Oh, I'm so confused!" She turned back toward the bunker, walking in long strides. "I don't want to walk tomorrow, Mikhail. Or the next day either."

"When then?"

"I don't know. I don't know anything. Let me alone." She began running and he stopped and let her go. Everything had begun so well today and now it had all gone wrong. He was deeply depressed.

CHAPTER ELEVEN

THE LOVERS

"GEAR DOWN."

The WASP co-pilot in the right seat of the B-17 obediently hit the switch and dropped the landing gear. "Gear down," she said as the wheels locked into place. The bomber swung off the base leg and lined up with the runway at Langley Air Force Base in Virginia.

"Full flaps," said pilot Claire Hunnicut. The co-pilot dropped the flaps and echoed the order. Claire eased back on the throttles, quickly checked the rate-of-descent and the airspeed—it was one hundred and fifteen mph—and began to flare out. It was the second time she had ferried a B-17—not counting that unforgettable afternoon with Mike—and she wanted to make a soft landing to show the hotshots at Langley that a WASP could fly.

The bomber settled onto the runway with barely a squeak of the tires and she smiled to herself. "Unlock tail wheel," she said. She let the bomber roll, then braked, chopped the port throttles, blasted the starboard engines, and pulled off on a taxiway.

Claire knew she should shake off her felt need to keep proving herself to the male officers at the bases she visited to ferry airplanes from factories to operational bases. But she wasn't alone in her feelings. The uniformed males still regarded the women pilots as curiosities and, when the women looked like Claire, as targets for seduction.

More than once, male officers and non-coms had made aggressive advances to her on various bases. One, a captain who had been drinking, had actually grabbed her at the entrance of a hangar and tried to pull her inside. She didn't scream or slap him in the ladylike way her mother would have favored.

She hit him in the nose with a short right cross from a balled fist and kicked him sharply in the crotch. As she walked away, she heard one of his friends laugh aloud as the offender, surprised and in pain, stood doubled over, blood dripping from his broken nose.

The men's reactions were partly due to their disbelief in the women's skills and partly due to jealousy. While the WASPS were civilians, they wore silver wings, were entitled to the same privileges that officers received on Army bases, and were paid two hundred and fifty dollars a month plus a per diem allowance to cover housing, food, and ground transportation.

A regular Army lieutenant got one hundred and fifty dollars a month, though an Army flier received an extra seventy-five dollars in flight pay—but only if he flew regularly. And the Army Air Corps men lived on their bases in barracks under tight military discipline while the females of the WASPS roamed the country, Canada, and sometimes the Caribbean to carry out their assignments.

Claire's current assignment, now completed, was to fly a radar-equipped B-17 from the Boeing factory at Seattle to Langley, where pilots and navigators received special training in radar bombing before going overseas.

That was a sore point with the WASPS, of course. Congress wouldn't allow the women to ferry aircraft overseas, much less fly combat. Some blamed General Arnold for the rule, but he claimed his hands were tied by Congress.

Claire had jumped at the Langley assignment because she wanted to pay a duty call on Mike's mother in Baltimore. As soon as she had turned off the B-17's engines and signed the necessary papers, she hitched a ride on a C-47 to Washington's Bolling airfield, where she changed from flight coveralls into a blouse, skirt, and flats and took a bus to Baltimore. A streetcar line ran close enough to the Gavin home in Roland Park to give her a short walk and loosen her legs.

Laura Gavin met her at the door. Claire could see Mike in her face —the wide-set eyes, the sharply-defined cheekbones, the generous mouth. She was, Claire judged, near fifty, but her voice was full, round, and youthful. Claire remembered that she was, or had been, a voice teacher.

"Come in, my dear, come in," Laura Gavin said. "I was so pleased when you wrote you were coming. Put your bag down; it looks heavy. It's called a musette bag or something like that, isn't it? Would you like to freshen up a bit before we sit and visit? I've made some tea."

They talked at length about Mike. Claire assured her, though she was exuding more confidence than she felt, that Mike was in a POW camp and would return when the war was over. Ultimate victory was assured; the Russians were winning now in the east and, soon, American and British troops would storm the French beaches to invade Germany from the west. It was just a matter of time.

Tears appeared in Laura Gavin's eyes. "He and I are all that's left of our family, you know, and I've worried about him terribly. He never wrote very much and, even when he did, he didn't say a great deal. We just didn't show each other a great deal of affection in our family; Mike and his father fought a lot. And then his father died. I've often regretted, particularly now, that we weren't more demonstrative. The closest we came to each other, I think, was when he was singing and I was playing for him, coaching him. Mike had, *has*, a fine voice. I wish you'd heard him sing."

"Oh, but I did," Claire said. She told him about Mike's performance at the Albany dance and how they saw each other afterward—though she omitted the part about her efforts to man-trap him, and how they, to put it politely, backfired. But she told his mother how Mike had taken her for a ride in a B-17 at Sebring though, again, she omitted—almost reluctantly—the dazzling, surreal sexual experience they had shared in the bomber's nose.

"He took you for a ride in his bomber?" Laura Gavin said. "Oh my. Was that, was it *legal?*"

Claire laughed. "Legal, I don't know. But I owe Mike a great deal, is all I can say. He was so, so sensible, and it was because of him that I got into the WASPS, doing flying jobs that used to be done only by men. It's been a wonderful experience."

"I can't *imagine* doing anything like that," Mike's mother said. "I can't imagine that they'd even *allow* women to do things like that."

"Well, they've held us under their thumbs for a long time, Mrs. Gavin. It's time we got out from under." *In more ways than one*, she said to herself.

When she left, they embraced and Claire promised to write.

Watching her walk away, Laura Gavin hoped not only that Mike would return safely but that, if and when he did—she always rejected the *if*—he would continue his relationship with this fine young woman. Claire was so strong, so self-reliant, and so lovely to look at.

Girls like Claire were so different from the women of Laura's generation. Asserting themselves in the way this girl had done would never have crossed their minds. It was simply the way the older women had been brought up. It didn't mean they were weak. Neither Laura nor any other woman of her acquaintance had protested when her son volunteered for the Army or Navy.

Though she was a relatively well-off Baltimore widow, Laura Gavin had grown up in a small Pennsylvania town, one of dozens of nearly identical towns spread throughout Pennsylvania, Ohio, and Maryland.

There, every able-bodied young man volunteered and left for his branch of the service when this huge, two-front war came to America. It was expected of them, and their mothers expected them to go. They would have been surprised and embarrassed if their sons had tried to evade the call to arms.

That didn't mean they *wanted* their sons to put themselves in harm's way, or that they didn't worry about them or feel anguish when, as now, they were reported missing. Laura Gavin sat down at the piano and, as tears began running down her cheeks, softly began playing the Rachmaninoff.

On the bus back to Bolling, Claire closed her eyes and tried to sort out her feelings. Mike Gavin had become a mythic figure to her, an idealized man, almost a hero, from a distant past. She no longer knew whether the things she remembered about him, or invested in the memory, were real or partly imagined.

She hoped he would return; part of her wanted to see him. But another part was reluctant to meet the real man; it might be a disappointment. Spontaneous moments of magic can't be resummoned and she didn't want anything ever to spoil her memory of that unforgettable afternoon.

Mike would forever be something of a magician in her memory. He had set her straight; he had set her on a new and rewarding path; and then he had opened a line of communication between herself and Buddy Bryce. Buddy wrote her almost every week in a laborious scrawl. They were funny letters, sometimes sad and self-revealing. She had come to know him so well.

She had immediately recognized him as a classic type of Southern male—irreverent, humorous, sly, steeped in Southern lore and myth, absurdly defensive about his place of origin and upbringing, but a romantic young man, a boy really, who was steadily opening his heart to her. And his loyalty to Mike was touching. One of his letters to her was frank about his ambiguous position:

> Well, I hope Mike gets back soon. He and I have got a lot to catch up on. He's lost a lot of time and rank and I'll have to tap into the ol' boy network to try to get him up to speed. I never thought I'd be such good buddies with a Yankee, but, with Mike, I am. And of course I want to ask him what his intentions are regarding a certain beautiful-looking young woman from my part of the country, God's country. He may have the inside track and all that, but unless you have made a true commitment to him, Claire, I want to put my hat in the ring. Or is it my glove? I'll have to look up the rules of Southern knighthood, I guess. I miss Mike and, tell you the truth, I miss you too. Take care of yourself, girl, and watch those cylinder-head temperatures. What a crazy thing to be saying to a woman! Keep writing and I'll do the same.

Flying had filled the void in Claire's life and made her a new person. Those who knew her now would never have associated this brisk, cheery, and competent young woman with the drawling Southern belle and man-trap who had delighted in manipulating and humiliating dozens of young men a few years ago.

She sometimes wondered why she was so disinterested in forming relationships with the men she met. Service in the WASPS didn't require a vow of chastity, and an occasional, discreet liaison wouldn't have been frowned upon.

But, she decided, the challenge of ferrying these airplanes—large and small, fast and slow—was too important and too exciting to waste time and energy on random romantic encounters.

And there were still two men in her life, even if they were far away. One was in a German prison camp (she insisted on believing) and one was a major and squadron commander of a bomb group in England. Maybe both of them were myths that would dissolve when the war was over. Like the WASPS. With all the men coming home and aircraft production shut down, she'd be out of a job, an exciting job.

She wanted the war to be over, but she would regret it all the same.

"You're missin' out on all the goodies, Mike-boy," Buddy said, fingering the oak leaf on his collar. He looked around quickly after he heard himself say the words; it wouldn't do to have word get around that the new commander of the 443rd squadron was talking to himself. He held his hands over the cheery glow of the potbellied stove in his tiny office.

"You're missin' out, though, son." The thought disturbed him. Buddy knew that his promotion was the result of merit. John Sloane had had nothing to do with it, though he knew that ol' John's helping hand would now be used to push him still higher.

For the first time, he realized that Sloane's goal of making Buddy commander of a bomb group, and a colonel to boot, was realizable. If he didn't get his ass shot off leading the squadron, of course. Those squareheads had no respect for American rank.

And who was that lunatic German who had actually flown into the beehive and taken on the whole damned Eighth Air Force over the Elbe near Magdeburg the other day? Him and his wingman. So long as the squareheads had that much nerve, they'd be dangerous. And the Jerries were getting better and better with their anti-aircraft guns. That 88 mm. of theirs was a wonder and they were shooting up some new kind of big rockets now.

A few days ago, Buddy had lost three planes from his squadron. Not one was hit by fighters. All three were shot down by flak. And then there was the problem of dumb-ass, freaky accidents. The week before, he thought it was all going down the drain—his ship, his crew, his promotion, even his ass—when a random flak burst hit him over France on the way in and set afire some of the incendiary bombs he was carrying in his bomb bay.

His bombardier tried unsuccessfully to jettison the bomb load over a forest and his crewmen had tried everything they could think of to get rid of the burning, dripping mess that threatened to set fire to the fuselage. He had had to leave the formation with his bomb bay doors open and dive for home, with 88s tracking him until he reached the Channel. He briefly considered telling the crew to bail out but decided to tempt fate and try for the big emergency landing field on the coast. The water was too cold to ditch the B-17 in the Channel. Five minutes after they landed, the ship blew up.

There was just no free lunch. You could have all kinds of big plans and have them wiped out in a flash. And now, just when he ought to be enjoying the favors of the English nymphs, he found himself thinking about Claire. The sight of her standing, laughing, in Mike's arms outside the officers' club that day at Sebring hung in his mind and wouldn't go away.

It was such a surprise to see Mike and a non-com in fatigues actually embrace and then to see the non-com's cap come off and reveal Claire's long blonde hair. Mike had smuggled her aboard his plane that day—that had become common knowledge—but, uncharacteristically, he wouldn't tell Buddy what had happened. Which obviously meant that it had to have been a major event.

Buddy had envied Mike that experience and tried hard to suppress feelings of jealousy. Buddy knew at the time that Claire was a man-trap, but she was so gorgeous and desirable. And maybe a knowledgeable Southern boy like himself could win her heart. Mike had never said he was in love with Claire, and Claire had been silent on that issue, too. So, Buddy decided, he wasn't intruding into Mike's territory by making a play for her now.

Life was so damned complicated; just when you got something you thought you wanted, you found it wasn't enough. Well, prison camp might not be fun, but at least Mike didn't have to worry about combat and women.

Mike was lying on top of her in the snow, but they didn't feel the cold. It was as if the snow were a field of cotton. Galina murmured that it was the first time for her and it was wonderful and he said that, in his heart, it was really the first time for him, too. Her blue eyes looked up at him adoringly and then went out of focus as she came.

He came, too, in a hard spasm, and he woke to find that he had fouled the covers of his bunk with sticky semen. Groaning, he reached for a towel and mopped himself and, as best he could, the bed. Afterward, he sat up and bent over, his head in his hands, his elbows on his knees.

What in hell am I doing in this crazy place anyway? he thought. *It isn't even my country and I don't speak the language—well, not much of it. There's no future here for me, and the girl I'm in love with is a cold-hearted bitch of a virgin who could care less about me. Well, she isn't really cold-hearted and it's unfair to say she's a bitch, but she's a pain in the ass all the same. And now I'm having wet dreams by myself when, if I had any sense, I'd be enjoying myself with Anna or Olga or one of the other girls who've been making eyes at me.*

Maybe the best thing would be to get out of this crazy place. Get in my Yak and fly westward as far as I can and then bail out and take my chances. He snorted at the thought. *Sure, and spend the rest of the war in a German prison camp or, likely, be shot as a spy.*

Piss-ant. It was cold in the room. He got up, pulled his heavy clothes on, and walked outside. It was 3:00 A.M. and as dark as a wolf's gullet. He began trudging toward the night-bomber field. He'd already made a jackass of himself, chasing after this girl, a regular *pokazukha*. Why change now? She was probably sleeping peacefully in her bunker; he hadn't talked to her in three days and he didn't know whether she had been flying or not.

But he'd go over and hang around anyway. Like some big dumb dog.

The flak fragment was red-hot; it was like being burned by a piece of molten metal. Galina screamed in pain as a large fragment plowed into her thigh and a second one gashed her cheek. She grew faint and the PO-2 wobbled as she relaxed her grip on the controls.

"Galina! Galina!" Valya shouted through the interphone. "Are you all right? We're falling!"

The sound brought Galina to consciousness and she pulled the nose up in time to avoid the birch trees below. The PO-2 careened over the snow-covered landscape. More flak bursts followed. But she was out of the searchlights now and streaking for home.

She felt her left leg growing wet as the blood flowed down it. The bottom of her boot felt soggy when she touched the rudder pedals. She fought to stay conscious. With no parachutes and not enough visibility to make a crash-landing, survival lay in getting home.

The thigh and leg were numb now, like a block of wood, and she wanted to go to sleep. If only Valya could fly the PO-2; as a navigator, she'd had no pilot training, though the biplane, being a trainer, had a separate, synchronized set of controls in the rear cockpit.

She couldn't, so Galina would have to stay awake. She squinted to keep her eyes in focus but her mind drifted away. What was she going to do about Mikhail? He had frightened her with his protestation of love—when was it?—three, four days ago. His words and his kiss had made her feel so warm. And so threatened. The threat wasn't to her body, though she had felt it yielding to his touch; it was to her mind, her heart. She wasn't ready for such an emotion. It was like a huge wave building up offshore. She could see it gathering and mounting in the distance and, if she didn't run, run hard, it would roll in and engulf her.

Right now, she felt as if it had stolen up on her unawares and carried her away. She was rolling in its embrace and the motion was making her very sleepy.

"Galina!" The stick between her hands rapped her sharply on her knee and woke her. Valya had jerked her rear-cockpit stick sideways to get her attention. Galina struggled back to wakefulness. The PO-2 was falling off on one wing and only a few feet above the trees.

She righted the airplane, took a deep breath, and saw the hooded landing lights of the field ahead. They had real landing lights now. It had become dangerous to keep oil drums flaring to mark the airstrip; it was an invitation to enemy night fighters to attack the PO-2s while they were landing. So the VVS had brought in a portable generator and connected it to hooded electric lights that were visible only if an airplane made a low approach and was ready to land. They were so pretty, she thought, glowing in the dark like that. So pretty.

"Galina!" Another rap on the knee from the stick. She opened her eyes, concentrated with all her might, eased the throttle back, and pop-popped in for a bouncing landing. As the biplane slewed to a halt, she fainted.

Mike ran to the plane and pushed himself through the group of women who were crowding around. Jumping up on the wing, he peered into Galina's face. It was as white as chalk. He reached into the cockpit, unbuckled her harness, grabbed her under the arms, and gently pulled her out. Taking her in his arms, he followed the women who ran ahead of him, nervously pointing to the bunker used as an infirmary.

The doctor was a middle-aged, stocky woman. She turned up the two oil lamps that illuminated the room and motioned to Mike to put Galina on the table in the center of the little room. Galina's trousers were soaked with blood. The doctor motioned Mike away but he shook his head, refusing.

Galina's trousers were stripped away. There was a long gash in the blood-soaked long johns underneath. The doctor quickly snipped the wool away and exposed a wound that was still bleeding heavily. The doctor put a tourniquet above the wound and then, with Mike's help, pulled off Galina's heavy jacket and woolen vest. The doctor swabbed one of the girl's arms and inserted a needle that she quickly hooked up to a bag of saline solution. She handed it to Mike with a motion to indicate he should hold it aloft.

The doctor examined the leg carefully and then probed the wound with an instrument. Galina moaned as the steel entered her lacerated flesh. The doctor looked up, nodded, and spoke to Mike in Russian. From the few words he could understand, he gathered that no bones were broken.

The doctor picked up a telephone and spoke quickly. Mike's eyes narrowed; she had spoken too quickly for him to understand all of it but he recognized the words *krovi* and *bol'nitsa* for "blood" and "hospital."

Valya touched his shoulder. *"Yey nado krovi,"* she said, pointing to the inside of her arm. *"Bol'nitsa.* Dakota."

"Field hospital," he said, understanding. "She has to go to a field hospital to get a transfusion. In a Dakota." Dakota was the name given to the U.S. Army Air Corps C-47. Hundreds of the mid-size, twin-engine transports had been sent to the Russians by America.

Half an hour later, a Dakota landed on the field and, with Valya holding the saline bag, Mike carried Galina into the airplane and climbed aboard. The pilot looked at Mike askance but Mike impatiently motioned for him to take off. Twenty minutes later they landed at a field hospital in the rear and Galina was placed on a rolling stretcher and taken to a small operating room.

Mike rolled up his sleeve and offered his arm to the surgeon. "Blood," he said. The surgeon shrugged. Mike made a ring of the fingers of one hand and said "O." The surgeon nodded and motioned Mike to a seat. A sample of his blood was taken along with one of hers and given to an assistant.

Mike waited while the doctor checked Galina's pulse and looked in her eyes. Minutes later, the assistant returned and spoke to the surgeon. The blood samples had been cross-matched and Mike's was acceptable. The surgeon nodded and motioned to Mike to sit next to the table on which Galina lay. The surgeon swabbed her arm and then Mike's and set up a transfusion.

While the transfusion was going on, the surgeon treated Galina's wound and sewed it up. Thirty minutes later, the transfusion was complete and Galina was placed on a stretcher and rolled to a ward. As Mike began to follow, the surgeon tried to block his way. Mike brushed the doctor aside roughly and followed the stretcher to a large ward.

As Galina was placed in it, she opened her eyes. Valya spoke to her at length in Russian, motioning to Mike and pointing to his arm. His sleeve was still rolled up and a piece of tape had been placed over the site of the transfusion puncture.

Galina looked at Mike. He bent close to her. "My blood is in you now, so now I'm part of you, Galishka. You can love me or not love me. Whether you do or not, I'll always be a part of you. Just as you're a part of me." He kissed her on the cheek.

As he turned to leave, two soldiers wearing the armbands of the military police blocked his way. One held out his hand and demanded Mike's papers. Recognizing the gesture, Mike shrugged and spread his palms. The MPs took him by the arms and started walking him away. Catching up, Valya spoke rapidly to them. Minutes later, in the administrator's office, one of the MPs phoned Major Borisenko. An hour later, Viktor showed up, his hair uncharacteristically askew and his eyes swollen with sleep.

"Borisenko is mad at you and, since he holds me responsible for you, he's mad at me, too," Viktor said as they walked to the regiment's captured Opel Blitz, which was sitting nearby. "He's wondering, and so am I, if you've gone around the track . . ."

"Around the bend," Mike offered.

"Around the bend, thank you," Viktor said. "I wake up in the middle of the night one night to go to the latrine and you're not in your bunk. I get up another morning and find you with a swollen jaw and a cut on your cheek. Another night you're gone again. And this morning, before dawn, Borisenko gets a call from the MPs who say you're pushing doctors around at a field hospital eighty kilometers from our base."

"It was only one doctor."

"Forgive me for overstating the problem," Viktor said as the car bounced along a dirt road. "The war can't simply stop because of one romance, you know. Even if it's the Russian virgin and our eccentric American having the romance."

Viktor sighed windily. "If it wasn't for the help you give to my idiomatic American English, I'd take you up on your earlier offer and ship you off to the infantry. But I suppose we can wait until Galina gets well. She'll be all right, incidentally; she should be back in her own bunk in four or five days."

"Thank God for that."

"We don't talk about Him around here. Unless, of course, you mean Comrade Stalin. Meantime, we're on the flight board; we take off two hours from now. Can you take the time to help me shoot at some Germans this morning?"

"With pleasure," Mike said gratefully.

They were in luck. They caught a flight of Stukas attacking Russian positions in one sector at the western edge of the Ukraine. The Luftwaffe's ancient, gull-wing two-seaters had been retired from their original role as dive-bombers when the aerial battle over Dunkirk had showed how vulnerable they were to fighter attack.

No pilot who had to dive steeply, dive-brakes extended, through ten thousand feet at 120 miles an hour could hope to survive with

350-mile-an-hour Spitfires nearby to pick them off. Now the old Stukas, equipped with two 20-mm. cannons in front and two 7.9-mm machine guns in the rear cockpit, were used for low-level ground attack.

But the half dozen Stukas making the attack when free-hunters Viktor and Mike arrived had no visible protection from high-flying ME-109s or FW-190s.

"We'll separate," Viktor said. "I'll take the one on the extreme right. You take the one to his left. Now."

They dived on the Stukas. The rear gunners, seeing them coming, opened up with machine gun fire and the familiar blue tracers arced up to meet the Yaks. Mike laid his gunsight on the rear gunner, pressed the firing button, and walked his cannon shells and machine gun bullets up the canopy. Viktor, meantime, was doing the same. Both Stukas heeled over, one to the right, the other to the left, and crashed.

Viktor broke to the right and Mike to the left. Each made looping circles to catch another pair of Stukas climbing off their targets. Catching his quarry in a climbing turn, Mike shot him down with one burst. As he banked and climbed away, he saw a Focke-Wulf diving from above on Viktor's tail.

"*Napravo!*" Mike shouted on the fighter frequency, "Break right!"

Viktor sheared off and Mike banked hard to intercept the FW. As he did, tracers from above ripped the fabric of his left wing. *The Focke-Wulf's wingman!* He tightened his turn, took a snap-shot at the FW in front of him, and pulled his nose up hard. The second FW shot past him, firing blindly.

Mike climbed, barrel-rolled, and looked around swiftly. One Focke-Wulf was trailing smoke and plunging toward the ground. The other, apparently the one that had tried to attack Mike, was fleeing westward.

Mike wiped his face with his glove and glanced at his watch. The whole thing had happened in less than two minutes.

In their second sortie of the day, Mike shot down a JU-88 bomber and Viktor caught a Heinkel. Afterward, Mike walked over to Galina's bunker to ask for news of her. He had become conversant enough with the Russian vocabulary to speak the language in at least a basic manner. Understanding what was said to him was harder, of course, but he usually could do it if the speaker spoke slowly.

Valya spoke slowly and distinctly. "We had word she'll return this evening. Come tonight. If she's feeling well, I'm sure she'll want to see you."

Mike thanked her and nodded. *I'm not all that sure*, he thought. *Knowing her, she'll probably resent my giving her my blood.*

After their evening meal, he and Viktor went to her bunker. Galina was propped up in her bunk with extra pillows. Little presents from her sister officers were piled around the bunk.

She was pale, but Mike had never seen her more beautiful—or so it seemed to him. She smiled when he and Viktor approached. She greeted Viktor and joked with him when he bent to kiss her hand. Then, looking at Mike, she patted the bunk beside her and told him to sit down.

"How are you feeling, Misha?" she asked.

He blinked. He was unused to be called something with an "ish" in it. "I'm okay. The question is: how are you?"

"I'm very well, Misha. I'm walking; I'll be back on flight duty next week. Don't frown like that, please. I'm almost recovered. You must remember that I have my duty to perform just as you have yours."

Her hand strayed to his blouse. "You have another uniform, don't you?"

"Yes, of course. Why?"

"Your jacket is much too large on the sides. It needs to be taken in. Bring it to me tomorrow, bring them both if you can, and I'll alter them for you. I'm a good seamstress and I have nothing to do but walk around a bit and rest."

"Well, all right. Thank you. I'll do that."

"We also should do something about your hair."

Back at their barracks, Viktor broke out his vodka supply and two glasses and stared at Mike in the half-serious, half-joking manner he often affected—a manner, Mike recognized, that sometimes revealed Viktor's underlying feelings as well as Viktor's ability to see the humor in them.

"I just don't understand it," Viktor said heavily.

"Don't understand what?"

"Why she prefers you to me."

"Oh."

"Well, it's very obvious now, isn't it?" He mimicked Galina's voice. " 'Bring me your jackets tomorrow, Misha, and I'll alter them for you. I'm a good seamstress and I have nothing else to do. Also, we should so something about your hair.' "

Mike grinned. "You don't need the help. Your jacket fits fine and your hair looks good."

"That's true, of course. But it doesn't alter the fact that Galina prefers you to me."

"Well, that's the way the ball bounces, I guess."

Viktor shook his head. "Hardly a useful explanation, is it? I'm simply saying that it makes no sense. Just consider the facts, please. I'm better-looking than you, aren't I?"

"Yes."

"I'm taller than you, aren't I?"

"Sure."

"More athletic looking, wouldn't you agree?"

"I guess I would."

"More dashing looking, with my dark eyes and hair?"

"Oh, yes."

"You don't even have a mustache, do you?"

"No, I don't."

"I'm cleverer with words, aren't I?"

"Yes, you are."

"I've had more experience with women, haven't I?"

"I'm sure you have."

"And yet she prefers you to me."

"I guess she does."

Viktor sighed and filled their glasses. "I hope this matter doesn't give you a swollen ego."

"I'll try to keep it under control."

It snapped cold. It was a glacial cold, colder than Mike had ever experienced. Making the conversion from Centigrade, Mike figured it was thirty below zero Fahrenheit on the ground. A chilling fog shrouded the field.

Snow fell steadily, and a large truck towed a heavy roller that compacted the white surface and made it as hard and flat as concrete. Water, oil, and gasoline were drained from the airplanes following their missions and heavy covers were wrapped around engines to keep them from freezing solid. One truck was fitted with a shaft that fit over the propellers and acted as a crank to help start balky engines.

Despite their glowing potbellied stoves, the bunkers were cold and the occupants routinely wore heavy clothes by day and night. Mike chafed at the enforced inactivity. The men were sleeping, playing cards, or, if it was certain there would be no flying, drinking.

So, despite a disgusted look and roll of the eyes from Viktor, Mike bundled up in his long, fleece-lined flight jacket and padded leather trousers, pulled on his fur-lined boots, cap, and gloves, and trudged off to the night-witches' bunker. He banged on the metal door until it opened a crack. A woman's eye peeped out and the door was promptly shut again.

Mike stamped around in the snow, swinging his arms, until the door swung open again and Galina came out, as heavily-dressed as he.

"I can't invite you inside," she said. "Some of the girls are not dressed. Do you want to walk a short way?"

"Yes, please."

They set off together. Cautiously, he slipped an arm around her shoulders. She moved closer and placed an arm around his waist, creating the physical linkage that young lovers have always used.

"This is to keep me warm, yes?" she said.

"Not entirely," he answered. She laughed. They walked silently for a while. The icy fog embraced them, shutting out all sight and sound.

"I didn't think," he said. "We could get lost."

"No. I brought my compass. I know the way back."

"How is your leg, your thigh?" he asked.

"It's very good now. The main problem was the loss of blood. But you restored the loss. So now I am fine."

Now they were walking beneath heavy evergreens and birches. He stopped, moved in front of her, and kissed her mouth. When they broke apart, she looked up, her blue eyes luminous.

"That was very nice. It made me very warm."

"It made me very warm, too. I'm still very warm."

She sighed. "Now you will want to fuck me, won't you, Misha?"

He recoiled in shock. "Don't say that, Galina."

"Why not? Is it a bad thing for me to do?"

"We're not talking about the thing to do, just the thing to say."

"Well, is it wrong to *do* the thing?"

"Not necessarily. Certainly, not if you're in love."

"Have you done it before?"

"Yes, I have."

"Were you in love?"

"No."

"Aha. So it was bad."

"Not really, no."

"This is more of your crazy American logic, perhaps. I should do it only with someone I love, meaning, I suppose, you. But you do it with anyone you please, you don't have to be in love. Because you're a man, of course. Pees-ann, is what I say to that."

"It's piss-ant, not pees-ann, as I've told you, and you shouldn't be saying it anyway. But you've got us off on the wrong track, Galina. I was talking about the word you used, that's all."

"What you are saying is that you want to fuck me but you're ashamed for me to say it. That's not very honest, Mikhail."

He tramped around in a circle, flapping his arms in frustration, making a deep path in the snow with his boots.

"That isn't it at all!" he shouted. "It's just the *word*, that's all! There are good words and bad words for everything, aren't there? You say you hit the target, you completed the mission, you had some casualties, you mean you killed some people, some of your people were killed. One of your friends gets killed, you say 'she bought it.'

"Fuck is a crude word, a disrespectful word for making love. i want to make love to you respectfully, Galina, be part of you, inside, outside, everywhere, taste you, smell you, feel you with all of me." He fell to his knees. "Don't you understand, really, don't you? Are you trying *not* to understand? I love you, Galishka."

He held out his arms. Impulsively, she plunged down in front of him and they embraced in their bulky coats.

"Oh God, I think I love you too, Misha," she said in an anguished voice. "I've tried very hard not to love you, because I see no possible future for us. But yes, I love you, Misha. I wish I didn't, but I do."

She drew back and looked at him. His eyelashes, she saw, were covered with frost. They kissed again. "All we have, or can ever have, are minutes like this, even if they're in the snow." Then she smiled. "This wonderful thing you don't like the word for. This love-making. You'd have to teach me. But where and how would we do it?"

"Somewhere where we can be alone, all alone. Maybe we could get a pass together and go to a hotel or inn in one of the towns around here."

She made an exasperated sound. "*Sumasshedshiy.* Crazy person. Where do you think you are? New York City or Brooklyn, perhaps? There are no hotels or inns in those villages and, even if there were, they wouldn't let us in. Even the hotels in Moscow are for visiting foreigners only. Russians can't stay in them."

"We'd need to find someplace where it wouldn't be quick or hurried. I wouldn't want to sell you short."

"Sell me? Why would you want to sell me?"

He groaned. "It's an expression. I wouldn't want to short-change you, especially the first time."

"I know it would change me, but why would it be short?"

"I mean short-change you, cheat you."

"Cheat me. Now I understand. Your kind of English is truly crazy."

"You make it sound crazy; you make *me* crazy."

She laughed and nestled against him, kissing him again.

"So where will we go for this wonderful love-making?" she asked.

"Is there any way we could get the women to move out of your bunker for an hour or two? Or let us have one of the rooms to ourselves?"

"The women's bunker? Oh my God, not a chance, impossible. What a scandal!"

"Well, we can forget the men's bunker. I wouldn't want them to know in the first place, and even if that were okay, which it isn't, I wouldn't trust them to stay away. Your commandant wouldn't lend us her front door key, would she?"

"What key? Never mind, I understand you. No, of course not. So what can we do? Try it here in the snow after all?"

"No, geez, you'd freeze that beautiful little rear end of yours at thirty below."

"And you"—she pointed timidly between his legs—"that would freeze, too."

He nodded. "Freeze and, in this cold, probably break off like a lollipop—what you call an ice lolly."

She gasped and then giggled. "An ice lolly? What a thought! So many times I've sucked an ice lolly." Her face turned crimson at the thought. "I didn't mean . . ."

"Well," he shrugged, "that's part of making love too, you know. People do it."

"I've heard of that. It sounds so strange. One of the girls even told me that men sometimes, with their tongues . . ."

"Go down? That's an expression, too, but it's pretty literal. I can see you understand. Yes, that happens, too. It's all part of it, not necessarily at the beginning."

"Some of it seems strange," she said. "But all of it will have to wait, it seems. All we can do here is kiss." She took his hand and placed it over her breast. "You can touch me here, if you like. I would like you to do it. But my clothes are so thick, and you have your gloves on."

She pulled him to his feet. "I know something we can do. Stand behind me." He obeyed. "I'll unbutton my coat just a little. You take your glove off quickly and put it down inside. Feel me."

He did. Her breasts were small and firm. The nipples felt like soft, erect buttons.

She sighed. "Oh, that is *very* nice. I'm going to unbutton a little further, Misha. Come around quickly and put your head down. I want you to kiss my breasts. But only for a moment; otherwise they'll freeze."

He sank his head into her breasts, inhaled their fragrance, and fastened his lips gently around a nipple, sucking. She drew her breath in sharply, making a hissing sound through her teeth. As he sucked and kissed, she arched her back, thrust her chest out, and held his head tightly. "Now the other, Misha, quickly." He complied.

She moaned. "It's lovely, Misha, but my skin is freezing; it's so cold it's burning now." He pulled away and she buttoned up quickly, shivering, and moved against him. "Oh, poor Misha," she exclaimed. "I can feel you against me now; your lolly is sticking out. It's very stiff. What can I do, my love? Do you want me to take it out?"

"No," he whispered. "I told you, it would freeze."

"My mouth is still warm, Misha. If you would like me to do that, my mouth would keep it warm."

He groaned and seized her hand as it moved downward. "No, Galishka, that's not the way for us to start, not the very first time. It will just have to wait. Spring will come. Then we can come out here in the woods with a blanket."

"We'll be bitten by mosquitos."

"I don't care."

"I hope now that it happens. I want it to happen." She looked at him confidently and nodded vigorously. "You will see; I will fuck as good as any woman you have ever known; more than that, better."

"Stop it, Galina."

"You don't believe I will fuck better than others?"

"Yes, of course, but . . ."

"Then why are you afraid to say so? Say so!"

"All right!" he yelled in frustration. "Yes, of course! You will fuck better than Cleopatra or Salome or Nefertiti, better than the greatest queens and courtesans in all the world's history!"

"Well, then, you will see."

"Yes, we'll both see. In the spring."

She huddled close to him and said softly: "Of course, you know we may not both be here in the spring. One of us could be transferred to another place." Her voice sank lower. "Or one of us . . ."

"Don't say it," he said in a loud voice. "Don't even think it. We

have to be together. We *have* to be.'' They were shivering uncontrollably in the cold. They huddled even closer together, heads down, arms
about each other, and began walking slowly to the women's bunker,
two small figures in a vast landscape of snow and ice.

CHAPTER TWELVE

FINAL PLANS

IT WAS COLD in the tiny slate-roofed cottage in early spring in 1944, but then it was always cold in a country without central heating. The fireplace in the small living room offered only a limited amount of heat, but the middle-aged man sitting at the oak table nearby didn't mind.

General Dwight Eisenhower, Supreme Commander of the Allied Expeditionary Forces, pulled on his suede and leather jacket. He was wearing an old shirt and GI trousers. On his feet were a pair of shabby straw slippers left over from his years in Manila. He was worried and irritated. The irritation flowed from the fact that he came on weekends to Telegraph Cottage, nestled in a ten-acre wooded tract twenty minutes from London, expressly to get away from worry.

He got plenty of that, plus constant interruptions, at his headquarters on Grosvenor Square. Telegraph Cottage, which his naval aide had found for him at thirty-two dollars a week, was the perfect retreat. It was small and simple, it had a rose garden in which he could paint, and there was a nearby golf course on which he could take a ball and club or two and play a few holes. Out back he did a little plunking, from time to time, with his .22 pistol. In the cottage he kept a stack of paperback cowboy novels; reading simple-minded Westerns was an antidote to worrying.

But even here there was no escaping the worry that now dogged every waking hour and confused his dreams. His face knotted into a ball in a way that someone who didn't know him might have found comical. It was impossible for Eisenhower to conceal his feelings—and, in private, his temper. His large, mobile face changed expression and color with every emotion. His bald forehead wrinkled. His eyes could turn quickly from bright and sunny to icy blue. His large mouth widened, compressed, turned up or down.

If his face had been a meterological instrument, one glance would have told the observer whether the weather was turning fair or foul. Today, it forecast heavy weather.

The invasion of France, code-named Overlord, had to be launched very soon. It would be the biggest and most complex military operation in history and success was far from assured. For the hundredth time, he reviewed the multiple parts of the problem.

As an amateur painter, Ike sometimes liked to think in visual terms. If you looked at the way the coast of France extended westward, he thought, the area called Brittany jutted out into the water like the head of a short and stubby dragon. If the dragon's tail turned straight up, the tip of the tail was the Cotentin peninsula. The coastal area of France immediately to its east was Normandy. Across the English Channel, a thin strip of water, lay England.

The first landings would be made in Normandy. A vast number of soldiers and quantity of equipment had been built up over two years to invade the continent. But only a handful of divisions, five or so, could make the initial landings. The area was small and heavily-defended, the weather was often bad, and, against all reason, there was a serious shortage of landing craft.

Ike swore, threw the cowboy novel he had been reading into a corner of the cottage, and started pacing around the room. The problems were enormous. First, there was the choice of a site. To begin with, it had to be within overnight sailing distance of ships leaving from England's southern ports. The eastern ports were too exposed to German attack.

The site had to be within range of day fighter planes based in England. The beach had to be hard enough to hold tanks and the surf couldn't be too high at that spot. Inland, the ground had to be flat enough for airfield landing strips.

The obvious site was Calais near the River Somme. It was the closest point to England, separated from Britain only by the narrow

Straits of Dover. It would provide a straight shot to Antwerp. It was perfect; it was also perfectly obvious.

That's why the site couldn't be Calais, though an enormous program of misdirection code-named Fortitude, complete with dummy tanks, ships, and airplanes, troops marching around, faked radio messages, and planned leaks, had been set in motion to convince the Germans that the Allies would indeed invade there.

Misleading the Germans was crucial to success, because they had far more army divisions available than the Allies could land in a few days. It was vital to keep the enemy divisions spread out or concentrated in the wrong place.

But where was the right place? The area north of Calais was too close to Germany and German reinforcements. The Brittany peninsula to the south was too far away. So it had to be Normandy, in between the two. Troops landing at the eastern base of the Cotentin peninsula could push westward across it, seal it off, and take the port of Cherbourg.

But, when you couldn't take Cherbourg immediately without destroying it, and you had to have a port for unloading supplies, what do you do? Surprisingly, the answer came from Prime Minister Winston Churchill. The little PM offered a dozen ideas a minute, most of them bad, but this time he had come up with a good one. Build huge artificial harbors out of concrete and use tugs to tow them into place near the Normandy beaches.

The harbors were being built now. He hoped they would work. A second piece of innovative technology was a giant pipeline that was being fabricated to lay across the bottom of the Channel to supply fuel to the Allied armies.

Another reason for picking the base of the Cotentin peninsula for the initial landings was Caen. Lying a short distance inland, Caen was a major communications center with relatively flat ground around it. And the bulk of the German defenses were clustered to the north.

Then, Ike ruminated, there was the question of *when*. That depended on a whole bunch of goddamn things. He held up a muscular hand and, as was his habit, ticked off its fingers, one by one, with the index finger of his other hand.

One, the landings would have to be about dawn, so the invasion fleet could sail under cover of darkness the night before and have a day of daylight to get onto and past the beaches.

Two, it would have to be at low tide; the Germans had studded the beaches with steel obstacles capped with Teller mines in the areas between high and low tide. Only at low tide could they be seen and cleared away.

Three, while you didn't want the night of embarkation to be too bright, you needed *some* moonlight so you could make paratroop drops or glider landings behind the beaches. So it would have to happen during a half-moon period.

Four, the invasion had to be staged late enough to promise decent weather but early enough to give the Allies a summer to fight in.

Combining these factors, you wound up with a couple days in May and the first and third weeks of June.

Then there were the frigging political problems. He had threatened to quit unless it was agreed that British as well as American commanders would be under his control. The Brits had bickered and chafed but finally acceded.

Not that this would solve the problems of dealing with prima donnas and turf protectors. He got along fine with British Navy Admiral Sir Andrew Cunningham and Royal Air Force Chief Marshal Arthur Tedder. He was genuinely fond of Churchill, at whose country home, Chequers, he had spent several pleasant weekends.

But British General Alan Brooke, who constantly tried to undercut him, was a pain in the ass. The biggest pain, of course, was British General, soon to be Field Marshal, Viscount Bernard Montgomery, who liked to be called the Lion of Alamein because of his North African victory over Rommel.

It would be more descriptive to call him the Peacock of Alamein, Ike reflected sourly. Montgomery, a sharp-nosed man with darting, restless eyes, was vain and overly self-assured; he had won in North Africa not because he was smarter than Rommel—he wasn't, not by a long shot—but because the RAF bombed and destroyed Rommel's supply ships and ultimately gave the British a three-to-one superiority in men and materiel. Even then, Montgomery had let Rommel get away.

Ike wanted to fire Montgomery, but the British lionized him. They had been through hell for four years of war and they needed heroes and victories. So Monty became a hero and even the dismal escape of their army from Dunkirk in 1940 was going into British history as a "victorious retirement."

Montgomery wasn't the only peacock in a general's uniform, of course. There was Ike's own man, Georgie Patton, a brilliant, hard-driving tank commander whose personal behavior kept getting him in trouble. First there was the day he slapped the soldier who said he couldn't stand shellfire. Then he had to make a dumb-ass speech about how America and Britain would rule the world after the war. That became a huge embarrassment in the two nations and nearly forced Ike to fire him.

Now there was a huge wrangle over air support. On that one Ike faced opposition not only from the Brits but from his own air commanders. On two things Ike was adamant. First, the Luftwaffe had to be absolutely defeated by the time of the invasion. That goal had almost been reached and, give him credit, Doolittle's Eighth Air Force had been killing off the German fighter force by forcing it aloft, day after day, to defend German cities and plants.

Second, every available airplane—heavy bombers, medium and light bombers, fighters, whatever—*had* to be used in support of the landings. On D-Day, a huge umbrella of fighters would cover the ships and landing crafts while bombers of every weight and size attacked German ground defenses. It would create a huge traffic jam in the air, with maybe eleven thousand planes flying around in a small area, but it was necessary. There was no disagreement on that point, but everything else was the subject of bitching and yelling.

Before and after D-Day, Ike wanted the heavies taken from their regular high-altitude missions against strategic targets and sent in at low-to-medium altitudes, where they were highly vulnerable to anti-aircraft fire, against German bridges, guns, and troop concentrations in Normandy. He also wanted the newly-discovered V-1 rocket sites to be knocked out.

And at least six weeks before D-Day, Ike wanted his staff's Transportation Plan to be carried out. The big bombers would carry on a sustained bombing of all rail lines and marshalling yards in France and the Low Countries that could be used to resupply German troops resisting the invasion. The air forces would make it impossible for the Germans to bring up reinforcements.

How could anybody object to that? Ike asked himself. But they did. RAF Air Marshal Sir Arthur Harris made the strange complaint that his heavies, which operated only at night, weren't accurate enough to do the job. And General Carl "Tooey" Spaatz, the grizzled chief of the U.S. Strategic Air Forces, wished the invasion force Godspeed but insisted on continuing with his Oil Plan, which was dedicated to destroying Germany's synthetic oil refineries by daylight.

Well, the Oil Plan was important, Ike muttered to himself, but it would have to be laid aside until the invasion was secure.

Even Churchill was giving him problems on this one. His War Cabinet objected to putting all air power under Eisenhower, even temporarily, and the Prime Minister was concerned over the "slaughter" of French civilians from the bombings. He was going directly to Roosevelt with his case.

Well, let him, Ike growled to himself. He'd either have the Transportation Plan, including the use of the B-17s and B-24s, or he'd resign. He picked up a baseball glove sitting on a nearby table and walked to the door of the cottage.

"Mickey!" he yelled. His aide, Sergeant Mickey McKeogh, bounced into the room. "Get a ball. We'll play some catch," Ike said. He'd throw a few high, hard ones.

It was almost unbelievable, Buddy Bryce reflected, but it was true, and he wasn't sure he liked it. It had happened too damn fast. He had barely become used to the oak leaf on his collar when General Sloane drove onto the base from Wing headquarters with newly-cut orders giving Buddy a temporary promotion to lieutenant-colonel and transferring him to the 300th Bomb Group as its commander.

"Desperate times, desperate measures, Buddy-boy," General Sloane inveighed. "The 300th has become our biggest fuckup, was all along, and it's paid the price for it, this time worse than ever."

Flying its habitually loose and sloppy formation, the 300th had been hit by a mass of fighters. The Luftwaffe turned up only occasionally now. When it did, it struck in "wolf packs" against the most vulnerable bomber groups and then fled the scene before the escorting American fighters had time to react.

This time, thirteen B-17s went down, taking with them the group commander and two of his squadron commanders. Another ten B-17s were badly damaged and unable to fly. Crippled and without leadership, the group was stood down by Wing.

"And the men's morale is lower than a rat's ass," Sloane said, waving his cigar disdainfully. "So the problem's gotta be fixed quick. This is no time to have one of our groups outta commission. Things are brewin', you know what I mean. I'm not tellin' you any official secret when I say we're gettin' ready for the invasion. Right now we've got the 300th stood down and it needs fresh blood.

"So we went 'round and 'round at Wing—everybody's got his favorite, y'know—but your record is real good and I got some help from some of the ol' boys of our persuasion. So you're it. Congratulations, son."

Sloane stuck out a meaty hand and Buddy reluctantly shook it. But he also shook his head. "Gen'l, I really appreciate this, you know I do, but Kee-ryst, this is awful fast. I don't feel ready."

Sloane waved his hands dismissively. "You'll do fine. Nobody's ever *ready*. Even the new Popes don't feel *ready*. You just do it, that's all. You know howta fly. You know howta lead in the air, right?"

"Yeah, I guess I do."

"That's the big thing. All you gotta learn is how to lead on the ground. You gotta good personality. Start tough. Make the bastards *work*. Get them *up*. Then get them some goodies, some rewards. You'll do fine. Now go pack your B-4 bag. I'm drivin' you over there now in my staff car."

"Now?"

"Now."

When he arrived, Buddy reflected, you'd have thought the 300th was a cemetery with a few airplanes parked around it. People walking around, heads down, eyes on the ground. Talking in whispers. Uniforms sloppy. Planes dirty. Food lousy. Buddy had always thought of himself, accurately, as an easygoing ol' boy. He couldn't imagine himself turning into a martinet, the kind of officer who nit-picked everything and was instantly hated by his troops.

But here he was. He already had his nickname. He found it scrawled on the door of the officers' club three mornings after he arrived. *Bastardly Bryce*, it said.

Buddy took Sloane's advice literally. He made a quick tour of the base, then called the group together and chewed them out. Officers, non-coms, and all ground personnel were assembled outdoors by the tower and Buddy got up on a platform with a bull-horn.

"I didn't ask for this job but I got it and I'm gonna do it," he shouted. "And you're gonna obey my orders or I'll send you where the dogs don't bark. Either that or the infantry; maybe both. First off, I want you to clean up, all of you. *Today*. Wash, *shave* for God's sake. I wanta see clean uniforms, ties, shined shoes. *Today*.

"I want you to clean up your barracks. *Today*. You ground personnel: clean up the hangars, the airplanes. *Today*. You cooks, clean up the damn kitchens and improve the food or I'll put you on permanent KP peelin' potatoes and washin' pots and pans. *Today*. You gunners, clean those guns. *Today*. You pilots, you have the reputation of flying the worst, sloppiest formation in the whole damned Eighth. You're a goddamn disgrace and I won't tolerate it. It's all gonna change, startin' tomorrow. We're startin' practice flights at 0700."

They glared and grumbled and whined. A few defied him and he called the MPs and had them taken off the base. Yelling and beating on them and working them unmercifully, he got the pilots flying a fifty-percent tighter formation within three days. Three days later they improved another twenty-five percent.

On the seventh day he called Wing and reported the 300th was ready to fly missions. Two days later they hit a "noball" target near St. Omer; it was nothing more than some kind of new rocket emplacement with 88s clustered around it. They flew good formation and hit the target and weren't bothered by fighters. But the AA fire was extremely accurate and they lost one bomber and had three shot up.

And then they got a biggie. The men groaned when they saw the map. *Berlin.* They encountered heavy, almost terrifying flak over the city but Luftwaffe fighters, looking for a quick hit-and-run target, passed over the 300th and hit the group ahead of them, knocking down six B-17s and damaging four. Buddy's group returned intact with no losses and only two injuries.

"What did I tell you?" Buddy crowed at them afterward. "We flew tight formation and the poor-ass 302nd didn't. And *they* got hit by the FWs instead of the 300th. We did our job and got out with our skins because we fuckin' well *flew* better."

That time, he got a few grudging nods, even a smile or two. And then, following General Sloane's dictum, he got them some goodies. A few miles from the base and set well back from the road, he noticed an abandoned building sitting in a patch of weeds. Inquiring, he found that it had been an ice cream plant.

The next day, he had the machinery hauled out of the building and moved into a hangar on the base. An engineering officer, a skilled mechanic, and a sergeant who had once worked in an ice cream plant bought, found, and made parts to restore it to working condition. The base supply officer was assigned the job of locating a regular and reliable source of eggs. Powdered milk was in abundant supply, some whole milk could be obtained from the farms ringing the base, and the 300th was well stocked with sugar.

So, within three weeks, homemade ice cream was on the menu in the mess halls and available at the non-coms' and officers' clubs. The men loved it.

Examining the sugar stocks in the base warehouse gave Buddy another idea. The monthly whiskey ration ran out regularly within a week's time.

"That's ridiculous," he told his adjutant, a bespectacled and earnest former bank officer named David T. Potter whom Buddy nicknamed Dee Tee.

"Don't they know a war's on?" Buddy demanded. "We need

booze, Dee Tee. I'd a whole lot rather have sour mash bourbon, some good corn whiskey, but if all they know how to make on these islands is scotch, well, then, let's find some scotch. You look through the 201 files and find me a wheeler-dealer."

"A what, sir?"

"A wheeler-dealer, Dee Tee. A dog-robber. A hotshot salesman. On a base with three, four thousand people, there's bound to be one."

There was. His name, appropriately, was Wolf. Master Sergeant Timothy B. Wolf, a tubby, bright-eyed chief supply clerk and former traveling salesman from Oklahoma whom Buddy dubbed Timberwolf. Buddy, Dee Tee, and Timberwolf discussed the problem and Buddy gave the ex-salesman carte blanche to visit other base warehouses and strike any deals he found advantageous.

"Colonel," Timberwolf told Buddy after a week's survey, "it's not a matter of money, you might say; it's a matter of barter, making trades. Now trade opportunities are, you might say, marginal with other bomb groups. They get pretty much the same stuff as we do. Oh, once in a while you can run across a good deal. I found a nice load of A-1 spark plugs on a dock that a ship salvage crew overlooked. Okay, any one of our bomb groups will wanna trade for some of them."

Wolf waved a chubby finger in the air. "But whatta *we* want? That's the question. Even as hard as good spare parts are, it'd be a hard sell to squeeze much scotch outa other groups. They run out just like we do." He rose on tiptoes. "*But*," he intoned dramatically, "the *distillers*. They're short of the stuff we're long on, you might say, and vice versa."

"The distillers," Buddy repeated. "You mean the Brits?"

"I mean the *Scots*," Timberwolf said, his eyes alight. "They got the scotch, right? I visited one of the gentlemen yesterday. He's got scotch, all right, he rations it out and he gave me a nice cold smile when I said I wanted about fifty cases. He could give me two, he said, and that'd be stretching it. So I said uh-huh, that's nice, but, by the way, when's the last time he's seen three hundred pounds of sugar or a hundred cartons of American cigarettes—not those crumby coffin nails the Brits smoke, those Players—and maybe even a few pounds of real coffee and tea?"

Dee Tee looked concerned but Buddy grinned. "That opened his eyes some?"

"You might say it did," Timberwolf said. "He practically dropped his teeth. Give me the word, I'll scoop up the cigarettes; we got a fair amount of non-smokers and every man gets a carton a week from

Camels or Chesterfields. They'll contribute when they know the deal. I can scrounge the rest. It'll be a three-way trade to start. Part of our new spark plug inventory'll go to the 302nd for extra sugar and coffee. Then the commodities trade to the Scotsman plus a couple pounds of butter as a gift to his wife. And he hands over the scotch. I'll set up a regular supply."

"I don't think Wing would approve this kind of thing," Dee Tee sniffed.

"They're real busy at Wing," Buddy said. "No use addin' to their worries. Go sic 'em, Timberwolf. Take a truck and driver, two trucks, whatever you need."

"Thank you, sir. The deal is as good as done, you might say."

Two days later, as they were eating their ice cream, the men of the 300th heard that the new colonel had miraculously replenished their liquor stocks. Overnight, all of the Bastardly Bryce signs and scrawls disappeared from the base.

That was nice, but Buddy felt edgy. His group was being sent almost daily into France now to knock out rail lines and bridges. The Seine bridges north of Paris had been destroyed. The air crews welcomed these kinds of missions because they were short. There was no fighter opposition and turnaround time was four or five hours.

But the invasion of Europe was near. Buddy wished he knew how it would affect his bomb group.

A feeling of savage joy and an almost uncontrollable impatience surged through Josef Stalin's heavy chest. For a moment, the violence of his emotions produced a roaring in his ears and made his heart beat heavily. He struggled to control himself and lighted his pipe with shaking hands.

The old-fashioned clock on the mantel struck midnight and the Man of Steel nodded rapidly. Yes. Yes. A new day was beginning. A day of victory, a day of retribution and revenge.

He strode to the long map table and bent over the big map of Belorussia, White Russia, the last part of the Soviet Union still in Fascist hands. In the south, the Crimea had been liberated with heavy German losses. To the north, the German blockade of Leningrad had been broken. Now, in the early spring of 1944, the Ukraine, the immense, fruitful breadbasket of the empire just south of Belorussia, was back in Russian hands.

Stalin reflected grimly. For a time, when the Germans first invaded, it appeared that the White Russians and Ukrainians would side with the Germans. Many greeted the invaders with ritual offerings of bread and salt. If they had turned against the Soviet state, en masse, the Nazi victory would have been assured.

But Hitler was stupid. He treated even friendly Slavs as sub-humans. His SS imposed a harsh rule on the peasants and killed everyone who broke even the smallest rule. Several villages were literally exterminated, with men, women, and children herded into churches and burned alive to pay for the assassination of a single German soldier.

And so the disillusioned Ukrainians and White Russians swung about, despite their hatred of the Soviet state, to fight against the Hitlerites.

By now, more than four hundred thousand miles of territory taken by the Fascists had been recovered. The Third Reich was trapped between the Eastern and Western powers and the resources of the Nazi state were being squeezed dry.

And finally, after a year of timidity and delay, the *soyuznichki*, the little allies in the West, had given him a date for their invasion of France. It was June 5. When it happened, the hysterical Austrian corporal would start moving divisions and tanks and aircraft to the West to stop it.

And that would create a splendid opportunity for two giant Soviet blows. The first would drive the hated Germans out of Belorussia, that immense and mysterious land of swamps, marshes, lakes, and forests. He pushed a marker along the map. The front was long, six hundred and fifty miles from north to south, but the weakest spot—and thus the target of the Soviet assault—would be the Wehrmacht's Army Group Center commanded by Field Marshal Ernst Busch.

Army Group Center had only four hundred thousand men remaining and had lost large numbers of tanks, artillery pieces, and aircraft due to combat and transfers to bolster other German defenses. The Soviet advances to north and south had left the German center invitingly exposed.

Stalin absent-mindedly tore up two cigarettes and stuffed the tobacco in his pipe. The Russian campaign would begin shortly after the Anglo-American invasion in the West. He would send two million men and thousands of tanks against the four hundred thousand Hitlerites of Army Group Center. In the air, his efficient commander, Novikov, would throw an estimated eight thousand combat aircraft against the enemy's one thousand.

He paced the floor of his office. The campaign had to have a name. Something taken from history. He considered several, then stopped.

He had it. *Bagration*. The name of a Czarist general, true. But Bagration was a Georgian, like himself. And Bagration was the general who stopped Napoleon.

He began pacing again. So Operation Bagration would surround and crush the enemy's doomed Army Group Center and drive the Fascists out of Belorussia within a month. He stopped and bit the stem of his pipe sharply as the feeling of joy surged through his body again.

Then, *then*, the great Soviet army would sweep like a flame through Poland and East Prussia, through the German heartland, into Berlin itself. He would tell his commanders to tell the men to *enjoy* the conquest. They would be encouraged to take their revenge on the Germans, *all* the Germans, since it was their troops who had raped Russian women, burned down villages, killed peasants, shot commissars, and hanged partisans.

The motto and guiding theme of the advance would be *blood for blood*. He nodded grimly. In past years, he had ordered the deaths of millions of people without passion or any particular ripple of emotion. Now, starting with the execution of fifty thousand German military and political officers, he would kill, degrade, and impoverish millions of Germans and he would enjoy every minute of the experience. Soviet soldiers found in German prisoner-of-war and concentration camps were, of course, tainted. They would be sent to penal camps in Siberia.

There was a knock on the door. "Enter," Stalin said, walking back to the map table. His generals trooped into the room. First was Zhukov, his favorite and, he thought uneasily, his possible competitor. Then Vasilevsky, the head of the general staff. Following him, Bagramyan and Chernyakhovsky, who, respectively, would command the First Baltic Front and the Third Belorussian Front to the north. And Zakharov and Rokossovsky, respectively commanding the Second Belorussian Front in the center and the First Belorussian Front to the south. Also Novikov, whose five air armies and detachments from eight long-range bomber corps would directly support the ground assaults. And, of course, Molotov The Hammer, his foreign minister.

Within an hour, they had reviewed the general strategy. The northern and southern fronts would act as a giant pincers and the central front would smash inward to complete the destruction of the enemy. They would surge forward like huge tidal waves. First, the northern armies, then the central ones, then the southern fronts. Clearing a path for each frontal group would be one or more air armies.

Stalin felt a tickle of perverse humor. He loved to pit his generals against each other. In his thinking, the competition forced them forward, regardless of risks and losses. And it sometimes offered unwitting amusement. As now. He ordered Zhukov, who was nominally the overall commander, to supervise the operations of the two northern fronts. He ordered Vasilevsky to oversee the advances of the central and southern frontal groups.

As he announced this elaboration on his original plan, he watched the two generals bristle reflexively and glare at each other. Stalin puffed on his pipe to keep from smiling.

Still, he had one worrisome concern. Rokossovsky's front of combined armies would face fanatical enemy resistance in the southernmost part of the sector around Bobruysk. It was important to have a clear agreement on exactly how the Russian assault would be launched, and Rokossovsky was as strong-willed and independent as Zhukov, sometimes even more so.

"Rokossovsky," Stalin called. "Come here." He placed his finger on the map. "Where do you propose to break through the enemy's defensive positions? Here at the Dnieper bridgehead? That's the logical place."

"At that spot, Comrade Stalin," the coarse-faced general said. "And here." He pointed to a second spot.

"The defense should be breached in one place, should it not?"

"I believe it must be breached in two places, Comrade Stalin."

Silence fell over the room. Stalin scowled. "Explain yourself."

"If we breach the defense in two sectors," the general said, "we bring more forces into the attack. By doing that, we deny the enemy the possibility of transferring reinforcements from one sector to another. This gives us an important advantage."

"You call that an advantage?" Stalin demanded contemptuously. He pointed to the door. "Your thinking is confused. Go sit in the outer office and think it over."

Rokossovsky opened his mouth to speak, closed it, turned on his heel, and left the room. The outer office was dark and silent. A clock ticked; it was 1:30 A.M. The general sat for a moment, then sprang to his feet and began pacing. He was expected to return and agree to one blow from the bridgehead. The Man of Steel would be satisfied and the meeting would go on.

If he opposed Stalin further, the dictator's legendary fury would explode over him and he might soon find himself demoted or worse. But if he agreed, given the swampy terrain and the heavy defenses the Germans had built up in the south, the Soviet forces would suffer heavy and unnecessary numbers of casualties. They might even be stalled and pushed back and he would be held to blame. The enemy might be badly outnumbered but—he hated to admit this, even to himself—the average German soldier, even today, was worth two, three, perhaps as many as four Russian soldiers.

The door opened and Rokossovsky was summoned. Walking from the semi-darkness into the light was momentarily blinding and he couldn't initially see the Supreme Commander's face with any clarity. But the voice was clear enough.

"So, Rokossovsky. Have you thought it through?"

"Yes, Comrade Stalin."

"Well, then, do you agree now that we should strike a single blow?" Stalin pushed the map marker across the table.

Rokossovsky took a deep breath. "Two blows are more advisable, Comrade Stalin."

Stalin's voice lashed at him like a whip. "But that would dissipate our forces from the very beginning!"

"Theoretically, perhaps, Comrade Stalin," the general said stolidly. "But moving through the swampy terrain and forests makes for slow going, and enemy defenses will take a heavy toll of a single attacking force. Two simultaneous blows will throw the enemy into confusion."

Stalin shook his head. "You're being stubborn and mule-headed, Rokossovsky." He pointed to the door. "Go out and think it over again."

The general left for a second time. He walked back and forth in the dark outer office like a caged lion. Five minutes later, the door opened and Molotov appeared. "Where do you think you are and who do you think you've been talking to, Rokossovsky?" Molotov said harshly. "You have to agree with Comrade Stalin; that's all there is to it. Now come back in."

Stalin looked up from the map as he reentered. "So what is better?" the dictator said. "Two weak blows or one strong blow."

Rokossovsky pulled himself to attention and looked straight ahead. "Two strong blows are better than one strong blow."

Stalin scowled. "Which blow should be the primary blow?"

"Both blows should be primary."

A heavy silence settled over the room and the generals braced for the expected explosion. Stalin glared at the map for a long minute and then looked up at Rokossovsky, squinting.

"You really believe this, after all I've said?"

"Yes, I do, Comrade Stalin."

Stalin abruptly waved him aside. "All right. Do it your own way."

There was an audible exhalation of breath among the assembled men. "However, I want a full rehearsal of your operation. Select a remote forest for it. Run through the whole thing, coordinate the actions of your army, division, and regimental commanders. Zhukov, you will supervise."

Stalin walked to his desk and sat down. "Now we will review air support. Novikov, tell us what you are doing."

The air commander stepped up and reported. He was working with Marshal Zhukov on the overall plan. He and his subordinate commanders were working closely with each army staff to assure close, carefully-timed frontal support of the ground assaults. He now had 13,428 planes in the VVS inventory. Between 8,000 and 9,000 would take part in the Belorussian campaign. About one-third would be Shturmoviks. Soviet fighters would outnumber German fighters by an estimated ten to one.

The night bomber regiment would be concentrated in the center to knock out enemy communications and concentrations and soften the enemy defenses for the advance of the Second Belorussian Front. Other bombers and fighters, including the free hunters, would be clustered to the south in support of the First Belorussian Front.

Seventy new hard-surface fields were being built for the medium bombers and the fighters. They would be based as close as possible to the fronts but, because of the many swamps, bogs, and forests of Belorussia and the need for long, hard runways, they would have to be located where such open spaces were available.

"Fortunately, this is not the case with our night bombers, the PO-2s," Novikov said. "They can fly from short, grass fields, so they'll be able to move up quickly, even day by day, as we advance. Scouts are being sent ahead to find suitable spots as we speak."

"How will they sustain themselves?" Stalin asked.

"Comrade Stalin, this women's regiment will create such shelter as they can—in villages, if any are nearby, in dugouts and huts they find or can make for themselves; if nothing else is available, in slit trenches covered with canvas. As the weather warms, they may sleep on the ground under their airplanes. As circumstances dictate, they may be required to subsist on cold rations."

Stalin frowned. Hundreds of thousands of packaged food rations had been sent by America, as had nearly eleven thousand combat and transport aircraft and thousands of trucks, cars, and other equipment. The U.S. A-20 twin-engine Havoc attack bomber was—he hated to concede—better than its counterparts in the Soviet inventory. The P-39 Bell Aircobra, while useless as a high-altitude fighter, was, because of its 37-mm. cannon and maneuverability, perfect for ground attack. And Russia could hardly have survived without the Dodge and Chevrolet trucks.

Now the Americans were asking why Stalin hadn't told his people about the vast amount of equipment and supplies Russia was receiving through the U.S. Lend-Lease program. He disliked being forced to admit that the Soviet Union was accepting so much aid from a capitalist nation but, he supposed, he would have to do it.

But that would wait a bit. Stalin tapped his pipe in his hand.

"You have found the 'night-witches' "—he liked the enemy's term for them—"to be more useful than you originally thought."

"I admit it, Comrade Stalin," the air commander said. "They can take their airplanes where no other kind of aircraft can go. They allow us to harass the enemy twenty-four hours a day. Unquestionably, our Shturmovik ground-attack aircraft is our greatest aerial asset—and I should make it clear that some of our women are flying as gunners and even as pilots—the physically stronger ones—of the Shturmoviks. Just as they are members of tank crews and sniper teams on the ground.

"But I digress. Next to the Shturmoviks, I rank our PO-2s as perhaps the most useful of our air combat types. Of course, our fighter aircraft clear the air of enemy fighters and make it possible for these others to operate. But in terms of carrying the fight to the enemy, the Shturmoviks and PO-2 biplanes are our greatest assets. We will work them very hard in this campaign."

Galina banked over the grassy field and tried to measure it with her eye. The partisans had reported that it was flat, and several of them were waving at her now from below. They had even attached a sheet to a long pole to show her which way the wind was blowing.

She turned into the wind, eased the throttle back, and let the biplane sink. She knew she could get down all right. But would there be enough room to get out again? The only way to find out, unfortunately, was to find out.

Landing, the biplane bounced a few times and rolled to a stop. The ground was soft, perhaps dangerously so. She stood on the brakes and ran up the engine, showering the area behind her with mud, to turn and taxi back to the end of the small field. She would need the longest possible run for takeoff.

Galina talked for a few minutes with the partisans, two men and a woman. They had built wooden shelters and lean-tos in the forest that flanked two sides of the oblong-shaped field. Bogs lay to the other sides. It was a murky, sinister sort of place, hard to get to on the ground and easy in which to find concealment. Which, of course, was why the partisans had been able to survive in it with German forces nearby.

She walked into the woods with the partisans and looked at the shelters. It would be a primitive and marginal place for several hundred aircrews and ground personnel to live, sustain themselves, and resupply and repair their airplanes. But she and six other PO-2 pilots had been dispatched to fly to and look over a dozen small grass fields close to enemy lines that the partisans thought might be suitable for air operations.

She walked back into the open and reflexively looked up. Two Yaks sped by; no enemy aircraft were anywhere in sight. A low mist rose from the swamps and drifted across the field. The woods behind were dark. She shivered; it was the sort of place described in childhood fairy tales and populated by wolves and goblins.

But it would probably suffice if she could get the PO-2 off the soft ground with something to spare. She had to allow for the extra weight of the bomb load. She walked along the edge of the field, picking a tall pine tree as the point of no return for takeoff. It could only be an estimate, but it was an important one to make. If the airplane wasn't light in her hands and ready to take flight when she reached the pine tree, she would chop the throttle and, hopefully, have enough room to stop. If the biplane wasn't ready to take off at that point and she tried to extend the takeoff run any further, she would crash into the trees.

The attempt was nerve-wracking but necessary. She started the engine, held the brakes, pushed the throttle to the stop, and, when the brakes began to slip—they slipped too soon on the PO-2—she began rolling. The old airplane rolled and rolled, bouncing a bit when the wheels struck an uneven spot, but settling back down again.

Take off! Take off! she muttered. The big pine tree was coming up. Now! The biplane bounced, lifted slightly, and sank again. She chopped the throttle, held the stick back in her lap and, when she felt she could do it without flipping on her nose, began applying increasing pressure on the brakes. She lurched to a halt very close to the trees.

She lifted her goggles onto her helmet, pulled a handkerchief from her jacket pocket, and wiped the perspiration from her face. She glared at the trees towering in front of her.

Pees-ann! she spat. Then she uttered the nasty and objectionable four-letter word that Mikhail didn't like her to say. It was especially satisfying to say because it was objectionable. She shouted it three times at the trees.

Then she swiveled the biplane around, taxied it back to the starting point, and turned it around again. Cutting the engine, she told the partisans that this field was just too short and soft. She might come back and try it again when the ground hardened.

Meantime, she needed people to act as human brakes. Hold her wings and tail while she ran up the engine to its highest output, then, upon her signal, let go.

Within five minutes, she had six men and four women to help her. She positioned them carefully, told them to hold tight, and started the engine. When its popping became a roar and the little aircraft shuddered so hard she thought the engine might tear loose, she lifted her arm and the partisans, spattered with mud and grass, fell flat.

The PO-2 jumped forward, rolled, bounced a few times, and, before she reached the pine tree, took wing. She cleared the trees, banked around, waved at the bedraggled people below, and headed for home. Her home that *was*, but would no longer be.

The news that the mixed regiment was to be broken up came as a crushing blow. She knew that it had to happen sooner or later but it was a surprise and shock when the order came. She had resolved to be calm when she and Mikhail were able to meet and talk about it, but she broke down and cried. Tears sprang to Mikhail's eyes and he was unable to speak for a few minutes and, for a time afterward, only brokenly.

"But this area we're going into is so damn big!" he protested in anguish. "How will we find each other again? How, Galishka?"

"Have faith that we will, Misha dear," she replied, nestling against him. "Have faith. We know the number of each other's regiment. Keep asking others you meet if my regiment is near; I'll do the same. We'll find each other."

"Oh God," he said, holding her tight, "how will I know you're all right?"

"Misha darling," she said, smiling sadly, "you've got to give up this crazy idea of trying to protect me. You can't do that any more than I can protect you. And there's no point in telling each other to be careful. You know that. We'll find each other somehow. Meantime, my dear Misha, go with God."

"I thought you didn't believe in God," he said sullenly. "Your Comrade Stalin doesn't."

"I've come to believe in many things I didn't believe in before."

She leaned back in his arms and smiled. "I didn't believe I would ever like you, and now I love you. I didn't believe I would ever want to make love to a man before marriage, and now I can't wait for it to happen. I didn't believe you would ever learn to speak Russian, and now you do it even without thinking. Do you realize we've been speaking in nothing but Russian for the past five minutes?"

"I didn't, no."

"I have to go and pack now, Misha. One of my comrades, Olga, has found a suitable field northwest of here, and we're leaving today. I love you. Kiss me again and we'll say goodbye. For now."

Packing her things, Galina's cheery bravado faded. She wondered if she and Misha would really find each other again. Belorussia was so immense. And, after that, there would be Poland and East Prussia. She desperately wanted to be reunited with him, though she knew, as she had always known, that their relationship was doomed.

Mikhail refused to accept that fact, and his enduring naiveté was one of his most endearing traits. He had become a highly capable combat pilot, brave and resolute, and a very quick student of Russian language and customs. But he hadn't grasped the fundamental difference in their cultures, or didn't want to.

He was too American—too, she said the word to herself with a feeling of surprise—too *free* to ever be a Soviet citizen. He wanted to think and act for himself. She had been, and still was, intensely patriotic. She and her comrades were, after all, defending Mother Russia from the Hitlerite invaders.

But how would she and her comrades have felt and behaved if the shoe had been on the other foot, if it had been the Soviet Union that had invaded Germany, rather than the other way 'round? The two powers were traditional enemies; it could have happened the other way. Would she and her sisters have fought with the same ferocity as invaders rather than defenders? She wondered. *No;* she had to be honest with herself. They would not have fought the same way. She probably wouldn't have fought at all.

When The Great Patriotic War had been won, would she feel as patriotic about spreading the gospel of socialism throughout the world? No. Would she then be willing to leave her homeland and go with Mikhail to America? Yes, she concluded, she would. But there were two giant obstacles. First was the fact that Soviet citizens were not allowed to emigrate or even to travel within their own nation. Second, even if she could get out, and she were willing to leave her family, wouldn't they suffer because of her defection? She would find no happiness with Mikhail in America if her father lost his job in

Moscow and he, her mother, and her sister were sent into Siberian exile.

So it was hopeless. All she could hope for was that she and Mikhail would survive the combat to come, that they would find each other again, and, before he left the Soviet Union, that they would enjoy the idyll both of them wanted. It would be lovely if he gave her a baby she could raise and love and name Mikhail. The regiment would be scandalized, of course. She sighed. It was hopeless.

Viktor looked at Mike sympathetically and poured two more glasses of vodka. It was late at night and they were alone in the tiny room assigned to the squadron commander. "Men have died of many things, Mikhail, but not of love. That's an old . . ."

Mike smiled faintly. "It's an old saying of Shakespeare's. The way it goes is 'Men have died from time to time, and worms have eaten them, but not for love.' "

Viktor nodded grudgingly. "Sometimes you surprise me, Mikhail Stepanovich. For someone who's what?—twenty-two now?—you've done a considerable amount of reading. That should help console you. But please don't worry. I have every confidence we'll find Galina's regiment again. This campaign shouldn't take too long. Not with the forces we're able to assemble now."

"I don't even know where we're going; I couldn't find Belorussia on a map of the world."

"All you'll need is a map of the sector, comrade, and that will be provided. But let me instruct you; I've done so much of it over the last few months it's become second nature."

Mike shrugged. "Go ahead."

"You've heard the term 'Tsar of all the Russias.' "

"I suppose I have. Yes."

"Well, 'all the Russias' meant three Russias. The heartland of Muscovy, Moscow, where I come from, is known as Great Russia."

"Of course."

"Of course. The other two create the peripheral western parts of our empire. The Ukraine, which was known as Little Russia. And Belorussia, to its north, called White Russia."

"Why is it called White?"

"Some say because many of the people are of light, fair coloring. Some say it's because the Mongols were thrown back at that point, so the border became the white line of defense against the dark Asiatics."

"I've learned a little about the Ukraine. It would probably be a beautiful place in the summer. What's special about Belorussia other than the swamps and forests I keep hearing about?"

"It's been a battleground for centuries, Mike. Armies of Germans, Great Russians, Poles, Swedes, even Lithuanians have tramped over it. The people of the inhabited areas have suffered very much during this war. Reports are that Minsk has been almost completely destroyed and that nearly all of its people have been killed or wounded or driven away.

"But," Viktor said, brightening, "there are other things to be said about Belorussia. Such as the fact that the people are obsessed, there's no other word for it, with potatoes."

"Potatoes?"

"Potatoes. They call it their second bread. They have songs about potatoes. Their principal folk dance is called the *Bulba*, meaning, of course, the potato. They supposedly have more than one hundred recipes for dishes made with potatoes."

"That sounds pretty odd. Is that their only oddness?" Mike asked, sipping on his vodka.

"By no means. Their houses have only two windows facing the street."

"How many should they have?"

"Why, three, of course. As we have in Great Russia."

"That makes sense."

"And then there's the fact that the bear is a popular hero in Belorussia."

"The bear?"

"Yes. The bear is depicted in Belorussian mythology as a friend of man. They even have a bear holiday; they call it *Kamayeditsa*. People traditionally eat a dish of potatoes and beans and then lie on the grass and imitate the movements of a bear."

"You're kidding."

"I swear I'm not."

Mike forced a smile. "I appreciate your little song-and-dance to cheer me up. I admit that you have a colorful country, or set of nations, republics, empire, whatever you call them, call it. But you never say much, anything, about the Baltic nations up north."

Viktor peered around instinctively and looked faintly embarrassed. "At the time of the last tsar, the Soviet Union was called the 'prison of nations.'" He held up a hand. "I'm not saying I believe that, mind you. I'm just giving you a little history. Well, you know how Comrade Stalin concluded that so-called non-aggression pact with Hitler before the war began. And then Germany and the Soviet Union jointly partitioned Poland in 1939 . . ."

"You jointly *invaded* Poland."

Viktor frowned. "All right, invaded. And then, under the terms of the pact, we annexed the Baltic nations—Estonia, Latvia, Lithuania. That was in, um, 1940."

"You mean you seized them, took them over."

Viktor sighed. "The official explanation is that the matter of nationalities is a transient question. According to the principles of Marxism-Leninism, nations and national boundaries are transient matters in world history." He shrugged. "To some extent, it's true. The German knights occupied Estonia in the thirteenth century and built the only Gothic architecture you'll find in the Soviet Union. That area has changed hands at least twenty times over the centuries. I've studied the history, a lot of it in your Library of Congress in Washington, by the way. Lithuania once had an empire that extended all the way down to the Black Sea. The Lithuanian tongue has words in common with the Hindus in India."

"I didn't know that. But did it give you the right to grab the Baltic nations back in 1940?"

Viktor looked at Mike for a long minute. "No," he said. He paused. "Michael, no one is more determined to defeat Germany and destroy that tyranny, humiliate all those arrogant people, than I am. I say that in all seriousness. But," his voice dropped, "it's still true, Mike. We're still the 'prison of nations.' "

Viktor's face clouded. "I'm not happy to admit that. And I'm not happy to tell you another thing. But I think I must."

"What is it? Is it something about Galina?"

"Only indirectly. Borisenko was visited a few days ago by one of the air army commanders of the VVS. Novikov has ordered them to visit all the front-line regiments to brief them on the campaign ahead and to assess their readiness."

"So?"

"So, during the conversation—the colonel who came was an old friend of Borisenko and they talked of other matters over a bottle of wine—it seems that your chief air commander in Britain has persuaded Comrade Stalin to designate several air bases here for what they are calling shuttle missions. The three are Poltava, Mirgorod, and Piryatin, all near Kiev. Preparations are going ahead now, Borisenko said. Very shortly, your bombers will be able to bomb very deep into Germany, into areas they can't now reach from England, and then fly on and land at Russian bases. They'll refuel and rearm here and then bomb eastern German targets again on the way back to England."

Mike got up and began pacing around the room. "So there'll be American Air Forces personnel here in Russia. There are probably some at those bases already."

"Yes. And if we can get you to one of those bases—Borisenko and I would find a way—that would be the way to get you repatriated, sent back to your own bomber group."

Mike grimaced as if in pain. "My God. That all seems so, so *foreign* to me now. A funny word to use, I suppose. But I'm used to being a fighter pilot now. And how could I leave now, anyhow? We'll be moving northeast of here tomorrow or the next day, you said."

"As part of the Sixteenth Air Army, supporting the First Belorussian Front. Galina's regiment has been moved farther north, near Orsha."

"So how could I just up and leave you, leave . . ."

"Galina."

"Yes, Galina. We love each other, damn it! If I did that, we'd *never* find each other again."

Viktor put his glass on the table. "You could elect to become a Soviet citizen, of course. Our government would be delighted to have an American pilot—an ace like yourself . . ."

"Defect."

"It wouldn't really be defection. Well, perhaps it would."

"I don't see how I could do that."

Viktor shook his head. "You really couldn't, Mike. You could but you shouldn't. You just wouldn't fit into our society, learning to think in two contradictory ways, talk two different ways, watch every minute what you say, what you do."

"No, I wouldn't. And I love my own country, not incidentally. I *want* to go back. But not now. I'm not a deserter. I didn't come here by choice. But I *am* here and I'm fighting the Germans just as hard as I'd be if I were back in my bomb group. Probably harder. I think I'll just leave things the way they are for now. If it's all right with you and Borisenko."

"It's fine with us, Mike," Viktor said. "You're a fine pilot, a real asset to the VVS. There's one big problem, however."

"What's that?"

"Later, you may not be *allowed* to leave. Don't forget; you're dug yourself rather deeply into our culture. You've learned our ways, the way we think and act; you know a great deal now about our equipment, our tactics and techniques, even our language. The people up above may decide later that you know too much to leave, to be allowed to leave."

"Oh hell, Viktor, I'm just one little guy, one pilot, among thousands and thousands. How would they even know about me?"

Viktor smiled. "There are still some things you don't quite understand about our society. Mike, *they know about every single foreigner in the Soviet Union*. They know who you are and what you're doing, just as they know about every Frenchman or Pole or Czech who's flying for us. I simply don't want you to be denied the chance to leave when you're ready to."

Mike waved a hand in dismissal. "I'll just have to hang on for a while and take my chances. Maybe those shuttle missions won't even come off."

In his bunk that night, Mike's mind raced through a series of fantasies before he fell into a fitful sleep. He had seen an A-20 overhead. He would find out where the A-20s were based and steal one. No, first he would find Galina and take her to the A-20 base. They would escape together. But, if they were attacked by Russian fighters, she wouldn't be able to use the machine guns; she'd had no training in gunnery. Okay, she'd pilot the plane, she was a good pilot, and he'd be the gunner.

Oh, *piss-ant*. The range of the A-20 was too short to get them to England. No, he would get hold of Galina somehow and steal a B-17 at one of those shuttle bases. He'd have to steal it because, if he didn't, they'd never let her aboard. He'd fly the B-17 all the way back to England and land it at his old base.

But then they'd send Galina back to Russia. Of course, she probably wouldn't be willing to leave Russia with him anyhow.

Shit, shit, shit! There was just no good way out of this mess, not if they were ever going to be together. He would just have to wait. It was the only thing he could do.

Waiting was horribly hard for Supreme Commander of the Allied Expeditionary Forces Dwight Eisenhower. The clock was ticking, and now May was drawing to a close.

The Anglo-American bureaucracy planning the invasion of Europe now numbered 16,312 men and women, not counting the staffs of the American and British armies and air forces. Yet all they could do was plan, investigate, advise, and write reports. Not one of them could actually *act*.

That responsibility fell on him alone and he found the burden almost unbearable. The garden at Telegraph Cottage was alive and aromatic with azure, purple, and red rhododendrons, but he hardly noticed.

He sat behind his easel trying to paint a tall pine tree. It was one of his favorite ways of taking his mind off the pressures of the coming invasion—the horribly complicated invasion that had to come off on schedule or be postponed for another year.

The thought of postponement was intolerable, unthinkable. If that happened, America's prestige would plummet, the delicate alliance he had crafted with the British would fall apart, and there would be an open break with Russia. Stalin would sacrifice the lives of untold millions of his people to crush Germany and very possibly swarm all the way across Europe. That suffering continent would find itself under the heel of a new tyrant and the Allies would be back where they started, but with a new and immensely stronger enemy.

Ike listlessly made another few strokes with his brush. Then he scrawled the word *baloney* at the bottom and put his brush away.

CHAPTER THIRTEEN

THE INVASIONS

JUNE 5, THE day set for the invasion, had come and gone, if you could even call it a day. The wind was shaking Eisenhower's trailer near the coast with almost hurricane force. The rain was lashing sideways, the Allied Supreme Commander noted gloomily, and it was as dark as the bottom of a coal mine.

The invasion ships had set out and been recalled. The English Channel was so rough that supporting naval gunfire would be inaccurate, the men would be too seasick to fight, landing craft would flounder or capsize, and the surf would be too high for the landings.

As bad or worse than all these, the clouds had descended to a few hundred feet off the ground and, even at ground level, visibility had fallen too low to provide air support for the ships and troops. Without the overwhelming firepower of the air forces, the fragile landing force would be thrown back into the sea.

Ike declared a twenty-four-hour postponement with no hope that the next day or two would be any better.

Problems had been multiplying for weeks. The first ones were small but alarming. A jerk of a sergeant, dreaming about his girl friend, had sent secret Overlord documents to her address in Chicago instead of to the War Department in Washington.

He hadn't even wrapped the package properly. The papers fell out at the post office and a dozen postmen learned more than anyone should have known about the plans and probable date of the invasion of Europe.

A U.S. Army major general and a U.S. Navy officer babbled about the invasion plans at separate parties. Both were sent home.

Then came the big problems. Congestion at England's southern ports, where landing craft and ships were loading for D-Day, had become so bad that supplies from America had to enter at the northern ports. This meant that the goods had to be shipped to the south on England's overburdened railroads, temporarily denying the British badly-needed supplies of food.

The warehouses, depots, and heavily-loaded ships in the southern ports were, of course, bulging with invasion equipment and supplies. Though they were surrounded by barbed wire and guards—or perhaps because of it—it was hard to believe the Germans wouldn't know about them. And intelligence reports said the enemy was about to start launching its jet-propelled V-1 flying bombs against England. If they landed in numbers on the warehouses and ships, Eisenhower reflected, you could kiss the invasion goodbye.

Next, RAF Chief Air Marshal Sir Trafford Leigh-Mallory, commander of the Allied tactical air forces and every bit as imposing as his name and title, said a key part of the invasion wouldn't work. Leigh-Mallory had become convinced that the scheduled air drop of the U.S. 82nd and 101st Airborne divisions on the Cotentin peninsula to protect the Utah Beach landings would end in a "futile slaughter" of perhaps seventy percent of the American paratroops and glider troops.

Leigh-Mallory's argument alarmed Ike but, the more he thought about it, the risk had to be taken. Without the air drop to protect it, Utah Beach could turn into a bloody failure and jeopardize all the landings.

Next, the cranky "tall asparagus" who had declared himself leader of all French forces, le grand Charles De Gaulle, was sulking and refusing to broadcast an appeal to the French resistance to sabotage the railroads the Germans were using. Ike had even invited De Gaulle to his war room June 3 and shown him the maps and plans for the invasion. De Gaulle began criticizing them and lecturing the Supreme Commander on how it should be done. Ike had nodded gravely and said he wished there was time to make the changes the eccentric Frenchman recommended.

Even Prime Minister Winston Churchill had created a worrisome distraction. He announced that he would personally participate in the invasion by going on one of the British warships. Aghast, Admiral Sir Bertram Ramsey appealed to Ike to stop him. Ike told Churchill that, if his ship was hit, another four or five would have to drop out of line to save it instead of doing their assigned jobs.

Churchill said he was going anyway. Ike said that, as Supreme Commander, he was ordering Churchill not to go. Churchill smiled and said that, while Ike was indeed Supreme Commander, he had no authority over personnel assignments aboard His Majesty's ships.

Ike was momentarily checkmated, but the King came to the rescue. If the Prime Minister was participating in the invasion, the King said, he would go along too. Churchill protested, wrote complaining letters, sulked, and finally backed down.

Finally, after two years of planning, the huge operation, the biggest and most complex amphibious military invasion in world history, was ready to begin. Nearly 200,000 men were ready to make the assault. They would be put ashore from 6,840 transports, landing craft, and special-purpose vessels.

The invaders would be supported by 6 battleships, 23 battle cruisers, 122 destroyers, and 260 PT boats. Twenty-five flotillas of minesweepers would clear the mines from the landing areas.

Overhead would be 5,409 fighters, 1,645 light and medium bombers, 3,467 heavy bombers, and 2,316 transports. Intelligence said the Luftwaffe had only 300 aircraft in the area, about a hundred of them fighters.

The soldiers had been issued special invasion money, gas masks, vomit bags, cigarettes, toothbrushes, extra socks, food rations, and extra rounds of ammunition. To care for the wounded, 15 hospital ships were ready with 8,000 doctors, 800,000 pints of plasma, 600,000 doses of penicillin, 100,000 pounds of sulfa, and thousands of tons of other medical supplies.

The whole operation was leaning forward. If it didn't take the decisive step very soon it would fall on its face and, like Humpty Dumpty, smash into a thousand pieces. June 5 had been picked because British Group Captain J. M. Stagg, the meteorologist, had predicted good weather for the first week of June. On June 3, Ike had driven to Southwick House, Admiral Ramsey's headquarters near Portsmouth. In the mess room Captain Stagg greeted him with bad news. The high pressure system was moving out and a low was moving in. There would be storms, heavy clouds, Force Five winds, and high surf.

Ike looked at the windows, hoping to see a ray of light. They were dark, and the wind and rain rattled the glass. The day passed, and then the night. June 4 and 5 were no better. Then Stagg reappeared, smiling. The rain would stop by midnight and the winds would diminish. The weather wouldn't actually be what you called *good,* he said. The seas would still be rough and clouds would hamper aerial operations somewhat, especially for the heavy bombers. But low-flying fighter-bombers probably could get under the clouds well enough to operate the night of June 5–6.

Ike looked around. Should they wait a bit before deciding? Admiral Ramsey shook his head. The naval task force had to know within a half-hour if it was a go for June 6. And, because of tidal conditions and supply problems, any further postponement would push the invasion back to June 19. Stagg said the long-range weather predictions were for worse weather by that time. Ike grunted in frustration. What would the weather be like the day of June 6 in the Channel and over France? Stagg shrugged. "I just don't know," he said.

Ike sat back in his chair and looked around. Every face was turned toward him. "It's a helluva gamble," he said. "But I don't know how long you can hang this operation out on the end of a limb and let it hang there."

He waited a moment and said: "The order must be given." Ramsey rushed out to tell the U.S. and British fleet commanders. Thousands of ships left their ports and began moving toward France through the rain-swept seas. Ike went back to his trailer and tried to sleep. At 3:30 A.M. he rose and returned to the mess room at Southwick House. The admirals and generals convened.

Soon after, Stagg appeared again. The weather would clear within a few hours, he said. But, by June 7, the Channel could become rougher. Ike sighed. That meant that the Allies might get the first and second assault waves ashore and then be unable to reinforce them.

Soon, the ships he had dispatched would reach their point of no return. There was no clear indication of what to do, but the decision had to be made now. Ike took a deep breath and said: "Okay, let's go."

The generals and admirals left. Ike sat alone in his armchair. It was early morning, June 6. The invasion was on. Now even he couldn't stop it. For the first time in two years, and for a period of days, he would have nothing whatever to do but wait.

He took a piece of paper from the table and began scrawling a press release on it. It would be used if things went wrong. It said that the landings had failed and that he had withdrawn the troops. The end of the press release said "The troops, the air and the Navy did all that bravery and devotion to duty could do. If any blame or fault attaches to the attempt it is mine alone." He stuffed the note in his wallet and prayed earnestly that he wouldn't have to use it.

The Allied landings caught the German Army by surprise. Two of the three division commanders in the landing area were away attending a war game. Rommel, watching the storm strike and, convinced there could be no invasion in such weather, had gone to Germany to celebrate his wife's birthday and see Hitler.

The Desert Fox, as an admiring German public called him, had begun to suspect where the Allied landings would be made. To prevent them, he had moved the 352nd infantry division up to the Normandy beaches and his 91st Airborne to the Cotentin peninsula.

He wanted to move the 12th SS and Panzerlehr divisions and a rocket-launching brigade into the area. That would be enough to defeat any amphibious landing.

Hitler had refused the requests. So Rommel decided to fly to Berchtesgaden and make his appeal personally.

But, against all reason, the Allies hit the Normandy beaches at dawn on June 6 and threw the defending German troops into confusion. In Rommel's absence, his chief of staff tried to move the 12th SS division into position but the order was canceled by Commander-in-Chief West Rundstedt because Hitler's headquarters hadn't confirmed it.

At eleven o'clock in the morning, Rundstedt frantically put in a call to Adolf Hitler to ask that the 12th and Panzerlehr divisions be released to him. But, he was informed, the nocturnal Supreme Commander was asleep and couldn't be awakened.

At 2:30 P.M., Hitler agreed. But when the divisions tried to move, they found rail lines smashed, bridges out, and roads blocked with debris. As they struggled to get through, they were strafed and bombed and suffered heavy casualties.

Rommel reached his headquarters by late afternoon, checked the situation, and immediately asked that six divisions stationed in Brittany, central and southern France, and the Channel Islands be sent to the Normandy beachhead.

Despite the damage they would suffer from aerial attacks on the way, they would still have enough strength to throw the invaders back into the sea, Rommel argued. Hitler refused. The Normandy landings were a feint, a sideshow, he said; the main landings would come soon northeast of there at the Pas de Calais.

Still, a single Wehrmacht division nearly derailed the invasion. The Americans stormed ashore at Utah Beach, near the base of the Cotentin peninsula, without serious opposition. But at nearby Omaha Beach, the U.S. 1st Infantry Division, known as the Big Red One, unexpectedly ran into the German Army's battle-seasoned 352nd Division.

The 352nd smashed forward, pinned the Big Red One down on the beach, and was on the verge of driving it back into the sea and splitting the invasion forces. But, thinking they had already repulsed the invasion, the German commanders stopped. They had received no directions from above and didn't know what was happening in other areas. The Americans regrouped.

Next morning, Eisenhower appeared off the beach in a British minesweeper and anchored offshore to receive a personal report from General Omar Bradley. Overall, the news was good. Twenty-five hundred men had been lost but 156,000 Allied soldiers had managed to get ashore at five points. The airborne troops, 23,000 of them, had landed inland in Normandy.

But there were serious problems. At Omaha Beach, only one hundred of twenty-four hundred tons of supplies had made it ashore and the beach was still under fire. The men were nearly out of ammunition. Of thirty-two amphibious tanks launched at Omaha, only five were ashore.

. All five divisions ashore suffered the same problems in varying degrees. The 82nd and 101st airborne troops were creating havoc in the German lines but the divisions hadn't come together as coordinated fighting forces.

But things would improve. Ike lifted his binoculars to his eyes. Tanks and trucks were rolling inland now. He looked around. Tugs were towing the huge artificial harbors toward their destinations. Overhead, the sky was filled with combat airplanes, none of them German.

Ike allowed himself a grin. Soon, American forces would seal off the peninsula and take the deep-water port of Cherbourg. Southeast of there, British forces would take the critically-important town of Caen and open the way to Paris. At a meeting of Allied leaders three weeks earlier, Montgomery had walked around like a boastful giant on a huge map of France he had laid on the floor and promised that he would take Caen in a day and then "crack about" inland.

One thing, at least, seemed certain, Ike thought: Now Stalin would end his carping that the Western allies were hanging back. From now on, there would be an unselfish spirit of cooperation between East and West.

"Kee-ryst, Dee Tee, this is a funny one." Buddy brandished the teletype field order from Wing that had just chattered out of the machine. "We're goin' to Russia!"

"Yes sir," Major D.T. Potter said. "I called Wing on the scrambler to get some details. It's called Poltava. It's a Russian base in the Ukraine. It's one of these shuttle bases General Spaatz has set up. There's a very big force, over two thousand '17s and '24s, going to Berlin. Our Wing, we estimate about one hundred and fifteen '17s, will peel off and hit the synthetic oil plant at Ruhland, south of there. Then you'll go on to Poltava and land and stay overnight. Refuel and rearm. You'll hit another target on the way back."

"A twofer, huh?" Buddy said. "What about fighter escort? It gets lonesome without our little friends."

"They'll be there, Colonel," Dee Tee said. "You'll have seventy P-51s with you. All the way in and out."

Buddy nodded. "Well, it'll be somethin' new, anyway. Sounds like we'll have a drinkin' party the night we get to—what's the name of that place?"

"Pol-tah-va."

"Poltava. Okay. Listen, Dee Tee, put a couple bottles of scotch aboard my plane, will you? I oughta give one of their majors or colonels a present or two, we're such good friends now."

Walking back to his quarters, Buddy looked around the field with a feeling of satisfaction. He wouldn't have imagined it possible, but he had become a leader of men after all. He had improved the skills of the air crews and instilled the men with pride. A half dozen new B-17Gs had arrived to fill out his group very nicely. He had forty-two planes on the base now, all clean and shipshape.

Mike would be proud, Buddy thought, though it would be understandable if he felt a little jealous. Buddy had always seemed to play second fiddle, somehow, when Mike was around. Even when they flipped for it, Mike got the first pilot's seat. Then he got Claire.

Buddy pulled his cap off and rubbed his head. He wished sometimes he could disconnect the damned thing and have one of his crew chiefs rewire his brain. He had so many contradictory thoughts and feelings, more than a simple ol' S'uthe'n boy was supposed to have.

Mike was never far from his thoughts; Buddy still talked to him—that is, to himself—surreptitiously sometimes. He still felt bonded to Mike with invisible steel bands. He also wanted the pleasure of being able to show Mike that he, Buddy, could outstrip him at something.

For one thing, he wanted Mike back so that he, Buddy, could compete, man to man, for Claire's affection. He couldn't forget that Mike and Claire had made love that afternoon aloft in the B-17 and that the experience must have been a humdinger. The thought was intimidating. He didn't want to come up short—an unfortunate choice of words—in that kind of contest.

Nor did he know whether the Claire he thought about nearly every day was a real person—as intelligent, beautiful, capable, decent, and desirable as she had become in his imagination—or simply a romantic illusion he had concocted out of loneliness and nostalgia. He wouldn't know until they could meet and see each other and talk and touch.

And what would she think of him? Perhaps, thousands of miles away and traveling through environments that were as alien to her as his were to him, she had conjured up an equally imaginary man. But they were getting to know each other in their letters. It was frustrating not to be able to really tell each other what they were doing—the censors neatly snipped away any such references—but they were able to chat and joke and reveal something of themselves. Her last letter gave him a nostalgic pang.

. . . Well, Buddy, I guess I can't tell you what I'm doing except to say that I'm awfully busy, busier than I ever was before, and that's saying a lot. I suspect you can say the same. I do hope you're well and that you're being careful. I know that's a dumb thing to say, but I feel better saying it anyway.

I still like what I'm doing, I do love ███████████, but the other day I found myself thinking, wouldn't it be nice to pull off these coveralls and take a bubblebath, the way I used to do in the old days, and put on a pretty dress and makeup and maybe stick a gardenia in my hair.

Sound like a real Southern Belle with a capital B, don't I? Well, I'll never be *that* person again; she wasn't very nice. But I wouldn't mind *looking* like her now and then. I feel like you might be a bit disappointed when you see today's Claire, short hair, no lipstick, coveralls (like I said), work shoes, broken fingernails, blisters on her hands from wrestling some of these big you-knows around. I may not look as good to *you*, but, unless I miss my guess, you're going to look pretty imposing. Not that you were ever bad-looking, you were nice-looking, but you've come up in the world and a man seems to improve with authority and confidence, and let's not forget that uniform. I've seen a few of those battle-blouses of yours, I hear they're called Eisenhower jackets, and they're really sharp looking.

But I'd like to believe that it's who we are inside, what we've become, that's really important, and I have to say that I think we're both bigger and better people than we were before, and you're a much sweeter person than I thought I knew.

Got to fly now. Literally.

Love,
Claire

It was the first time she had signed her letter with "love." It didn't necessarily mean anything, but it *was* the first time she'd used the word. He wondered if she was *making* love to anyone; if she was, he didn't want to know about it. He recognized that the old double standard didn't apply like it used to and, in wartime, it was often wham-bam-thank-you-ma'am (or man) on both sides within a day, a night, sometimes even an hour of meeting.

But when you cared about a woman, or thought you did, you didn't want someone else sharing her. Women probably felt the same way about men. Mike once quoted something from Shakespeare that stuck in his mind. It was from *Othello* and he wasn't sure he remembered the exact words, but it hit the heart of the matter. Othello said something like: "By heaven, I'd rather be a toad and live on the vapor of a dungeon ['vapor of a dungeon,' no Greenville boy would think up words like that] than share a corner in the thing I love for other's uses."

But he and Claire hadn't made any kind of a pledge to each other, so both were free. And, in one sense, that was good, Buddy reflected. For it was just about totally impossible for a jumpy American flying officer who had just come off a raid and was probably going to fly one the next day to say no, ma'am to a milky-skinned English blonde who walked up at a party, batted her big blue eyes at him, and sweetly offered him milk, cookies, mothering, and sex. A lot of married Americans suspended their vows under the pressures of combat and that kind of temptation.

The English girls weren't the kind of man-traps that the Southern belles were. Most didn't have any money and a lot of them made their own clothes, so they weren't as smart-looking as the American girls. But they weren't as demanding, either; they tended to be kind of simple and open. Many of them were very appealing—they had lovely smooth skins—and they were attracted to the Americans, who were bigger and bolder and had better teeth and more money than the English boys.

That's how Buddy had taken up with Peggy. She was sweet and loving and childlike, and he could keep her separate in his mind from his feelings about Claire. Peggy was wonderful in bed, and she was interesting in other ways as well. The odd way she used words, for instance. In bed, she had said that, "if you keep doing that, you're going to send me mad." How do you "send" somebody mad? Once she playfully poked him in the ribs with a finger and said "keeks!" Keeks! What kind of word was that?

He had tried hard to teach her to talk right. She couldn't even pronounce where he came from. She said "You-knighted Staysts" instead of "Yew-natted Stets," and she laughed when he tried to correct her. As he said, she was childlike.

Buddy saw her once a week or so, in Cambridge, where she lived, or in London, or, on the rare occasions there was a party, on the base. Lately, she'd been pestering him to grow a mustache. It would look "smashing," she said. Smashing. He had thought about it but he had seen the way the gunners on one of his bomber crews had acted to their pilot when he grew a mustache. They pointed to his mustache, grabbed their crotches, and whimpered.

If he grew a mustache, they'd do it to him, too, Buddy reflected. They just had no respect for authority, no damned respect at all. He bet the Russians did.

Josef Stalin stared at Novikov, whom he had told to stay behind as his other generals trooped from his Kremlin office. It was June 21, the eve of the third anniversary of the unspeakable day on which the Germans had invaded the Soviet Union. That invasion, which the Hitlerites had grandiosely named Operation Barbarossa, had been repelled.

Tomorrow, in a savage celebration of that anniversary, Operation Bagration would smash into the remaining enemy forces with overwhelming power and drive them from the sacred soil of Mother Russia.

Yet, aggravatingly, new invaders were arriving today. The Americans would land at Poltava within hours. They would mingle with his air commanders and pilots. They would bring airplanes for their shuttle missions that the Soviet Air Force coveted but didn't have, the four-engine B-17s and the speedy, advanced P-51 Mustangs.

The Americans would be wearing uniforms that made the Russians' uniforms seem shabby. They would bring food and drink that the Russians couldn't obtain. They would walk and talk and laugh boldly and confidently and say what they wished, as no Russian would dare to do. And, doing so, they would spread the virus of their spurious freedom.

Stalin had never wanted the Americans in Russia, and certainly not on the soil of the ever-rebellious Ukraine. But they had kept demanding bases for shuttle bombing, and the demands had become impossible to refuse. The Americans had supplied the USSR with large quantities of essential weapons and supplies, and now they and the British had invaded France. He had to agree, or at least to appear to.

Stalin filled his pipe while his chief air commander waited. Perhaps it was time, on this historic date, to make it clear that an ally was not necessarily a friend. You might accept help from someone who faced a common enemy, but that didn't mean you had to invite him into your house. If he had the bad taste to demand an invitation, perhaps you should make it clear, in your own way, that he wasn't welcome.

The dictator lit his pipe and motioned to Novikov to sit down.

A deadly wall of black hung in the sky ahead, and Buddy was glad when the Wing leader turned away from Berlin instead of following the main force into the writhing curtain of flak. Despite the admonitions of the leaders, the bomber command channel was alive with cries and curses as angry or panicked pilots cursed or called for help.

Fighter groups darted about nimbly on the periphery of the bomber stream, chasing or being chased by other fighters. The blinding sun moved to the left and out of Buddy's eyes as he swung his group southward. For a moment, at least, it was a relief. A new curtain of flak began to appear ahead of them as they approached Ruhland. The lead bombardier of the lead group had dropped smoke bombs to mark the target and their long white trails stretched vertically from twenty-five thousand feet all the way to the ground.

Flying over them gave Buddy a familiar but unsettling moment of vertigo. Flying at high altitude created no sense of height because you were disconnected from the ground. But looking down the white rope of smoke somehow created that connection. As it did, it gave Buddy an instant sense of disorientation. It was like touching a live wire.

He shook his head and concentrated on the target ahead. The routine had become automatic. The bomb bay doors were open and sub-zero air was swirling through the cabin. The co-pilot set the engine

RPMs at emergency war power and they made a horrible grinding noise. The bombardier fed him minute changes of course and then engaged the clutch that coupled his Norden bombsight to the plane's autopilot. Vapor trails of condensed ice crystals streamed rearward from the engines of the airplanes ahead.

The planes rose as the bombs fell free, and Buddy reclaimed the controls and left the target in a slow bank, losing altitude. The navigator gave him a course to Poltava. The P-51 escorts closed in. The flak had stopped and there were no enemy fighters around.

But there was a German fighter-bomber, a JU-88. It was trailing the formation from far behind, flying well out of firing range. Its presence had been reported by the tail gunner in the B-17 flying tail-end Charlie in the low squadron of the last group.

Buddy shrugged when he heard a brief conversation about it on the bomber channel. No problem. If the P-51s were too low on gas to double back and shoot it down, he was sure the Russians would go after it in their little Yaks or whatever they called their fighters.

Poltava was fun. It was a grubby kind of a base and, by the time everyone landed, there were B-17s parked all over it. But there was a regular receiving line and everybody exchanged gifts and slapped everybody else on the back. The Russians yelled and laughed and, when they went inside to a big sit-down dinner, they knocked back vodka and cognac as if they were drinking water. People kept jumping up and down, toasting each other.

Buddy hadn't been with such a bunch of carousers since the time Old Miss won the Sugar Bowl. Or was it the Cotton Bowl? Things were getting fuzzy and he couldn't remember. Near midnight, a soldier rushed into the mess and said something to the head Russian, a general named Perminov.

Perminov raised a hand and said in English: "German aircraft have crossed our front lines and are headed toward this area."

Well, so what? Buddy thought. Any Luftwaffe crazies who get through will get themselves shot full of holes by the ack-ack and the Yaks. Minutes later, an air raid siren went off. Buddy looked at Perminov. The Russian commander just chug-a-lugged another shot of vodka, so Buddy relaxed.

The soldier ran into the mess hall and spoke to Perminov again. The Russian shrugged and dismissed him. Then the soldier ran in with a third message, waving his arms as he spoke. Perminov looked up and spoke in a loud voice: "I think we should go to the slit trenches."

Bewildered, Buddy trooped outside with the others and went

down into a deep slit trench. After standing there, shoulder to shoulder, with the others for what seemed like ten or fifteen minutes, he wondered if they were playing some kind of silly game—a summer camp snipe-hunt or something.

Then he heard the heavy drone of airplane engines. A moment later, night turned into day and Buddy realized the Germans had dropped illumination flares. The field was bathed in a stark, white light. A whistling sound followed. Buddy looked up, open-mouthed. A series of shattering blasts erupted across the field. Catching a glimpse of the attackers, someone yelled: "They're JU-88s, and I saw a big Heinkel, a 177, just then."

Bombs continued to fall. Antiaircraft guns started firing, but their fire was sporadic and no German planes came down. The ground shook with the bombing. It was scary; it seemed to suck the breath out of you. And it went on and on. At length, Buddy checked his watch. A whole goddamn hour had gone by and the Germans were still bombing the field.

Where in hell are the Red Air Force fighters? The sound of the engines stopped and he started to climb out of the trench. Someone pulled him back. Now there was a new sound.

"They're coming back at low level," an American shouted.

The German bombers swept back over the field and raked it with machine gun fire. When they left, the Americans and Russians climbed out of the trench. The field was a wasteland. Forty-seven B-17s, including Buddy's, were flaming hulks. And three hundred thousand gallons of precious high-octane gasoline, brought here from halfway around the world, had gone up in flames.

Buddy looked at the Russians and screamed: "What the hell's happened here? Where was your goddamn air force? Where *were* the bastards?"

As the B-17 wing was flying eastward to Poltava, Mike's Yak squadron crossed beneath it, flying westward toward the new day-fighter base. The sight of the familiar Fortresses shocked Mike, infusing him with a sense of guilt, and his Yak wobbled out of formation for a moment.

I should turn right around and follow the B-17s to their shuttle base, he thought. *That's what I should do. But if I tried to, somebody would take me for a deserter and shoot me down.* It had been a rash decision to stay with the VVS, he knew; if he had gone by the book, the U.S. GI book, he would have accepted Viktor's offer to spirit him to Poltava or one of the other new shuttle bases.

But, nearly a year ago, he had opened another book, and he had been following it faithfully ever since. He had become a member of the Red Air Force and he was fighting the same enemy that Buddy and his other American friends were fighting. He wondered how Buddy was doing. He even imagined for a moment that maybe Buddy was one of the pilots in the B-17 formation that had just passed.

Wouldn't it be great to see him again? Buddy would have changed some, of course. By now, he was probably a captain or, to really stretch reality, even a major.

The thought gave Mike a pang of regret. If Michael Gavin held a military rank, it was still that of a lowly first lieutenant in the Eighth. His recently-acquired rank of senior lieutenant in the VVS was honorary and temporary. Not that it mattered. He had rationalized his decision to stay with the Red Air Force instead of seizing the chance to rejoin the Eighth by saying that they were fighting the same enemy and, by now, he was doing it better by flying the Yak.

That might be true, Mike knew, but it was still a rationale. It allowed him to avoid a moral conflict and, at the same time, satisfy his real reason for staying. He couldn't bear to leave Galina. It would have been different if Galina were an American or even an English girl and he had just waved goodbye to her with some reasonable chance of returning and finding her safe. But if he had left, he would never have found her again.

Even worse, he would never know whether she had survived. Whatever she was doing right now, it certainly wasn't safe. He had come to admire and respect the women who were flying combat, but it was terribly hard for a man who loved such a woman.

It wasn't right for a woman to put a man through that kind of torture.

Flugkapitan Hanna Reitsch drew herself up to her tallest, looked beseechingly at her Supreme Commander, and spoke passionately. "I know it is very late, mein Führer. I believe we could have destroyed the invasion if our Suicide Group had been activated. There have been so many delays. But now we ask your permission to launch our attacks. The Suicide Group is not a stunt, mein Führer. It is a collection of brave and clearheaded Germans who offer their lives to insure a future for our children."

Silence fell over the tiny room in the Führerbunker below the ruined Berlin Chancellery. General of the Bombers Werner Baumbach, who had been given nominal control of the operation, shuffled his feet in embarrassment. *These neurotic scenes have become grotesque,* he thought. A new "ram Commando" was being set up at Stendel to ram the American B-17 bombers with fighters. Another officer wanted to form another group of suicide pilots who would wear Army uniforms and crash their planes into targets.

And Hanna, who deserved the highest respect for her flying skill and bravery, if not for good sense, had formed her Suicide Group to fly the almost unflyable V-1 bombs into strategic targets.

Nor are these schemes the only thing that's become grotesque, Baumbach thought. Adolf Hitler looked as if he'd been given a magical old-age elixir. In a year's time, he had grown gray-faced and stooped. His voice was a rasp, and his hands shook so badly that he had to use a rubber stamp to affix his signature to orders.

At last Hitler spoke, his voice hoarse and tired. "Hanna, I cannot be bothered with such things. I will have none of this. I listened to you only because of my regard for you. I have no more time now."

After the meeting, Baumbach ordered the suicide pilots to be scattered to the four winds. Some were sent back to their original units, some left for new flying schools that were being set up, some went to replacement depots. He was sorry for Hanna Reitsch who stood, head down and depressed, in the ruined, bombed-out garden of the Chancellery. But he was relieved to be rid of at least this one nightmare.

He envied the fighter commanders. All they had to do was take off, go shoot at the enemy, and return. They led a much simpler life.

The ground crew, several of them women, pushed and pulled the Focke-Wulf from its camouflaged lair in the forest. As it moved into the open at the edge of the field, the pilot emerged and quickly scanned the sky. Seeing nothing but a few drifting clouds, he jumped up on the wing, climbed into the cockpit, and waited nervously while a female crewman helped him fasten his safety harness.

General of the Fighters Adolf Galland walked from the improvised headquarters shack that had been built under the trees and watched. The female ground worker was rather pretty in her form-fitting black jumpsuit with that inviting zipper in front. At another time, he would have approached her when she went off-duty and explored the possibility of a little diversion.

A cool June breeze caressed his face with the scent of the flowers and herbs that grew wild at the edge of the woods. He inhaled; it would be very nice to lie in the flowers with the girl. There had been so little beauty in his life during the past year.

He sighed and looked at the Focke-Wulf. It looked as if this unit might get four to six fighters aloft today, as other units, similarly distributed within wooded areas near the front, were attempting to do. It was a pitiful substitute for the comprehensive plan that High Command Air had worked out to the tiniest detail for the support of the German Army in France.

But the plan didn't arrive until the second day of the invasion. Not that it would have made a great deal of difference. The emergency airfields that had been set up in France had already been bombed, and front-line conditions were unbelievingly primitive.

It was, Galland reflected, strikingly like the collapse of the French Air Force when the Luftwaffe blasted a path for the German invasion of France and the Low Countries in 1940. Like the French, the Luftwaffe Fighter Corps had lost its bearings because of disrupted communications. High Command didn't know where their units were or, if they had arrived at their appointed designations, what shape they were in and what they needed.

On the way to their action stations, nearly half had become involved in dogfights, suffered heavy losses, and become separated. By this time, most of the pilots were inexperienced. They knew little about navigation and bad-weather flying. Many got lost and many crashed. The repair squads were overworked and lacked necessary parts. Fuel was running short. Everything fell into chaos.

So, on the Western front, the Luftwaffe retired to a form of jungle warfare. Squadrons were broken up and the planes were hidden in wooded areas with the help of camouflage netting. If the concealment was poor, the forest would be carpet-bombed a day or two later by the Americans.

Galland told the Supreme Commander firmly that he must withdraw at least two surviving fighter groups from the front and begin building up a reserve. Hitler, inexplicably, agreed. Speer would supply new airplanes from his underground factories and Galland would train, however incompletely, new pilots. His goal was to have two thousand fighters available for the defense of the Reich by September.

For now, he was visiting the "jungle" units on the Western front to see if they were achieving anything worthwhile in the face of the Allies' overwhelming air superiority.

He wished the pilot would get the *verdammt* Focke-Wulf in the air. The boy had had only sixty hours of training, hardly enough to teach him aerobatics, much less how to survive in mortal combat.

The FW's propeller began turning at last. The fighter began rolling along the ground. Then Galland's ears, acutely tuned to distant engine sounds by years of experience, heard them approaching. *Gott!* Reflexively, he raised an arm and prepared to shout at the FW pilot, though his conscious mind told him it was too late.

The rolling Focke-Wulf had just raised its tail when the two American P-47s streaked low over the trees. The leader's cannon shells walked along the ground and into the body of the fighter straining to take off. The Focke-Wulf blew up in a red ball that hung in the air and showered debris over the field.

Knowing what would happen next, Galland took a few long steps into the trees and threw himself on the ground. The P-47s stood on their tails, climbed, rolled quickly around, and raked the forest with cannon fire. By the time they had left, one ground crew member had been killed, a second had been wounded, and another Focke-Wulf had been wrecked.

Galland brushed himself off. He hoped he would have better luck leaving in his own plane. Though when he got back to his headquarters, he would probably find another blockheaded complaint that the Luftwaffe's fighter pilots had become sniveling cowards. Where is the Luftwaffe? they would cry. He wished they would come and see for themselves.

Where *is* the Luftwaffe? General of the Infantry Hans Jordan asked himself as he peered out the slit of his concrete blockhouse near the front lines in Belorussia. He hadn't seen an airplane bearing a Maltese cross in days.

For that matter, he wondered, where is our leadership? Turning up the wick on his oil lamp, he made an entry in his diary. It was, he noted carefully, June 22, 1944.

Ninth Army stands on the eve of another great battle, unpredictable in extent and duration. One thing is certain: in the last few weeks the enemy has completed an assembly on the very greatest scale opposite the army, and the army is convinced that that assembly overshadows the concentration of forces off the north flank of Army Group North Ukraine . . .

The army believes that, even under the present conditions, it would

be possible to stop the enemy offensive, but not under the present direc-
tives which require an absolutely rigid defense. There can be no doubt,
if a Soviet offensive breaks out, the army will either have to go over to a
mobile defense or see its front smashed . . . The army, therefore, looks
ahead to the coming battle with bitterness, knowing that it is bound by
orders to tactical measures which it cannot in good conscience accept as
correct, and which in our earlier victorious campaigns were the causes
of the enemy defeats . . .

These truths had been pointed out time and again to the commanding general and chief of staff, but neither had the courage to argue
them with the Führer. From what Jordan had heard, the Supreme
Commander sat regularly at a map table and, like a child playing
with toy soldiers, moved markers around that represented divisions
which hardly existed. Even when they did, the markers were placed
hundreds of miles from the actual sites.

That was a special kind of insanity. Another kind came regularly
over the Russian radio frequency. The Russian high command didn't
even bother to code its transmissions. For the coming battle, it gave
orders in the clear, often warning the local commanders that "if you
fail to take your objective, it will be very bad for your health."

Jordan knew what that meant. He had seen Russian soldiers and
former officers, terrified and disheveled, advancing with linked arms
over minefields while machine gunners behind them ensured that
they wouldn't break and run. When anyone did, he was immediately
cut down. If he didn't, he was frequently blown into the air by the
explosion of the mine he stepped on.

Jordan closed his diary, put it in his map case, and turned down
the lamp wick. If that's how the Russians treated their own soldiers,
he reflected, one can imagine how they treated enemy prisoners of
war. It would be better to die in battle. That's what he expected to do.

Galina opened the package of rations and looked at them with dis-
taste. She recognized the words printed on the package as English.
These things had been a mystery until the existence of America's
Lend-Lease program had been announced in a terse bulletin. Of
course, it was hardly a secret that the Soviet Union was receiving aid
from the capitalists. Otherwise, how could one account for the Dakota transports they used regularly, the Bell Aircobra ground-attack
aircraft, the old Curtiss P-40s, and the Dodge and Chevrolet trucks?

And now cold food rations. She pulled a tough cracker from the package and nibbled on it disinterestedly. When she had eaten it, she would open the little tin of potted meat, some kind of preserved pork product, she judged. The only thing worth eating was the hard chocolate bar that came with it.

Present conditions were the worst the night bomber regiment had endured. She and the others wrapped themselves in their blankets after a night's work and slept under the airplanes, but all of them were covered with mosquito bites by daybreak.

Galina's hands were blistered and, like the others, she was dirt-smeared and smelly from digging protective slit trenches and from the peculiarly pungent sweat that broke out on her body when searchlights and heavy ground fire bracketed her biplane.

Drinking water had been delivered in large bladders but there wasn't enough for bathing. So they had to stay dirty and smelly. Unlike the ground soldiers and even the Shturmoviks, the night-witches had been attacking the enemy along the central front for days. Every night, they glided silently over the Fascist lines and bombed the command posts, supply depots, and the zigzag trenches that had been dug to repel the coming Soviet attack.

The enemy's rapid-firing cannons and flat-trajectory 88-mm. guns were numerous and deadly and it was terrifying to be caught in the blinding searchlights. Her *Ved'ma* had been punctured with fifty holes, by count, and Valya had been gashed in her left arm by a flak fragment. Galina was, of course, exhausted.

But they had been lucky. Two of the girls had been killed and three had been wounded. Five members of the regiment had formed an honor guard and fired pistol volleys over the grave of the comrade whose body had been recovered.

Galina wondered if Misha was all right. She judged that he hadn't had much to do except get settled on his new Yak airfield and wait for the order to begin the big attack. She often thought, with longing, of the time when she would lie in his arms. If it were happening now, all she would want to do would be to cuddle close to him and sleep. After she had bathed, of course.

He would probably grumble "pees-ann" and be disappointed, but he was sweet, he would understand.

For now, she would eat what she could of her unappetizing rations, wrap herself in her blanket, try to sleep, and wait for the next order to attack.

*   *   *

"Well, you were right about the potatoes," Mike said in Russian, moving his spoon through the watery soup in his tin dish. "Potato soup and potato bread. I thought I was tired of cabbage but I'd even welcome seeing a green leaf in here today."

Viktor and Boris Gusarov grinned. "I'm sorry we couldn't supply beefsteak and champagne," Viktor said. "That's one of the horrors of war. But we do have music with our meals now that Boris has unpacked his saxophone. I seem to remember an old Russian saying: 'If music be the food of love, play on,' or something like that."

"I keep forgetting that Shakespeare was a Russian," Mike said. He turned to Boris. "So, what are you going to play for us? Something happy and American? 'Roll Out the Barrel,' perhaps?"

"Aha!" Boris said. "Now we turn the tables. Mikhail. Your 'Roll the Barrel' is, in fact, taken from an old folk song from this region."

"If Viktor had said it, I wouldn't believe it. From you, I do. So play whatever you like."

Boris launched into "Chattanooga Choo-Choo," riffing through the intervals and imitating the diverse instruments of a big band. When he had finished, he wiped the mouthpiece and looked appealingly at Mike.

"Do you really think you'll be able to send me all these big-band recordings? When you return to America?" he asked.

"You bet I will," Mike said. "A great big, carefully-packed crate of records. Tommy Dorsey, Glenn Miller, Woody Herman, Harry James, all the big guys. I'll figure out some way to get them to you."

"That would be wonderful," Boris said.

"There could be a problem," Viktor warned. "Anything coming here from abroad would be, um, examined very closely. Perhaps for quite a time."

Boris' face fell. Mike frowned. "They wouldn't let the records in?" he asked.

Viktor looked around instinctively. "At the proper time, perhaps I could make some inquiries. Through one of the diplomatic friends my father has kept in touch with. The diplomatic pouch, perhaps. Particularly if you could manage to buy a second set for the, um, the go-between."

"Provide an incentive."

"Yes, an incentive."

Boris smiled. "Anything you can do, you know I'll be most grateful." He looked around the old hut they had been sleeping in. "It's too bad we don't have a piano, and Nadia to play it."

Mike looked gloomily at him. "And Galina to . . . *be* here."

"Of course." Boris lifted the sax and fingered the keys. "What was that song you sang to her at the dance that first night, after the first one? 'I Can't Get Started,' wasn't it?"

He lifted the sax to his lips and began playing. Mike closed his eyes and began singing to himself.

> I've gone around the world in a plane
> I've settled revolutions in Spain,
> The North Pole I have charted
> But I can't get started with you.

A siren went off. He opened his eyes and Boris stopped playing. Viktor stood up. "I think the balloon's gone up. The waiting is over."

CHAPTER FOURTEEN

BREAKING THROUGH

OPERATION BAGRATION STRUCK the German armies in the East like a series of tidal waves. On June 22, the attack of the Third Belorussian Front folded back the northern flank of the German positions. The next day, the Second Belorussian Front caved in the German center. On the third day, the First Belorussian Front smashed through the fortified positions of Hans Jordan's Ninth Army.

Within days, huge Russian pincers extending from the north and south began to close on the four hundred thousand German soldiers caught between them. As the jaws narrowed and the defenders became packed closely together, thousands of airplanes, one-third of them ground-attack Shturmoviks, blasted them unrelentingly.

At night, as the Germans tried to retreat under cover of darkness, the PO-2 bombers, now reinforced by American-made B-25 Mitchell and A-20 Havoc medium bombers, struck at their columns, river crossings, and vehicles.

The defeat of the last German forces still on the soil of Mother Russia was now a certainty. The only question was whether the invaders would be killed, captured, and routed within one, two, or, at most, three weeks.

Limp and exhausted, Galina and Valya slept beneath their biplane in their blankets as a groggy mechanic worked to repair the aircraft. After flying four sorties on the preceding night, with five-minute turnarounds for refueling and attachment of bombs, the *Ved'ma* had staggered home with one hundred holes in it. One wing had been reduced to little more than a skeleton and the tail stabilizer was in tatters.

The VVS had sent a supply of parachutes to the front in a Dakota with orders to wear them. But the women, after conferring among themselves, decided that it should be an individual decision.

"We're flying at low altitude anyway," Valya said. "Bailing out at night under those conditions, with heavy fire all around you—how much chance would we have? And if we came down in the Fascist lines, after the way we've been bombing them, how long do you think we'd live?"

"Without the parachutes, we can put some extra explosives, stick grenades at least, in our cockpits," Galina said. "Right now, it seems to me, every little bit helps. And the parachute shifts when I bank the plane. That could throw me off." She sighed wearily. "I'd like to get this over with."

"We're agreed then?" Valya asked. "No parachutes. What one of us does, the other ought to do, too."

Galina nodded. "No parachutes. Not unless we get orders to start flying higher or something else changes."

Something changed the following day. Sleeping openmouthed under her biplane, Galina was wakened in the morning by Major Kravchenko. "I'm sorry to wake you, Comrade Lieutenant," the older woman said, "but we've had orders to start flying day missions as well as night ones. The Hitlerites are crowded along the Berezina River. There's a traffic jam there, trying to get across. VVS wants every available bomber to hit them. Briefing's in one hour. Eat your food ration, get your gear together, and report."

Flying in the daylight was always a shock to the night-witches. Flying at night produced its own distinctive kind of terror—the ominous, creepy nature of the darkness one had feared since childhood, the difficulty in seeing the ground, the ever-present danger of crashing, the horror of suddenly being caught in blinding searchlights and struck by red-hot crimson tracers.

Flying combat in the daylight held different, but equally frightening terrors. You were, Galina and Valya agreed, so terribly *exposed*. Everybody could see you, including gunners on the ground and predators in the air. You were a tiny, poorly-armed, and pitifully slow biplane whose only chance of survival lay in maneuverability, skill, nerve, and a large measure of luck.

But daytime flying offered an almost unbelievable, wide-angle spectacle. The airplanes were like a dense swarm of locusts over the battlefield. Nearly all of them were Soviet airplanes, Galina was glad to see. Though among them, from time to time, she caught sight of a Messerschmitt or Focke-Wulf bearing a Maltese cross.

When one streaked into view, she was caught between fright and admiration at the valor of the hopelessly outnumbered German pilots.

"There's the target!" Valya shouted over the interphone. "Drop just short of the river bank. Mind we don't drop on our Shturmoviks."

Thousands of German soldiers were densely packed along the river bank trying desperately to get across in boats, barges, and rafts. A bridge had been knocked out. Some, crazed by the constant bombing and strafing, were floundering in the water.

For an instant, Galina felt pity for the dying Germans. But, in the same instant, she remembered that terrible day in Stalingrad when she saw barges and boats packed with screaming Russian civilians—women and children—trying to cross the river while German fighters and fighter-bombers mercilessly strafed and bombed them into bloody rags.

Grimly, she pulled the release wire and dumped her bombs on the German troops. The motto for the destruction of the Hitlerites had come down from above: *Krov' za Krov'*. *Blood for blood.*

A Focke-Wulf streaked close to her nose and she banked sharply away. A Yak whistled down from above and blew it apart. But a terrible barrage came up from the ground and one of the shells struck the Yak. The fighter spiraled away, trailing smoke.

Now tracers of different colors—blue, red, yellow—were coming up from all types of weapons, big and small. Anyone on the ground who had a gun was firing at the airplanes above. Twisting and turning, she reversed her course and dived for the treetops. She had to swerve quickly to avoid an oncoming squadron of low-flying Shturmoviks who were heading for the river to pound the German troops and the remaining concrete emplacements.

Viktor's face was ashen. His eyes were dull; the sardonic light that so often sparkled from them had gone out. Mike had never seen him so shaken. "Borisenko is dead," Viktor said in a harsh voice. "Ground flak hit him. He crashed on the way back. An ambulance plane was sent to bring his body back."

"I'm sorry," Mike said. "Really sorry, Viktor. He was a good guy. A good friend of yours." Viktor nodded. Mike asked: "Who'll command the regiment now?"

"They've told me to take over. I've already been given the rank of major." Viktor smiled mirthlessly. "I wanted the promotion." He shook his head. "But not this way."

He looked up. "You'll be a flight commander now, Mikhail. For your *para*, Gusarov will be your wingman." He started to walk away and then turned back. "One more thing. We'll be moving west. Two days from now; I'll want your help making an inventory of our equipment and supplies. I also may need you to go and take a look at the field they've picked out for us."

"All right. What are you going to do now?"

"What I'd like to do is get drunk," Viktor said. "I'll do that later. Right now I need to check the board, see who's available. Then get on the phone and find out what our orders are."

Stalin smiled and squeezed his thick hands together. The battle reports had come in. It was July 4, the day that the curious Americans called their Independence Day, the day they celebrated their independence from the British they now fought beside in the West.

Operation Bagration was over, except for mopping up here and there. The Germans' Army Group Center, the vaunted force of highly-trained Fascist soldiers who had led the march on Moscow in 1941, had been crushed—more than crushed, exterminated. According to the reports, nearly three hundred thousand of the Hitlerites had been killed, wounded, or captured.

Mother Russia had been liberated. The savory feasts of Poland, East Prussia, and Germany—Berlin itself—now lay open before the vengeful Soviet soldiers.

He would, of course, go home and turn on the Telefunken radio in his dining room to pick up the short-wave broadcasts and listen for confirmations of the reports.

He also wanted to check on events in the West. He had heard that the Americans and British were stalled, nearly a month after they invaded Normandy, just a few miles inland. At places called St. Lô and Caen. He was getting a lot of double-talk from the Allied representatives in Moscow about it.

Stalin compressed his lips in disdain. The *soyuznichki*, the little allies, were still playing Alphonse and Gaston and bowing to each other, being careful not to offend each other's sensibilities, and shrinking back from the need to throw all their forces into the battle, brutally and headlong, as the Russians did, regardless of casualties.

"That sonofabitch!" Eisenhower shouted angrily. "He was going to take Caen in a day and go 'crack about' inland, he said! In one god-damn day! That was seven weeks ago and Montgomery's still sitting there making excuses! Now he's claiming all he was supposed to do was tie up the Germans there while *we* did the fighting!"

Air Marshal Tedder, disdaining support for his countryman, nod-ded sympathetically. But he wished Ike would order Monty more strongly to his face to get off his duff and attack. Some SHAEF of-ficers suggested that Montgomery be sacked and made a member of the House of Lords or perhaps Governor of Malta.

Churchill privately agreed, but Monty was too popular with the British for such a move to be made.

Ike glowered at his advisors. After seven weeks of fighting, the Allies had moved only twenty-five miles inland along an eighty-mile front. It was too small an area in which to maneuver or bring up the divisions waiting to debark from England. The newspapers were talking about a stalemate.

The main pressure points were at St. Lô, directly south of the origi-nal landing point in Normandy and, to the east, Caen. After weeks of stalling, Montgomery had, with great fanfare, launched a campaign called *Goodwood* to break his British troops out of the strategic area. Though he was assisted by an enormous aerial bombardment, he had lost 401 tanks and 2,600 casualties and called off the offensive.

"It took seven thousand tons of bombs to help him move seven miles!" Ike shouted. "Does he think we can go through France with us dropping a thousand tons a mile to help him along?"

Meantime, with Montgomery stalled at Caen, Bradley's U.S. First Army to the west was forced to struggle through hedgerow country. The Americans hadn't planned on plowing through terrain filled with sunken roads, tall banks, and hedges. The Germans punctured the soft undersides of the Sherman tanks as the tank drivers tried to climb up the steep sides of the banks. A U.S. sergeant finally solved the problem by making steel tusks out of abandoned roadblocks, mounting them on the front of a tank, and watching it bore through one of the banks. Soon, all the tanks were fitted with steel tusks and things went faster.

But Bradley needed help to break through to a point where he could unleash the flamboyant Patton's Third Army to race ahead and outflank the enemy. The plan, called *Cobra,* depended on air power. Bradley told Ike he needed a very small area, twenty-five hundred by six thousand yards, pulverized by bombs. Twenty-five hundred, heavy, medium and light bombers would be made available for the task.

"We go in at *what,* Dee Tee?" Buddy asked incredulously.

"At twelve thousand feet, sir. At about half your normal altitude." The 300th Bomb Group adjutant handed Buddy the yellow paper he had just torn from the group's teletype machine. "I checked by scrambler, Colonel. Seems some other bomb groups have done the same. Wing was pretty testy. Said just follow the damned order, don't ask questions. What it is, is we're hitting the German troop positions again and our army is so close to them and . . ."

"Yeah, I know the situation," Buddy said. "Saw it in the war room." Since the landings, every bomb group had its own war room with a big map of the continent and markers that were moved according to reports from Wing. The Third Army, under Georgie Patton, who carried pearl-handled pistols and peed in front of his troops and talked like a good ol' boy, wanted to break out of St. Lô, and he needed the heavies to lay the biggest bomb carpet ever on the German defenders.

"Goddamn touchy thing," Buddy said. "Miss a German factory by a few hundred yards and drop your load in a pasture and it's too bad, you didn't carry out the mission, but the only casualties are Herman's cows and the village idiot. But miss the target here and you hit your own soldiers. Goddamn touchy."

He pointed accusingly at his adjutant. "So you have to go in low, even if ol' Betsy wasn't designed to do it at that altitude. Even if every goddamn 88-mm. flak gun in France can blow holes in you. Even then, how do y'know you're dumping your hundred-pounders on the bad guys instead of the good guys? Tell me that, Dee Tee."

"They say you'll see a line of purple smoke markers on the ground, Colonel. And the pathfinders will go in first and drop smoke bombs. The white trails hang in the air and they'll help form the bomb line, they say. Just bomb beyond the line, but as close as you can."

Buddy grunted. "You haven't been there, Dee Tee, no disrespect. And none of the dog-soldier paddlefeet who thought this up have been there, either. It all sounds fine and maybe even looks fine for a few minutes, but the minute the squareheads see purple smoke markers they go get themselves some purple smoke markers and begin burnin' them. Whose markers do you bomb on, Dee Tee?"

He held up a hand. "After the first one or two bomb drops, there'll be so much haze and smoke you won't see the ground markers anyway. Have to hope the white aerial markers don't blow away. Hope *we* don't blow away."

"Wing says we have a pledge from the Army that their artillery and tanks will conduct counter-artillery fire against the German tanks and antiaircraft batteries," Potter said. "And the Eighth will send in fighter-bombers ahead of you to suppress the flak guns."

Buddy shrugged and smiled a faint smile. "Nothin' to worry about then."

"I hope not, sir."

But there was, of course. The weather was poor. Briefing was at 3:15 A.M. and they should have taken off by 5:15. Clearance came at 8:15. Buddy led the mission. The group got every possible B-17, forty-eight of them, off the ground.

Neither he nor any member of the Eighth Air Force had ever had such an experience. The mission was a mess. Visibility was bad and they encountered two problems on a scale they had never seen before.

First, there were so many airplanes in the air in so small a space that you had to look out above, to the sides, and below to avoid collisions and keep from bombing a friendly plane below you or being bombed by one above you.

Second, Buddy found, the enormous turbulence of propwash created by the multitude of airplanes made the big bombers almost impossible to control. Sweat ran down Buddy's face and chest as he manhandled the control column, struggling, with the aid of his co-pilot, to hold the wings level. One and then the other wing of the airplane kept stalling out. It was like flying through a hurricane full of strange and unpredictable air pockets.

Two pilots in the group, dizzied by vertigo induced by the roiling air currents, fell out of formation.

Below, the ground kept winking steadily as guns fired. At first, the flashes were frightening—under normal circumstances they signaled that flak was coming up—but Buddy realized the guns on the ground were firing at each other. Bradley had made good on his pledge. No flak rose to bring down the slow and vulnerable low-flying bombers.

But it was questionable whether the mission would succeed. The bombardier complained that he couldn't tell exactly where to drop the group's bombs.

"Just beyond the smoke markers," Buddy said testily.

"Pilot, there seems to be a couple of sets of smoke markers and the wind's blowing so I can't tell which is which," the bombardier said. "I'm afraid we'll bomb too short and hit our own guys."

"Then bomb long, damn it."

"That might not get the job done right, pilot."

"Better than hitting our own people, bombardier. Just do it."

They bombed long and, banking carefully to fly between two bomber groups, headed back for England.

Buddy stumbled out of the B-17 after landing and was still cursing and mumbling to himself on the jeep ride back to headquarters. "Sprained both my damn wrists trying to hold the airplane," he told Potter. "We bombed long; I don't know what we hit. Probably Herman's cook and his pots and pans. Visibility was lousy. Have you had any reports?"

"Yes sir," Dee Tee said. "Results were fair. We have to go back tomorrow."

"Oh, whoop-to-do," Buddy said. "I'll have to go to the flight surgeon, tape up my wrists. This point, I'd just as soon be goin' back to Frankfurt, Leipzig, places where we at least fly right."

The second day's mission over St. Lô was successful. The German troops were stunned and paralyzed by the huge bombardment and Bradley's forces punched through their lines.

"We finally did the job right," Buddy sighed.

"Our own groups did, sir," Potter said. "Unfortunately, another group dropped short. Killed about thirty of our own men plus an American general. General named McNair. He was there as an observer."

The group was called out for another medium-altitude strike against German troops and tanks on August 8. The target was Caen; the bombardment was a desperate effort to get Montgomery moving again and allow Patton's fast-moving Third Army to sweep north and link up with Canadian and British forces driving southward.

"Wing says General Montgomery will make the same promise that General Bradley did," Potter told Buddy. "His guns will conduct counter-artillery fire against the German guns and suppress any flak. You'll go in at fourteen thousand feet."

"Makes me real uncomfortable, after St. Lô," Buddy said. "With all those planes and all that propwash, it'd be a real horror if Montgomery doesn't keep that promise."

He didn't. The mission was a disaster. Heavy propwash made the B-17s and the B-24s stagger in and out of formation almost uncontrollably. As they neared the target, the floundering bombers were met by a thunderstorm of intense, accurately-placed 88-mm. flak. With a loud crack, Buddy's Number One engine shattered. As the co-pilot feathered the propeller, Number Three was struck and began throwing oil.

A ship blew up alongside and two bombers collided in another group. Flak rattled through the fuselage of Buddy's plane and Number Three began trailing black smoke. Buddy hit the fire extinguisher. They were on two engines and still had a full bomb load. The ship began losing altitude.

Buddy called the deputy flying on his right wing and told him to take over as group leader. After they pulled out of formation, Buddy's bombardier salvoed the lead ship's bombs in an area he swore was held by Germans. Then, dodging flak batteries that began tracking them, they dived for the Channel and home.

When the group returned, Buddy counted four ships lost and all but ten so badly riddled that no mission could be mounted the following day.

Within a week, the Americans and Canadians had joined forces, defeated a German counterattack ordered by Hitler, and destroyed or routed the bulk of the German armies left in France. By August 17, Patton's tanks had raced eastward and were only forty miles from Paris.

All Buddy knew for sure was what he spouted angrily at General Sloane when his friend and mentor visited the base. "I figure I got two personal enemies now, Gen'l Ol' Stalin or whoever's idea it was to let the Germans bomb my airplanes at Poltava, he's one. And that phony Limey bastard, Montgomery. He didn't suppress the German flak at Caen; hell, far as I could see, *he* was firin' at us, too."

Stalin allowed himself a diversion. Red Army units were deep in Poland and would soon move against Warsaw. Other units to the north crossed the border into East Prussia. To the south, a huge Red Army force of nearly a million men and fourteen hundred tanks were crossing the Danube into Rumania.

Even the *soyuznichki* in the West were, at last, defeating the Hitlerites. The Germans had evacuated Paris and the counterattack ordered by the demented Hitler had led his troops into a trap at a place in

France called Falaise where, radio reports said, ten thousand Fascists were killed, fifty thousand were captured, and, regrettably, as many as forty thousand escaped.

Neither the British nor the Americans displayed the overwhelming power of the Red Army on the ground. The British were good, even admirable, at defense. Once they took a position, made themselves comfortable, and boiled water for tea, they were almost impossible to dislodge. But they were exceedingly cautious and slow when attacking.

The Americans, Soviet observers reported, were more easily dislodged from defended positions. But they were startlingly good at mobile warfare. The tank columns of their General Patton were moving with lightning speed to outflank the Fascists. It was something to keep in mind for the future.

For now, Stalin diverted himself by making awards for valor and skill in battle. Such awards were useful for two reasons: they created heroes and models for others to emulate and, at the same time, they created an image of Josef Stalin as an all-seeing, all-wise, and benevolent leader.

Hundreds of awards were given out to common soldiers and officers in the Army and Air Force. Awards were given for distinguished service in the support services, including the medical service. Nearly half of the doctors and medical assistants, he noted, were women. There were also special categories of awards to foreign volunteers and to the women's combat groups.

Stalin went over the list of VVS candidates with Novikov, paying special attention to the women, since they were a visible symbol of the Soviet Union's unity and its total commitment to winning the Great Patriotic War. Of thirty Hero of the Soviet Union awards given to Air Force women, twenty-three were given to the night-witches.

Other honors would follow. PO-2 regimental commander Major Marina Raskova, who had been killed in action, would be buried in the Kremlin wall. Lilya Lityvak, a Yak ace, would have a memorial built to her in the Donetsk region.

Stalin nodded as award candidates were named from the French, Polish, and other foreign air units.

''There is another foreigner, an American with a Russian background, who has distinguished himself,'' Novikov said. ''He is a Yak pilot flying with the 450th Air Regiment of our Fourth Air Army. His name is Gavronov, Mikhail Stepanovich Gavronov. He has downed fourteen Fascist planes. Recently he was given command of a *zveno* when his superior, a Major Markov, succeeded to command of the regiment. Markov is on the regular list for an award."

Stalin puffed on his pipe. "Is Gavronov the one who came to us after a bail-out from a Flying Fortress?"

"Yes, Comrade Stalin, the same."

"What does the regimental commissar say about him?"

"That he is a very good pilot, very aggressive. He has learned our language well enough to speak it with some fluency, not well enough to read or write it very well. He disavows interest in political ideology. He has a close friend and mentor in the new regimental commander, Markov. Gavronov is apparently enamored of one of the night-witches. I have her name here. Tarasova. Her regiment is in another sector at this time."

Stalin squinted at the air commander. "Give the American a Hero award. We want the world to know how young men from all over the world came to the Rodina to fight for the socialist cause. This could be particularly useful in the case of an American. Can we make more out of this? With his background, will he apply for Soviet citizenship? Can he be persuaded to?"

Novikov shrugged. "At this moment I don't know, Comrade Stalin. I'll inquire."

"If he shows no such interest, I want you to keep a close watch on him," Stalin said. "All of the other foreigners we're giving awards to are members of organized foreign units, aren't they?"

"Yes they are, Comrade Stalin."

Stalin frowned, pulled on his pipe, and thought for a moment before speaking. "But this one is part of a Russian regiment. He has learned our language, formed close friendships with Russian officers, learned how we train and fight and, perhaps, how we look at things. He knows our equipment."

The dictator puffed on his pipe. "If such a man does not become one of us, he could become dangerous. Particularly an American. When we defeat the Fascists, the only powerful nation besides ourselves will be America." He looked at Novikov with hooded eyes. "I do not want this Gavronov to return to America, do you understand?"

"Yes, Comrade Stalin."

"I also want a thorough investigation made of these two intimates of the man . . ."

"Markov and Tarasova."

"Investigate them thoroughly. History tells us that, when our victorious Russian soldiers returned from Paris after the Napoleonic wars, many brought back the virus of individualism. That's what comes from contact with foreigners. Never forget it."

"Yes, Comrade Stalin."

They had run out of gasoline and were grounded. Major Viktor Markov sat at the oaken desk in the office he had set up in the half-wrecked Polish mansion the regiment had commandeered. He smiled wryly; the glint had returned to his eyes.

He would never forget the death of his friend Borisenko, but, like all pilots, he accepted it after suffering through the initial surge of grief. Then, as others had learned to do, he stored it in the back of his mind to examine at another time.

"You expect, from time to time, to run out of serviceable airplanes, even of pilots," Markov said. "But aviation fuel? You might as well talk about running out of vodka." He pretended to shudder.

Mike smiled. "Assuming I get through this war alive, I wonder if I'll ever be able to live normally again."

Viktor raised his eyebrows. "You don't feel that our Russian ways are normal? How strange. You have to admit our new accommodations are comfortable."

"They are," Mike said, looking around at the scarred wood paneling. "You don't often see houses this big in the East; brick and stone, too. The people who lived here were plenty rich. I wonder what happened to them."

Viktor shrugged. "Fortunes of war. The owner probably made his fortune from the sweat of the farmers or from Silesian factory workers. Millions of people have been dispossessed; most didn't deserve it. He probably did."

Mike looked out the big window that faced southward. "I'll say one thing; this is beautiful country. Look at those mountains; I couldn't believe it when we flew down here."

"The Carpathians," Viktor said, turning to look. "Very beautiful, very big and rugged. The whole area is beautiful. Hills and valleys, but a great deal of level grassland, too. We can fly off of grass fields like these. Some very dense evergreen forests. Up north, many small lakes. You'll also see some very old castles."

A cool autumn breeze filled the room with aromatic scents. Viktor inhaled. "Turpentine, I think. Very fresh-smelling, from the evergreens. And there's something else."

"I believe it's jasmine," Mike said. "My mother always liked jasmine. I guess I'm surprised. I thought Poland would be a dull sort of place. The Poles seem to've been looked down on by practically everybody. Certainly the Germans. By the Russians, too, I gather. Even in my country. They're called Polacks; they work in the mines and machine shops. Looking around, I don't see why."

Viktor nodded. "Poland's like many of the countries in the East; it's been torn apart many times. It's been a big nation, a little one, no nation at all. Technically, it doesn't even exist at this time."

"Because you and the Germans invaded it and divided it up before the war."

Viktor sighed. "You needn't remind me, Mikhail. It was bad enough that it happened. The fact that we did it in collaboration with that unspeakable Hitler . . ." He snorted in disgust. "Poland has had a long, difficult history, Mike. It's been fought over by the Germans, the Turks, the Swedes, the Russians."

"Now it will belong to you," Mike said.

"I suppose it will."

Mike sat straight up. "What was that?"

"What?"

"Out the window. I saw a biplane. I'm sure I . . . Look, there's another!"

Viktor turned. "A PO-2. You're right. It's landing over there somewhere beyond those trees. Perhaps the night bomber regiment is here. It would make sense. The VVS says there's to be a heavy buildup of all forces in this area. Apparently a flanking move against the Fascists. Or a diversion to draw the Hitlerites away from their center."

Mike stood up. "I've got to go find out."

Viktor rose. "Of course. I'd like to call on a friend as well. There's nothing to do here until supplies arrive. I'll tell Gusarov to man the telephone. We'll take my car."

They walked quickly to Viktor's new car, a German Kübel. When the regiment moved, the Opel Blitz had to be left behind. The previous owner of the Kübel, a German major, had been found dead in the driver's seat. The assumption was that he had been shot by a partisan as the Germans were evacuating the area. The Kübel, Mike told Viktor, looked and drove like an American-made Willys Jeep.

After making several wrong turns, including one into a blocked road, and bring stopped by a sentry who demanded identification, they came onto a clearing and found the PO-2 regiment.

Viktor located Major Kravchenko while Mike waited impatiently. Dirt-smeared, weary, and exuding an unpleasant body odor, she told an unhappy story.

Her air crews and aircraft were in bad shape. The biplanes were tattered, oil-smeared, and lacking necessary spare parts. Like the Yak regiment, the night bomber regiment would be grounded till supplies arrived. They were out of gasoline and oil and, more importantly, food. The women were not only exhausted and unwashed but starved.

"We've been living on boiled corn, little else, for the past month."

"That's all?" Viktor asked. "No bread, no meat of any kind?"

"Not even potatoes."

"I'll round up everything we can," Viktor said. "We have bread, potatoes, barley soup, flour for making dumplings. Two of our sergeants have shot some wild hares. I was about to send a hunting party into the hills to bring back some wild pigs. We also have the American C- and K-rations. We'll share with you."

"Whatever you have we'll be grateful for," Kravchenko said. "Now that we're grounded for a bit, perhaps our supplies will catch up to us." She looked about. "I have to find shelter for my girls. We've mainly been living in dugouts we've scraped out in the woods."

Viktor pointed to a small village lying to the east. "The peasants will house you. There are also a couple of large houses, mansions really, in the area. We're quartered in one of them." He paused. "Um, Major, may I see Larissa?"

Kravchenko smiled sadly. "I'm sorry. She was sent to a hospital in the rear for surgery. A chest wound. We're hopeful she'll be all right. We haven't heard anything, of course."

Viktor lowered his head and looked at the ground. "Please let me know, if you can, when you hear something," he said in a low voice.

Fear flooded through Mike. "Galina?" he asked.

Kravchenko pointed to an area where six planes had been parked and crew members were stringing camouflage netting. "Over there, Comrade Lieutenant."

Mike ran to the spot and found Galina tying an end of a net rope to a pole. "Galina!" he shouted.

She looked up, startled, began running toward him, and fell. He picked her up. A grin showed through a face that was pale and streaked with oil. "Misha!" she said delightedly. It was clear that she was exhausted.

She was wearing her medium-weight leather jacket over a pair of stained coveralls. As they embraced, he was shocked at how thin and frail she had become. "Misha," she murmured, leaning against him.

"When's the last time you ate?" he asked. She shook her head. "Slept in a bed?" Another head shake. "Took a bath or showered?"

She shook her head again. He picked her up in his arms. "Your regiment's stood down till your supplies arrive. You're not going anywhere today or tomorrow, either. I'm taking you with me."

"I can't, Misha," she said weakly.

"Yes you can." He carried her to the Kübel, where Viktor as waiting. "I'm taking her back, for now."

Viktor hesitated, then said: "Wait." He strode to Kravchenko, who had been watching, and spoke quietly to her for a moment. Mike saw the woman spread her hands in apparent frustration, then drop them and nod.

Viktor returned. "It's all right. Galina must be back here in the morning. Meantime, you're on your honor, whatever that means. Get in the car."

As they drove back, Galina fell asleep in Mike's arms.

"It'll only be for tonight," Mike said. "Do you suppose, would you be willing . . ."

"I'll move one of the wooden beds and a mattress into my office," Viktor said. "She can use that, you can, both of you, whichever. And she can use the washroom. I'll tell Gusarov to keep the men away."

Viktor smiled ruefully. "Ordinarily I'd be jealous. Right now, I think I feel only pity. The witches have had to put up with hardships far worse than ours. That's the penalty for always being up on the front line, operating out of places no one else can get into. I hope you don't have visions of a night of passion and burning romance."

"I don't," Mike said curtly.

When Viktor and Boris had carried the wood-plank bed and mattress into the office, Mike laid her on it and went to the washroom. In one corner there was a crude toilet, doubtless an innovation at the time it was installed. In the other sat a large slipper-shaped metal tub with handles at the ends. The owner of the house, wanting only the best, had had a drain installed in the tub. It was connected to a pipe that led into a small garden.

In the center of the room was a flat-topped wood-burning stove. Mike placed birch logs atop the glowing embers inside, picked up a bucket, carried it outside, and filled it with water from a hand-pump that pulled water from the well behind the house.

Methodically, he dumped buckets of cold water in the tub, then heated bucketfuls atop the stove and poured them into the tub until the water was the right temperature. He unwrapped the piece of yellow soap he had been hoarding and took his towel, together with one of Viktor's, into the washroom. There was no such thing as a washcloth, so he rummaged through his bag until he found a clean undershirt. That would have to do. As an afterthought, he pulled a blanket from his bed and carried it into the washroom.

Satisfying himself that everything was ready, he picked up Galina and carried her into the room. She woke and asked in a weak voice: "What are you doing, Misha?"

"You're going to take a bath," he said.

"I can't," she murmured. "Too tired."

"I'll help," he said.

Ignoring her weak protests, he pulled off her boots and coveralls. Beneath them, she was still wearing a pair of dirty longjohns. They came off too. Her breasts were smaller than he had remembered and her ribs protruded sharply through her white skin. He half-sat her on a wood stool and, holding her up with one arm, pulled her panties off with the other hand. Her triangle of pubic hair was soft and black.

Mike had looked forward to this moment with great longing. Every time he had thought of it, almost always at night after going to bed, he had grown hard; he had had to dismiss the sexual fantasy from his mind so he could sleep.

But now, undressing her, he felt only tenderness. For the moment, she was simply a beautiful, though emaciated, girl-child who badly needed a bath. He placed her carefully in the warm water, commanded her to close her eyes tightly, and soaped her hair. Then, testing the temperature of the water in the bucket atop the stove to ensure that it was right, he poured it over her head. He had to do it three times.

When he was satisfied that her hair was clean, he began scrubbing her body with the soapy undershirt. He soaped all of her, carefully washing her underarms, between her legs, and, lifting her, in the cleft of her buttocks. He scrubbed every dirty toe and the places between them.

By now the water was nearly black. Mike unplugged the drain and let the water flow out. When the tub was empty, he plugged it up again and painstakingly refilled it. It took nearly half an hour before he was satisfied that Galina was clean.

Carefully, he lifted her from the tub, placed her on the stool, and dried her body with his towel. Soon, her skin began to glow and her eyes opened. "You are bringing me back to life."

He nodded and lightly kissed her mouth. "A comb," she murmured. "I need a comb."

"I'll get one." Retrieving his own comb from his room, he finished drying her as she slowly combed her hair. Her eyes were closing again and the motions became slower. He picked up his blanket, wrapped it around her, carried her into the office, and laid her on the bed. He carefully arranged the blanket to cover her, closed the door, and went back to the washroom.

He heated more water, found a brush, cleaned the tub, then, piece by piece, scrubbed her filthy clothing: the panties, longjohns, socks, coveralls, even her helmet liner. Bringing a chair from the office, he draped the wet garments across it, placed it near the stove, and fed fresh logs into it.

Viktor met him outside the office. "How is she?"

"She's exhausted," Mike said. "I washed her and she's sleeping again."

"You should feed her."

"I will. But I don't think she'd even be able to eat right now. I'll watch her and see."

"I've put away a few fresh eggs," Viktor said. "You can have them for her. When she wakes. A dish of fried eggs, potatoes, and onions would be good for her." He smiled. "I'm becoming so selfless I hardly recognize myself."

Mike grinned. "Your true character is finally showing itself, that's all."

When night fell, Mike lay beside her. Galina instinctively moved closer to him and he put his arm around her and fell asleep holding her. At daybreak, hearing the bustle of the men, he woke and took Viktor's eggs to the cook.

The dish recommended by Viktor was soon prepared and Mike carried the smoking plate of food and a tin cup of hot, sugared tea to the office. Galina was awake, the blanket tucked up around her breasts. He had never seen her eyes so blue. She smiled at him. "Thank you, Misha. You'd make a wonderful orderly. Maybe you could transfer to my regiment and continue this line of work."

"Only for you, Galisha," he said. "Here's breakfast. Eat it slowly, please. I'll get your clothes."

"The food was delicious," she said after she had finished. "And clean clothes, too. Everything but our night of love. You could have, you know . . . *taken* me during the night, if you'd wanted to."

He smiled ruefully and shook his head. "We have an old American saying: It takes two to tango. You weren't ready for the dance."

"I must get back to the field," she said, looking worried. "Kravchenko will have my head."

"Viktor told me that your comrades have been billeted in the village over there," Mike said. "Maybe you could come back tonight."

"Knowing our major, I think I'd better be a good girl and stay wherever I'm supposed to stay tonight," Galina said. "Tomorrow, though. I'll try."

While she dressed in her clean clothes, Mike went to the cook and cajoled him into supplying a small bag of sugar buns he had baked. When she saw his gift, her eyes widened in delight. "Oh, this is wonderful."

"Give a couple to Major Kravchenko with my compliments. Maybe that'll soften up the old girl. But eat at least two of them yourself."

They kissed and hugged each other closely before going outside. The men eyed them enviously, wrongly assuming the obvious.

"May I borrow your car, Major?" Mike asked Viktor.

"Why not?" Viktor said. "You've taken everything else."

When he returned to the mansion after taking Galina to her airfield, Viktor was at his desk in the office. "I've just heard that our supplies are coming in today. By truck and Dakotas. To the other air regiments in the area as well. Gasoline, oil, parts, food—everything, they say. We haven't received any orders to fly, however. There seems to be a general regrouping."

"Galina's regiment will be getting their supplies too, then."

"I'm sure they will."

Mike walked alone through the beautiful fields and woodlands until he heard the sound of the Dakotas arriving in late afternoon. The trucks arrived an hour later and the men labored to stow the fuel and parts in a makeshift dugout and move the foodstuffs to the kitchen. Mechanics began working on the Yaks.

There was a festive air at the evening meal and the cook served *kolbasa* and *pierogi*. Rations of vodka were drunk afterward and Gusarov played his saxophone while another flying officer squeezed his accordion to the accompaniment of folk songs rendered by pilots from various regions of the empire.

At the end of the evening, at Gusarov's insistence, Mike sang the "GI Jive." After ten minutes of coaching, the men sang along, mangling the words and dissolving in laughter as Mike translated the lyrics' references to bad food and senseless military routines.

Later, Mike asked Viktor: "Will it be all right if I keep the bed set up in your office till after tomorrow night?"

Viktor looked askance. "So you have ambitions after all."

"We hope to get together tomorrow night."

"I would be Ivan the Terrible if I said no, wouldn't I?" Viktor grumped.

"Yes, you would."

Ambition died in the morning. Having drunk more than usual, and with no military duties to perform, Mike slept late. He was awakened by a familiar sound. When he realized what it was, he swung quickly out of bed and ran to the window.

The PO-2s were taking off, their tiny engines pop-popping. Mike dressed hastily and ran to the door, looking for the car. It was coming down the dirt road. It braked to a halt and Viktor got out. "You saw them take off," he said.

"Yes I did. What in hell's going on?" Mike's voice became anguished. "They aren't *leaving*."

Viktor smiled gently. "I'm afraid they are. By now they'll have left. I was there just a few minutes ago."

Mike's voice dropped. "What happened?"

"Kravchenko said they'd just received urgent orders to go to a prepared field north of here, some one hundred and fifty kilometers. It seems there's some fairly heavy fighting up there. They'll join a Shturmovik regiment. The Shturmoviks will work on cleaning out the sector by day and the witches will hit them at night to keep them from regrouping."

"How many kilometers did you say?" Mike asked.

Viktor shook his head. "Don't even think about it, Mike. By the time you'd get there, they'd probably be gone again. The witches are like gypsies, always on the move. Besides, you belong to this Yak regiment, Comrade Senior Lieutenant. We should be getting our orders today or tomorrow. It's too bad, but personal matters have to be —wait a minute. I nearly forgot. Kravchenko gave me a note to give to you. From Galina, I'm sure."

Viktor fumbled in the pocket of his jacket and handed it to Mike. "It's in our alphabet. If you have any trouble understanding it, I'll . . ."

"I'll figure it out, thanks," Mike said, taking the note and putting it in his pocket. He went back to the office, disassembled the bed, and reassembled it in the large room being used as the officers' barracks. Then he sat on the bed, smoothed out the note on his knee, and painstakingly deciphered the Cyrillic letters. It read:

Misha, my love,

The Rodina calls again and we are off. I'm terribly sorry about the interruption in our plans. Still, I must tell you that I treasure the memory of our hours together, the way you took care of me, even to washing my clothes. I must tell you that I can't even imagine a Russian man doing such a thing.

Valya was awestruck when I told her. Yes, I told her, I may tell all my friends, I'm very proud to be cherished to such a degree and in such a lovely way. I will look forward to doing the same for you, and other lovely things as well.

I will not mention the one thing because you do not like me to use the disrespectful American word for it. But I must confess I use that bad word from time to time, while flying, when I become angry over something. I use the other term as well, the Piss-ann word you say that I say incorrectly. (I can't think how to spell it.)

I'm desperately sorry to leave so suddenly, my love, but don't despair. The Rodina is an immense place, as you've learned. But we are all going to the same small country to crush the Fascists once and for all. In that place, we will surely find each other.

I love you,
Galina

CHAPTER FIFTEEN

SURPRISES

Dawn brought a terrible surprise to the West on December 16, 1944. Two German panzer armies of twenty-four divisions struck an American corps of three divisions in the Ardennes forest of Belgium without warning or any advance artillery barrage.

Two U.S. divisions were smashed and, all through the area, the Americans retreated in confusion. Communications were disrupted so badly that accurate reports of what was happening were still lacking hours after the first assault.

Air power couldn't be used against the attackers or even to conduct aerial reconnaissance because nothing could fly in the fog, mists, and snow.

The Germans had pulled the same trick they had used to outflank the British, French, and Dutch armies and race all the way to the English Channel in a ten-day dash in 1940. This time, they struck through the forests toward Antwerp, the critically-needed, deep-water seaport that the Allies had only recently taken and had repaired for bringing in supplies.

If the German panzers got there, they would split the Allied armies, reclaim the port city, and change the whole course of the war in the West.

Allied Supreme Commander Dwight Eisenhower stood outside a bleak and cold barracks in Verdun, the site of monstrous carnage in World War I, and glowered at the fog and falling snow. Bad weather had so often frustrated him. He tried to puff on his cigarette, but it had become too soggy to smoke. Ike swore and threw it away. The elements seemed to be conspiring against him in all things, large and small.

Except for its timing in bad weather, the surprise strike by the German panzers made no logical sense. With ingenuity and determination, the Germans had built a strong defensive wall west of the Rhine that stretched all the way from the North Sea to Switzerland.

The German generals had pulled together one hundred infantry battalions from fortresses in the rear and sent eighty to the western front. Another twenty-five Volks Grenadier divisions had arrived in October. Units had been moved skilfully from one sector to another to patch holes in the front.

The Wehrmacht would be at full strength to resist an Allied campaign to cross the Rhine in the spring. It was foolhardy for the Germans to waste their painstakingly rebuilt resources in a high-risk attack of this kind.

The Allies had been held up throughout the autumn by a scarcity of supplies due to a lack of deep-water ports, by bad weather that had grounded airplanes and immobilized tanks, and by the interminable squabbles between the American and British commands.

Ike walked into the squad room of the barracks and, as his commanders filed into the room, warmed his hands at the potbellied stove. In a sense, he knew, the surprise attack by the Germans was his own fault.

He had failed to realize that the man in charge of German strategy wasn't Gert von Rundstedt, the cautious Wehrmacht commander in the West, but Adolf Hitler, who would try and do anything that crossed his mercurial mind.

And part of Ike's fault certainly lay in his failure to force Montgomery to obey his orders. The British peacock, obsessed with the desire to win glory by leading a single thrust across northern Germany into the industrial Ruhr, had tragically wasted the lives of British and American paratroopers at Arnheim in his abortive Operation Market-Garden.

Then Montgomery had frittered away valuable weeks by ignoring, delaying, and deliberately misinterpreting Ike's repeated orders to take Antwerp so that badly needed supplies, particularly ammunition, could be brought in to reequip stalled Allied troops. Many of Ike's commanders, including Air Marshal Tedder, blamed Ike for not nailing Montgomery to the wall.

So the Germans had been given far too much time to restore their strength. Intelligence said that the Luftwaffe fighter force had been substantially rebuilt, too, though the American air forces still greatly outnumbered it.

And Allied intelligence was worried and puzzled by the surprise appearance of the unbelievably fast ME-262 twin-engine jet fighters that would greatly damage, if not completely halt, the Allied air offensive, if the jets were thrown against the B-17s and B-24s. But only a few of the ME-262s had been seen and they had been used only for reconnaissance.

That was a question to be answered another day, Ike reflected. The Ardennes attack was very serious. But it was also a great opportunity. Ike had come to recognize something that Stalin knew but Montgomery didn't; it was more important to kill Germans than it was to drive spearheads through enemy lines.

Ike looked at the expectant faces sitting around him and said formally: "The present situation is to be regarded as one of opportunity for us and not of disaster. There will be only cheerful faces at this conference table."

They quickly agreed on tactics. They would have to hold their north-south line at the Meuse River. There were huge supply dumps across the river at Leige that contained ammunition and, most important, gasoline for tanks. Lack of reserve fuel would be Rundstedt's key weakness. Deny him that and his attack would die.

Bastogne, therefore, was a critical pressure point. The 82nd and 101st Airborne divisions were ordered to get there as fast as possible. Patton was to turn his tank columns northward and attack the Germans on their southern flank. Montgomery was to attack from the north.

Meantime, there was a critical shortage of Allied infantry. After the meeting, Ike sent word back to Com Z, the headquarters of the noncombat operation in the rear, to find him men in non-combat jobs who would step up and fire a rifle. He offered soldier-criminals serving court-martial sentences a pardon and a clean service record if they volunteered. All those who were serving fifteen-year sentences at hard labor volunteered.

Ike also took a radical step and sent a circular to black troops in the rear asking for volunteers who would be willing to fight in infantry units that would be integrated "without regard to color or race."

Ike's chief of staff, General Walter Bedell Smith, icily reminded him that this directly violated War Department regulations. In addition, if integrated front-line units were formed, Smith said, the present policy of segregation in non-combat units could hardly be defended. Chastened, Ike withdrew the circular.

Ike then retreated to the Trianon Palace in Versailles, where he was guarded so closely that he felt like a prisoner. Reports had spread that American-speaking Germans in American uniforms and driving American jeeps had penetrated the lines and were ordered to assassinate Eisenhower.

After two days of being cloistered, Ike exploded. "Hell's fire!" he shouted. "I'm going out for a walk. If anybody wants to shoot me, he can go right ahead. I've got to get out of here!"

He opened a back door, brushed his guards aside, and began tramping through the snow. When would the damn weather let up? he growled. When it did, the U.S. air forces would rain hell and destruction on the damned Germans. Then we'd see who'd shoot who!

With General Sloane's, Dee Tee's, and Timberwolf's help, Buddy had created a group football team in an adjoining pasture with goal posts, field stripes, bleachers, banners, and imported footballs and uniforms. Cajoling other group commanders, he had succeeded in forming a league of five teams.

The 300th's team was, of course, called the Rebels.

The team practiced and played between October and December missions in good and bad weather. Group personnel and bewildered Britishers sat in the stands, clapping and cheering.

Buddy even organized a squad of cheerleaders from surrounding villages. Peggy, her blonde hair flying, became chief cheerleader.

Occasionally, a player who hadn't returned from a raid had to be replaced, but casualties had been light in recent weeks. On December 18, the weather shut down so completely that the team was able to practice every day for five straight days.

After a hard day's practice during which Buddy put himself in to run a few plays at end, he returned, sweating and wheezing, to his quarters, to find Dee Tee dancing about nervously.

"General Sloane's called you twice," he said. "Wants you to call him right back. On the scrambler."

Buddy wiped his face with a towel, slung the towel around his neck, sank into his chair, and picked up the phone. Sloane came on the line immediately.

"Buddy-boy, I got a surprise for you," he said with a distinct note of satisfaction in his voice. Buddy tried to think what it could be. American beer? Scotch? Dancing girls from the Windmill in London? Another visit from the Glenn Miller band? Another Hollywood sex bomb? What was left to ask for? It couldn't be Claire coming over; that would be *too* much.

"Weather's clearin', son," the general said. "You're leadin' the Wing and, here's the best part of all, I'm gonna fly with you." Amazed, Buddy struggled to reply. Finally, he said: "Uh, why that's fine, Gen'l."

"Gonna come over tonight. Jus' find me a place to bed down. Gonna fly command pilot with you, sit in the right seat beside you. Time I got out and flew. Wanted to check up on you anyways."

"You say we're leadin' the Wing, Gen'l?"

"We're the fellas with the fuzzy balls tomorrow," Sloane said. "No need to go inta details. We're on scrambler and all, but I still don't liketa talk too much on the phone. You'll see the field order right soon on your teletype."

"Sounds, uh, real good, Gen'l," Buddy said.

"Don' it though," Sloane said. "See you tonight."

The field order described the target, altitude, bomb load, prescribed time over target, and order of battle, and Dee Tee fed him the rest. A huge force of fighter-bombers would swarm over the Ardennes at first light to blast the German tanks and troop positions while C-47s dropped ammunition and food to encircled American defenders in the forest.

The heavy bombers would fly farther to the east to bomb railheads and roads being used to reinforce the German Army. Other groups would strike German airfields to keep the Luftwaffe from interfering with the aerial effort to wipe out Rundstedt's army.

As predicted, December 23 dawned clear and bright. Heavy mists still shrouded the field as the sun rose but, when the sun's warmth penetrated to the ground, the fog vanished as if by magic. With Buddy leading, thirty-six B-17s took off, assembled, and headed east to link up with other groups and Wings.

Leading the group on autopilot, Buddy felt like an only son being watched over by a doting father. When he looked sideways at Sloane, the older man's eyes creased over his oxygen mask in what was obviously meant to be an encouraging smile.

Buddy and the general had placed their D-ration chocolate bars by the windscreen to gnaw on when they were on the return trip and could descend to ten thousand feet and remove their oxygen masks. Buddy had stuffed a fresh pack of Camels in an inside pocket so he could offer the general one at that moment. After you wiped the frozen crust of saliva from your lips, a cigarette tasted wonderful in the thin air. Buddy smoked very little, only a few a day, but he always savored the one he smoked on the letdown. The whole crew lit up when Buddy gave the word and the aroma filled the airplane.

Leading the missions had become so familiar to Buddy that the experience would have become boring if it weren't for the satisfaction he felt at the skills he had acquired. He had learned all the tricks and subtleties of a master pilot.

He knew how to lead a formation and how to fly close formation on someone else's wing for long periods without exhausting himself or straining his back. He had learned how to make minute, fingertip changes in throttle settings to move forward, back, up, or down without disturbing the intricately-interwoven matrix of a combat box of thirty-six or forty-eight heavy bombers.

He knew how to adjust the autopilot so that it flew the airplane in calm or rough air without jiggling enough to disrupt the formation. He knew how to relax physically and conserve energy while staying alert on a ten-hour mission.

He knew all these things, and he knew how to impart them to others insofar as teaching could help someone to learn. He also knew how to dispel fear, his own and his men's, and how to cajole and inspire them. He was no longer surprised by what happened in the air.

Until this moment.

Without warning, eight hundred Luftwaffe fighters fell on the bombers of the Eighth Air Force. The first shout of alarm came from the bombardier as flashes winked up ahead of them. Almost simultaneously, a waist gunner called from the right side. Waves of Messerschmitts and Focke-Wulfs ripped through the formations head-on in line-abreast, company-front formations. Other waves struck from the flanks.

Groups of escorting P-51s and P-47s sped to the scene, but not before the lead groups of bombers had taken severe battle damage. Buddy's ship shook with the pounding of his gunner's heavy machine guns. The familiar sound of stones being thrown against metal signaled that they had been hit throughout the fuselage. One waist gunner went down. The Number One engine began spurting oil.

Keeping a firm grip on his nerves, Buddy reached over and hit the button to feather the propeller, called to the crew to stop shouting, and looked sideways at Sloane. The old man's eyes were wide with surprise and terror. Buddy's skin was prickling and his heart was pounding, but he felt a perverse tickle of satisfaction. *The general had considered this a milk run,* Buddy thought. *The old boy is finding out what it used to be like every damned day, apparently still can be.*

It was his last thought. Something struck him in the head and he felt himself falling through the sky into a deep, heavy fog. He kept trying to pull the handle of his parachute but it was fused to his chest somehow; he couldn't get it free. People were shouting and crying in the background. And then there was a lot of annoying talking. Finally, their voices faded away.

His eyes opened. Sloane was sitting beside him. He smiled broadly as Buddy came awake. "All I seem to do is sit 'side you in hospitals," Sloane said. "Way we met back in the States, after you shot up that Viking and they shot you back, remember?"

Buddy wiggled his fingers and toes and tried to raise his left hand to his head. Pain shot through his shoulder and he grunted. He cautiously raised his right hand. His head was bandaged.

"How bad am I hurt, Gen'l?" he asked.

"Head wound, son. Tiny fracture there, kind of a bad crease, gettin' better. You've been out, in and out, quite a while. Your vision a little blurry? Yeah; doctor says it'll clear up. It'll be fine. Pretty bad hit in the left shoulder, though; piece of a cannon shell, came right through the side window, thick, bullet-proof glass and all."

"Bullet-resistant, not bullet-proof," Buddy croaked.

"Anyway, tore up your shoulder some. Not gonna be playin' end again, least not for a long while. They had to rebuild that cuff in there. You'll get seventy-eighty percent mobility back after a while, lotta rest, lotta physical rehab, all that."

Sloane leaned forward, smiling sympathetically. "Long and short of it is, you're goin' home, Buddy. To Walter Reed in Washington, first of all. When you get out, R&R, rest and recreation, for thirty days. See Claire, see if you got something goin' there."

Buddy shook his head. "Hate to leave the bomb group. I really do."

"I know, son. Can't be helped. You've done a hell of a job here, son, hell of a job."

Buddy nodded, wondering irrelevantly why Sloane, like Senator Claghorn on Fred Allen's radio show, always said everything twice. He did it twice again.

"You're goin' further, Buddy, you're goin' further. You're not through by any means, not by *any* means. This war'll be over pretty soon, matter a months now, the damn fool Hitler scared hell out of us in the Ardennes, but we've cleaned up that pocket. They've lost, it was 220,000 men, G-2 says, about half killed and wounded, the other half prisoners. Plus about 1,500 tanks and big guns. A damn fool trick. And the Nazi bastards shot 'bout a hundred of our men, unarmed prisoners, in a field at a place called Malmedy."

Sloane shook his head and sighed. "Anyway, like I told you before, we're gonna form a separate service now, Buddy-boy. No more Army Air Corps. We'll be the U.S. Air Force. Need you to stay in, Buddy. Grow with it, grow with ol' Uncle John. I'll help you."

He grinned and pointed to a new ribbon on his uniform. "You've already helped *me*. Did it the hard way, sorry to say. But you did it. Forced me to *do* the job for once, not just sit 'n talk about it. And I did it. Flew us back, had a lotta trouble keepin' you from grabbin' at the controls, fallin' over inta them. Lost another engine, had another man hurt, we shot down two Jerry fighters, put out a fire in the bomb bay, skimmed back over the Channel, couldn't bail out because a you and the other wounded, made a belly-landing at the coast. Saved the ship. The whole damned smear, as the guys from New York say. So they're givin' me the Silver Star to go with my DFC. Won't hurt the ol' 201 file a bit."

Sloane patted Buddy's good shoulder in a fatherly fashion. "You get well and all, and there'll be nothin' but good things ahead, son, good things ahead. I'll keep in touch, believe me."

Adolf Galland, former General of the Luftwaffe Fighters, sat in a rickety chair in a patch of weeds at the edge of a grass airfield at Munich-Riem, lighted one of his long Brazil cigars, and stared straight ahead. In the distance, shrouded by thin clouds, lay the Alps, their shadowy outline as unreal as the war that the Luftwaffe was still trying to fight.

Near him, on a crude table, sat a field telephone. Beside it was a cracked coffee mug and a half-eaten piece of coarse army bread smeared with jam. Around him, for the most part sitting silently or dozing in an odd assortment of old chairs, were the last of Germany's greatest flying aces. Every man wore a Knight's Cross; every one had scored dozens of victories. Some, like Galland, had flown in the Spanish civil war.

Close by Galland sat Oberst Johannes Steinhoff, a superb ace with

176 kills to his credit, now director of training for Kommando Jagdverband 44. If it seemed odd for a former fighter group commander to be supervising the training of pilots for a squadron, it was odder still for a legendary general like Galland, whose face adorned a million postcards and the pages of penny magazines throughout Germany, to be commander of the squadron.

But it was a unique squadron; not only were its members the most accomplished fighter aces of the era, the aircraft they had been given to fly was the Messerschmitt 262, the wonderplane that flew as much as 150 miles per hour faster than even the newest American Mustang, nearly twice as fast as the old ME-109, nearly three times faster than the B-17 Flying Fortresses that were destroying the Reich.

Steinhoff looked at his rakish leader and wondered what he was thinking as he sat waiting for a call from ground control to say the Viermots, the Boeings, had crossed the Channel and were on their way, escorted by hundreds of fighters, to pound Germany's ruined cities into rubble.

Was he wondering, as Steinhoff often did, what this dwindling number of pilots from the past—expert though they may have been— thought they were doing? In his diary, which he would turn into a book if he survived, Steinhoff had compared these last Luftwaffe aces to dayflies, destined to flit through the day and then, unable to feed, die, when the dream fades into oblivion.

Was the general thinking about his dismissal as General of the Fighters by Reichsmarschall Göring? Was he, more likely, thinking about the huge victory the Luftwaffe would have won had the cowardly Göring and the deranged Führer allowed them to amass a thousand or even one hundred of the new jet fighters to attack the Boeings a year ago?

Galland, in fact, was thinking of none of these things. He was thanking his lucky stars that his and Germany's nemesis, Adolf Hitler, had got wind of Göring's plot to blame him for the Luftwaffe's failure to stop the bombing of Germany.

Göring was trying to salvage his own reputation. The bombings had all but destroyed Germany's transportation system and now were threatening to cut off its fuel supply. One recent report signaled what was to come. The Panzerlehr division had to abandon fifty-three of its tanks when they had run out of fuel.

Göring's plot to make Galland the scapegoat for Göring's failures had driven the former fighter general to the brink of suicide. The SS was tapping his telephone and had beaten up his orderly. Göring had convened a hand-picked investigating commission to fix the blame on Galland for the decline of the Luftwaffe.

Galland had even picked the night on which he would shoot himself. But his latest girl friend, Monica, had taken a personal risk and told Armaments Minister Albert Speer of her lover's plans. Speer immediately phoned Hitler who, already disgusted with Göring, flew into a rage, dissolved the investigation, chastized Göring, and phoned Galland to reassure him. From now on, Galland would be free to do what he wanted to do: fly.

And, Galland reflected wryly, get himself killed. The ME-262s would create havoc when they attacked the bombers, but they were so hopelessly outnumbered, and so vulnerable to enemy fighters when taking off and landing, that, sooner or later, they would all be shot down. All the aces realized that.

Galland shrugged. To be killed at this time, under these circumstances, was nothing. Soldiers were being killed everywhere; millions more would undoubtedly die before this stupid war ended.

There would be no easy ending. The Führer had angrily rejected Rommel's advice to sue for peace. Now Rommel was dead, forced to swallow poison or be court-martialed and have his family punished for suspected complicity in the officers' plot to kill Hitler.

The American President Roosevelt had announced that there would be no negotiated peace; Germany would have to surrender unconditionally. And, Galland heard, Stalin had told his commanders that "everything would be allowed" when Russian troops entered Germany. Those who died in battle would be lucky.

The Vistula is Poland's main river. It rises in the interior, runs through the capital city of Warsaw, and meanders northward to the Gulf of Danzig. The bank of the Vistula was the high water mark of the Russian advance westward until January 12, 1945.

At 5:00 A.M. that day, amid thick, falling snow and freezing temperatures, the first assault wave of nearly two million men supported by forty-one thousand artillery pieces and six thousand tanks thundered across the Vistula and plowed westward toward the Oder, which forms the boundary between Poland and Germany east of Berlin.

Because visibility was zero on the first day of the attack, none of the six thousand combat aircraft assigned to support the armies was able to fly. But artillery was clustered so thickly that, in some sectors, there were five hundred guns along each mile of front. And the thick snow covered the rolling Russian tanks and made them hard to see.

The Soviet commanders knew that the Germans would fight with increasing ferocity as the war reached their homeland, but the Germans were outnumbered six to one in men and ten to one in armor and artillery. In aircraft, the estimated advantage was seventeen to one.

The Germans had virtually no reserves to bring up, and they were repeatedly placed in self-destructive positions by their Supreme Commander who tried to give detailed battle orders to units far away and who believed that the real objective of the Soviet attack was not Berlin but Prague.

Stalin's northern and southern frontal armies moved to block off any German reinforcement of the center forces where the Soviet weight was concentrated.

Rolling westward, the Soviet armies took the ruined capital city of Warsaw five days later and found a shattered and embittered populace. Some 250,000 Poles had died needlessly there because, months earlier, Stalin had urged the anti-Communist Home Guard to rise against the Germans. After a few token air drops, he stopped supplying the Poles. Unobstructed, Hitler's Stukas repeatedly dive-bombed the buildings held by the Guard and German troops moved in to crush the uprising.

By doing so, the Germans rid Stalin of Poland's anti-Communist movement before they, too, were destroyed.

Poznan, east of Berlin, was encircled by January 25. The Silesian area in the south, second only to the Ruhr in importance to Germany for industrial production, fell by January 29. To avoid destroying the factories, Stalin's army commander created a huge encirclement with an opening, making sure the Germans saw the opening. After the Germans retreated through it, Russian tanks, camouflaged with lace from a nearby textile mill, attacked the escaping troops. Atop some of the tanks, Russian soldiers sat and played accordions. Within a few days, Soviet armies had reached the Oder and were only fifty miles from Berlin. And then there was a lull.

It was hard to reconcile the contrast between the beautiful mountains on the left and the carnage below them and to the right, Galina thought as the night bomber regiment flew northwestward in bright daylight toward their new field on the Oder.

As she looked to the left from her open cockpit, she saw peace, quiet, and unspoiled nature. It was early spring and the snow had melted except for high places and sheltered spots in the hills.

To the right, there lay a vast area of wreckage and ruin. Many of Silesia's factories had been left intact. But near them lay the wreckage of still-smoking tanks and trucks, the carcasses of dead horses being picked over by starving peasants, and a landscape covered with the bodies of soldiers, most of them German.

Public buildings, churches, and most of the houses and huts in the villages had been burned to the ground by the retreating Fascists.

But nothing seemed, or could be, as terrible as the camp they had encountered near their last airfield. The place was called Oswiecim; the Germans, she was told, had called it Auschwitz. The women of the regiment had been told to stay away from foreign villages and encampments. But there had been so many whispers and so much rolling of the eyes about this place that she and Valya had decided to go and see for themselves.

She had smelled the unpleasant smell of death before, but the concentration camp at Oswiecim exuded a stink that was almost beyond endurance. Inside the gate, lying on the ground, were a collection of living skeletons, clad in filthy striped pajamas and crying out feebly. In one huge room there were ovens and mounds of clothing that revealed what the ovens had been used for.

In another room they found stacks of naked, emaciated bodies of dead men that were piled nearly to the roof. They backed out hastily and Valya bent over and vomited. They began walking rapidly to the gate and then, without thinking or even realizing what they were doing, started running.

When they had calmed down and were walking again, they talked about what they had seen.

"If there was ever any doubt about the barbarity of these Hitlerites, any doubt at all, that place is the final proof," Galina said bitterly. "I hope they take pictures of that place and show them all over the world."

"They will, you can be sure," Valya said. "It was horrible."

"Nothing like that has ever happened before in history," Galina declared. "Nothing. And this is the twentieth century. It's unbelievable that human beings of any country, any race, can treat other human beings like that."

Valya walked silently, looking at the ground. Galina looked at her. "You don't say anything, Valya." Valya shrugged.

"What are you thinking, Valya?" Galina asked. "I know you. You're thinking *something*."

Valya looked around before she spoke. "I come from a village near Kiev, you know."

"I know. What does that have to do with anything?"

"I wouldn't say this to anyone else, Galina," Valya said. "But . . ." She stopped and shook her head.

"But what, Valya?" Galina said. "You know you can say what you want to me. I'm your friend, not the commissar, for heaven's sake."

Though they were alone on the roadway, Valya spoke in a low voice. "In the Ukraine, it was only twelve, thirteen years ago, Galina, we had the collectivization program. Peasants thrown off their lands. Many thrown into wagons and sent to, they say, Siberia. All the crops confiscated by the army. Thousands, millions of people, left to starve."

"Did you really see anyone starve?" Galina asked.

"Oh yes. Many of them. It was terrible. We were lucky, my father worked in a factory. We had enough to eat, not as much as we wanted by any means, but enough for the family to live. But the farmers had their grain, all their food, taken away from them. Those who resisted were shot; some were hanged from trees and scaffolds. No wheat for bread, not even a kernel of corn."

"How did they stay alive?" Galina asked.

"Most didn't. Those who did, my father said, were the ones who had learned about plants."

"Plants?"

"Yes. Nettles, linden leaves, grasses, tree barks and roots. Acorns. Even uncured sheepskins. They made soups from old cattle hooves and horns that were lying around. There wasn't a dog or cat left, of course. Still, the soldiers came and searched the barns and cellars; they even prodded the ground with sticks and bars, looking for grain that the *kulaks* might have hidden away."

Valya looked searchingly at Galina. "Then there was the purge. You come from Moscow. You must have known about that."

Galina nodded. "The arrest of the intellectuals. Yes, I know about that. The police came and knocked on the doors at night. In the morning, the people were gone. An old professor I knew, and his wife. In Moscow, it was quite frightening for a time. We tried not to think about it."

She paused. "Isn't it odd, we've known each other all this time, we've flown together and been shot at together, grown so close, but we've never talked of these things before."

Valya nodded. "It isn't a good thing to talk about. Today it's only because we've been to that terrible camp and seen what the Hitlerites did there. But, honestly, is it really any worse than what"—she choked momentarily, unable to say the dreaded name—"what some of *our* people have done?"

"It was for a different reason, a cause," Galina said unconvincingly.

"Did that make it right? To do?"

"No," Galina said.

"Let's not talk of this anymore," Valya said. "I hear we're taking over an old country house up at the border."

They were pleasantly surprised to find the rumor was true. They moved into a weather-beaten old house that had once been owned by a prosperous farmer. It was in disrepair, with paint flaking from the walls and creaking, sometimes rotten, floorboards. But, to the night-witches, it was a place of incomparable luxury.

They were sheltered from the weather, in itself a blessing. But there was even more to be thankful for. The previous occupants, who had evacuated the area in a hurry, had left behind sacks of flour and a bin of potatoes. The afternoon they arrived, the cook served them potato cakes and bacon fat.

In the living room downstairs, there was a large stone fireplace. At night, they sat around a roaring log fire and sang songs. Galina wished she could hear Misha sing again. She wondered where he was and how soon they would find each other.

The Yak regiment had taken over an abandoned German airfield near the Oder. The ground had thawed enough so that the shell craters could be filled in by old men, boys, and women from a village that adjoined the field. The villagers were glad that the Germans were gone, but they resented being dragooned for the task and hoped that the Russians would leave soon so that they could plant potatoes and grains in the field. Planting season was almost over.

The air crewmen were billeted in the villagers' homes, many of them little more than thatched-roof huts. Viktor told the men sternly that there were to be no rapes or instances of brutality. After the German occupation, the villagers recoiled instinctively from anyone in uniform.

Mike had become Viktor's de facto deputy, and they watched the activity on the field from the church they were using, like the Germans before them, for their headquarters. Large boxes and crates had been unloaded from trucks and transport planes and were stacked around the Yak fighters under the camouflage nets.

Some mechanics were pulling off engine cowlings and removing engines with cranes while others lay under the fuselages and installed long metal tubes.

"This doesn't make any sense," Mike said.

Viktor said: "Ours not to reason why, ours . . ."

"I know; it's an old Russian saying. But turning a light little Yak into a fighter-bomber for ground-attack . . ." Mike shook his head in dismay.

"The way they explained it to the regimental commanders, it seemed logical, at least at first," Viktor said. "There aren't enough Fascist fighters left to require a large number of us to maintain high cover. We have air superiority now, especially since they've transferred so many units to the Western front. Apparently their cities are being bombed into the ground over there."

Mike felt a twinge of guilt or regret, he didn't know which. "By B-17s," he said. "My group, where I'm supposed to be."

"In any event, the new Yak-3s and the LA-7—it has a big 1,850-horsepower engine—are better than our Yak-9s for dogfighting," Viktor said. "Both of them fly over four hundred miles an hour, forty or fifty miles an hour faster than we do. If we still need air superiority fighters, they'll do the job.

"But the biggest need is for ground-attack aircraft. The 37-mm. cannons they're putting on our Yaks will hit a great deal harder than our old 20s. And we'll be able to carry up to eight hundred pounds of bombs on those fittings they're putting on the underside of our wings and fuselage."

"Yeah, but we don't have the armorplating the Shturmoviks do," Mike said. "We'll get cut to pieces by ground fire. If we do run into enemy fighters, we'll be too slow and clumsy to dogfight with them. We'd be better off flying Shturmoviks for this kind of job."

Viktor looked pained and stared at the mechanics as they worked. "We're a Yak regiment and all our men take pride in flying the Yak. We're fighter pilots. It would upset them a good deal to be put into Shturmoviks." He sighed. "But you're right. If we begin to lose many Yaks when the campaign begins, they may come to the same conclusion."

"When is it supposed to start?" Mike asked. "We've been sitting here, it seems like weeks. If I'd known where Galina was, is, I'd have tried to visit her. We've got all this strength now; what's going on?"

Viktor smiled. "Your Will Rogers used to say he only knew what he read in the newspapers. We don't have any newspapers here, just orders and rumors. I hear there's some sort of argument going on at the top. Who's going to get the glory for taking Berlin? Who's going to be pushed aside? And who's this who's coming up the path? Captain Prune-Face himself."

It was Captain Spirin, the regimental commissar. His thin, ascetic face, framed with little round eyeglasses, was, as usual, impassive. He had spoken to Mike very little in the previous months, but he always seemed to be somewhere in sight. Mike disliked him instinctively. He had never seen Spirin smile and the commissar had few, if any, friends in the regiment.

Spirin walked up the steps. He was carrying a small case. Viktor invited him inside and indicated a chair. Spirin remained standing. He placed his case on Viktor's desk, opened it, looked up, and spoke formally.

"I have the honor to notify you, Comrade Major Markov, and you, Comrade Senior Lieutenant Gavronov, that you are recipients of awards approved by Comrade Stalin himself upon the recommendation of Comrade General Novikov. As of this minute, you are both Heroes of the Soviet Union. A notice to this effect will be posted on the orders board. There will be a general ceremony before the assembled regiment in a few days."

Spirin opened the case, pulled out two medals hanging on ribbons, and held them up for Viktor and Mike to see. Viktor flushed with pleasure; Mike looked baffled.

"I greatly appreciate this award," Viktor said with equal formality, "and I will treasure it. It is, of course, a tribute to the men of the regiment more than to myself and, most certainly, to my predecessor, Major Borisenko, who created the discipline and skill that we embody today."

"A similar award is being made to Major Borisenko posthumously," Spirin said. He turned to Mike. "And what is your reaction, Comrade Senior Lieutenant?"

Mike stuttered uncertainly. "It's a surprise, a very big surprise. I thank you, of course . . ."

"You should thank General Novikov and Comrade Stalin, not me."

"I will, I mean I do. But it's a surprise, my being a foreigner. And everything," he concluded lamely.

Spirin nodded. "You raise an important point, Mikhail Stepanovich. You have become, in virtually every respect, a Russian. You know our ways, our culture, you even speak our language now. You could have returned to your own military group at one point—I am sure that possibility did not escape you—but you chose not to.

"You have served us well, and we have done you the honor of designating you as a Hero of the Soviet Union. We are prepared to do you the further and even greater honor of allowing you to become a Soviet citizen. Will you accept that honor?"

Stunned, Mike looked at Viktor, who was watching him closely, eyes narrowed. Did Viktor move his eyes from side to side almost imperceptibly? Mike looked back at Spirin. The thin face told him nothing, but Mike knew that he was standing in an ideological minefield. He cleared his throat and spoke.

"Comrade Captain, this is too much to absorb at one time. First, this enormous award"—he indicated the medal Spirin was holding—"now this *other* suggestion, honor. I have grown to, I mean to say, I have a great respect and affection for what I have seen and found here. Still, I've never felt I was turning my back on my own country. I am confused. Please give me time to sort out my thoughts."

Spirin stared at him for a long moment, light reflecting from his round eyeglasses. "Very well, Comrade Senior Lieutenant. Tell me when you have, as you say, sorted out your thoughts. I hope it will not take you too long a time."

The commissar nodded and left. Viktor watched him with concern.

"This is dangerous," he said. "For you and, potentially, for me. If you turn this down, well, something bad could happen."

Viktor groaned. "Things just don't turn out as they're supposed to. You want good things, then when you get them, you find the price is too high. I wanted the promotion to major, but not at the expense of Borisenko's life. Now comes the Hero award, a very important, you might say, key to the future, my future, certainly, and it's compromised by *this*, our national paranoia about foreigners."

"I don't want to hurt you," Mike said. "What should I do?"

"Stall. You're too busy. You haven't had time to think. Stay out of his way."

"It would help if we'd get our battle orders."

"It would. The conversion of the aircraft will be finished in a few days. By then maybe our orders will come. Spirin can't pin you down on a matter like this while you're fighting. Let's hope the campaign starts soon."

It would be a race to seize Berlin. Stalin was sure of that now. He had assumed all along that, at the propitious moment, the Western allies would try to capture that prize before the Soviet armies did. Now he was certain of it.

Eisenhower had sent him a message that said explicitly that the Americans and British did *not* view Berlin as their primary objective.

Instead, having crossed the Rhine, they would drive eastward on a broad front, thrusting to the north and south and holding in the center. This would leave Berlin to the Russians.

Stalin curled his lips contemptuously when he had read the message. Did the American general really think that the Supreme Commander of the *Stavka*, the Soviet forces, was *that* stupid?

The message, very obviously, was a crude attempt to mislead him. Its true meaning was the exact opposite of what Eisenhower said. He picked up his telephone and told the operator to summon Marshals Zhukov and Konev. They were his toughest and most capable generals; they were also the fiercest competitors among his commanders.

Both would have to fly nearly a thousand miles from the Eastern front to Moscow for the conference. Stalin lit his pipe and pondered. He would exploit their jealousy of each other. This would lead each of them to do everything humanly—and inhumanly—possible to be the first to capture Berlin. Their fierce competition had pushed the Soviet forces through Belorussia with unprecedented speed. Frantic to be the first to his assigned objective, Zhukov had thrown his armies headlong against the embattled Fascists; he had brutalized his commanders, demoted several, and sent others to penal brigades for failing to move fast enough.

Georgi K. Zhukov was Josef Stalin's kind of man. Even so, Ivan Stepanovich Konev, the onetime political commissar, a better-educated and, in some ways, cleverer general, was close behind. And he could be barbarous, too. When a German division had refused to surrender to him, Konev had unleashed his saber-wielding Cossacks to cut them down. The Cossacks had even hacked the hands from the Germans who raised them in a last-minute surrender.

Competing with each other for the biggest prize of all, the city of Berlin, the still-beating heart of the Fascist monster, these two fire-breathing stallions would outstrip the Western allies, win the race for the Soviet Union, and, at the same time—how had those British fellows, Gilbert and Sullivan, put it?—provide a little innocent merriment.

Meantime, Stalin started to compose a message to send back to Eisenhower. In it, he said he agreed with the Allied Supreme Commander about the military insignificance of Berlin. The Red Army, he said, would concentrate instead on taking Dresden.

The following day, the two generals rolled into the Kremlin compound in their field-gray staff cars, weary and anxious, just as the gilt hands of the clock face on the Great Savior's tower showed 5:00 P.M.

Climbing out of their cars, Zhukov and Konev smiled broadly at each other, shook hands, and walked into the elevator, chatting amiably, hating each other.

Both knew that the subject for the conference had to be Berlin. Zhukov had already been given a clear indication that he had been chosen for the honor. Command of the First Belorussian Front in the center, standing due east of Berlin, had been taken from Rokossovsky and given to him. Rokossovsky, an able general, had been relegated to a supporting role as commander of the Second Belorussian Front in the north.

Konev commanded the First Ukrainian Front in the south. He was seventy miles from Berlin, about twice the distance of Zhukov. But Zhukov's forces would have slower going against the concentrated German defenses in the center.

They walked into Stalin's familiar conference room and were joined immediately by the seven members of the State Defense Committee, including Molotov and Beria.

Stalin walked in a minute later, dressed in a mustard-colored uniform without epaulettes or any insignia of rank. On the left side of his chest hung the gold star of a Hero of the Soviet Union. One of his favorite British Dunhill pipes was clamped between his teeth.

Sitting down, he said quietly: "The *soyuznichki* intend to get to Berlin ahead of us. They are already near the Elbe. So, comrades," he said, looking at the two marshals, "who will take Berlin? We, or the Western Allies?"

Konev spoke quickly. "We will, and before the Anglo-Americans."

A small smile played over Stalin's pockmarked face. "So, is that the sort of fellow you are?"

The smile vanished. "Your forces are in the south," he said crisply. "Wouldn't it require a major regrouping for your forces to take Berlin?"

Konev recognized the bait and the trap; it was Belorussia all over again. "Comrade Stalin," he said, "all the measures will be carried out. We will regroup in time to reach Berlin."

He had planned to say more but Zhukov intervened. "May I speak?" he asked. Before Stalin could answer, he said smugly: "With all respect, we of the First Belorussian Front need no regrouping. We are ready now and we are aimed directly at Berlin. We will take Berlin."

Stalin smiled a small smile again. "Very well. You will both stay here with the general staff and prepare your plans. I expect them within forty-eight hours. Then you will return to your fronts with everything approved."

Stalin stood. "The dates for the beginning of your operations will attract our special attention." He nodded and left the room.

Forty-eight hours later, the sleepless generals appeared in Stalin's conference room. Only the Generalissimo was present. He pointed a finger at Zhukov, inviting him to make the first presentation.

"The First Belorussian armies are at my fingertips, Comrade Stalin," the stocky marshal said. "Four field armies and two tank armies will make the main thrust; additional armies will be employed in support. We will open our attack with at least two hundred and fifty artillery pieces for each kilometer of front; the opening barrage will be made by eleven thousand guns, not counting small-caliber mortars."

He held up a finger and smiled. "The enemy will be stunned. But he will also be blinded. I will launch my offensive in darkness. At the instant of the attack, I will switch on one hundred and forty high-powered antiaircraft searchlights. They will be trained directly upon the enemy positions. The enemy will be able neither to see nor to hear. We will destroy him."

Konev's plan was equally innovative. He would make a dawn attack under cover of a heavy smoke screen laid down by low-flying squadrons of aircraft. He would employ the same heavy density of artillery in his opening barrage. Here he exercised a bit of one-upmanship.

"Unlike my neighbor," Konev said, "I plan to extend the opening barrage. I will saturate the enemy positions with artillery fire for two hours and thirty-five minutes."

He added an emotional appeal: "Berlin is an object of such ardent desire for us that every one of us, from general to common soldier, wants to see it with his own eyes and have a part in capturing it by force of arms. We are overflowing with this desire."

Nodding, Stalin approved both plans. The primary responsibility for capturing Berlin would be Zhukov's, he said, because he was closer to the city and had larger forces at his command. But, Stalin said, he would transfer two armies from the Baltic and East Prussia to reinforce Konev. And, Stalin noted with hidden amusement, Konev had craftily massed his tank armies on the right wing of his forces so that, after breaking through the enemy lines, he could turn northward toward Berlin and perhaps crash into the city before Zhukov got there.

To make it clear that, no matter what he said, he expected the two marshals to race each other to Berlin, he summoned them to the map table, bent over a map of the region, and began drawing a boundary line between the two marshals' army groups.

Peering at each as he did it, Stalin drew the line westward from their present positions to the town of Lubben on the Spree River, sixty-five miles southeast of Berlin. Then he stopped drawing and raised his pencil.

The meaning was clear; if he had continued the line, it would have become a boundary that Konev could not cross. Now there was no line of demarcation.

Konev was overjoyed; Stalin had read his mind. Zhukov looked at the two suspiciously. The Generalissimo smiled, thanked his marshals, and told them their plans would be incorporated into a general directive that he would issue immediately. The date for the attack would be April 16.

Adolf Hitler studied the map of the Eastern front, noted the heavy buildup of Zhukov's forces opposite Berlin, and decided he had been right all along. It was a clever feint. The primary Soviet attack would come far to the south, he told his generals in his cramped conference room in the bunker beneath the Chancellery in Berlin.

Colonel General Ferdinand Schörner, one of his least talented generals, said he also had seen through the plot. "Mein Führer, it is written in history. Remember Bismarck's words: 'Whoever holds Prague holds Europe.' "

Hitler's eyes flashed. He immediately promoted Schörner to field marshal. Then he ordered the transfer south of four veteran panzer units, an important part of the armored forces that Colonel General Gotthard Henrici needed to stop the Russian attack on Berlin. Henrici shook his head in dismay.

At his headquarters, Zhukov assembled his commanders around a large relief map of Berlin. Each objective was neatly numbered with a flag. The marshal looked at his officers and, pointing to them in turn, said: "Who will be the one to reach the Reichstag first? And what about the Chancellery? Who will be the first? Will it be you? Will it be you? Or you? Who will it be?"

One of his commanders burst out: "If I get to 106, maybe I'll catch

Himmler!" Another said: "I'll get to the Chancellery! I'll get the monster Hitler himself!"

Outside, Zhukov's troops watched in awe at the long procession of heavy guns being wheeled and towed toward the front. And there was truck after truck carrying huge searchlights, each accompanied by a crew of uniformed women.

Claire landed at Bolling, changed her clothes, washed her face and hands, and adjusted her makeup. She botched her lipstick and swore as she wiped it off and reapplied it. Her hands were trembling and she told herself it was silly to be nervous.

She and Buddy Bryce had been corresponding for a year or more. Aside from that, they had had two phone conversations, courtesy of General Sloane. That was really the extent of their relationship. It was foolish to imagine it as something more, she told herself as she rode an Army bus to Walter Reed Hospital.

She and Buddy would meet again after all these years. They would look and be very different than they had seemed at that long-ago party at Hendricks. They would, very probably, find themselves a bit disappointed because each had conjured up an unreal image of the other through their letters. Buddy's last letter, stowed in her musette bag, had been particularly appealing.

Claire,

I've thought a lot about what you said in your last letter, our growing into bigger and better people. Here you've gone and done things that no woman was ever supposed to do, be able to do. I'll bet your mother's been having kittens over the things her daughter's doing. It must have been awful tough for you to handle all the stuff you've had to handle—I mean, learning to do things that women *haven't* done except for maybe Cochran and Earhart. Learning to put up with all the flak from the men you've had to deal with. I'm ashamed to admit it, but back then I'd probably have been one of those same men, a lot more interested in getting you into bed than helping you do your job. Not even wanting you to be doing that kind of job.

Tell you the truth, though, it's been tough for me, too. I'm the guy, remember, who always was the squadron————(I won't use the Army word for it but you know what I mean). Mike and I—there I go talking about our buddy Mike again, I want to get past that obstacle where you're concerned—anyway, Mike and I were always looking for trouble, not trouble exactly, but some kind of way to thumb our noses at authority, show how smart and, well, smartass we were.

Now, sometimes I wonder how it could have happened, *I'm* the authority now. I'm the head man here, I enforce the rules, sometimes make them. I'm responsible for telling people what to do. I get all teed off when these junior birdmen screw up, try to pull swifties on the old fox, and I have to remind myself that I was just exactly the same way a few years ago, and I looked at the older guys at the top—they were only a couple years older—as if they were boring old graybeards. It amazes me that they can think of me that way today, but it's more important that I understand how they think about themselves.

I found out a long time ago that you don't get people to do what you say just by giving orders, not if you're really any good at your job. You have to make the orders make sense. You have to train your people, make it tough for them, don't even think about being popular, because if you're popular, that almost automatically means you haven't done your job right. We've had commanders who were so nice to their men that their men were allowed to get sloppy—and, because of that, they got killed.

But you can't just be a hard-ass, excuse the expression, either. You have to make it clear that you understand their feelings and, when they've done things right, you have to find rewards for them. Old John Sloane gave me good advice on that early on.

I think it's probably the same way, to a great extent, or ought to be, in civilian life. I like the way things have turned out for us, Claire. I like the thought that we're both stronger people because that means we're more understanding people, too. People who've had to stretch, people who've developed deeper, it's not easy for me to find the right words, *things* to fall back on. *Resources.* Maybe people like that can find each other interesting to be with.

Love,
Buddy

The bus went through the gate and drew up to the formal entrance of the main building. She got out and looked around. Her heart leaped. At the top of the steps, one arm in a sling, stood a man with a mop of curly hair and a wry grin on his freckled face. He seemed much older than she had remembered. And he seemed taller; she realized it was because he was so thin.

At the top of the steps, Buddy looked at her twice before recognizing her. The soft Southern belle was, my God, gone forever. The girl standing there was unquestionably Claire—he could tell by the way she held herself—but she was a very different woman. This one was leaner in the body and firmer in the face. Her hair was short, which was too bad because he liked long hair on a woman.

But there was an undeniable magnetism about her and, though her movements as she walked up the steps suggested self-reliance, even a kind of toughness, they were unquestionably feminine.

They stood for a moment, nose to nose, smiling at each other. And then they embraced, two strangers who realized that they had come to know each other very well.

CHAPTER SIXTEEN

FINAL FLIGHTS

THE LIGHT WAS blinding and the noise assaulted her ears with a volume of sound louder than anything she had ever heard. Galina felt a new and sharp sense of fear. It was as if every sense was being battered and overwhelmed. The little PO-2 biplane rocked in swirling, turbulent pre-dawn air.

The PO-2s were the leading edge of the vast offensive launched April 16, 1945, by ten Soviet air armies, more than two million ground troops, and sixty-five hundred tanks and guns.

The thought that the regiment of little biplanes was actually the vanguard of the forces to cross the Oder and crush the German Reich was awesome and humbling. It was also frightening.

The artillery and troop positions the PO-2s had been ordered to attack were savagely defended by batteries of 88-mm. antiaircraft and rapid-firing 40-mm. cannons that filled the sky around them with orange and red explosions. Two PO-2s blew up immediately and one turned over on its back and, trailing flames, spiraled toward the ground.

The antiaircraft fire faltered, though it didn't stop, when the Russian artillery barrage began. The enormous sound of the massed Soviet guns shook the earth and inflamed the sky. At the same time, huge searchlights, pointed directly at the German positions, snapped on and created an ocean of white light.

"Thirty seconds more," Valya called. "Steer two degrees to the right."

"I can't see!" Galina shouted, struggling against panic in the nightmare of blinding light and deafening sound.

"I can see. My head's in the cockpit," Valya called. She peered at the compass and turn-and-bank indicator on the instrument panel and checked her stopwatch. "Straighten up now. Right wing up a little. Now. Pull the wire."

The bombs fell free. As she had done a hundred times before, Galina banked sharply, hit the throttle, and pushed the nose down. A giant explosion erupted above her. She heard the flak fragments puncture the wings and fuselage.

Valya cried out. "What is it, Valya?" Galina cried. "Are you hit?"

"My arm," Valya gasped. "I'll try to bind it up with my belt."

"We'll be home soon," Galina said. "Just hang on." There was another explosion, and another. The plane slewed sideways and, as she recovered, a sharp pain shot through the left side of her torso. She kept her nerve and remained clearheaded, but it hurt her to breathe in or out.

"Pees-ann!" she swore. She still wasn't sure that it was a swear word, but she had grown accustomed to using it as one. The new wound was probably trifling, but it made her angry. It meant that both she and Valya would have to go to the mobile hospital the VVS had set up behind the lines and receive first-aid.

She had counted on being healthy, even though she would be weary, when she returned from the pre-dawn sorties. The forecast was for heavy early-morning fog that would ground all aircraft till at least noon.

And she was determined that she and Misha would use those early morning hours to make love. It would be senseless and stupid to wait any longer. She had suggested it and he had agreed.

They had been reunited the previous afternoon. Major Kravchenko was briefing them in the bunker dug at the edge of their new airfield when they heard the familiar snarl of the Yak engines coming in to land. It had been rumored all day that Viktor's Yak regiment would arrive to encamp in a nearby clearing and the rumor, for once, was proven true.

When she heard the sound, Galina's head snapped up, as did those of several of the women. One was Larissa, who had recovered from her chest wound and had rejoined the regiment. Larissa would be happy to see Viktor again. It wouldn't take *them* long to find a place to make love; you could be sure of that.

At that moment, Galina resolved to tell Misha—oh God, she hoped he was all right; the thought sent a surge of panic through her—she would tell Misha that it was time for *them* to do it, too. How many chances would they have?

What was that old Russian saying? Misha always joked about Viktor's inexhaustible supply of Russian sayings. "Old too soon; smart too late." In wartime, it should be amended to "Dead too soon . . ."

"Comrade Lieutenants, and I must particularly mention Galina, Larissa, and Valeria, you will pay attention." Major Kravchenko's eyes were angry, her voice sharp and reproving. "This is a historic moment. We have been given the honor of being the first, the *first*. Do you understand what that means? We, a regiment of women, are leading the final attack on the Hitlerites.

"That should be enough to galvanize every one of you," she continued. "And, if that isn't enough, try to remember that we are now a Guards Regiment."

Chastened, Galina dropped her eyes. A general had come to their last airfield, assembled them, and told them that they had been named an honored Guards Regiment in belated recognition of their skilfulness, bravery, and devotion to duty. After the award was announced, their new regimental flag was unfurled and every member of the regiment approached, knelt, and kissed it.

Kravchenko spoke in a softer voice. "Your duty comes first, Comrades. You know that. However, following the briefing, you may, if you wish, go and join your male friends in the Yak regiment for an hour. *One hour*. No more. We fly tonight."

The PO-2 had drifted slightly to the right and Galina moved it back on course and leveled the wings. She realized she was tired, but she was determined it wouldn't keep her from her rendezvous. She had been thinking and dreaming about making love with Misha for months now. She knew it would be wonderful, even though Misha had amused her by becoming nervous and telling her not to expect too much the first time.

"This isn't something you can hurry, you know," he said.

She and Larissa had been practically neck and neck as they ran to the Yak field. Valeria was a few steps behind them.

Viktor, who always seemed to have an extrasensory apparatus that told him when women were near, was the first to see them. He barked a command to Mikhail, who tumbled out of the cockpit of his Yak and started running toward Galina.

"I can't believe it!" he shouted. As he took her in his arms his voice fell to a whisper. "I just can't believe it. I thought I'd never see you again."

"I'm here, my love, I'm here," she said. "Stop talking and kiss me."

They rocked back and forth together, mouth to mouth, and then held each other closely without speaking. Finally he spoke: "I hope we can spend some time . . ."

"Listen, Misha," she said. "We're flying tonight. Leading the offensive. It's a great honor. You were scheduled to replace us at dawn, but the weather report is for heavy fog by then. We think the forecast is accurate; you can feel the temperature dropping already."

He held her face in his hands. "Why do I care about a weather report?"

She placed two fingers over his lips. "You will if you keep quiet and listen to me. If it works out as they've forecast, I'll be finished my sorties by dawn and you won't be able to take off until noon. That will give us five or six hours together. I'll wash up and come to you. You find us a place to be alone. Inside or outside, I don't care. We'll make love then. It's time, Misha. I don't want to wait any longer."

His heart beat faster. "I don't want to wait any longer either and I'll find a place, but—are you sure?"

"Don't be silly, darling," she said. "I want you. How plain do I have to be? Shall I say I want you to fuck me?"

She giggled as she felt him recoil. Leaning back in his arms, she said: "This is *really* silly. Now I'm the one who's acting as the aggressor and suddenly *you've* become the prim virgin."

He smiled. "I'll make it even sillier. I'll say, this is so sudden. I'll find us a place, Galishka. I won't be able to budge Viktor out of his quarters. He'll be in there with Larissa. We may wind up outside after all. If that's the best there is, I'll borrow some extra blankets—Viktor can't deny me *those*—and make us a nest in the woods over there. And I'll be waiting for you to land."

"As you always have."

"As I always have."

It hurt worse now when she breathed and she was feeling very tired. That rekindled her anger; she was damned if a stupid flak wound was going to keep her from making love with Misha. She would simply get first-aid treatment. They would bind it up and then she would wash up thoroughly. She knew she had blood on her chest because she could feel its wetness. It felt cold in the night air and she began to shiver.

"Valya, are you all right?" It was hard for her to speak.

"I'm all right, Galina, just a little dizzy," Valya said. "Turn five degrees to the right—the right, not the left, Galina. You should see the oil drums at the field in about two minutes. Galina?"

"I heard you. Oil drums in two minutes."

"What's the matter with your voice, Galina? Are you all right?"

"I'll be all right. Let's—save our energy."

They landed hard and bounced. Valya grabbed the dual-control stick in the rear cockpit and helped Galina hold it back tight as the biplane thumped onto the grass a second time and settled in. After they had taxied a few yards, Galina collapsed, her vision and coordination gone. The PO-2 slewed around in a circle and Valya, turning the ignition switch, cut the engine. People started running toward the plane.

"Oh, God, no!" Mike yelled. He sprinted forward, pushing others out of the way. *This happened before,* he thought. *Goddamnit, once was enough! Enough!*

When he reached the biplane, Valya had crawled out and fallen on the grass. Mike noted, automatically, that the PO-2's fabric was punctured in at least a dozen places. He climbed up on the wing, as he had done before, reached into the cockpit, and dragged Galina out. Her flight jacket was soaked with blood and her face was a chalky white.

She recovered consciousness as he laid her on a stretcher two women medics brought to the plane. Her eyes opened and saw him. One small, cold hand reached up to touch his cheek.

"Pees-ann," she whispered. Her eyes half-closed and her hand slipped onto her chest. One medic yanked open Galina's jacket and cut open her underwear. Galina's breasts and torso were saturated with blood. There was a jagged hole under her heart. Her eyes were half-open and fixed. The older medic felt for a pulse in her throat; the other felt her wrist. They looked at each other and began turning away.

"Wait a minute!" Mike shouted, summoning up the useless words that people use in such circumstances, knowing they are useless. "Don't just leave her! *Do* something! Take her to the hospital!"

The older medic looked at Mike. "I'm sorry. The lieutenant is dead." They turned to Valya, who was holding her arm and weeping. Two crew members started to pick up Galina's stretcher. He batted their hands away and fell to his knees beside her on the wet grass.

Dawn was breaking but the rolling fog was too heavy for the sun to penetrate. In the gray light, Galina's face seemed made of ivory. He felt for her pulse. There was none. He placed his mouth against hers to see if she was breathing. She wasn't. He sat up and looked at her for a long moment. Then he gently closed her eyes. One eyelid started to open again and he applied gentle pressure to close it.

It was as if she were a doll, a beautiful doll dressed in military flight clothes, clothes that needed cleaning up. But, he realized as he watched, this really wasn't Galina at all. This was a shell; the real person, the vibrant woman he loved, was gone.

Two strong hands grasped him beneath his armpits and pulled him to his feet. "Go back to your quarters, Mikhail Stepanovich," Kravchenko said. "There's nothing for you to do here." She breathed a ragged sigh. "We've taken very heavy casualties tonight. Five of my crew members, my *girls*, are dead. Seven more are wounded. We have to take care of the wounded and get ready to fly again.

"I liked Galina, I *loved* her," Kravchenko said, unaccountably glaring at him. "We're not like you Yak men and your casual male friendships. Here we are close, very close to each other. Galina was one of my daughters."

The older woman took Mike by the shoulders, turned him around, and pushed him in the back to start him walking toward his airfield. When he had left, Kravchenko gestured curtly to the stretcher-bearers to remove Galina's body. She couldn't bear to see the girl's face turn that detestable blue-gray color she had seen so often.

When Mike arrived at the Yak field, Viktor was waiting at the door of the barn the regiment had commandeered. "I heard," he said. "I'm very sorry. Larissa made it back all right; I gather many didn't. Larissa won't be coming to stay with me this morning; she said it wouldn't seem right. I agreed. How do you feel, Mike? That's a stupid question. I mean: Are you all right? Can you function? They expect this fog to lift around noon."

Mike stood silently, head down, for a few minutes. "I don't know how I feel," he said. "Mostly numb. How I'll feel later I don't know. Don't care." He looked up. "You're asking if I can fly?"

He shrugged. "Sure, why not? What else would I do? Sit here and look at—what? I'll fly."

The Luftwaffe intercepted the message sent to the American bomber groups by U.S. General Carl Spaatz on April 16, the same day that the Russians launched their offensive against Berlin.

Major Paul Hofmann read the transcription and chuckled mirth-lessly. The principal part of Spaatz's message read:

The advances of our ground forces have brought to a close the strategic air war waged by the United States Strategic Air Forces and the Royal Air Force Bomber Command. It has been won with a decisiveness be-coming increasingly evident as our armies overrun Germany.

So, Hofmann mused, from the American point of view the air war was over. There would be no more bombing of German cities by the Flying Fortresses. The British Lancasters had stopped their indiscrim-inate area bombing earlier.

German industry was in ruins; the gasoline tanks of German tanks and airplanes were starving for fuel. The American and British ar-mies were reported to be near the western bank of the Elbe but showed no sign of marching on Berlin. From the East, a vast horde of Russian barbarians had crossed the Oder and were advancing on the suffering, battered capital city of the Reich.

The Luftwaffe had hoarded enough gasoline to supply some two thousand combat aircraft, all but one or two hundred of them bomb-ers, to help repel the Eastern invaders. After a dozen sorties or so, they would run out of gas.

So it was doubly ironic, in these final days, that a handful of Luft-waffe pilots were flying the incomparable ME-262, the jet fighter that represented a giant leap forward in aviation technology—one that consumed a crude, low-grade fuel that was still available.

Yet Hofmann's jet fighter group had been severely depleted by the masses of American fighters that had tried to defend the B-17s and B-24s. Though the 262s could sail through their formations with ease, there were so many enemy airplanes in the sky that 262s were shot down by lucky, random hits or in collisions with other airplanes. Many of the 262s were being caught by free-ranging American fight-ers as the jets were taking off and landing.

The losses had little to do with the pilots' skills. Oberst Johannes Steinhoff, who was unbeatable in the sky, had crashed and burned on takeoff when the wheels of his 262 had hit a bomb crater. General Adolf Galland was wounded and shot down a week later by a P-47 Thunderbolt that fell on him from above just after he had shot down two American medium bombers. Both men had survived but were out of action.

Oberst Karl von Moltke, who had succeeded them, died when his

262 collided with a Flying Fortress. Most of the flyable jets were lost in that aerial battle.

Now Hofmann commanded a squadron of seven ME-262s. They were being flown by the best of the Luftwaffe's surviving fighter pilots. They, like him, wanted to keep flying the superplane until the last possible moment. It was absurd, considering their present situation, but flying the 262 gave him and the others a towering sense of superiority.

And they had the freedom to spend their final days doing what they wanted. Hofmann's unit had become a band of free-lancers, operating from an autobahn adjacent to a wooded area. Orders coming from above were so confused and fragmentary that they couldn't sensibly be understood, much less obeyed.

There was really only one place left to go and fight. Hofmann was from Berlin; he had gone to the *gymnasium* there and, later, studied architecture until this ridiculous second world war had started. He had lost his younger brother there when his family home had been destroyed by the Amis' bombing. His parents, thank God, had escaped to the south.

Berlin was also the home of two other members of the squadron. There might be no doubt as to the outcome of the Russian invasion but Hofmann decided—and his squadron mates agreed—that they would do what they could to make the enemy pay the highest possible price for desecrating the city.

So, early the next morning, they would take off to attack the oncoming Russian bombers and fighter-bombers. They could easily pick them off from above and then speed away before the Red Air Force's high-cover fighters could intercept them.

But, he warned his fellow pilots, they would have to be very careful, as well as lucky, not to get shot down by their own flak. Though the German war machine was in fatal disrepair, the volume and accuracy of its antiaircraft fire had never been greater. As one captured Ami bomber pilot had told them: "You could walk on that stuff."

Hofmann smiled at the briefing and told his squadron mates to shoot down at least one hundred of the barbarians before falling to their own flak. If each of us can get ten, he said, it will have been worth it. After all, who wants to live forever?

Mike flew his first series of sorties like a robot. The thump of the big 37-mm. cannon was heavier than the 20-mm. guns the Yak had carried before it had been refitted. Skimming over the ground, he and

Boris, his wingman, punched holes through tanks and into artillery batteries. Mike tried to summon up a feeling of vengefulness or at least satisfaction at smashing the enemy, but his emotions were dead.

So were any normal feelings of fear. The hailstorm of flak that came up to meet them was heavier than anyone had ever seen in low-altitude operations. The danger of collisions was equally great. There were so many Soviet airplanes at all altitudes that each regiment flew within strictly-drawn channels.

Viktor had told the pilots at their briefing that there would be as many as two hundred Soviet airplanes per mile of front. In all, he had said, the VVS would put up seventy-five hundred aircraft for the assault on Berlin.

When he ran out of ammunition and knew that his *zveno* would be low on fuel, Mike turned, with Boris still on his wing, and headed for home. It took perhaps fifteen minutes to rearm and refuel the Yaks. Then they took off and returned to the front. They flew six sorties before nightfall.

Within three days, the ground forces had advanced so far that the Yak regiment was ordered to move up. Being closer to the front consumed less fuel and allowed more sorties to be flown. But the regiment had lost seven airplanes to antiaircraft fire.

"You were right," Viktor told Mike. "Without the armorplate of the Shturmoviks, we can't withstand much fire from underneath. But there isn't much we can do about it." He shrugged. "Except hope that we can knock out those ground batteries."

It was evening and they were sitting, with Boris Gusarov, in the ruins of a bombed-out house that was being used for shelter. A tarpaulin had been stretched overhead to keep out wind and rain, and camouflage netting had been strung over it. Viktor had taken over a small storage room for his office and personal quarters.

Viktor turned up the oil lamp and looked at Mike hesitantly, obviously unsure for a moment whether he should say what he had on his mind.

"What is it?" Mike asked.

"I thought you would like to know. A message came from Major Kravchenko that her regiment had a graveside ceremony for the girls, the women, who were lost that night. They pay tribute to the, um, the ones who were lost, and then they fire a salute with their pistols. I thought you would like to know."

Mike nodded. "Thanks."

"Well, let's have a drink," Viktor said wearily. "And go to bed. We'll be flying again in a few hours."

Viktor waited till Boris left for the common room that was being used as sleeping quarters for the pilots and turned to Mike. "I also wanted to tell you. Spirin has been nosing around again, wanting to talk to you. I told him you weren't feeling well and this wasn't the time to raise the question of citizenship again. Try to stay away from him till we figure something out."

"It isn't important."

"It *is* important, Mike," Viktor said severely. "I don't want to see you thrown into a labor camp, or worse. You may be officially a Hero, but I don't like the way they're watching you."

Of course, considering the losses we're taking on these low-level missions, Viktor thought, *it may not matter.*

Mike's emotional shell cracked open on his next sortie. As they neared the German positions, three sleek, gray-green airplanes of a kind Mike had never seen flashed by them at a speed he could hardly believe. By the time he swiveled around to look for them, they had swooped onto a *zveno* of Yaks nearby and shot down two of them.

Mike hesitated, decided against evasive action—they might easily plow into another VVS formation—and grimly put his gunsight on a German artillery battery. His cannon thumped and he saw an 88-mm. artillery piece fly into pieces. As he started a wide turn to the left, as prescribed, the gray-green ghosts flashed by again.

A cannon shell smashed his instrument panel and, beside him, Boris' Yak blew up in a cloud of red and black. Reflexively, Mike fought to regain control of his Yak and turned for home. The appearance of the ghost-like enemy airplanes had dissolved the Russian formations. Planes were milling around in all directions like frightened geese.

His windscreen was covered with oil and Mike could hardly see when he skidded in for a landing. Once again, the regiment had taken heavy casualties. Hollow-eyed and pale, Viktor asked him if he could confirm the report that Boris' plane had blown up. Mike said he saw it happen.

"These new enemy fighters seem to have some new kind of propulsion system," Viktor said. "They have no propellers. I've asked VVS about them. They say they know about them; there are only a few left, they say. They hope to capture one to study."

Mike nodded, went into the barracks room, and sank down on his mattress. They hadn't had time to assemble their bunk beds; mattresses were laid in even rows along both sides of the room. Some of the pilots were stretched out, sleeping. A few, like Mike, were sitting on their mattresses with their heads in their hands.

Boris' mattress was beside Mike's. Protruding from Boris' bag at the head of the mattress was the end of his saxophone. Mike reached over, took it out, and began polishing the metal against his sleeve. He looked at it for a long time. Boris was, *had been*, a fine, promising young musician. He had possessed, Mike believed, a prodigious talent. Men died—and women, too, he reminded himself—every day. But it seemed a peculiarly terrible thing for a musician's talent to die, too.

Mike adjusted the mouthpiece and tried to blow in the instrument. It made a honking noise and a pilot sitting nearby looked up and glared at him. Mike carefully replaced the saxophone in Boris' bag. Then he bent over and, after a while, began crying quietly in hard, painful sobs. He cried for Galina, for Boris, and for himself.

It was already a good morning's work. The 262 contained an hour's worth of internal fuel but, in the first twenty minutes of combat, Paul Hofmann's *ketten* of three jets had shot down thirteen of the Russian airplanes. Most of them had been Yaks. They would have registered at least three more kills if the armorplating on the accursed Shturmoviks hadn't been so thick. The damned things were like porcupines.

It was time to return to their landing area. It might, by now, be under attack, but there was no place else to go. The Luftwaffe ace led one last strike on the Yaks and Shturmoviks swarming about below. He and his two wingmen blew up another Yak and an American-made Aircobra—he hadn't seen many of those—and swung away.

He looked up to ensure that an LA-7 wasn't diving on him from above. When he looked down again it was too late. A Yak was coming head-on. He plowed into it and there was a giant explosion. He felt an instant of pain before the world disappeared.

Fits of weeping overcame him from time to time and Mike had to go outside and tramp around in the darkness to avoid being seen by his fellow pilots. Once, the bloodless Captain Spirin had tried to approach him but Mike snarled angrily and waved him away. Before he walked outside again, he saw Spirin talking animatedly to Viktor.

That night, Viktor drew him into his room and asked: "If you're going to fly I need to assign you a new wingman. But I don't want to risk him if you're really not up to it."

"What else is there for me to do?" Mike demanded.

"But can you, you know, function all right?"

"Yes."

In the morning, the battered regiment of Yaks, now fifty percent smaller than when it arrived at its present field, took off. Three of Mike's four-plane *zveno* survived the expected hailstorm of flak, knocked out concrete pillboxes and artillery batteries, and returned to the field.

As he neared it, he saw streams of black smoke rising from the ground. He told the pilots on the fighter channel to overfly the field so they could see what had happened. The field had been heavily bombed and strafed. It was pitted with craters. A dozen Yaks lay wrecked and smoking. The house lay in ruins.

Mike circled the field, looking up and around carefully. The enemy aircraft had left. He told his fellow pilots to peel off and land one at a time. "Be very careful," he said.

The first Yak struck a crater, cartwheeled, and burst into flame. The pilot struggled out with his uniform afire. The second managed to land safely. The third landed on a nearby road and ripped off a wing when it struck a tree. Mike opted to land on the field, did his best to avoid craters, jinked sideways at the last instant to avoid one, and then, as the nose came up and his view of what lay ahead of him vanished, settled onto the grass.

He was down safely, he thought. But, at the last possible moment, one wheel struck a crater and he nosed over, crumpling the propeller and one wing and striking the bridge of his nose against the windscreen.

Viktor, his face smeared with soot, walked toward him as he climbed quickly from the cockpit. "Well, that makes it just about complete," he said. "The third *zveno* was gassing up and rearming when a squadron of JU-88s arrived. Those Germans must have brass balls. Or did. I'm sure our people have caught them by now."

"They knocked out everything, it looks like," Mike said.

"Everything," Viktor said. "We'll have three or four Yaks left; maybe ten pilots. We lost our stores of fuel, parts, everything."

"What happens now?"

"We managed to reconnect the phone wires and get through to one of our mobile command posts. We're to wait for further orders." Viktor flung his hands up. "Who knows? Maybe we'll be given rifles and told to start walking." He looked at Mike seriously. "It wouldn't be a bad idea for you to do just that. When we get a bit further to the west.

"Meantime," he said, "the news isn't all bad. There are two good things, in fact. Our nosy commissar friend, Spirin, is dead. Blown right off his feet just as he was writing a report; probably telling his superior that it's time to arrest me for consorting with foreigners."

"What's the second good thing?"

"They didn't hit my vodka. Let's open a new bottle and have a drink."

Sitting in his command post in a commandeered castle on the Spree River, Marshal Ivan Stepanovich Konev called Supreme Headquarters on his new high-frequency telephone.

Stalin was on the other end within seconds. Konev reported with satisfaction that his tank armies were advancing deep into Germany in a northwesterly direction west of the Spree and were almost south of Berlin.

Stalin interrupted him. "Things are going hard with Zhukov," the dictator said. "He's still hammering at the defenses east of Berlin on the Seelow Heights. Could we route his mobile forces through your sector so he could strike at Berlin from the south?"

Konev spoke quickly. "Comrade Stalin, that would take a lot of time and complicate things as well," he said. "We're in good shape; I can turn both my tank armies north toward Berlin. Let me offer a reference point for the maneuver; the town of Zossen. It's about twenty-five kilometers south of the city."

"What map are you looking at?" Stalin demanded.

"The scale is one to two hundred thousand."

"Hold on." In a moment, Stalin came back on the line. "I have it. Do you know that Zossen is the headquarters of the German General Staff?"

"Yes, I do."

"All right. Turn your tank armies toward Berlin." The phone went dead. Konev shouted with delight, clapped his hands together, and called his tank commanders on the high-frequency line. He told them to turn quickly northward, not to worry about counterattacks from the flanks. They would obey but he knew what they would be thinking. *Disregard the danger of counterattacks on my flank? Easy for you to say, Comrade Marshal. It's not your flanks they'll be attacking.*

Konev hung up the phone and sat back. If he moved fast enough, he could beat Zhukov to Berlin. It would be he, not his adversary, who would be in the history books as the conqueror of Berlin.

* * *

"We will take that ridge now! *Now*, do you understand?" Marshal Georgi Zhukov shouted at his commanders. His heavy face was red; veins stood out on his forehead and his neck bulged over the collar of his tunic.

He saw his victory slipping into Konev's hands and it made him frantic. The mighty forces of the Second Belorussian Front were stalled at the village of Seelow, east of Berlin. Just over the hill, still tantalizingly beyond his grasp, was the Küstrin-Berlin highway and an open road to the capital.

To make matters worse, the Supreme Commander had embarrassed him by phoning and reproving him.

"If you can't get the job done, maybe Konev can," Stalin had said. When the dictator hung up, Zhukov called in his commanders and exploded.

"Who's holding us up?" he yelled. "A bunch of amateurs, that's who. Luftwaffe parachute men without infantry training. Some of them are boys; those prisoners we just took were what?—sixteen, seventeen years old. My God, their officers are former pilots! *Pilots!* And *that's* the bunch that's holding us up!"

"Comrade Marshal, they also have hundreds of 88s looking down the ridge at us," one of his commanders said quietly. "And even if most of those paratroops are only partially trained, they're dug in with machine guns and those damnable *panzerfausts*, the bazookas. They're taking a heavy toll of our tanks."

"*I* will take a heavy toll of my commanders if that ridge isn't taken today!" Zhukov shouted. "A lot of you will be in penal companies tomorrow if your units don't get through today! Be warned!"

"We have a lion on our hands," one commander said softly to another as they left. "And it seems Comrade Stalin has stuck a thorn in his paw. We'd better take whatever losses we have to and get it done. Or he'll have the two of us leading infantry assaults the day after."

A new assault began hours later. Russian guns and mortars began pounding the hillside, searchlights snapped on, and hundreds of tanks clanked forward. The heavy guns plowed up the earth and forced the teenagers in their foxholes to press hard against the earth. Then a huge roar erupted behind the frightened paratroopers and hundreds of German 88s with depressed barrels fired point-blank into the approaching tanks.

The Russian tanks were blasted, caught fire, blew up. The infantrymen who ran forward from the tanks were cut down by machine gun and rifle fire. There was another assault and then another. Russian tanks were destroyed by the score and the bottom of the slope was littered with dead Russian infantrymen.

But, after repeated batterings, the German fire began to wane. Many guns had been shattered, some ran out of ammunition. The youngsters in their foxholes continued to destroy Russian tanks with their *panzerfaust* bazookas, but innovative Russian tankmen tore bedsprings from all the beds they could find in the surrounding villages and mounted the springs on the front of the tanks. If the bazooka shells didn't bounce off, the bedsprings at least cushioned the shock of the explosions.

The technique proved to be effective, the tanks came on, and the parachutists had to retreat. When, mindless of its losses, the Russian war machine continued to grind forward, the parachutists and former pilots broke and ran.

Zhukov sighed with relief. The race was on again.

The remnants of the Yak regiment arrived in a transport at a village south of Berlin near the Teltow Canal. When they climbed out of the Dakota, Viktor Markov was met by a Colonel Vladimir Lisov, a burly, hard-faced man with muscular arms and hands.

They exchanged salutes and shook hands. The survivors of the bombed-out Yak regiment had been transferred south to a reconstituted Shturmovik regiment, part of Krasovsky's Second Air Army, attached to Konev's First Ukrainian Front.

Lisov was the regimental commander; Viktor would be second in command. His men would have one day, no more, to familiarize themselves with the handling of the heavily-armed and heavily-armored tank-killer.

Immediately after landing, they attended a two-hour briefing by Lisov on flying the airplane, following proven Shturmovik techniques in combat, and on the mission they would fly the following morning. They would give support to General Pavel Rybalko's Third Guards Tank Army in an assault against the fortifications on the northern bank of the Teltow Canal.

"It'll be different, we can be sure of that," Viktor said when they left the briefing. "At least you've flown the airplane once; I gather it handles like a truck."

"It's surprisingly maneuverable; it turns pretty tight," Mike said. "But you're right, it's heavy in the hands and it'll feel a lot more so when you're used to the lightness of the Yak controls. But there's one very good thing about it that we ought to emphasize to our people."

"The armor."

"Yes, the armor," Mike said. "The Yak's a piece of cardboard compared to the Shturmovik. Tell the men there's a good reason why the plane's so slow and heavy. It's slow and heavy because of the armorplate underneath and behind the pilot. He gives up speed but he gains a lot of personal safety."

Mike had found he could function, even talk clearly when he had to. Inside his chest, however, lay a large, cold stone. It hurt to breathe and he could eat very little. Sometimes, a shimmering crescent of a kind he had never seen before appeared in his line of vision. His mother had periodically suffered from migraine headaches and she once told him that a shimmering object appeared in her line of sight when a headache came on.

Mike didn't experience the migraine headache—his headaches were the result of vodka hangovers—but he realized that he was being afflicted by part of the migraine syndrome. It would have been crippling if one had come on when he was flying. But it happened only when he was free to think, and he found he could usually rid himself of it by massaging his temples for ten minutes or so.

He was wretched, but he could function and, because Viktor needed him, he did.

There was no airfield, as such, for the Shturmoviks. They would use a paved highway for takeoffs and landings. The airmen were billeted in villagers' houses. Some of the German villagers had been shot by the approaching Russian ground troops; their bodies had been thrown into the woods.

Mike's emotions were in a state of ferment. He welcomed the new combat assignment because its pressures would demand complete concentration. There would be no way to think of anything else. He disliked the idea of occupying the homes of civilians who had recently been shot—murdered was a better word—but, at the same time, his feelings for the Germans had crystalized into an icy hatred. It was the Germans who had brought Adolf Hitler to power and supported him. It was the Germans who had started this unbelievably horrible war. It was the Germans who had killed Galina.

Mike disliked the days but he hated the nights. Combat would keep his mind occupied during the days, but there was no defense against the dreams that came at night. Except, only briefly, the stupor provided by vodka. Before going to bed, he drank his vodka ration and cadged an extra quarter-pint or more from Viktor. Viktor worried that Mike was drinking too much to be alert during the mornings, but he gave him what he asked for.

Still, as he had done so many times before, Mike woke at three o'clock, weeping. He had been talking to Galina in a dream and she had suddenly disappeared in a fog. He called and called to her and began crying. A fellow pilot called to him and told him to please shut up. He sat up and held his head, which was aching horribly. He wished dawn would come soon. He could get in the new Shturmovik, the flying tank, and kill Germans.

The obstacles facing the tank army were strong ones. On the northern bank of the canal there were windowless houses whose walls were a meter or more thick. Part of the bank was occupied by reinforced concrete factory buildings whose blank sides faced the canal. The canal itself was wide and deep and the bridges that were still standing had been mined.

Enhancing these natural obstacles were trenches, concrete pillboxes housing heavy guns, self-propelled guns, and dug-in tanks.

To defend the canal, the Germans had herded fifteen thousand soldiers together into a small area. They had mortars, five hundred machine guns, and thousands of *panzerfaust* bazookas.

The Germans waiting for the assault of the mighty Russian force facing them—heavy artillery, mortars, *katyushas*, Shturmoviks, and hundreds of thousands of savage soldiers—knew that theirs was a last-ditch stand. If they were defeated, Berlin, close behind them, would be open to the barbarians. And if they broke and ran, they would be caught by waiting SS men and dragged off to SS tribunals, after which they would be shot or hanged.

Contemplating his fate, one fifteen-year-old boy in the Volkssturm battalion began weeping. The elderly man beside him, a white-haired World War I veteran, spoke sternly. "Stop that crying. I'd say you were acting like a girl, but some of our girls are putting the men to shame."

"I don't want to die," the boy protested. He looked at the old man with angry, tear-filled eyes. "I'm too young to die."

"If you die, you'll know you died defending the Fatherland," the old man said. "What better death can a man ask for?"

"It's easy for you to say," the boy said bitterly. "You're old, you've lived your life. I'm only fifteen." He began snuffling again.

"Let me ask you something, young man. Can you go back and live yesterday if you want to?"

"Of course not."

"Can you go forward and live in the future?"

"There won't be any future."

"That's not what I'm asking you. Can you, right now, jump into the future?"

"No, of course not."

"Then the only life you have, that you can live, is right now, this minute, isn't it? Isn't it?"

The boy shrugged. "I guess."

"So it really doesn't matter whether we live ten years or a hundred years. All we know of life, all we can live of it, is the present moment —right now. A Roman emperor said that a couple thousand years ago. Think about it. Life is just this little piece of time we're living now. It's the same for all of us."

Someone pointed and yelled. "Look! Those planes are coming again!"

Absorbing heavy losses in men, tanks, and airplanes, General Rybalko's tank army crossed the canal, smashed through the defenses, killed most of the German defenders, and plowed on toward Berlin. Later, the marshals would argue who got there first. Other Russian ground forces flowed around them westward to surround the city and drive toward the Elbe.

Mike's Shturmovik was hit by an 88-mm. shell on his seventh sortie. The explosion blew away the instrument panel and the left wing of his airplane. His left arm was punctured by flak fragments in three places. He bailed out at low altitude, landed hard, and broke his forearm.

The following day, Colonel Lisov was killed leading a Shturmovik formation and Viktor became regimental commander. When Mike returned from the mobile hospital unit with a light cast on his arm and his arm in a sling, Viktor drew him into the room of the house he was using as his office and sleeping quarters.

"This is your chance," Viktor said. "I'm ordering you to take it. You see those artillery and infantry units going by? They're heading west; they'll meet very little opposition in that direction. The hard fighting will be north of here, on the outskirts of Berlin."

"What are you saying?" Mike asked.

"I'm saying that it's time to bail out, literally, Mike. Out of Russia, the Soviet Union, back to your people. Walk west. Our VVS reports say your people are at the banks of the Elbe. You can be there in a few days, a week at most. Rejoin your people. Here." He rummaged about in a closet.

"I've packed some things for you, a light bag with a couple days' food rations and some vodka. And here. You have an arm in a sling so it's clear you've been wounded. But you should carry a weapon for looks. This is the rifle we've joked about. It's a 7.62 bolt-action Mosin Nagant. There's ammunition in the pouch if you really need it. Leave now, Mike."

They stared at each other. "Come with me," Mike said.

"I can't. Your people would only send me back and you can imagine what would happen to me then. But I wouldn't leave, anyway. I'm a Russian for good or ill, probably both, and I love this huge disaster of a country." He smiled faintly. "Well, it's not really a country. It's an empire, one that'll grow a lot bigger now."

"I'll never forget you."

"You'll forget me, Mike. There's an old Russian saying. Only women and elephants never forget."

Mike grinned in spite of himself. "Actually, I think that's from, let me think, Saki. And I think it says women and elephants never forget an injury."

"Really? Somebody must be peddling bogus Russian sayings."

"Somebody certainly has been." Mike's face softened. "I'll never forget you, Viktor. And, with this new alliance we have, our countries will be friends. We'll be able to travel, see each other."

Viktor shook his head slowly. "No, Mike, no. You've learned so much about us; try to understand one more thing. We've become immensely powerful. The fool Hitler did what no one on earth could have done; he drew all the parts and pieces of the Russian empire together. He made people who hate each other fight side by side. He made us strong. And America will be our next enemy, Mike. You capitalists.

"We have no experience with what you call freedom, my friend. Many of us wouldn't want it if we had it. When the day comes that our republics break away, if it comes, we'll be in complete confusion; maybe we'll have civil wars, and that will be very dangerous to everyone, including you. I hope with all my heart that what you say is true, that your nation and mine will someday become friendly, that we'll be able to think and talk freely and visit each other.

"But I doubt that it'll happen in our lifetimes, Mike. Until it does, we'll be the same suspicious, paranoid, repressed Asiatic people we've been for a thousand years. I'd quote you another old Russian saying about how the more things change, the more they're the same, but you'd probably claim we stole it from the French. You're such a skeptic."

Mike's voice faltered. "I don't know what to say." Tears came to his eyes.

"Don't say anything, Mikhail. Take the rifle and your bag and go." They embraced briefly and Mike turned and walked away.

Flugkapitan Hanna Reitsch felt strangely helpless. She had been wedged, feet first, into a rear section of the fuselage of a Focke-Wulf 190 fighter that had been outfitted as a two-seater. A Luftwaffe sergeant flew as pilot in the front cockpit. Oberst-General Ritter von Greim of the Luftwaffe occupied the rear seat. Hanna lay on the metal spars inside the fuselage behind him.

Greim had been summoned to the Berlin Chancellery by Adolf Hitler. Obviously, he had to get there, but how? Berlin was surrounded by Russian armies and under heavy fire. The only hope was the Gatow Airport, unaccountably still open.

He had asked Reitsch to accompany him because she had made earlier test flights in and out of the city, landing on the roof of the flak tower near the Chancellery in a helicopter. They had planned to use the helicopter on this flight but, the previous night, the aircraft was destroyed in an American bombing raid. Still, she knew the compass headings to all possible landing points, so it was helpful to have her present.

They landed at Gatow safely, only to find that all streets and roads leading to the Chancellery were blocked by Russian troops. Before they could decide what to do, the sergeant left in the Focke-Wulf. To have remained would have invited its early destruction.

"We really have only one option," Hanna told Greim. "There's a Fieseler-Storch on the field. We'll fly it to the Brandenburg Gate and try to land there."

Greim sighed and nodded. "It's a desperate solution but I can't think of anything better. All right, Hanna. But I'll fly. I know you're a wonderful pilot but you haven't had any experience flying under fire. I have."

"With your permission, I'll stand behind you," she said. "If anything happens I'll be able to reach the stick and throttle over your left shoulder."

The waters of the Wannsee shown like silver as they buzzed

through the gathering twilight only a few feet from the surface. It was beautiful and deceptively peaceful. Brushing the treetops beyond, they thought they might be able to slip through the defenses without being seen.

A series of explosions shattered the illusion. Greim screamed in pain as an armor-piercing bullet smashed his right foot. He collapsed in his seat, fainting, and the small reconaissance airplane began drifting toward the trees.

Hanna reached across the general, grabbed the stick and throttle and, standing, managed to pull the plane back on course. Gasoline was streaming from the wing tanks. The air became thick and dark with sulphur fumes and smoke, and visibility fell nearly to zero.

Thinking quickly, she turned the Storch onto the compass heading for the flak tower, knowing she would intercept a broad highway running east and west. The Brandenburg Gate lay at its eastern end. There it was! She turned east, skimmed along the highway, closed the throttle, eased the stick back into Greim's stomach, and plopped onto the ground by the Gate.

Aware that an artillery shell or mortar could smash them any moment, she jumped from the Storch and pulled the semiconscious general out. The area around them lay in ruins. Bombed-out buildings stood like stark skeletons. Gun pillboxes squatted, smashed, with the dead gunners presumably still inside. Smoke swirled through the street.

A moment later, a German lorry pulled up. Within minutes, they were ushered into the underground Führerbunker beneath the Chancellery. Greim was taken to the bunker's operating room, where a surgeon treated his wound. Afterward, he was placed on a stretcher. As he was carried two floors below, Hanna walked beside him. Rounding a corner, Magda Goebbels, wife of the famed propaganda minister, came out of a doorway. The two women stared at each other in amazement and then embraced. Sobbing, Magda asked Hanna to come see her and her six children in their bunker quarters after Hanna had seen the Führer.

Hitler shook Greim's hands with both of his own and turned to Hanna. "Brave woman!" he said emotionally. "There is no one braver than you. You give me confidence that there is still loyalty and courage in the world."

The reason for the summons became clear. Göring had betrayed him by sending him a message saying that, without objection, he would assume command and negotiate a surrender with the Allies. Enraged, Hitler had ordered Göring's arrest.

"So, Colonel-General Greim," the dictator proclaimed, "I appoint you Chief of the Luftwaffe and promote you to the rank of Field Marshal forthwith."

In severe pain, Greim stared speechless at the Supreme Commander. To be ordered to a place from which they would probably be unable to escape, and to be told he headed an air force that no longer existed! Obviously, they were now living, as Guderian had recently remarked, in *Wolkenkuckucksheim*, cloud-cuckoo-land.

Upstairs, Frau Goebbels told Hanna that she had chosen to remain in the bunker with her children and husband rather than try to flee to safety. Magda's six children, ranging in age from four to twelve, peeked at the famous woman pilot from their double-decker bunks like inquisitive birds. For several days, in an eerie atmosphere of fantasy, Hanna told the children stories about her flights and, sometimes, repeated their favorite fairy tales. When the youngest one cried at the crash of the Russian shells bursting overhead, she told them that the sound was Uncle Führer defeating their enemies.

Hanna Reitsch had become inured to the prospect of death, but she felt an almost unendurable anguish at the plight of the children. She felt a secret disdain for Hitler's mistress, Eva Braun, who spent most of her time in their quarters polishing her fingernails, combing her hair, changing her clothes, and lamenting about "poor, poor Adolf."

At midnight April 28, Hitler staggered, white-faced, to the entrance of Hanna's room. He held a telegram in his hand. "Now Himmler has betrayed me, too," he whispered. "Even he is negotiating with the enemy. You two must leave here immediately. I have news that the Russians will storm the Chancellery tomorrow morning."

An Arado 96 had landed at the east-west axis, he said; it was waiting for them in a blast bay. As they prepared to leave, Magda Goebbels wrote a letter to her son for Hanna to take with her.

In it, she said, the "glorious ideals of Nazism are approaching their end and with them everything beautiful and noble and good I have known in my life." The children were too good for the world that would follow Germany's defeat, she wrote, "and a merciful God will understand my reasons for sparing them that sort of life."

An armored car took Hanna Reitsch and Greim to the airplane, where they were greeted by the sergeant who had flown them into Gatow. A dispatch rider urged them to take off quickly. The axis was clear of craters for four hundred yards, he said. With shells landing nearby, that could change any minute. They took off safely amid thick smoke. The whole city seemed to be afire.

As Russian tanks and troops approached the bunker two days

later, Magda and Joseph Goebbels poisoned their six children and themselves. Eva Braun bit into a cyanide capsule. Adolf Hitler shot himself through the roof of his mouth with a .380 Walther pistol in much the same manner that one hundred and one of his generals had already done. Hanna Reitsch lived on to write her memoirs.

CHAPTER SEVENTEEN

THE ROAD HOME

THE TROOPS THAT Mike accompanied on the road west were drunk. They were, apparently, from all parts of the Soviet Union. Some were dark, some blond, some swarthy and fierce-looking. Some even had yellowish skin and almond eyes.

They moved in trucks and on foot. Some of the vehicles towed guns, but there were far fewer than Mike had expected to see.

Only a few men and officers had seemed to notice him at all. Seeing his arm cast and sling, and noting that he was wearing a Hero medal and carrying a rifle, the few who approached him treated him with respect.

An artillery lieutenant, his face flushed and eyes dilated, looked him over and said: "Shot down, were you? Well, it's good to see that you wanted to pick up a rifle and join us. Shows you're one of us. If we'd had more of that spirit, we'd have won long ago."

The man's name was Tukachevsky and he had a long black mustache and glittering black eyes. He was from the Kuban, he said. He added proudly that his father had been a Cossack. He said that his father and mother had been killed by the Germans along with other people in their village. His sister had been raped. His eyes became as hard as agates as he told the story.

Mike cautiously noted that the troops straggling along the road didn't seem prepared to do battle if a German force were to appear. Tukachevsky shook his head and laughed.

"Oh, no," he said. "The Fascists that aren't dead in this sector are already prisoners. We're the second wave, in a manner of speaking. Didn't you know that? The first bunch did the fighting. They had the tanks and heavy stuff. We were supposed to be the backups. Weren't needed that much, not here. We're just being sent out to occupy the area, you know."

He gave a braying laugh. "And have fun." His face became hard. *"Blood for blood.* That's what the higher-ups said. These squareheads burned our villages and killed our men and raped our women, didn't they? Now it's our turn to pay them back. We're not just *allowed* to do it, we're *told* to do it. You didn't know that?

"You people in the air force are in a world of your own, I guess. No, here it's blood for blood. *Everything* is allowed. Comrade Stalin said that himself."

The lieutenant pointed to a tree. The body of a young man hung from the end of a rope. A sign scrawled in German was pinned to his trousers. "We didn't do that one. His own people did it. The SS strung up, hung soldiers who'd been separated from their units. Kind of people they are."

Approaching a village, the troops ahead broke into a run with shouts of glee. By the time Mike reached the first row of houses, one was on fire.

"Most of us had never seen houses built like this, made of brick instead of wood, roofs of tile instead of thatch." Tukachevsky said. "Their barns are like mansions, cut from solid timbers. The roads are even paved. Our men, some of them are just *kulaks*, peasants, tried to set fire to the bricks. Finally, they learned the house would burn if they set fire to the rafters. They set fire to the barns, too; I hated to hear the cows mooing inside, but"—he shrugged—"I can't stick my nose into everything."

There was a cacaphony of discordant musical sounds. Looking ahead, Mike saw that a piano had been dragged into the street and two soldiers were atop it, stamping on the keys. The sight made him feel sad. Ahead, a toilet had been wrenched from its fittings inside one of the houses and thrown through a window.

Within a few minutes, furniture littered the roadway. One Russian, a bottle of cognac in his hand, was wearing a formal, long-tailed morning coat. Another carried a woman's fan. A third soldier stripped and dressed in women's silk underwear, putting his own clothes on over it.

Screams broke out in several of the houses and shots rang out. An old German struggled briefly with a Russian soldier in a doorway until another soldier yanked the German's head back by the hair and shot him with a pistol.

A naked German girl ran from the back of one house toward the woods. A rifle fired and she fell into a field of tall grass.

By the time they left the village, every house was afire and nearly every female above the age of puberty had been raped, some by a dozen or more men. Some of the women were strangled afterward. At least two dozen men had been shot. Soldiers shot at but missed a small boy who escaped into the woods.

Sickened but powerless to stop the carnage, Mike walked on, his head down. At nightfall, they camped in a second village.

"Don't sleep outdoors, for God's sake, Lieutenant," Tukachevsky yelled as Mike moved toward the base of a tree. "You VVS people obviously don't know how to take care of yourself. Walk into one of the houses and take the best bed. And anything else you find there. Be careful walking in, though. Some old Herman might still have a gun. Join the fun, Lieutenant!"

Not wanting to draw attention to himself, Mike poked his head into the doorway of a small brick house backed up by a garden and stand of oak trees. It was quiet inside. The furnishings were modest but neat. There was a small couch in the living area and he thought he'd bed down there. But, to be safe, he decided to explore the rest of the house.

Quietly, he moved into the back. There was an indoor bathroom and two small bedrooms. One was empty. So was the second. But he heard a noise in the closet. Moving quickly to the side, he drew his pistol and jerked the door open.

A thin blonde woman in her thirties shrank away from him. She had a bruise on the side of her face and, he saw, the front of her dress had been torn. *"Bitte,"* she said pleadingly. *"Bitte."*

"I won't hurt you," he said in Russian. She shook her head uncomprehendingly. He repeated it in English and she cocked her head, half understanding but puzzled. He opened his hands and smiled a small smile reassuringly.

The woman edged out of the closet, looked at him carefully, and then ran to the window at the front of the house and peered outside. *"Bitte,"* she said again. She ran back into the bedroom, closed the door, moved to the bed, and pulled her dress off over her head. Then she took him by the hand, unbuckled his belt, and hurriedly began pulling his jacket off.

What in hell? he wondered. Then he realized what she was doing. Sizing him up as less dangerous than others who would enter, she wanted him to go to bed with her. He could have her body and, if she pleased him, he might spend the night with her. By doing this, she could use him as a shield against being gang-raped and injured or killed.

By now she was naked. She climbed under the covers and held out her arms to him, though the expression on her face was one of fear rather than of passion. He stood still for a moment, uncertain as to what to do. A voice shouted outside and the woman cried out to him.

Uncertainly, he removed his arm sling, stripped off his clothes, and got into bed. The woman moved quickly against him. She was trembling so hard her teeth were chattering. Instinctively, he put an arm around her and patted her shoulder and back.

Soon, her trembling stopped. As he lay quietly, she turned her head and looked at him in the darkness. Then, apparently coming to a decision, she began kissing his neck and slowly stroking his body. It had been a long time since he had had sex. He was to have made love to Galina, but that joy had been snatched away. Should he remain celibate in her memory? Would it matter? Nothing mattered really. Now the woman was kissing his body, slowly moving downward. For an instant he thought of stopping her and saying that he hadn't bathed in days. Now she was *there* and, as her warm mouth closed on him, he felt himself grow hard. *The thing has a mind of its own, a mind without a conscience.* The front door crashed open and heavy footsteps approached. The woman quickly pulled Mike on top of her, opened her legs, and slid him inside her.

Mike pulled the covers up as the bedroom door opened and a swarthy soldier stuck his head in. "Ah, comrade," the man growled. "So this church pew is taken. Will you be long?"

"It's been a long time for me," Mike answered. "I was wounded. I'll be here all night." The soldier growled in disgust and left.

"*Danke,*" the woman breathed. "*Danke.*" She tightened her grip on Mike's back and began rocking with him. Soon he came and they lay together quietly. Within a short time he was asleep. A sound woke him just before dawn as a second soldier, dead drunk, stumbled into the room. Mike ordered him away and the man left.

The woman gratefully drew him back to her again. Afterward, he sat up and looked at her. Fear returned to her eyes. *"Doch erschiessen Sie mich nicht!"* she whispered.

"Don't do what?" he asked in English.

"Don't kill . . ." she said haltingly.

"Kill who?"

She placed a hand on her breast. He felt a weary surge of sympathy. "I'm not going to kill you. *No kaput.*"

Tears filled her eyes and she threw her arms around his neck.

"Wait," he said. It was daylight and he would have to leave. Others could enter at any time. He rose, went to the back window, opened it, and looked out. There was no one in the garden and the trees were thick enough in the back for hiding.

"Quick," he said. *"Schnell."* Understanding, she rose and quickly dressed. He handed her her shawl, which she tied around her head. Then he rummaged in his bag and gave her a chunk of bread and sausage. It wasn't much but it would sustain life.

He leaned out the window again. Still no one. He motioned for her to get out. She nodded, kissed him quickly on the cheek, looked at him warmly, and climbed out. Bending low, she ran to the cover of the trees.

Mike peed in the toilet, splashed water over his face, dressed, and went outside. He fell into the straggling column alongside Tukachevsky.

"So you took my advice and had a good night," the man said, grinning. "Was it good?"

"It was very good," Mike said.

"Did you slit her throat afterward?"

Mike hesitated for an instant. Then he smiled and answered firmly, "Absolutely. From ear to ear."

"Good, good," Tukachevsky said. "You're learning. Did you set fire to the house?"

"No, I forgot that."

"Never mind. Others will come along; someone will take care of it."

They had to move aside for a column of men in ragged uniforms who were traveling in the opposite direction. The men were accompanied by guards. "Who are they?" Mike asked. "They don't look like Germans."

"They're Russians," Tukachevsky said. "They were prisoners of the Fascists."

"Why the guards? And why should they hang their heads like that? They ought to be glad."

Tukachevsky snorted. "They shouldn't have let themselves be taken prisoner. That's what our commanders say. And any of them who don't look bone-thin—well, our commanders say they must have been collaborating to be so well-fed. And anyway, they've been consorting with the enemy. They could be infected with, with bad ideas."

"So what'll happen to them?"

Tukachevsky shrugged. "They'll be tried. Some will be shot. Some will go to labor camps. Maybe some, a few, will be freed."

Later in the day, the columns took a right turn into a dusty road and they walked through a burned-out village. It was silent and desolate. A few bodies were sprawled in the roadway. Mike flinched when they walked past a wooded area. The naked bodies of a half dozen women were hanging from the trees by their ankles. Their throats had been cut.

Pleading illness, he stopped at the side of the roadway and vomited. He tried to vomit again, but only retched dryly, when they came upon a band of freed slave laborers, mostly Poles. They were starving and in rags. They smelled terrible and looked like skeletons. Most of them, too weak to walk, were lying by the roadway.

When Mike and a few others stopped to look at them, a captain wearing a medical insignia angrily waved them away. The emaciated men had been doing forced labor in an underground factory making 88-mm. shells for the Germans, he said. A medical unit would be along soon to attend them. Anyway, he said, most of them were dying and beyond help. So move along.

Hours later, an excited gabble broke out among the men up ahead and they began running forward. Another village to burn, Mike thought. More women to rape, more old men and children to kill. Are we such a low order of creatures, he wondered, that, lacking social restraints, we quickly learn to brutalize and murder each other? It seems we are—Germans, Russians, and, probably, Americans, too. And wasn't it the British who had been so notoriously brutal to their seamen and who had beaten and killed participants in Gandhi's nonviolent freedom movement in India during the days of Empire? It was something to think about later.

Now cheering broke out ahead. They were coming to a river. The men beside him began running and he joined them. Standing on the near bank—Mike's heart swelled so suddenly he felt it might burst— were a dozen American soldiers. They had just climbed out of small boats they had rowed to the eastern bank.

Mike realized it must be the Elbe. The Russian and American

soldiers were grinning and slapping each other on the back. Mike walked up to an American corporal.

"Corporal," he said. The American recoiled, startled, to hear a Russian speak English.

"Ivan!" the corporal said, extending his hand. "You speak English."

"I ought to," Mike said. "I'm an American. I'm Lieutenant Mike Gavin. I'm a pilot, I was a B-17 pilot with the 205th Bomb Group, First Division, Eighth Air Force. I want to return to my unit."

The corporal's jaw dropped. "I gotta get the sergeant," he said. He turned and pulled his sergeant away from a Russian who was trying to embrace him. "Sarge!" the corporal said excitedly. "This guy says he's an American."

"I just explained to the corporal that my name is Michael Gavin . . ." He repeated what he had said.

The sergeant's eyes crinkled skeptically. "Well, you *sound* like an American, Ivan, but some of us fought in the Ardennes and we ran across Germans who spoke good English, too." His eyes widened at the thought and he turned to the corporal. "This guy might be a German. Or a spy, a plant of some kind."

"Sergeant," Mike said, "stop the horseshit. Just take me to your commanding officer. I'm an American officer and I fucking well want to be repatriated. Now."

"Geez," the corporal said. "He sure *sounds* like a real American. I never heard a German talk just that way before."

"We'll see about that," the sergeant said sternly, putting his hands on his hips. "Okay, Lieutenant, who's Minnie Mouse's husband?"

"Mickey, for Christ's sake."

"And who always says, wait till next year?"

"The Dodgers."

"Here's one you won't get. Whatta we drink with rum, huh?"

"Coca-cola. I'll sing the 'GI Jive' for you, too, if you want. You don't? Then get your ass in gear and take me across the river, okay?"

CHAPTER EIGHTEEN

EPILOGUE: THE GENERAL

THEY LAY QUIETLY together for a while, his arm around her shoulder, her head on his chest. He felt drained, more from the talking than from the sex. Shifting images flickered across the ceiling as a breeze stirred the trees outside and the lights of passing cars illuminated the leaves.

She stirred and looked up. Her eyes were a clear blue in the half-light, as blue as Galina's had been.

"What happened when you got back?" Kathy asked. "You must have confused them."

"I did. They couldn't go to the Army manual and find a case like mine. For a while they didn't know whether to court-martial me or give me a medal or just drop me in a deep hole. Then the intelligence boys got hold of me. I was like a big box of candy to them. They couldn't get enough. They wanted to know *everything*. They'd interrogate me for hours and they'd study the transcripts and what I'd said would raise new questions and then we'd start all over again.

"After a week of it, I bitched that I wouldn't say another god-damned word until I'd called my mother and contacted my friend Buddy. They didn't know who he was. Piss-ant, I told them they were supposed to be hot-shot intelligence people—go find him.

"My mother was, well you can imagine. I told her I'd be home soon, at least for a visit, and I told the G-2 people they'd better arrange it. Two days after that, Buddy showed up himself. He was a bird colonel, I couldn't believe it. He waved some papers around from General Sloane and I was a free man for a while. We got drunk and, well you know how that goes. A lot of backslapping and maudlin stuff."

"You moved into intelligence afterward, didn't you, Michael?"

"Yes, I told them about my odyssey over a period of months, then I joined them. Went to various schools, war colleges here and abroad. Buddy became a brigadier, no less, and his unseen hand has guided me along. I went up in rank very fast, as he had. Later, I was attached to the White House for a while, then the National Security Council, supposedly became a Russian expert on weapons, culture, the whole bit."

"And you've taken up the cudgel for women in the service."

"Yes, I owed that to Galina. I'm not sure that a woman should be forced to go and fight in a war but, where no heavy lifting is concerned, I believe that women in the armed services should be able to qualify for combat positions if they want to. Certainly in the air forces. Otherwise, they'll always be second-class soldiers, lagging behind in promotions. Women don't have the quick strength that men have, but their stamina is as good or better than men's. They're certainly as smart as men, and, with today's aircraft, physical strength isn't necessary.

"Also," he said, warming to the subject, "there isn't a distinct 'front' in combat today—if there ever was. A woman pilot flying a transport in support of troops can get shot down just like an F-16 pilot. If women can drive and vote and do any kind of civilian job, they ought to be able to do the skilled jobs in the military, too. Including flying in combat."

"You've certainly spoken eloquently on that subject," Kathy said. "But, if you don't mind changing the subject, going back a bit, I apologize if this pains you very much, did you really ever get over Galina? The loss of her?"

"Not really. The sharpness of the pain lessened after a while, of course. For a long time, a very long time, I'd see a slim figure walking in the distance and my heart would stop. I'd want to run to her and look her in the face." He laughed drily. "In fact I did that a few times. The women took me for a lunatic. One ran away screaming."

He paused, thinking. "Or there would be a face in a crowd, blue eyes like hers, like yours, and my mind would turn to mush. Or I'd hear the sound of an old airplane engine; nothing really sounds like that old pop-popping five-cylinder engine of the PO-2, but I'd hear an old single-engine trainer and tears would start running down my face. Or there'd be a breeze and it would bring a scent to me—the turpentine smell of a pine woods, or a rush of jasmine from somewhere, and I'd die inside. For the thousandth, millionth time."

He took a deep breath. "The acute part of it faded after a few years. I even tried marrying a girl, probably because her voice sounded a little like Galina's. A very bad idea. We were divorced a year later. I was sorry I had put her through that. Then later, much later, I managed to find a certain happiness in thinking about Galina, the good times, the funny things. Every soldier knows how you can manage after a while to forget the horrible things about war and just remember the good things, the fun times. I was able to do that with Galina."

Kathy said: "Of course, if she'd lived, you wouldn't have been able to get her out of the Soviet Union. Or, if you'd done it somehow, you were such different people from such different backgrounds, you might not have been happy at all. You must have thought of that."

"I know," he said. "Everything you say is true. We might have been miserable, separated or together. But that's all irrelevant somehow. We were just *interrupted*. In the first flush of love."

"So she'll always be young and beautiful," Kathy said. "In your mind, your heart." She rolled sideways, pulled a Kleenex from a box, and rolled back inside his arm. At length she asked: "What about Claire?"

"She married Buddy. After my mother died, I spent some time with them down at her family home in Albany where they live. She looked wonderful; she was a great match for Buddy, more than a match in some ways. When her father died, she took over his cotton business—the WASPS had been disbanded by then, of course—and she made a real success of it. I stayed with them for a month or so the first time."

"Was it, well, *odd*, staying there with both of them?"

"You mean, was I the bastard at the family reunion? Well, it could have been that way. Claire and I had that passionate night and day together, but it was only a night and day. And she didn't belong to Buddy then, or to me, for that matter. By then she was her own woman. When I saw her later, Buddy was probably a little edgy, seeing her kiss me and I'd kiss her back and hug her. But the saving thing was: we all loved each other. Each of us loved the other. It wasn't a *ménage*-whatever, and nobody wanted it to be. But we've seen each other many times, and kept in close touch."

"And they're still getting along well together?" Kathy asked.

"In the sense you mean, yes. But Buddy's old now, like me, and he's got a bad heart. He had a bypass, all that, but it's in pretty fragile shape. He's retired, of course. The last time I saw him, he didn't look too great. I don't like to say it, but I don't think he's going to be with us very long."

"If that happens," Kathy asked, "is there a chance you might move in with, marry Claire? I don't mean to sound unfeeling or be offensive and, of course, it's none of my business. But you fascinate me, General Gavin, and you've told me so much already."

He chuckled. "You'd have made a great interrogator. None of the intelligence services have ever thought of using *your* technique, your tiny needle and where you inject it. I don't mind answering. If Buddy dies before I do, it seems likely he will, I'll certainly spend time with Claire. And it's certainly possible we could get together again, for friendship, mutual comfort, love, I don't know. But that's all speculation. I don't want to hurry Buddy offstage for that to happen, if it would. Any more questions?"

"Just a couple. Whatever happened to Viktor? Do you know?"

"Yes. As a matter of fact, I managed to see him on a mission to Moscow the year that *glasnost* broke out. It turned out that he was arrested when the VVS found out I was missing and he hadn't reported it. He wound up being convicted of anti-Soviet activities and was sent to a gulag for seven years. Worked in a clay pit and mine.

"As you'd expect," he continued, "he lost some of his teeth and contracted chronic bronchitis, among other things. He spent years in exile after his release but managed to get back to Moscow through an old girlfriend. It seems she had risen pretty high in the bureaucracy and found out about him when she was assigned to investigate Stalin's misdeeds. So, in the end, his womanizing saved him. He was promoted up the ladder, his medals were restored, and he's back on a government pension. I owe him a hell of a lot and I'm trying to get him to come over here for a visit."

"That would be lovely," she said. "One more question. Your bio says you live in Rehoboth, Delaware, now, near the beach. Do you live alone?"

"Except for my dog, yes. I like walking the beach, looking at the ocean, winter included. It's nice, even though it's a little off-center for me. I still get called back as a consultant, etcetera; I might have to take a small apartment in Washington."

"Really? I have a small apartment in Washington, as it happens. I'll be decommissioned soon, probably take a job teaching nurses at a hospital there. As your friend Buddy would say, I'd admire to have you come stay with me."

He raised himself on one elbow and looked at her. "That'd be lovely, Kathy, but why put a hold on your life with an old man like me? Even for a little while? I'm very flattered that you're interested enough in me to make an idyll like this possible. But anything between us would be very temporary because of our age differences. You're just a girl in her, your . . ."

"Try thirty-six," she said. "Don't slide back into male paternalism, Michael. I'm a free-thinking woman and *I'll* decide what I want to do and when, and who with. Whom with. I know this is very temporary, as you put it, but I want to be with you some. And if you feel up to it, we can make love like this every couple days."

He laughed. "Who am I to say no? If I have a heart attack, after all, you're a nurse. And, to quote one of Viktor's old Russian sayings, what a way to go. We'll spend some time with each other, then. You're a lovely woman, Kathy. Being with you seems to help fill up an empty space inside me, somehow. You're quite a kick."

"I know why and so do you," she said. "Galina was a brave and bold woman. I think I am, too. And I have eyes like hers."

"Yes, you do. Just like hers."